S0-AWN-910

Threads West
An American Saga

Maps of Fate

REID LANCE ROSENTHAL

BOOK TWO

ROCKIN' SR PUBLISHING
Cheyenne, Wyoming

© 2012 Reid Lance Rosenthal
http://reidlrosenthal.com
www.reidlancerosenthal.com

ALL RIGHTS RESERVED. Reid Lance Rosenthal © 2012.
No part of this book may be reproduced, stored in a retrieval system, or trans-
mitted, in any form or by any means, without the prior permission in writing of
the publisher, nor be otherwise circulated in any form of binding or cover other
than that in which it is published and without a similar condition including this
condition being imposed on the subsequent purchaser.

PUBLISHER'S NOTE:
This is a work of fiction. All characters, places, businesses and incidents are
from the author's imagination. Any resemblance to actual places, people, or
events is purely coincidental. Any trademarks mentioned herein are not author-
ized by the trademark owners and do not in any way mean the work is sponsored
by or associated with the trademark owners. Any trademarks used are specifi-
cally in a descriptive capacity.

Book Design by TLC Graphics, *www.tlcgraphics.com*
Cover by Tamara Dever; Interior by Erin Stark
Proofreading by: Tami St. Germaine

Outside and inside cover photo credits:
woman's portrait: courtesy of the Ida May Miller family
flag: ©iStockphoto.com/Blueberries
leather: ©iStockphoto.com/colevineyard
leather tooling: ©iStockphoto.com/belterz
scrolled leather: ©iStockphoto.com/billnoll
parchment paper: ©iStockphoto.com/ranplett
map compass: [2012] mike301. Image from Bigstock.com
Indian chief: ©iStockphoto.com/emyerson
Cover painting by: Debbie Sampson

Printed in the United States of America

ISBN: 978-0-9821576-3-3
Library of Congress Control Number: 2012902581

To my mother June who, among many gifts, passed on to me a love of and talent for writing. To my literary editor, Page Lambert, who cajoles, commends and scolds at just the right times, and who continues to teach me just how much I do not know about the wonderful craft of prose. To my daughter, Jordan, without whose artistic and technical skills this book would not be a reality.

And to America—her values, history, people, and the mystical energy and magical empowerment that flows from her lands.

Special Mention:

To Susan Murnon, whose overall period, location and other dedicated historical research is instrumental to the historical integrity of the series.

To Denise Winter, whose extensive expertise and incredibly detailed research in the clothing of the era is key to accurate portrayal of the times and characters who live in these pages.

To the great Threads West team, without whose enthusiastic belief in this series and unending efforts, this book would not exist:

Jordan Katie Allhands—Art, web and organization
Jani Flinn—Rockin SR Publishing
Laura Kennedy—Coordination, media and administration
Deborah Kunzie "Web Deb"—web design and programming
Devani Alderson—Social media
Erin Stark and Tami Dever—TLC Graphics
Tom Dever—Narrow Gate Books
The great folks at Midpoint Trade Books of NY

Threads West
An American Saga

TABLE OF CONTENTS

Threads West
An American Saga

Maps of Fate

INTRODUCTION

IN THE SPRING OF 1855, AMERICA IS ON THE CUSP OF HER GREAT westward expansion, reluctantly on the threshold of becoming a world power. St. Louis, gateway to the frontier, booms with an eight-fold population expansion from just a decade prior.

Fifteen hundred miles to the west is the lawless, untamed spine of the continent, the Rocky Mountains. The power of their jagged peaks, rugged territories, and vast resources beckon the souls of a few adventurous men and women, destined to love and struggle in the vibrant but unforgiving landscape of the West.

America draws individuals and families from all corners of the earth with the promise of land, freedom, self-determination and economic opportunity. Immigrants exchange the lives they know for the hope and romance of a country embarked on the course of greatness.

The revolt of Texas against Mexico, with the surreptitious aid of the United States, has resulted in vast new American terrain—unexplored western lands stretching from the Rio Grande to the Pacific, and north to the areas later to become the Kansas Territories and eventually Colorado and Utah—magnetic draws for the restless and ambitious, and those in search of freedom and future.

The brave, passion-filled characters of *Maps of Fate* set forth on a dangerous journey as they try to establish life in this unknown wilderness, swept unknowingly into the tumultuous vortex of momentous changes shaping the United States and the West between 1855 and 1875, the years ensconced in the *Maps of Fate* era of the *Threads West* series. Secret maps, hidden ambitions, and magnetic attractions inherent in lives forged by the conflicting fires of love and loss, hope and sorrow, life and death, shape their futures and the destinies of their lineage.

America is in transition, the lives of the characters shaken by events they cannot foresee. Spurred by a lust for gold, land, and the conquest of Mexican territory, a massive westward migration begins. Railroads and telegraphs will soon pierce this wild land. The first newspapers in the west roll off the presses in Leavenworth and Lawrence, Kansas, and Platte Valley, Nebraska. Opposing stands on slavery ignite deadly hatred throughout the Kansas Territories. The budding enmity between North and South flares into the winds of war, and the remote fringe of the frontier falls into virtual anarchy as most of the meager army troops assigned to protect this area withdraw to the East.

On the front range of the Rockies, newly spawned Denver City, built on the shores of Cherry Creek, booms with the impact of gold discovered in the Pikes Peak area and the Ouray, San Juan, and Uncompahgre mountain ranges. The Civil War erupts, and the fires of deadly tumult sweep west. Some of those manacled by the chains of slavery set their life sails to the winds of freedom. A Confederate Army mustered in Texas is repulsed by the Denver Militia. The broken treaties between the white man and Native Americans spread into bitter and contagious conflicts throughout the West. The "resolution" of the "Indian Problem" leaves families and hearts broken, forever staining the pages of American history.

Momentous change continues, igniting further greed and compassion, courage and treachery, rugged independence, torrid passions, and fierce loyalties. The discovery of gold in California and the meeting of the tracks of the Union Pacific Railroad from the east and Central Pacific from the west in 1869, underpin the rise of the robber-barons, cattle empires, and commerce, drawing hundreds of thousands to the Rockies and beyond.

A tidal wave of hopeful souls follows on the trail of the strong men and women of *Maps of Fate*. Throngs of those displaced by the devastation of the Civil War add to the torrent of humanity flowing west. In the third and fourth books of the *Threads West* novels (*Uncompahgre,* and *The Footsteps*), the first *Thread's West* generation born in the remote and sparsely settled west begins to mature and contend with this cauldron of events, their lives unsettled by personal tragedies, triumphs, loves, and loss. Colorado, Wyoming, Utah, and Montana evolve into separate and distinct territories and then achieve statehood. Law and order struggles as outlaws linger on the outer edges and range wars erupt between the landowners and the landless, sheep herders, cattlemen, and sodbusters. The clash of cultures, creeds and beliefs, and bitter rivalries over the control of scarce water resources, fuels further violence and cruelty.

These decades of the *Threads West* novels become the crucible of the American spirit. This violent but magical period in American history will affect forever the souls of generations, the building of the heart of the nation, destiny of a people, and the relentless energy and beauty of the western landscape. This is *our* story.

To be continued...

March 18, 1855

$\mathcal{S}$UNLIGHT ON STEEL

A LIGHT UPSTREAM BREEZE STIRRED THE SLOW-MOVING CURRENT of the Mississippi. The riffles sparkled in bursts of reflected sunlight, lapping against the thick planks of the barge's hull. The small steam paddle wheeler pulling it belched black smoke in time with the uneven chug of its engines. Two heavy braided hemp ropes stretched taut from either corner of the stern to the bow of the barge. The two vessels were making sluggish progress toward the west bank. Above the murmur of the current, the shouts of men, bleats of oxen and nickers of horses floated in the light wind of late dawn.

Zebarriah Taylor's tall, thin frame leaned against the corner bulwark of the port side of the barge. He occasionally glanced up from the smoke he was rolling to take in the scene. His green eyes, deepset in weathered features, carefully assessed the two wagons and teams that shared the barge with him. Now and then, he glanced at the three pack mules loaded with supplies from St. Louis. The animals fidgeted, shook their heads and stomped their hooves, shifting their weight from left to right. A muscular mustang horse stood perfectly still at Zeb's side, not nervous but completely alert, his eyes focused on something Zeb couldn't see far to the west and beyond the side of the river they were approaching.

"You see something out there I can't, Buck?" The tobiano did not change his stance nor look at Zeb. "Trouble, maybe?" One of the mustang's ears flicked, and he let out a soft whinny.

"Not going to let me in on the secret, are you? Well, never mind, I suppose we'll both find out soon enough."

Raised voices drew Zeb's eyes to the foremost wagon near the bow. He had surveyed the cargo-type rig as it trundled by him when the barge was loading. The wagon was solid, though older and makeshift with an arched canvas cover. His curiosity had been stirred by the couple who shared the driver's seat. Zeb sensed in the stocky, dirty, blond-haired man who drove the rig a discomfited unfamiliarity with wagons, lines and horses. They had only two horses, both older geldings. *Not enough*, thought Zeb to himself. A young, attractive, redheaded woman shared the driver's seat with the barrel-chested driver. The morning was chill, but not cold, yet she was bundled up, the somber grey shawl over her head not quite concealing semi-curly red hair, which peaked out from well-tailored, thick-knitted wool. Her shoulders were hunched as if the wagon was making its way into the teeth of a blizzard. She sat on the other side of the driving bench, as far from the driver as she could get. Zeb had seen the man's hands clenched tightly around the lines as they drove by and noticed the scars over his knuckles. The woman's jaw was tense and her complexion pale.

Zeb turned to Buck and ran a heavily calloused hand down the mustang's cheek. "Doesn't much look like married bliss to me," he confided to the horse. His reflections were interrupted by more raised voices coming from the front of the barge.

"I don't need any of your lip, woman. I will make these foul-smelling beasts do exactly what I want. I can handle this wagon just fine. I hate being out in the middle of this river. Reminds me of the last time I was on water and that was none too pleasant." The voice had a thick Irish brogue.

There was a pause during which the woman, out of Zeb's line of sight, must have spoken. "Shut your mouth, bitch!" Zeb heard the man shout. But the woman must have disregarded her companion's admonition, for the driver raised his muscular right arm over his shoulder, set to deliver a backhanded blow. Before he could swing, the woman jumped. On the far side of the wagon, Zeb caught a glimpse of high-laced boots with rounded toes. Her feet tangled in the hems of her heavy wool grey skirt and horsehair petticoats, and she almost fell to the barge deck. The driver, cursing, jumped from the near side of the seat and sprinted for the rear of the converted cargo rig, intent on intercepting his fleeing companion. She stopped in startled surprise as they met head-on at the tailgate, directly in front of the team pulling the second wagon. The frightened horses began to back up, lifting their forelegs nervously. Alarmed, the elderly couple in the rearward prairie schooner shouted.

Zeb wrapped the reins once around the saddle horn. "Watch the mules, Buck." He strode toward the couple, their struggles obscured from time to time by the shifting of the horses. When he reached them, the man had the redheaded woman pinned against the back of their wagon, one hand clenched on her upper arm and the other beefy paw around her throat pushing her head back into the canvas. The woman's wide blue eyes darted wildly from side to side. Surprised at how petite she was, Zeb was struck by the fear and loathing plainly etched in her features.

Zeb stood several feet back, reached out one long, lanky arm and jabbed the driver's broad, bulky shoulders tightly fit in a brown canvas jacket. "This barge is mighty cramped—ain't no place to have a fracas," Zeb said.

The man partially turned his head to size Zeb up out of the corner of one eye. His grip around the woman's throat seemed to tighten. Color was draining from her face as she gasped, her hands digging at the man's wrist, desperately trying to pry his fingers from her neck.

"Stay out of my business, coonskin," spat the man.

Zeb's right hand reached swiftly over his shoulder and behind his back. He silently withdrew his fourteen-inch blade knife from its scabbard. He stepped forward, leaned his chest into the man's back, and put the sharp edge to his throat. The man froze. Zeb pushed his lips so close to the man's ear that his dirty blond hair mixed with Zeb's long handlebar mustache. In a cold whisper, Zeb breathed,

"Best you take your hands off or in one second I will likely part your head from your shoulders, and I don't say things twice."

Zeb could feel the shock and anger radiate through the man. With one last shove against the woman's throat, the man released his grip and slowly straightened up. Zeb kept the cold steel of the knife pressed firmly against the flesh, just below the man's Adams apple.

"What the hell almighty is all this?" It was the barge captain.

"Nothin' much, Andy. Just makin' sure these teams don't get spooked."

Released from the vise of the burly hands, the woman's knees buckled and she almost fell to the coarse deck of the vessel. She caught herself with one hand on the wagon gate and slowly stood erect, struggling to breathe, her other hand frantically rubbing her neck. Zeb noticed the small band of freckles across the bridge of a delicate nose and the shape of her slightly parted lips as she gasped for air.

The man, still in Zeb's grasp, started to speak and began to turn his body. Zeb pressed the blade into the man's flesh, enough to indent the skin without drawing blood. He raised his forearm, bringing the man to his tiptoes and off balance.

"You would do well to keep your mouth shut. This barge needs to make the other side in one piece; otherwise we'll have bigger problems than this ruckus."

"Well, just hold on..." the captain began to speak.

Zeb cut him off. "If you want to know what went on, ask them in the wagon behind," he slung his head rearwards. "I suspect they seen what happened."

"And, you need to settle down," he said to the man, his knife still pressed against his thick neck. The woman had regained her breath, though she was still hunched forward massaging her throat.

"Is this your husband, ma'am?"

The woman shook her head with an unusual negative vehemence.

"Well, what is he to you?"

"She's my damn fiancée ..." the man's words died in a gurgle as Zeb drew the steel tighter against the man's windpipe.

"I weren't talking to you." He turned his gaze to the woman. There were tears trickling from the corners of her eyes. "You all right? Can you walk?"

She tentatively moved her head.

"Go on back there by the stern where that horse and three mules is. I'll catch up with you there in a moment, ma'am. After this gentleman gets cooled down a bit."

Zeb waited for the sounds of her boots to recede. With a sudden movement, he took the knife from the man's neck and took two long steps backward, the blade shining in the sun where it pointed from his still extended arm.

The stocky figure whirled. His face was scarlet and twisted and his eyes enraged. His hand began to run down the outside of his right trouser leg.

"If that's a boot blade you'd be going for, I'd think twice."

The man hesitated, and sized up Zeb and his stance carefully. His eyes flicked a glance at the brace of pistols, one cap and ball, the other a Colt Army revolver snugged in Zeb's belt, which anchored the waist of a well-worn fringed buckskin shirt that hung below his hips.

The burly towhead straightened up. "Nobody does that to Jacob O'Shanahan," he snarled through gritted teeth.

Zeb regarded him coolly. "I just did. Now git up in your wagon, have a little sip of whiskey and get unwound. This here crossing will be done shortly. You'll have far bigger things to worry about over the coming months."

Jacob hesitated and then gave a surly shrug. "Didn't catch your name, coonskin."

"Coonskin is my hat. I didn't mention my name."

Jacob leered, "Well, I'm sure we will meet up again, coonskin."

Zeb relaxed slightly, took another stride back and gestured with the tip of the knife, "Up to the front. And yep, I 'spect we will."

He waited until the man clambered back into the driver's seat so just his thick left shoulder was visible behind the front arc of canvas, and then turned and walked back toward the woman and his animals. She was leaning against the side of the barge. The long delicate fingers of one hand stroked Buck's neck. The horse seemed to lean slightly into her touch. She was trembling, still very pale. *Very beautiful.* The thought flitted across Zeb's mind along with a memory—another time, another woman. *Mebbe it's the rising sun shining auburn in her red locks.* A bruise was forming around her neck. One hand was spread across her abdomen just below the very pleasant shallow curve of her hips.

Zeb stood several feet away. "You alright, ma'am?"

The woman nodded her head slightly. "I'm Sarah, Sarah Bonney. Thank you for helping me I...I think I'm going to be sick."

Zeb moved quickly, "Lean out over the side, ma'am, you'll be all right."

Sarah clutched the lip of the gunwale with one hand, kept the other pressed against her belly, bent over the barge sidewall and retched. Zeb stood behind her, his hands resting gently on her square, but slight, shoulders, steadying the small heaving form.

When the nausea had passed, she turned and rested weakly against the bulwark. "I'm sorry—," she started to say, but Zeb interrupted.

"Nothin' to be sorry about. I got a bandana in the saddlebag." He walked to Buck, untied the rawhide fasteners on the flap and turned back to Sarah. "None too clean, but it'll do." He held out the reddish-brown square cut cotton cloth.

"You don't want my vomit on your bandana," Sarah protested feebly.

"Makes no never mind. I can just rinse it in the river when we get off. Take it." Zeb insisted.

She nodded thanks and Zeb noticed how the curled auburn tips of her hair caught the light and brushed against her cheek as she moved her head. He chided himself and stepped back respectfully.

"Miss Bonney, I am Zebarriah Taylor. Them who know me better call me Zeb. That accent of yours—English?"

Sarah looked up into Zeb's eyes and smiled pensively. "Yes, Mr. Taylor. I am from England. Liverpool, to be exact. I landed in New York just a month ago. It seems so much longer." A look of anger and something else shadowed her face momentarily. Her lower lip trembled, she blushed, looked out over the river, and then turned her head back to Zeb. "Are you headed west? Are you going with the wagon train?"

The last question seemed to carry a tone of hope. Her beautiful blue eyes dropped to the two raised purple scars that extended from below his left ear to his chin. He realized with a start it was the first time he actually cared that he had them. Lowering his chin, he angled his face so they were not quite as visible.

"Yes, ma'am, had some business back here, and some supplies to fetch in St. Louis," he nodded at the laden mules and new Grimsley saddles. "Now I'm headed west with the wagons, though I suspect I'll keep some distance for the most part. I'm working..." somehow speaking that word seemed foreign, and he hesitated, "... I'm helping some folks on the train." He paused again. "It was a bear that done those." He looked down at his thick, elk hide moccasin boots and scuffed one toe on the uneven boards of the deck.

"They make you look quite distinguished, Mr. Taylor...like someone who has had experience in life." Boldly, she continued, "Like your salt and pepper mustache. Sometime perhaps you shall tell me the story of your bear." Sarah took a breath and smiled. "If you want to, of course. What was your business back here? If you don't mind me asking." Some color came back into her face.

Zeb looked up and felt a grin grow under the bushy shadow of the handlebar curve of his heavy, long mustache. He raised one hand absentmindedly and smoothed a pointed tip where it tapered into the stubble just above his jaw. "One day I might just do that. Nope— don't mind. It was personal. My family was murdered twenty or so years back—the farm burned out by a mad-dog renegade. I lit out for the West. I had to come back and make my peace."

She looked shocked. Zeb took a deep breath, and his eyes flickered toward her wagon, "Is that man, Jacob, your betrothed?"

Sarah abruptly broke her gaze. Her smile vanished. "No...he's a... a traveling companion. He tells people that we are engaged to protect my dignity."

Zeb sensed a deeply bitter irony in the last statement, and he stood silent. *Seems we both have things we'd rather not speak of.*

"I better return to the wagon. It looks like we will be ashore soon." Over her head, Zeb could see the shallow draft steam tug had begun to veer away from the looming shore. The tow ropes had been run forward and cast ·to the bank where several brawny men were deftly tying them to haul harnesses on two braces of hitched oxen. They would pull the barge the last fifty yards to the very eastern edge of the frontier Zeb knew as home. He looked behind him. Half a mile distant across the chop of the river, square building shapes of uneven heights marked the edge of St. Louis. *I won't be seeing you again, ever—my head is settled,* he thought with satisfaction. To the north, two large white paddle boats with ornate rails and twin, tall, black stacks churned their way slowly down river.

He turned back, but Sarah was already halfway back to her wagon. Zeb watched her retreating figure for a moment and the slight side to side movement of her hips as she walked, her feminine sway visible even though ensconced in the thick wool and horsehair of her skirt and petticoats.

The memory returned. With an effort he shoved it back somewhere in the musty corner of his mind where it had slept until now. He felt Buck nuzzle the back of his head. The mustang seemed to have his head a bit cocked to the side, and his big brown eyes stared directly into Zeb's.

"What the hell you looking at, Buck? If I want to say more than five words to a woman once every ten years that's my business." Buck's ear flicked forward slightly.

"Wait 'til the damn ramps are all the way down!" Captain Andy shouted up front. There was a soft, muddy grating sound as the upward sloped leading-edge of the keel nestled into the muck and sand that was the eastern edge of the western half of America. Zeb couldn't see Jacob's figure, but he could see his hands pulling back harshly on the lines to the horses.

He reached into his leather shirt, retrieved a suede pouch hanging from his neck, dug out a wad of chew and bit off a chunk. He checked the over-under belly scabbard to make sure the .58 caliber Enfield musket and .52 caliber breech-loading Sharps rifle were snug in the leather, and spat down on the deck. Jacob and Sarah's wagon had begun to roll down the ramp into shore grass greening with coming spring.

Zeb watched as the rig creaked from side to side in the uneven boggy ground and made its way to the group of canvas-topped Conestogas and prairie schooners at the top of a slight rise two hundred yards from the river.

"Mighty interesting. Yep, mighty interesting." He turned to Buck and the mules. "You fellas ready to get back to the mountains?" Two of the pack animals brayed, and Buck tossed his head up and down impatiently, the hackamore leather squeaking in the brisk air. "Okay then, let's go home."

March 18, 1855

THREADS CONVERGE

By MIDMORNING, ALL THE WAGONS WERE ACROSS THE RIVER AND the beefy, red-haired wagon master, Mac had the train fully organized. He put Inga Bjorne and Rebecca Marx's prairie schooner third in line, where there was less dust. Johannes Svenson drove the wagon to teach the women how to use the lines and brake on the four-horse team. One of the two extra mounts purchased by Reuben Frank was tied to the back. The other, a powerful palomino of sixteen hands, pranced excitedly under Reuben.

Reuben twisted in his saddle and gazed back at the Mississippi. Dawn had retreated with a brilliant palette of indigo to the west and fire-orange flaring to the east. The Mississippi had a slight chop from the morning wind; the ripples reflecting the burgeoning day in a shimmer of color. The east side of the river had been the scene of frenetic activity around the forty-one wagons in the train, which contained several childless couples and a number of families. Two steam tugs dragged barges large enough to accommodate several wagons and teams across the river. The wagons were grouped in single file, pointed west toward the Rockies more than a thousand miles distant. Mac's shouted directions boomed over the murmur of the river and the chatter of the pioneers. The whinnies of horses, bleats of oxen and brays of mules echoed up and down the line of prairie schooners, Conestogas, and converted farm wagons.

Turning his eyes west, Reuben contemplated the enormous task ahead and recalled the look in his father's wise old eyes when he had selected him from the four brothers to fulfill the family's hopes and aspirations. He felt a momentary pang of doubt, then shook his head and searched for Zeb. A quarter mile to the south, he picked out a figure on a brown and white horse leading three mules. *As I would have expected*, he mused.

He turned his attention back to the front of the train. Mac was near the first wagon astride a stocky red sorrel that matched him well. The wagon master cursed as the excited horse shook its head and pranced sideways, then he waved for Reuben to ride over.

"Reuben, check those last wagons and make sure they're ready. Let's get this damned show moving. We're already late!" Mac bellowed.

Reuben's horse shifted with agitation. "Easy, Lahn," he soothed as he reached down and patted the thick, blond neck of the palomino. The gelding snorted, shook his head and stomped, his feet dancing a quarter circle. Reuben wheeled the muscular horse and cantered toward the rear of the line of wagons. He was not yet used to the deep trough of the western saddle, a far cry from European tack, but he liked the substantial feel of the heavy leather.

As he passed the rigs at the center of the train, his eyes widened when he saw that the pretty redheaded girl from the steamship *Edinburgh* sat on the driver's bench of one of the wagons. And that bully from the ship, Jacob, sat next to her. Sarah had a heavy shawl over her shoulders. Reuben thought she looked cold and unhappy in the cool of the spring morning. Jacob was busy with the brake. Reuben caught Sarah's eye and she seemed startled. But there was something other than simple surprise in her look. She smiled widely and waved. Reuben pulled down on the brim of his hat in return. The coincidence of Jacob and Sarah on the same wagon train, and the apparent fact that they were a couple, troubled Reuben. *Not her type at all. Very off*, he thought.

Reining up in a swirl of dust at the last wagon, a Conestoga, Reuben shouted to the driver, "Ready?"

"Let's go," replied the thick-set man with a ruddy face. He had just unfurled a several-foot-wide American flag from a knotty, barked pole he had lashed to the side of the wagon at the front rim of the curved canvas top.

As it snapped in the wind, Reuben thought the colors looked old, a version of the United States flag he had never seen. "Thirteen stars in a circle on the blue?" he inquired. "What does that mean?"

"This here...," the driver gestured, beaming, "was the flag my great-grandpappy carried in the revolution. That's just eighty-odd years ago, ya know. Family has been in Virginny since the sixteen hundreds. It was the first flag of this country called the Betsy Ross Circular. There ain't many of 'em around anymore. We usually just fly her on July Fourth, but we figgered what we're doin' is about as big as then, so—'cept for bad weather—this cloth is goin' to be full view to God and country all the way to the Rockies. I aim to fly it on a big tall post before I set the first foundation stone for our home-stead." Next to him, his buxom wife smiled and nodded. Two round-faced little girls peeked from between their parents.

Reuben was not fully sure of the man's meaning, but there would be plenty of time for that later. He eased Lahn alongside the wagon and fumbled in his shirt pocket. "Do you like jerky?" he asked as he leaned from the horse, holding out the treat to the children.

They giggled and hid their faces. "Come on, take it," Reuben coaxed. He took a bite himself and smacked his lips. "Umm, good." The children laughed shyly, and the older girl stretched out a pudgy hand and took the dried meat.

"Fine children," Reuben said, straightening in the saddle.

Their mother smiled. "That's Becky and Eleanor. I am Margaret Johnson, and this is my husband, Harris." Becky and Eleanor chewed contentedly on the jerky. "Perhaps you would join us for dinner one night, Mr...?"

"Frank. Reuben Frank. And, yes, that would be my pleasure. You can tell me more of the flag story."

Reuben turned in his saddle, raised himself high in the stirrups, felt the comforting press of the holstered Squareback Navy Colt against his right hip as he straightened his leg, and waved his hat in the air. Far to the front of the line of wagons, he heard Mac roar, "Move 'em out!"

March 18, 1855

OREBODING

ICE CLUNG STUBBORNLY TO THE BANKS OF THE SOUTH FORK OF THE Powder River as it flowed clear and cold in the half-light past the small Sioux encampment a thousand miles west of the Mississippi.

Eagle Talon was awakened by her fingers tracing feather-like down the ridged muscles of his abdomen. His eyes opened and he lay still, enjoying the touch of her small, somewhat calloused hands. The gentle gurgle of the river, muted by the thick skins wrapping the lodge poles, was soothing in the dim light of dawn as it seeped through the tipi's smoke hole. The chill of departing winter mixed with the last glow of warmth from the dying embers several feet from the thick buffalo robes of their bed. Her hands were more insistent now. She snuggled closer, pushing small, full breasts into the contoured muscles of his back. The slightly rounded belly in the fertile valley of her hips nestled into his buttocks, and her lips began to play softly at the base of his neck.

He reached back his hand and molded it to the barely noticeable bulge in her center where their child grew. She sighed. He turned slowly over to his wife and pulled the buffalo robe from her shapely brown body. The soft red-orange hue of the fire-glow accentuated the delicate, translucent nature of her eyelids, the angular bronze structure of her cheekbones and the fullness of her slightly parted lips over which she ran her tongue seductively. His lips first found the pulse of her neck and then her tan, distended nipples.

His hand gently rubbed the swell in her stomach. "Haven't I already done my work, woman?" he teased, smiling.

She started to push him away but her protest was smothered by his lips. "I want our child to have your eyes," Eagle Talon whispered, "and your wisdom and strength. A child to comfort us when we grow old and grey. But you? Even old, you will be beautiful."

WALKS WITH MOON LOOKED INTENSELY INTO HER HUSBAND'S EYES in the half-light. Sharp, steady, dark brown—they were the eyes she had seen in the dreams of her youth. She savored the warmth of his whispers. She had been awake that morning since the night's coals had faded, listening to her man's deep breathing, studying his sleeping, almost regal features in the subtle glimmer of smoldering fire.

She was the only daughter of Tracks on Rock, the tribe's medicine man. Eagle Talon was the sole son of the war chief, Two Bears of the Northern People. As small children, they had noticed each other during infrequent gatherings of the widely separated clans, often exchanging shy smiles when their parents were not looking.

Walks with Moon smiled into the warmth of their sleeping robes. She had never told her husband, but she had chosen him when they had known only five winters. And in the end she always achieved, in her own quiet way, whatever she wanted. Eagle Talon had finally succumbed. He had arrived leading a long string of horses toward the end of season of color, soon after her tribe had set up its camp the winter before last. Walks with Moon's heart had leapt. Without a glance in her direction, he had gone directly to the lodge of Tracks on Rock and requested permission to court her.

Her smile deepened as she remembered. Perhaps their parents had not been as blind as they pretended. The courtship lasted only four suns. Then, in typical brash Eagle Talon fashion, to the surprise of the village and delight of the gossipy older women, the handsome warrior rashly appeared outside the lodge of Tracks on Rock requesting Walks with Moon be his wife. He offered the staggering dowry of ten ponies, a finely crafted, polished antler tine breastplate, and a superb war lance. Her father had stood quietly, giving thought to what else he could ask for. That is, until her besieging stare caught his eye. He turned back immediately to Eagle Talon, grasped his shoulder and nodded his head once.

They had married soon afterward. As tradition demanded, her clan became his. She felt the pulse of pride at how quickly her man had proven his courage and skill in hunting and war party sorties that occasionally raided or retaliated against the competing Crow and Pawnee.

His prowess was not solely of the bow and lance. He had proven himself a statesman, too. Eagle Talon had single-handedly avoided bloodshed when Pawnee had night-raided the ponies of a tribe of Arapaho in the Valley of the Laramie, leaving signs to suggest her Oglala tribe was responsible. Bravely, he had negotiated a peace that had been approved unanimously by the elders of the Council.

The tingle of her husband's lips on her breasts brought her back. She felt her pout ease and moved ever closer in his embrace.

"What you say is true, husband," she breathed in his ear. Her fingers moved up his thighs and tightened gently around him.

EAGLE TALON TURNED OVER AND RAISED HIMSELF UP ON ONE ELBOW. He felt his chiseled face crease with a smile. He was sorely tempted. But there was much to do with the new sun, which was already making its presence known. He did not like to rush lovemaking with his beautiful wife. "I must rise, Walks with Moon. The Council meets today." He kept his tone soft, but firm.

"You mentioned the women are gathering to wash..." he laughed, "...and share stories, at the river today?"

"Yes, husband."

"Perhaps we can resume that part of this discussion, which requires no words, when the sun sets?" Eagle Talon let his finger drift over the curve of her hips, his lips pressed against her ear.

"I will look forward to that, husband."

He felt that primordial sense of man, family and love course through his being. His hands slipped up to her chin. Gently, he turned her face back over her shoulder toward his and kissed her lightly. "The first of many sons I am sure, Walks with Moon. I have much to do today. I must not linger."

He gently disengaged, kicked the last of the buffalo robes from their legs and stood. He pulled on the soft but heavy elk skin shirt that Walks with Moon had lovingly stitched for him during the winter. "You are strong, good and beautiful, my wife..." he grinned, "...and you sew well." He pulled the buffalo skins back over her, reached for his lance and war shield and moved to the tipi flap.

"It pleases me that you like your shirt, husband."

Eagle Talon paused, glanced back at her and nodded, then untied the leather thongs that held the flaps in place and stepped out into the morning. He could hear the activity inside the other tipis. Thin, grey wisps from dwindling night fires curled in slow tendrils from the smoke holes, dissipating in the chilled air. Uneven lines of snow had drifted into the hollows of ridges around the camp and the steeper banks along the river. The rim of the sun, rising over the sandstone ledges to the east, cast a dawn glow on the thick brush along the riverbanks. The leafless cottonwoods reached their upper-most branches into the first rays of the morning. *The season when life comes.* Eagle Talon sighed contentedly among the stirring village and the awakening earth, and the memory of Walks with Moon's touch on his loins. *Yes, the season when life comes. May it be so,* he whispered to the sky.

The flap of a tipi near him pushed open and an Indian with long grey hair, still broad-shouldered, but having lost the sculptured muscle of youth, stepped from his lodge. With some effort, Flying Arrow gradually straightened. One bony hand held a headdress with the feathers of many eagles, the other a long, thick staff with a heavy wooden burl at its head. Eagle Talon knew that staff had counted many coups.

The older Indian raised his arms to the now quickly emerging sun, the extended staff blending with the backdrop of leafless tree limbs behind him. He turned and slowly surveyed the camp until his eyes met that of Eagle Talon. He nodded a greeting, which Eagle Talon respectfully returned. Today was the Council of Chiefs. They would make plans for the coming season, promoting ideas as their own, never publicly admitting the heavy influence of advice from their wives, which carried considerable private weight in the matriarchal society of The People. Eagle Talon smiled, thinking of Walks with Moon.

It was time to make many decisions. Scouts would be designated to keep an eye on other bands of The People and competing villages of Pawnee and Crow. Other braves would begin the season's search for tatanka, and Walks with Moon's father, Tracks on Rock, would set a day a number of suns from this morning when the village would begin the ancient ritual of following the herds of buffalo located by the scouts.

The light breeze shifted from the east. Eagle Talon felt his brow furrow in concert with the uneasy stir in the morning air currents. There would also be talk of the strangers with white skins. There had been few of them up until now, but their sightings were becoming more frequent.

Eagle Talon had seen his first hairy-faced one when just a boy, twenty winters ago. Dressed in pelts and fringed leather leggings, the white man had bravely come into the village leading his horse and the two pack mules laden with beaver pelts and other skins. In the crook of his arm he carried a long wooden and blue metal object. He had moved with one hand raised, palm out, through the silent gathering group of The People.

As a boy, he remembered pulling on his father's loincloth asking, "What is he carrying, father? What is that?" He would never forget his father looking down at him, many feathers flowing from the sheen of his full black hair, their tips brushing his shoulder, the grip on his lance tightening, a somber darkness in his eyes.

"That is called a holy iron, son. It is the weapon of the hairy-faced ones."

The memory dissipated, and the promise of the spring dawn and later lovemaking were carried away by the east breeze; only to be replaced by a feeling of foreboding deep in Eagle Talon's spirit.

March 18, 1855

$\mathscr{S}$TRAINING AGAINST THE TRACES

JOHANNES COULD FEEL THE WARM AND SLENDER SHAPE OF INGA'S long thigh beneath his fingers, though his hand was separated from her flesh by her blue wool traveling dress and three horsehair petticoats. Inga looked at him coyly, a flush rising in her cheeks.

"Rebecca will see us, Johannes!" She glanced furtively to the side of the wagon, behind her, and then quickly toward the two wagons ahead of them.

He merely grinned then continued to gently slide his hand toward the "V" of her legs. "I think it will be a while before Mac gets things organized. Rebecca is no doubt behind the wagon, cursing the horses, and checking her trunks to see which of her gowns are still packed after Reuben ransacked them. Maybe we should wrap a blanket around us and see what happens."

"Johannes!" Her blush turned crimson, the deep pink of her high cheekbones offsetting startling blue eyes and bright blond hair. The hue crept up her throat, rising from the curve of her breasts and the tapered top of her laced bodice. Even through three layers of clothing Johannes noticed the swell of her nipples and knew that, despite her embarrassed protests, his idea held some intrigue. He leaned over, kissed her cheek and then moved his lips to her ear. "What color blanket should we use?"

Inga, her face now scarlet, her legs doing an involuntary dance, carefully smoothed the cloth of the dress over the tops of her knees, but she made no move to remove his hand, which was still slowly moving up her inner thigh.

Johannes' smile widened. He admired the beauty of her distinctly Scandinavian profile, like his, and the thin perfectly proportioned contours of her tall frame. He realized again that he reveled in the pleasure of simply sitting next to her. He was as surprised now at how he welcomed her warm, comforting energy, as he had been when their eyes first met on the train from New York to St. Louis just weeks before.

Above the sound of blood rushing in his own ears, he heard the hub-bub of noises around them. Mac, the fiery-tempered Irish wagon master, was fully audible, but somewhere out of sight ahead of the two forward wagons. Reuben had galloped by on Lahn toward the rear of the long line of wagons only seconds before, and the receding drum of the palomino's hooves could still be heard. The air reverberated with activity. To the rear, excited chatter echoed from every rig, their tongues and teams pointed with hope to the west, away from the rising sun and St. Louis, now on the other side of the slow swirl of the currents of the Mississippi.

"And what exactly is this?"

Inga jerked straight up, suddenly tense. The drift of Johannes' lips toward her bare neck froze. Standing to Inga's side, feet spread firmly on the ground, hands on perfectly curved hips, was Inga's mistress, Rebecca Marx. Her wide brown eyes were narrowed, and her normally full evocative lips pursed in a thin, tight line. The angry color in her cheeks accentuated waves of hair so dark as to be almost black.

"We are beginning a long, dangerous and dirty journey of one thousand miles. Reuben has totally disorganized my trunks, which are surrounded by dusty sacks of grain, we will have to contend with wretched wilderness, dangers, uncivilized behavior and horrible conditions for months. I doubt I shall even see my tea set until we get to Cherry Creek." Her voice took on a biting tone. "And you, Johannes, you have only one thing on your mind, always. There's no hope for you, but Inga, I'm surprised. Show some self-control. Your actions reflect on me."

Inga bit her lip and nodded, embarrassed as she surreptitiously removed Johannes' hand from where it had stopped in its travels up her leg. "Yes, Milady. Johannes and I were just talking..." her voice trailed off.

Johannes straightened up. Although Inga was very tall, almost six feet, Johannes towered a head above her. He was careful to keep the smile on his face. After all, Reuben was his best friend and for whatever reasons only the Lord knew, seemed to hold some type of attraction for this pretentious brunette.

"I was just leaning over to show Inga how to use the brakes on these prairie schooners, Rebecca." He caught her momentary grimace and felt some satisfaction. She hated it when anyone, particularly himself, addressed her as "Rebecca," rather than "Milady Marx." However, he noticed her reaction was far less hostile when Reuben called her by her first name.

"The grain is for the horses. This grass won't green for another month or more. No grain, weak horses. Weak horses, we walk. In that case your attire would likely be in tatters, Rebecca."

He let his eyes slide down the full length of her figure. She was resplendently swathed in a finely tailored black wool skirt and bodice, which clung to her petite body. Johannes presumed she wore at least four petticoats to achieve the explosive flair of the heavy material of the skirt. Her supple form needed no corset and though the bodice rose modestly to the base of her throat, the stretch of wool over her breasts concealed little of their perfect shape. The skirt's billows sported thin, dull red pleats that played off perfectly with the red bone buttons ascending the bodice from waist to neck in a double vertical line that centered narrowly in her cleavage. Long, thin black leather gloves disappeared into the swells of heavy silk false sleeves of muted red and black. The jaunty angle of her black wool hat, with its tapered front sun brim and fluttery red dyed ostrich plume, emphasized her almond eyes, high cheekbones and lips so well formed they were inviting even when pursed in a petulant line.

Johannes could literally feel the twinkle in his own pale blue eyes. "We probably won't be stopping for lunch or tea anytime soon. The Rocky Mountains are far away." He thought he had kept the sarcasm from his tone. The wince he felt in Inga said otherwise, as did Rebecca's darkening scowl.

She stamped her foot. "This is going to be an exceedingly long journey, Mr. Svenson. Inga, move over to the center, I am climbing up."

Johannes stretched out a long arm to offer her assistance, but she ignored it, pulling herself up to the wooden planks of the bench seat. Carefully arranging her dress under her she sat stiffly, back arched, nose slightly elevated, and stared straight ahead.

"As you wish, Milady," said Johannes with a chuckle and a slight pull on the front of his broad brim hat. He leaned over the side of the seat and looked far down the line of the thirty-eight wagons that stretched almost one-third mile behind them toward the river. He could make out Reuben standing in the stirrups next to the very last Conestoga, waving his hat in the air.

Mac appeared at a trot from behind the first wagon. His shoulders were far wider than the chest of the thickly muscled, red-sorrel quarter horse that pranced animatedly beneath him. His very full, light red beard was clearly visible against the faded grey wool of his trail coat and his hat was held high in one hand to shield his eyes from the sun. He rose in the stirrups peering intently back toward the tail of the wagon train.

Evidently, he caught Reuben's signal. He squashed the stained, well-worn hat over his mop of darker red hair and waved an outstretched arm, "Move 'em out!" he barked in a roar that startled the horses.

There was a buzz of exclamations and shouts up and down the line of wagons. The sounds of whips being cracked from the wagons pulled by oxen and leather lines slapping the backs of horses and mules reverberated in the morning air. Creaks of protest groaned from wood and metal. Puffs of dust erupted from the hooves of the horses straining against the traces of the forward wagons. As the beasts overcame the inertia of the heavy loads, their gaits evened with the first westward steps toward the new, and the unknown.

On the eve of March 18, 1855

RENEGADE

A THOUSAND MILES WEST OF ST. LOUIS AND FOUR HUNDRED MILES south of the Powder River, abrupt columns of granite rose like broken chimneys from the slopes of the foothills around the mouth of the Cache la Poudre River Canyon. Rugged hogbacks arched their red sandstone faces from the valley floor east of the canyon. The midday sun warmed pockets of grass, struggling to show the first spring green. Patches of leafless brush oak, bitterbrush and mountain mahogany meandered in and out of the boulder strewn hillsides, their thin branches poking from patches of old snow on the shadowed north slopes between scattered junipers and pine.

Black Feather made his way carefully through the grassy paths between outcroppings on the eastern ridge overlooking the valley. His tall, angular frame leaned slightly forward in a cat-like, half-crouch as he moved toward a figure that knelt, peering over the top of a boulder on the lip of the ridge. The heavy elk leather of Black Feather's leg moccasins, turned down mid-calf, made no sound as he climbed, even when the vegetation along the path gave way to crumbled granite. He moved with sinewy, deadly agility. From time to time he stopped, one outstretched, long-fingered hand and exposed bronze forearm balancing his frame against a boulder. He drew himself up a few paces from the man, who was engrossed and unaware of another presence. Below, farther than a bullet could fly, a faint wagon trail wandered through the heart of the valley.

The lookout was smaller than Black Feather. His thin, wiry body was covered in a dirty, heavy, cotton pullover shirt, which hung below the tops of his leather loincloth. Old bloodstains soiled one side and there was a jagged rip in the fabric across the lower back— no doubt a narrow escape from a knife blade. A sweat-stained, leather headband with a single row of beads kept his long unkempt strings of hair swept behind his shoulders. An ancient Enfield musket leaned, muzzle up and within easy reach, against the boulder that he hid behind.

Black Feather paused for a moment behind the unsuspecting figure. He raised his rifle and slammed the buttplate into the man's back between his shoulder blades with enough force to stun, but not kill or maim.

The man grunted and collapsed, the wind knocked out of him. He lay on his back on the ground, knees bent, struggling to regain his breath. His dark brown, almost black eyes stared up at Black Feather's swarthy features towering above him, fear evident in the rapid blinks of his eyelids and wildly darting pupils.

"Snake, I have told you many times. When you're on lookout you watch from the side of the rock not from the top. Even the white eyes can pick out your ugly face etched against the sky. We have been waiting here three days for prey. Far worse will happen to you if your stupidity causes that time to be wasted!"

"I understand," gasped Snake. "The rock was"—he wheezed— "too rounded to see well from the sides."

"Then find another rock. Get back on your feet. There will be wagons on this road and the men are getting restless."

Black Feather turned and trotted, almost jumping, down the slope, as a surefooted as a cougar.

He followed the base of the hill to where it turned south into a small draw. The warmth of the March sun radiated off the rocky faces from all sides, a natural heat-reflecting amphitheater. The picket line at the mouth of the little canyon strung an assortment of horses, big and small, several pintos, appaloosas, mustangs, and even a few stolen quarter horses, a new breed from the East. Each had a different brand, all were lean and muscular, and many had hairless scars along a flank or haunch. Two dozen men lounged here and there, one group still sleeping around a whiskey jug cradled between the saddles they used for pillows. Others were in small clusters talking. Three stocky men—one of them could be called fat—squatted, speaking Spanish, and passing a thick stick of jerky between them. They wore straw sombreros, and shawls or serapes whose bright colors had long ago faded.

The heaviest of the three rose as Black Feather moved toward them.

"Patron," he grated in Spanish, "the men become uneasy. We've had no spoils or women for weeks and no coffee for three days." His brown eyes squinted up at Black Feather between corpulent folds of wrinkled brown cheeks. His gaze was steady, but deferential. "May we have one small fire?"

"We need patience, not a fire, Pedro. We have spent three days here. I've never seen that wagon track go empty for more than a week this time of year, I'm sure there will be a group of white eyes traveling south after wintering at Fort Laramie. We shall strike quickly, take what we wish and head east." Black Feather's lips curled into a wicked sneer which grotesquely twisted the thin white scar above them. "Perhaps there will be women. Maybe even young women."

The two men laughed. Pedro's two front teeth were missing and the gap made a hissing sound as he cackled.

—————

IT WAS EARLY THE NEXT MORNING WHEN THEY CAME. FIRST LIGHT had not yet crested the buttes of the Pawnee Grasslands to the east. The horizon was a narrow, steel blue stripe that tapered into the spreading rose of a coming sun.

Black Feather was still in his bedroll, his long limbs pressed together to retain warmth under the two wool blankets. He heard gravel roll behind him. Swiftly sitting up, he spun in one smooth motion, a long, savage-looking blade in his outreached hand.

Snake had been bending down to report to him, but leaped back. "It's me, Snake."

Black Feather lowered the knife. "Speak."

"Wagons. Four of them headed south just as you thought."

"Get the men up. We will meet at the horses. Tell them to be quiet. No dust. Have Pedro send Hernandez a mile to the northeast. Tell him to walk his horse. I don't want to be surprised by a stray Cavalry patrol. Signal the lookouts up on the hill to stay where they are and keep their eyes sharp." Snake lingered for just a second. "Move," snarled Black Feather.

He rose and checked the loads in the .36 caliber 1851 Navy, Army issue Colt revolver, and his U.S. Model 1847 .45 caliber Smoothbore Musketoon. He paused for an instant to smile at the buttplate with the U.S. Army insignia. *Thank you, trooper. A fine scalp, a warm shell jacket, and a good rifle all at once made for a very good day.*

There was excited chatter as the men, standing near their horses, untethered their mounts. Several men were checking their firearms. Others honed the blades of knives or tomahawks.

"Quiet. Gather around," Black Feather ordered.

The conversation ceased immediately. "González, take three riders and position yourself down at the east end of the valley near Horse's Tooth Rock, just in case they try to run for it. Many Ponies, take two men and station at the west end of the valley. The rest of you follow me. No noise. Lead your horses and keep their hooves from the rocks. We will stop just below the crest of the hill. When I give the signal, mount and move down on them."

The men nodded, spread out, and began to ascend, each picking his own trail. They gathered again below the top of the ridge, out of sight of the unsuspecting wagons. Snake began to raise his head up over his lookout rock, then quickly retracted his body, glancing back at Black Feather. He sank to his hands and knees and edged one side of his face around the side of its rough edge. After a moment, he gestured.

Black Feather rotated his gaze around his men. "It is time. Mount up. We will do the usual. Kill the men first. Leave the women, unless they are trouble, and we will decide on each of them later."

Silently the band swung onto their horses. Black Feather waved his arm, and they advanced to the peak of the incline. He was in the lead, just his head peeking through a swale in the last contour. The front wagon was a prairie schooner with a man, woman and what appeared to be a younger woman sharing the driver's seat. Behind the prairie schooner was an older, smaller, canvas-covered supply rig. Driven by one man, its canvas was partially rolled up over the ribs from which corners and legs of furniture protruded. The last two were small cargo wagons with flat tarps. *Probably loaded with supplies, flour, powder, and foodstuffs*, Black Feather quickly guessed. The tail rig had two men. One appeared to have a rifle at the ready.

Black Feather surveyed the wagons again. He did not like surprises. Finally he was satisfied. *This will be easier than I thought. The food is needed, and it looks like they're moving their household so there must be some valuables.* A slight smile played on his lips. *And a young woman.* He raised his rifle horizontally above his head. The band of renegades crested the hill and began to descend slowly in a wide line of horses, weapons and men.

The wagons made considerable noise as the wheels bumped along the primitive road, hitting still frozen ruts where it was shaded. Black Feather's band continued to move without haste. They were now but one hundred and fifty yards from, and slightly behind, the wagons.

They still do not know we are here. They are close enough now that there is no escape. Using the barrel of his Musketoon he pointed to four of his men, then at the wagons, and slid his finger across his throat horizontally. The men nodded and raised their rifles. The four shots sounded almost as a single report. Both men in the rear cargo carrier slumped over. The driver in the third wagon toppled off the seat onto the ground and the rear wagon wheel rolled over his back. The man in the second wagon lurched, then steadied himself and positioned his rifle over the back of the wagon seat to use its edge as a rest. In one smooth motion, Black Feather coolly leveled his Smoothbore, brought the stock to his shoulder, and fired. The man's rifle dropped from his hands and his head slumped over the backrest, his body suspended by his chin caught on the rough, wood edge.

The driver of the family in the prairie schooner frantically slapped his horses with the lines. The team struggled into an uneven run and the wagon bounced wildly, its wheels rising in the air as they hit ruts and rocks. The tailgate sprung open and boxes and baskets fell out from under the rear canvas. Black Feather coolly reloaded and then spurred his black stallion diagonally across the valley. Three of his men followed. The chase was short. Two of the bandits halted the wagon team. The driver was middle-aged, and in good shape except for a slight potbelly that tightened the fabric of his overalls and suspenders. He wore a farmer's floppy, brimmed, brown wool felt hat. He dropped his old musket and raised both hands in the air in surrender.

His wife, of the same age, had short nappy hair, dark with touches of grey, under her wool sun bonnet and a pleasant but wrinkled face. She trembled uncontrollably, her mouth open and tears rolling from the corner of her eyes. She clutched her daughter, who was shaking like a leaf, her face buried in her mother's side. The girl's thin shape was just taking on the form of a woman. She had long blond hair and a clear complexion. Black Feather judged her to be in her early teens. He looked from one to the other, saying nothing.

The farmer began to speak in a cracking voice. "Whatever you want. Please take it. We have some valuable things here. We're just going back to our ranch down on the Big Thompson. The house was not quite finished so we spent the winter at Fort Laramie. Please, this is all we have."

The Smoothbore lay across Black Feather's forearm, its muzzle to the side of the stallion's neck, pointing at the man's head. "Thank you for your offer. But we already know that we can have whatever we want." Black Feather let his eyes slip to the hysterical girl.

"Now, wait just a…" The blast from the Smoothbore blew off the top of the man's head. The .45-caliber ball sprayed blood, splattering the women and the wagon canvas. The black stallion squealed in protest at the percussion and reared to the side.

The mother rose, her hands in the position of prayer in front of her chest, pleading, "Please..." A shot rang out from one of the men at the fore of the wagon team. The woman clutched her throat, bright red blood squirting from between her fingers, gurgled and fell backward into the wagon. The girl's sobs grew more violent, but the shock had stolen the sound from her.

She doubled over, her immature breasts pressed against her knees. She covered her head with shaking hands, her frame racked with hysterical shudders. Black Feather noticed the clear, smooth skin of her wrists and long fingers where they dug into her blond hair. Deep within him a grim, long buried memory stirred.

"Crow!" Black Feather turned to the man behind him. "Take her away from the wagons."

Crow kicked his horse forward. Black Feather reached out the long barrel of the Smoothbore and placed its length against the man's chest. "Do not hurt her." Crow nodded and urged his horse forward again. Black Feather pressed the side of the barrel, more firmly this time, against Crow's neck. "And do not touch her." A slight look of anguish flitted across the outlaw's face, but he looked in Black Feather's eyes and nodded.

Black Feather waited until Crow and the girl were one hundred yards away on the other side of the wagon. He climbed on the wagon seat, reached into the bed, and dragged the front half of the mother's body from behind the canvas. He checked quickly to make sure he was out of sight of Crow and the girl. His blade flashed in the sunlight and moved several times in a saw-like motion, its sharp edge making a swishing sound like a rough finger drawn back and forth across wet parchment. Black Feather rose, scalp in one bloody hand and the silver-red knife dripping in the other.

Hoisting the prize in the air, his bronzed arms lifted high, he tipped back his explosion of long, dirty, brown hair, shook the scalp and the knife at the blue sky that seethed with morbid pink-hued memory, and screamed in triumph; his muscular torso etched against the morning grey, his silhouette framed to the south by Longs Peak and to the west by Rawah Range. Around him, the unkempt members of his renegade band had gathered. They, too, raised their rifles and bows to the sky, joining his bloodcurdling howl.

He jumped from the wagon directly into the saddle on the stallion. "Men, strip everything of value. Don't forget the food, and do not fight over the scalps. We won't torch. Smoke would be dangerous." The band scattered with whoops and shouts except for Pedro, his lieutenant, who rode up beside him, awaiting orders.

He turned in his saddle and spoke sharply to him in Spanish. "Pedro, after the men have stripped the wagons, get the girl and bring her to me. Bind her wrists. Wet the rawhide first. I want it tight but not so that it marks her. She is mine."

Pedro puffed out his chest. "But we always share..."

Black Feather's fist, clenched around the hilt of his knife, struck out, delivering a meaty backhanded blow to Pedro's face. The paunchy man's voice died in a gurgle as he fell from his horse. Black Feather glowered down from the stallion as the fat man rolled back and forth on the ground, clutching his bloody nose and whimpering in pain. Black Feather watched with impassive detachment.

"One more word Pedro, and your scalp will join those of the white eyes on my belt. If I tire of her, perhaps I will give you a taste, or perhaps I will kill her."

Raucous laughter caught Black Feather's attention. He cursed and trotted over to where Crow and another outlaw with a toothless grin were roughly holding the girl's arms to keep her upright. Crow was fondling her breast and licking his lips. The heel of Black Feather's foot connected square with Crow's right temple. He staggered backward and released the girl who slumped to the ground.

"I told you not to touch her, Crow."

Crow was rubbing his head. "Shit, boss, wasn't doing nothing. You never been so particular before."

Black Feather silently dismounted and crouched in front of the girl's shuddering figure. One small pert breast was still exposed where Crow had ripped her blouse and chemise. He slowly reached out one hand toward her face, as if offering a first-time smell to a new horse. He gently pressed two fingers under her chin and carefully lifted her face toward his. The black pupils of her terrified eyes almost obscured their hazel color.

"What is your name, girl?"

She said nothing. Black Feather wasn't sure she could hear, or, if she could, if his words were registering. With his fingers still under her chin, he moved his thumb to remove the smear of blood from her cheek. Her skin was young and smooth. This gesture drew no reaction either. He stood, turned to his stallion, and untied the leathers holding his bedroll. From under the bedroll he drew out a black and tan wool coat with a sheepskin collar.

He knelt down to her. "It's well-worn but it has warmth." Her eyes remained vacant, her body listless. He extended the coat but she made no move to reach for it. Black Feather carefully drew the wool over her shoulders. He began to rise. The coat, much too large, slipped from one side, exposing her arm. He squatted, one long arm rearranging the wool to cover her. He remained squatting, staring at her, unsettling visions again trying to claw from the depths of his mind where he had long ago buried them.

Standing, he turned to Crow who had three fingers pressed against the purple welt that was rising above his eye. "Put her on the saddle behind me after I mount. Tie her to me if she can't hold on. Use that lariat if you have to."

Crow stepped forward to obey the command. Black Feather grabbed him by his shirt collar and pulled his face close to his. He gave the smaller man a savage look. "Gently." Crow looked astonished, but nodded vigorously.

Black Feather mounted and Crow hoisted the young woman, who was breathing in deep tortured gasps, into position. She slumped forward into Black Feather's back, her small white hands clutching the sides of the blue army shell jacket he had taken from the dead trooper.

"Will you hold on?" There was no response. "Crow, tie her off around the middle to me. Not too tight." Black Feather looked up and realized his entire band of cutthroats was dispersed in a loose circle around him. They were all staring, several with mouths agape.

He ignored them. "We will head out to the grasslands and then northeast to the Platte. Less chance of cavalry. Better chance of wagon trains, *bigger* wagon trains." He laughed. "Let's ride."

March 18, 1855

$\mathscr{S}$TRENGTH
OF CONVICTION

SIX HUNDRED MILES SOUTHEAST OF WHERE THE BLOODY CORPSES lay crumpled in the plundered wagons along the Cache la Poudre, and several hundred miles southwest of where Mac's wagon train had begun its westward journey, Israel sat hunched over, his sloughed shoulders forward, his curly salt and pepper head just inches from a yellowed newspaper. A pair of round spectacles, rimmed in a thin brass frame, hung from his wide nose. The pages were spread out on an old nicked table made of scrap lumber. The corners of the home-made table were worn, rounded like Israel's once broad shoulders. He squinted as he read, mumbling the sentences aloud in a low baritone, sometimes repeating unfamiliar words to get their gist.

His gaze raised to the far wall of the ramshackle structure he and his wife called home. Several used pots and ladles hung from smelted, square-head spikes over the weighty, cast iron wood stove. A few patches of colored fabric were tacked to the exposed rough studs of the twenty-by-twenty building, "To give the place some color," his wife had said.

Peeling the thick-glassed spectacles from one ear, and then the other, he cleaned the lenses with his shirttail, giving careful thought to what he had just read: "New York – January 17, 1855 – Slaves Find Help In Escape."

Mistress Tara had somehow obtained the glasses when she secretly taught him to read, and realized he was having difficulty seeing the print. He was about to don them again when he heard footsteps creaking on the broken steps to the rickety front porch at the only door of the one-room shack.

He hastily closed and folded the paper, covered it with a large, square, hand-carved wooden tray he kept on the table for exactly that purpose, and quickly stood. The sudden movement knocked the wobbly old chair over. Its rounded backrest, missing one vertical spindle broken long ago, bounced several times on the uneven, rough-sawn planks of the floor before it came to rest.

The door, hinged to the frame with strips of dried, cracked leather, swung open. The rounded figure of a woman, whose tired body and worn features belied her middle age, stepped over the threshold. Israel let out his breath, letting his shoulders relax. His wife's hair, all but a few wiry grey strands mixed with black, was tucked under a blue print bandana. Her face was full, round, and high-cheeked. She carried a wooden water pail in one hand and a burlap sack, its bottom bulging unevenly, in the other. She stood just inside the open door, her eyes darting from the chair, to the table, to Israel's face.

"How many times do I have to tell you, husband, if you're going to read them papers Mistress Tara smuggles to you, you best do it somewhere's else where the bosses can't walk in and catch you. That old black body of yours is way past time it could take twenty lashes."

Israel shuffled his feet. "Now, Lucy…"

"Don't you dare 'now Lucy' me," she wagged her finger at him, the digits crooked from years of manual labor. "You know it's against the law for our kind to read, and if we're caught, Lord knows it ain't pretty." She shut the door partially with her elbow, closing it firmly with a rearward push from the sole of her foot. She walked over to the table and dumped the burlap sack with a purposefully aimed thud in the square tray covering the newspaper. Israel backed up a step. Hands on hip, she faced him.

"You know, there's even some darkies would turn you in. This hovel they gives us is better than most, and sure 'nough there are others who would curry favor with the massuhs and get themselves a better roof. At least this place doesn't leak."

"Lucy, we've been doing other people's bidding since we was born. Reading these papers tells me what's going on out there in the world, even if they are months old when I get them. That anti-slavery paper out of Lawrence, the *Kansas Free State* is good, but this one..." He slipped the tray carefully off the yellowed paper, "*The New York Times* Sunday Edition, January 17, 1855, it's the best." He lovingly traced one crooked, calloused finger down the edge of the page.

"Takes me a long time to read it and there's words I have to sort out, so I understand what the writings 'bout, but one thing's for certain sure. There's changes comin' and I thinks they be comin' right quick." Israel looked closely at his wife. "Have you overheard the field bosses talkin'?"

Her hands still on her hips, Lucy pursed her lips. Her wide-set, brown eyes remained unwavering in their reproachful expression. She spoke in a low tone, with a glance at the door. "It just so happens, when I was cleaning the kitchen after serving dinner up at the main house the other night, I did hear talk. It was about folks called abolitionists and some men named Thomas and Quantrill. They particularly did not like some man I think was from Illinois. Lincoln, if I recall correctly. And then someone named Brown—they thought he was crazy," she paused.

"And, Mistress Tara has stopped taking supper with them." She shook her head slowly and wagged a finger at him, "But that's not our business Israel, that's white folks business. Our chore is to stay alive, have food on the table and make sure there's wood for that stove," she nodded at the grimy, 1735 Castrol cast iron cook stove in the corner, its black flue pipe ascending up to the roof in segments, some of which were bent and ill-fitting.

She sighed. "It's just turning spring, and summer will be here soon enough, I reckon. You'll be busy taking care of the horses and mules and other critter fixins. I thank God you're not in the field anymore.

There were nights you'd come home so tired and dirty you didn't even have strength to eat."

Israel walked slowly over to his wife. He was not a tall man, but he stood a head higher than she. He wrapped his arms around her back at her shoulders, pulled her toward him and kissed the top of her head where the brittle curls of her hair poked out from under the tight wrap of the bandana. Her unflinching, rigid posture loosened only slightly. "Lucy, we been married close to twenty-four years, and you're still the prettiest woman in the Oklahoma Territories."

She pulled away from him. "Stop feeding me that nonsense. I been listening to it since before we married. We both know it's not the truth. We are two dirt-poor, half-broken down old darkies. I was birthed here, you came here shortly after you was born, and this stuff about the world..." she gestured at the paper, "and reading all that nonsense written by a bunch of white folks living rich in some big city two months' wagon ride from here don't change nothing. They don't even call this Oklahoma. They call it the Unnamed Territory. They don't know nothing. We can't change them facts. Stop thinking of yourself and your notions. Think of me. Think of us. You get caught reading that paper and we get thrown out of this shack, what we gonna do?"

Israel felt his jaw set, and the muscles in his face tighten. He stared at his wife with unblinking eyes. She finally looked down. He took a step forward and very gently lifted her chin so that his gaze once again bore into hers.

"What we'll do, woman, is we will be free. And I'd rather be free and dead than alive and a slave. I am plumb fed up with 'Yes Massuh,' 'No Mistress,' and 'Yessir boss,' being told what to do, not getting paid and being only able to provide this, " he swept his arm around the barren interior, "to the single person in this life that I love."

"Free?" Lucy's voice rose in pitch and volume. "You're talking foolishness again. Look around you, Israel. You have two pairs of clothes, one set of overalls and one pair of old work boots. I got two work dresses, my church outfit, and one dress-up set for when I'm serving over at the main house. We got seven dollars saved up from that leather stitching you do for folks in town, and you are not supposed to be doing that. We got nothing."

Israel felt that tight, constricted, frustrated feeling. It was always like this, whenever they had these arguments, which had become more frequent over the past year.

"Lucy," Israel pounded his chest hard several times with one fist, "...we got this. We got heart. We got spirit." He raised his forefinger to his forehead. "We got brains. We got those things and we don't need nothin' else other than the freedom to put 'em to work for us and not for others."

Lucy exhaled in an exasperated sigh. She looked down at her feet, shook her head slowly and then shifted her eyes to him again, her voice softer, "There are times, Israel, when you say that with so much belly fire behind the words that you get me at least half-believing." She sighed again, and eased herself onto the only other chair in the room, rubbing her knees. "These old joints are achy today. Sure sign of weather coming in. I think I dislike spring more than any other season. You don't know what can happen from one day to the next."

She continued to rub her knees with her hands, gnarled finger joints wrapped around her knee caps. Israel noticed the slightly lighter appearance of her skin up to her middle forearms, the result of doing laundry in bleach, day in and day out, up at the main house. The faded sun of late afternoon filtered through the four pane window, the mullion making a cross-like exception in the beam that fell across the table, brightening the yellowed white of the newsprint.

His heart lurched as he saw a tear trickle down the wide curve of one of her cheeks.

"You know I'm proud of you, Israel. You are a good man, strong and smart..." She smiled gently. "And there was a time you was the best dancer on the plantation."

Israel chuckled, "If I remember right, we could sure shake a leg."

Lucy giggled, "Yes sir, we sure could." She looked down at her hands still moving in tight circles on her knees.

Israel knew she was thinking. "Lucy, I been reading about these things that the field bosses has been talking 'bout and what you been hearing over at the main house. I tell you there's a change headed our way. This Lincoln fellow, he's against slavery, and there's plenty more like him. Some say he may run for president, although most think he can't win this time anyway, but there's lots of folks angry. There was this agreement that was made between white folks from the North and South called the Missouri Compromise, 'cept for the state of Missouri. It dates back to about 1820, and stopped slavery above the thirtieth parallel. No one paid it any mind. They tried some tom-foolery with that compact in 1850, but that didn't go nowheres. Now there are those that want to extend slavery north of that. That line ain't too far above us, and north of it using slaves has been illegal.

"Now they just passed this new one last year..." He walked over to the table, sat down, put on the spectacles, folded back a few pages of the paper, ran one finger down the columns and stopped. "... Yep, the 1854 Kansas Nebraska Act. That set more folks off against one another. You heard about the shootings in the Kansas Territories few months back. There will be a lot more of that. There's lots of people that think there is going to be a war, slave states against the non-slave states mostly, the South against the North."

"Last time I checked Israel, we are considered to be in the South. Missouri and Arkansas ain't but a good day's ride north or east. And that is all slave country," she said with resigned sarcasm.

Israel made a fist and slammed it on the table, but with no real force, "And, that new law I tolds you 'bout just now—it made Kansas a Territory, and its free—no slavery—and it ain't much more than two or three days' walk."

He rose from the table, bent down on one knee in front of her, reached out his calloused, once powerful hands and wrapped them around one of hers.

"Look at me, Lucy. Have I ever told you wrong?"

Lucy's eyes held his. She shook her head slowly.

"That's right. No, I ain't. And I'm telling you, I don't read so good, but I've done read and overheard enough to know slavery ain't gonna last forever. It might be over sooner than you think. The trick is, we might be too old, and if all the darkies get free all at the same time, it's gonna be rough. Most folks like us don't think like I am talking. The Massuh's don't want us to have these thoughts that's why they say we aren't allowed to read. I'm telling you woman, we need to get out ahead of what's going to happen. We don't want to be where there's gonna be armies or worse yet, a bunch of godless bad men pretending to be armies like that Quantrill and Brown fellas you heard them talking about. They is in the paper, too."

Lucy looked at him intently. She blinked rapidly and another tear trickled down her opposite cheek. "Even if what you say is true, Israel, there's nothing we can do. This is all much bigger than us. It will all just be like before. Everything we do, everything we are, everything we have, our lives, will always be decided by others."

Israel reached up both hands, pressed them gently against either side of her face and held her head steady just inches from his own. "You're wrong, Lucy. We got four things way bigger than the white man's armies, or the Massuh's rules. You got you, I got me, we got each other. And we got the Lord. Ain't nothin' bigger. No one can take our spirit from us." He paused and looked earnestly into her eyes. "...If we don't do something with these gifts the Lord done give us, then we got no one to blame but us. Let me read you something."

Israel stood carefully, pushing down both hands on his raised knee to lift his other leg off the floor. He went to the door, opened it a crack and looked out. He made his way to the window and carefully surveyed the flat, wavy, undulations of the countryside, and the main house several hundred yards distant. He moved over to the bed, which was little more than a raised wooden platform topped by a thin mattress with strands of straw poking out from a threadbare cotton cover, overlain by several tattered, dark wool blankets.

He reached under the mattress and drew out a folded piece of old, ragged, brownish-yellow newspaper. "You know what this is?" He shook the paper, which crinkled in the stillness of the shack. "This is a printing of the Declaration of Independence. You know, July 4, when they have their picnic and such. This here paper is what happened when some white men decided they wasn't going to be slaves of other white folks in the seventeen hundreds. And this applies to all citizens of the United States of America and that's what we are part of."

Lucy shook her head again, "But that's the point, Israel. We ain't citizens."

"By God, we are. This paper says so and there's a bunch of folks that agree with it. I've been reading about—hold on a minute—let me find it." Israel carefully unfolded the paper, its brittle, compressed pieces reluctant to separate. He fumbled his spectacles onto his nose with one hand and held them there, "All men are created equal and endowed by their Creator with certain inalienable rights..." he bent his head closer to the print "...life, liberty, and the pursuit of happiness."

Israel slowly took off the spectacles, thoughtfully refolded the paper and slipped it carefully far back under the mattress. He turned to face his wife again. "Lucy, 'all men' means us! I think it's high time that Lucy and Israel grabbed their share of that 'equal' and that 'liberty'."

Lucy was wide-eyed. "Okay, supposing I was to say yes, Israel, what do you plan to do? You planning on going to Massuh Jim and askin' him to borrow his Sunday carriage for a day? Maybe tell him we just want to go for a ride in the woods and you'll be back by sundown, don't worry?" She chuckled dejectedly at the thought.

"No, Lucy, I think we bide our time, make ourselves a plan, concentrate on what we need, pick warm weather, and lite out one night. We head north, and get in touch with this outfit called the 'Underground Railroad.' Paper says it runs right up through the Kansas Territory. It's secret, on account of that Fugitive Slave Act the Southern states got through. Anyone helpin' escaped slaves can go to jail. But we'll find them—I know we will. We let them help us get ourselves west. You've heard Massuh Jim and his friends talk about the Rocky Mountains where they go hunting for elk once in a while. I've been reading up a mite on them, too. They are big, mighty harsh, and very few folks. There's free darkies out there makin' names for themselves like this fella I read of, Barney Ford. But, he was born free. We can't take no chances. We will go to the other side of the range and be far from what things I think are going to happen. We will do what we have to, and if we die trying then its far better than taking our last breath in this pile of wood we don't even own."

They stared at each other for several minutes and then Lucy broke into a laugh. Her body shook. "Oh, Lordy, Lordy," she gasped.

Her laughter infected Israel who finally had to sit down and hold his sides. Lucy had one hand over her chest trying to catch her breath. "You are crazy, Israel. You been crazy since the first day I met you. Maybe that's why I love you." She gasped for air and wiped the tears from her eyes with the tips of her fingers, "You figure out how us two old niggas is gonna do what would be impossible for a twenty-year-old, and Lucy Thomas will stand by her man. We will put our lives in the hands of the Lord and see what He decides." She shook her head in disbelief at her own words. "The Rocky Mountains? Don't know much about that place. Maybe you could read me some of those words so at least I know little bit about where we'll be headed when we die."

"Sure enough, Lucy. Sure enough. I will."

March 18, 1855

PRACTICALITIES

REBECCA'S HIPS AND SHOULDERS SWAYED WITH THE MOVEMENT OF the wagon. She had willed herself to not say a word to Inga and Johannes. Despite her rigid posture and the cold, stern forward immobility of her head, her eyes kept shifting sideways toward the two of them. There was no mistaking the shared glances and soft smiles between them, or the opportunity each took to touch the other, even if just insignificant brushes of fingers against legs or arms. It all gave rise to an annoying feeling she couldn't quite place, and that annoyed her even more.

Angry? Maybe a tad, she thought. *Jealous of Johannes? Impossible. Of Inga? No, she is my friend. Lonely? Never. Envious?* She felt her eyes widen with sudden realization, and sighed.

"Are you all right, Milady Marx?"

Rebecca diverted her stare from the two-track to the lanky, beautiful blonde next to her. Inga's exquisite Scandinavian facial features were anxious.

"Yes, Inga. Thank you, I am quite fine," Rebecca mustered a faint smile, and looked back to the road.

The trail here was well used, *if one could call it that,* sniffed Rebecca to herself at the bumpy, tracked ruts that had been worn by the wheels of many wagons. The lands within twenty miles of the west bank of the Mississippi, and south of Missouri River, whose course they were parallel to, were sparsely populated. Farm houses—some white, some red—and barns of the same color, or unpainted weathered grey or chestnut amber, peeked from the edge of fields and nestled in clusters of trees. The landscape was a gently rolling, never ending patchwork of cultivated farm lands, grassy pastures, and large clumps of leafless woodlands. Here and there a farmer stumbled behind a hand plow pulled by oxen or mules. Several stopped their work and stared—wistfully, it seemed to Rebecca—at the almost one-third-mile string of wagons creaking westward.

The day was warm for March. The rutted tracks wove through the trees and open areas, casting the prairie schooner in sun and shade. The clang and thumps of wheel and wagon parts and tools in the jockey box bolted to the side of the schooner was annoying, and Rebecca was uncomfortably surprised at the film of perspiration on her upper body when the blasts of sun cut through the humid air and fell on the black wool of her dress. *I shall have to pay better attention to the weather. Black may not be the best color for sunny days.*

After several hours of stony silence, broken only by her curt reply to Inga, Rebecca thought she had made her displeasure with the two lovers' antics clear, and she turned to Johannes. "When do you think we will stop for lunch?"

Johannes looked back at her over the top of Inga's head and smiled. "I was beginning to think the excitement of the trail had rendered you speechless."

Rebecca felt her cheek muscles tighten. *He really is an insufferable rogue, even if pleasant on the eye.* Rebecca appraised him with an aloof, unblinking stare. Johannes was a handsome, tall, well-built fellow, if a bit on the lanky side. His endless, often sardonic smile was set in a rugged Viking face framed by a shock of blond hair. His unwavering pale blue eyes had a rarely absent, sometimes impish, twinkle. He reminded Rebecca of a happy-go-lucky schoolboy on the verge of playing another prank, but she knew that under that beguiling manner lurked a worldly soul and quick mind. She had met men like him on her father's trading ships, mostly officers. Despite their outward jovial natures, they were cold, hard and decisive in a crisis.

She flashed a guarded smile. "The trip thus far has been pleasant. Such quaint little farms, and the weather is much better than I expected."

His expression of mild surprise at the civility of her answer was not lost on Rebecca. She decided to press the momentary thaw in their dialogue.

"So, Johannes, what times of the day do you think we will stop to freshen up and eat?"

"Truth is, it is not up to me. I don't believe we will be stopping except for very short breaks to tend and water stock. We are but a couple of hours into a journey of almost two months. Stopping for lunch each day could add weeks to the travel. The longer we are on the trail, the more danger. Simply said, delay increases our exposure to unpleasant events, such as floods and storms, or from parties adverse to our interests, or wanting what we have." He paused, "And I'm quite sure there are many of those between here and Cherry Creek."

Though Rebecca was reluctant to admit it, the rationale of his answer was irrefutable. She quickly mulled several counterpoints she could raise to make an argument, but found she could not quarrel with the logic. Her inability to intelligently respond added to her unsettled feeling. She realized with a start she had never thought of how basic day-to-day needs would be handled on the trail.

Her eyes flicked from Johannes, to Inga, and back to Johannes. "You mean we will not stop at all during the day?" A sudden thought struck her. "But... what do we do when we need to be... private?" She felt herself blush, and noted with satisfaction that Inga's head snapped up, and she turned widened eyes to Johannes.

Looking from one woman to the other, realization clearly dawning, Johannes cleared his throat. "Perhaps we will stop briefly from time to time during the day. The wagons and wheels will need to be checked periodically, and if we need water...," he nodded back to the three, thirty-gallon wooden planked casks securely lashed to the side of the prairie schooner, "there will be waste if the wagon is moving. According to Reuben's maps, as we get further west in the weeks to come water will become a far more scarce and valuable commodity. Sloshing water on the ground will not be a luxury we can afford." He flashed a smile at Inga. Rebecca's shoulders gave an involuntary jerk at the mention of "maps," but Johannes was so focused on Inga that he did not notice.

"When you ladies need those private moments, Reuben or I could accompany you for safety, or you can walk out into the brush and then catch up with the wagon. There are enough oxen-drawn rigs in this column that I think you could catch up easily at a fast walk." He paused and chuckled. "Of course, it depends how long you must be away from the wagon, and I presume that how you dress and in how many layers will be a factor." His eyes danced with amusement as he glanced at Rebecca.

Rebecca, still distracted by Johannes revelation, was unable to muster a snappy response.

"Oh, my," exclaimed Inga, "I've never given those basics any thought." She radiated such deep concern that Rebecca had to stifle a laugh, but her mind returned quickly to Reuben's maps. *Were they anything like hers?* She gave a quick thought to coaxing more on the subject out of Johannes. *No,* she smiled to herself, *I can learn more from Reuben.*

That plan settled in her mind, she turned to Inga. "Fine thing it is. We will be bouncing on this hard uncomfortable wagon seat for months, and that will mean more frequent needs for privacy than normal, with far less opportunity." She raised her eyes to Johannes. "Regardless of the hardship, I intend to dress as a lady."

Johannes shook his head slowly, practically beaming his amusement. "As you wish, Rebecca."

"Perhaps you should talk to Mac. Maybe you could convince him to be amenable to a scheduled series of stops each day for the ladies."

He snapped the lines across the backs of the horses, with a gentle touch Rebecca noticed. His eyes expertly checked the line attachments and collars as he spoke, "Understand, Rebecca, Mac is not one I would expect to endorse any delay. I believe if we didn't have to stop at all, he wouldn't. Each time we halt without the wagons in a circle as a defensive perimeter, we are far more prone to attack. If we stop in single file for more than just a few minutes, it must be only in an open area from which an ambush could be spotted in advance."

"How do you know so much about this, Johannes?" Rebecca was fully aware that Johannes was not keen on questions concerning his past, and when he popped the horses again it was with a bit more force than necessary. Then he turned to her, that grin once again creasing his lips. "Library books, Rebecca. I read many library books as a youth."

———

THE SOUND OF A GALLOPING HORSE MOVING ITS WAY UP THE LONG string of wagons toward them could be heard above the bumps, thumps and creaks of the prairie schooner. Reuben reined in on Rebecca's side of the wagon. Lahn was apparently displeased at the interruption in his run, and Reuben had to hold the palomino back several times.

Rebecca smiled coyly at him. "Mr. Frank, how pleasant that you join us. Your job of standing in the stirrups and waving your hat in the air has kept you quite occupied."

Reuben pulled on the brim of his hat before replying, "And good day to you too, Rebecca."

Promptly ignoring her, he and Johannes launched into a discussion about some river they would have to cross, while Rebecca discreetly studied him. He was a very attractive man, well built, in a sensuous, but wholly masculine way. His face was ruggedly handsome—wide-set green eyes, angular, square jaw, with dark brown hair that had a hint of curl. Her gaze dropped to his hands. They were large but not overly so, calloused, powerful, the fingers in proper proportion to palms.

Her mind drifted back to their chance evening encounter between the train cars weeks ago en route to St. Louis from New York. Their sharing the same Pennsylvania Railroad train west, had been a surprise—not all pleasant—to both of them. One evening a sudden jostling on the tracks had thrown her into him as they tried to pass one another between cars. Those hands had grasped her back to steady her, then their eyes had met and he had drawn her into him.

She remembered the kiss—her very first kiss, ever—the sway of the train, the sounds of the track, the energy that coursed through her body as his lips found hers, the fierce pounding pressure in her chest, the perfect fit and press of their bodies, and the strange warmth that spread from her stomach downward between her hips. Caught up in the moment, she had responded, pressing herself to his form, parting her lips to mold to his, and, to her own dismay, instinctively running her eager, searching tongue hungrily inside his mouth.

Fate kept throwing them unexpectedly together. They had noticed one another on many occasions during the Atlantic crossing of the *Edinburgh*, but their encounter on the train was the first time they had touched, and the feel, the smell, the magnetism of their bodies was one of her constant memories.

The rush of desire had surprised and scared her. Frightened by her own reaction, she had ended that kiss with an attempted slap to his face. He had caught her hand in a vice-like grip. Even in the twilight between the cars, she was struck that his eyes had changed from green to grey. She often wondered what color they might have become had she not pushed him away. She had seen him angry only one other time. She and Inga, and Reuben and Johannes had by yet another quirk stayed at the same upscale hotel on Fourth Street in St. Louis. She had swallowed her pride and asked Reuben if the men would assist her and Inga in the furtherance of their trip west. Johannes had been enthusiastic, Reuben far less so.

The day they were loading the wagon in St. Louis, she and Reuben had a thunderous argument—quite a public display. She demanded to bring all six of her oversized, ornate trunks. Reuben insisted on a limit of three, and when she refused, he dumped all six carry-alls from the rear of the wagon. One exploded as it hit the street, festooning the sidewalk directly in front of the hotel entry with her clothes, much to the delight of Johannes, amusement of onlookers and the sing-song laughter of the Chinese coolies Johannes had hired to help load.

Reuben was particularly frustrated by the one trunk she always kept double locked, and by her adamant, foot-stomping refusal to open it, coupled with a demand that he discard his "old, scuffed leather case" to make room. His eyes had flashed to grey. "No!" he had snapped with such force that she said nothing further.

They finally compromised on three trunks, one of which would be the one locked. The balance of her clothes, jewelry, tea sets—except one, four-piece setting—and valuables would be stored at the hotel until her intended return in the fall. Though she had never planned to travel beyond St. Louis, she had no choice. She was forced to go further west, if she was to keep the promise she had made to her father on his deathbed. To fulfill that vow, she had to follow the map he had left her to the mysterious piece of land bequeathed to him by the King of Spain in Las Colorades, on the flank of Las Montanas Rojas, the Red Mountains, in the rugged southwest corner of the Kansas Territory. The acreage was hers by inheritance.

The map, and other gifts of his, formed the secret, treasured contents of the locked trunk. She wished the business of his estate and related matters completed as quickly as possible. Her mother was frail, and their family finances in disarray after her father's passing. Her goal was to maximize monies from a sale of the property and make a speedy return to far more civilized environments. Rebecca had assured Mum she would return to their stately London row house by late fall.

Reuben moved one hand along the length of Lahn's reins, and as she studied the curves of his fingers, she found the tip of her tongue running over her upper lip. Was she never to have control of herself around him?

"You are looking a bit pink, Rebecca, are you okay?"

She stiffened and tore her eyes away, paused briefly to reclaim her composure, and then looked up at Reuben. "We were just discussing the daily routine. Is it true that we will not be stopping and the time ladies have for privacy will be limited?"

Johannes shook his head and chuckled. "Now you wish to compare answers?"

Reuben looked from Rebecca to Johannes, and then back to Rebecca. Inga nervously fidgeted, smiled sweetly up at him and interjected, "Good morning to you, Reuben."

"Pleasant day, Inga. You look very lovely this morning. Has Johannes shown you how to drive the team?"

"He has given me some instruction, but I'm afraid there's more to learn."

Johannes boomed out a laugh. "Then we shall just have to continue the instruction, won't we?"

Reuben chuckled, "I doubt you need that excuse, Viking that you are."

Reuben turned his attention back to Rebecca, "Apparently this is not the first time you've made this inquiry." He smiled, "Stops, when they occur, will be short-lived and sporadic. I would suggest setting aside some hardtack, salted beef, or jerky before we move out each day. Certainly nothing that needs preparation. We brought several water bags. You should probably fill them in the morning and keep them up front in the wagon with you for easy access. From here to Cherry Creek will be a very basic lifestyle."

Rebecca felt his eyes rove down her figure, his gaze lingering at her breasts, and again at her waist. Her heart skipped, and she was immediately annoyed with herself.

"You might want to consider a bit less on clothing, Rebecca. Layers of clothes are great for warmth but we are heading into months of higher temperatures, and they can get in the way and take far more time to deal with."

Rebecca narrowed her eyes. "Well, whatever the normal customs on these wagon trains," she said, pursing her lips, "I am a lady and I intend to be and look like one, each and every day."

"Suit yourself," Reuben shrugged. "I overheard Mac say something this morning. The phrase stuck with me. 'You can lead a horse to water but you can't make 'em drink'."

He turned his attention to Johannes. "We need to talk about some of the other wagons. Remarkably, there are two other passengers from the *Edinburgh* in one. By the way, I would be happy to switch out with you and drive a while if you want to get some time on a horse."

Johannes shook his head, showed a moment of curiosity, and then looked sideways at Inga. "Maybe later in the day. Right now I think

I must focus on teaching Inga...and Rebecca if she wishes..." he looked over to Rebecca with that teasing grin, "...to drive this team."

"It just so happens gentlemen, that I know how to drive a team, ride a horse, and shoot a rifle." Rebecca shot each of them a defiant look. "Rather well, actually."

Reuben and Johannes eyes met. Neither responded. Inga's eyebrows arched and she stared at her mistress.

After a long moment Reuben laughed, nodded at Johannes, and tipped his hat to Inga and then Rebecca, "I think you are in good, but mischievous hands. I will see if we plan to stop before evening. Mac is gonna do a roast tonight with one of the train's two pigs. It'll give us a chance to meet one another and become better acquainted. I think he also wants to make sure everyone knows his rules. When we make camp, we can figure out the sleeping and other arrangements."

Johannes smiled from ear to ear, looked at Inga and, knowing full and well that Rebecca was watching, winked at her. Inga blushed, smoothing the fabric of her dress where it draped over her knees.

Reuben slapped his thigh, released a low chuckle, and then gently spurred Lahn into a canter toward the head of the train.

March 18, 1855

$\mathscr{L}$UDWIG'S DIAMONDS

MAC COULD FEEL THE WOOL OF HIS JACKET BIND SLIGHTLY ACROSS his back as his broad shoulders moved side to side with the prance-like walk of his feisty mount. He heard the drumbeat of horse hooves behind him but, already familiar with the rhythm of Reuben's palomino, he did not turn around as the young man rode abreast of Mac's reddish mare, slowing his gelding to a walk.

"Much obliged for your help getting this outfit rolling this morning," Mac said, leaning over the opposite side of his horse and spitting a gooey, dark brown stream of chew into the ruts on the wagon road. "Seems you have yourself a hell of a horse there, too. Good looking animal."

"Wasn't much to it," replied Reuben. He reached forward and patted Lahn's shoulder. "A good horse indeed. He thinks like me." Mac watched Reuben shift in the saddle. "I like this western saddle, but it is much different than ours back in Germany. Puts pressure in different places," he said, grinning.

Mac suppressed a laugh. "I've seen them European saddles. Reminds me of some female sidesaddle. I'd go bareback before I sat my Irish ass in one of them."

The two of them rode in silence for several minutes. Sunlight filtered through the grey, coarse-barked trunks of oak, elm and beech where the two-track wound through stands of trees, the broken rays alternately brightening, then darkening the sheen of their horses' coats. Mac glanced at Reuben from time to time, sizing him up. Reuben was not an overly big man, maybe six feet. He was powerfully built in a sinewy way, with muscled shoulders that tapered to a slender waist. His body was built for action, his hands had seen work, and the steady level look from those green eyes didn't waiver.

"A fifty-two caliber Sharps rifle?" Mac nodded toward Reuben's scabbard.

"Yes, with Enfield adjustable ladder sights out to twelve-hundred and fifty yards." Reuben leaned forward and patted the exposed stock of the Sharps where it protruded from the heavy leather.

"I like the Army issue 1847 Musketoon, myself," Mac grinned, "but my favorite for close-in work is this..." he reached behind him and half drew out a shotgun, with a checkered walnut buttstock, "Colt Model 1855 Revolving Percussion shotgun. Five-cylinder, 10-gauge, side hammer, thirty-inch barrel. Brand, spankin' new. It can do some damage."

Reuben shook his head appreciatively and whistled, "Now that is some fire power."

Mac laughed, "Yep, a swiss cheese factory," then he grew serious. "We will be crossing the Gasconade River five days from now. It ain't as big as the Osage, in a few weeks, but it's our first sizeable crossing," Mac stated quietly. "Ever taken wagons across a river?"

"On the farm we had to drive the cattle across the river when we moved them from pasture to pasture. Every once in a while, we would have to get fence or other supplies, or the plow, to the other side and back, but I can't say I have a lot of experience." Reuben paused for a minute. "And to be honest, Mac, the Lahn is a slow-moving river. I have a feeling some of the water we'll be encountering is much more wild and powerful."

"Yep, you can bet on that. My right-hand man is going to have to learn how to traverse American rivers. Other stuff, too. I'll teach you. There's a trick to choosing the angle, which is pretty much based on current and depth, and finding the places on either bank that work. Preparation time before the first wagon hits the water might be more important than the actual ford. Pick a bad spot, or poor crossing points on either side, or misjudge the current, or what kind of bottom the river has, and you will lose wagons and animals, maybe people, sure enough."

"I'm eager to learn, Mac. Anything you want to teach this green-horn, you don't need to ask first. I think every bit of 'how-to' I can pick up will certainly come in handy when establishing the ranch."

"Where are you planning to build this ranch?" \

"A place called Las Montanas Rojas, the Red Mountains, in an area known as the Uncompahgre."

Mac whistled softly. "That's the very southwest corner of the Kansas Territories. Hell, that's the damn edge of the country, son. Makes the trek we are making look settled. Mexico still claims part of it."

"The less people, the more land, Mac."

Mac nodded. "I suppose you're right. How big a spread you plan-ning on?"

Reuben hesitated. "I don't know yet. It will depend on what I need to spend to stock up and outfit. Everything else will go into the land. I hope to have several thousand hectares, about a third in bottom ground, if I can find the spot. I have two maps prepared by a scout my uncle in New York hired. There was supposed to be a third, but it never arrived, and the scout disappeared. The farm—I mean ranch—won't really be all mine. It is for my family."

Mac felt his eyes widen. "Several thousand hectares? Why, that's almost five thousand acres. Where did you get that kind of stake, son?"

He could tell Reuben was carefully weighing his answer. He did not know his younger companion's mind was back in the kitchen of the farmhouse in Prussia, with his three brothers, Erik, Helmon and Isaac, and his ailing father, Ludwig, at their kitchen table. Reuben was thinking of his father's low, iron-firm voice and eyes boring into his. *I have sent money in advance to Uncle Hermann in New York. In addition, your work coat is back from Marvin, the tailor. There are six diamonds sewn in the hem. The money is for supplies and cattle. Lud-*

wig had paused. *The diamonds, however, are for one thing only, to buy our land. They are to be used for nothing else.*

Mac noticed the furrow in Reuben's brow ease and the tension in his lips slip into a bemused half-smile. He looked at Mac. "Well, maybe I will have to set my sights lower. We'll see. Time tells all tales."

Shrewd, too, Mac thought as he leaned over and spat. The sorrel jerked, not keen to the shift in weight, and the spittle fell short of its mark. Mac shook his head in disgust, ran the long fingernails of his huge powerful hand through the wavy, wild tangle of his beard and held them up for inspection. His fingertips glistened with wet-brown stain. "Can't you walk still and easy for more than a minute, Red?" He wiped his hand on his jacket. "Damn, that happens three or four times a day. If I didn't know better, I'd say you do that on purpose, you sorry excuse for a horse." Red seemed to roll back her eyes at her wide-shouldered master. She jerked her head up and down, tugging the reins through her rider's lax grip.

A chuckle rumbled from Mac's chest. "Yep, on purpose." He rubbed his hand affectionately on the beginnings of mane that sprang from between her ears. "You sure do what you have to, though, when we have to, so I suppose I can take your jokes from time to time."

Reuben's smile widened. "How long have you had her, Mac?"

Mac sighed. "Going on ten years, I reckon." He was silent for a moment recalling the day. "We was headed back to St. Louis from Cherry Creek. Twelve wagons filled with hides and such. Midsummer, if I remember right. There were a few Indians who didn't take kindly to white men even back then, but in those days, for the most part, folks got along. Most problems was from half-breeds. Cherry Creek was just a bunch of tents and lean-tos. Hell, there was generally more Arapaho tipis then white man huts. Things have changed now, and I think the change that's coming might be faster. Me and my brother, Randy, had started up a mercantile in a big field tent made of hides a Pawnee woman stitched together for us."

He laughed. "Cost us a mirror, a blanket and a rusty musket back from the damn revolution, and I had to bed her a few times, though, I didn't mind. Anyways, we had this crazy idea about bringing wagons back and forth for pay. Figured there'd be more and more folks headed west, and folks back East couldn't get enough leathers and furs. We figured right. We were busier than we ever thought. And it just gets more and more busy. Didn't have the money to buy a horse. Our folks brought us over from Ireland when we were wee tots. Good people, but they were dirt poor working and scratching a living out of some acres they cobbled together in the Ohio River Valley with my mother's dowry. The wagon strings from the East in them days might be ten or fifteen rigs once or twice a year, 'cept for the big ones carrying fools to California with pick axes and shovels. Now we're doing thirty to fifty rigs to Cherry Creek—sometimes three times between March and October if the weather lets us. And we ain't the only outfit getting people across. Those mountains are like magnets to folks." He paused and rubbed his chin.

"What happened the day you got Red?" prodded Reuben.

"Yep, well, got lost in some thoughts. Anyways, we seen heavy smoke from down river. We come around a bend. Seems two fool families tried to make the trek west to Cherry Creek on their own. Even back then there was safety in numbers. By what was left of their clothes, they were Mormons or some type of religious folks. Maybe they figured God would protect them. Folks who figure that are often real disappointed."

"What do you mean by what was left of their clothes?"

"Well, whoever hit 'em—might have been renegades or maybe a rogue band of Indians—they left no tell-tale signs, even pulled their arrows. They killed them all, took whatever they wanted, then burned everything including the bodies. Must've found oil for the lanterns and poured it over the remains of those poor pilgrims. Was a damn nasty, smelly scene." Mac felt his nose involuntarily wrinkle as he recalled the stench of burning flesh. "You couldn't even tell if those children was boys or girls 'cept judging by the size of the bodies they could not have been much more than five, six, or seven years old. Their killers must have thought they took all the horses and mules— I guess one of the two rigs had mules judging by the tracks." Mac saw Reuben was obviously transfixed by the story.

"There was a stand of cottonwoods right close. The outlaws must have hidden in those trees. While we were working the shovels trying to give those remains a decent burial, out bolts this mare. She was glad to see us, but she was mighty jumpy. There was more white in her eyeballs than brown. She could hardly keep her hooves still. She just skittered around while we got the pilgrims settled, God rest their souls. Then I took a handful of grain and a rope, and caught her. Tied her to the back of one of the wagons. I rode her from time to time. There was a bit less ruckus each time. Guess we got to be friends."

Mac leaned down, rubbed Red's shoulder, straightened up in the saddle and spit out his wad of chew, wiping his mouth with the back of his sleeve. "So, are ya willing to be my assistant?"

"Assistant?" Reuben looked puzzled.

Mac chuckled. "Sure, you know, Lieutenant, right-hand man, go-to hombre. Need me to spell it out in German for you, son?"

Reuben was obviously surprised. "Well, Mac, I appreciate the offer. The truth is, I'm learning. I think you may need someone older and more experienced to back you up."

Mac peered into Reuben's eyes. He said nothing. The muffled clop of the horse hooves in the fertile Missouri soil were the only sounds. He gave his next words careful thought, "Reuben, I liked you first time you and that tall blond-haired Norwegian, or whatever he is, came in the livery stable back in St. Louis when you were looking for horses and a wagon. You don't get much chance to gauge a man out here. Things happen fast. You have to figure him quick, and size him up right, or there will be hell to pay." He paused, and reached a meaty hand into his coat. He bit off a huge chunk of the chew stick, savoring the sudden burn of tobacco and cherry flavoring. He extended the chew to Reuben who shook his head.

"Don't chew, eh? That's a habit you have to pick up. It can be an awful good friend on the trail. Clears your nose and helps you think." He stuck the tobacco back into his coat and turned his eyes back to Reuben.

"I know you're green, but I figure you for a quick study. You got brains and fire. That's a rare combination. I think you got guts, too. But I figure you'll have plenty of chances to prove me right or wrong on that score over the next two months. I'm more interested in the man who backs me up, than whether or not there are things he needs to learn. You up for the job?"

Reuben held Mac's eyes with a steady gaze. "I don't suppose there's any pay involved?"

Mac slapped his thigh and Red did a sideways prance, alarmed at the clap of flesh meeting canvas-denim. "Whoa there, you cantankerous critter. Now that's exactly the question I'd expect from a Hebrew fellow. No. No pay." He tried hard not to laugh, but finally burst out with a loud guffaw and Reuben joined in.

"My father taught me well, Mac. Used to go to the cattle auctions with him."

"I hear you Jewish families all stick together. I guessed, but it figured, you being from Prussia, and that last name Frank, and all. Makes no nevermind to me. Not interested in the God you worship, just your grit."

"Fair enough," Reuben extended his hand. Mac leaned over and shook it, his massive paw engulfing Reuben's. *That's settled*, he thought, feeling a sense of satisfaction.

"Mac, do you stop the wagons during the day so folks can rest up, and the ladies can have some privacy?"

Mac felt a stir of annoyance. "We have a schedule to keep, son. We get to these rivers too late and we'll be fighting snowmelt from the mountains. It's easy to get jammed up for a week." A sudden thought struck him. He shot Reuben a sly smirk, "That pretty little dark-haired thing put you up to asking me?"

The reddening in Reuben's dark complexion gave him away. "You poking her, son?"

"What?" Reuben looked astonished.

Mac started to laugh. He couldn't control himself. His laughs boomed off the trees and a flock of starlings resting on their journey north, squawked in protest and flew from their perches on the barren limbs of several oak trees, the combined beat of their hundreds of wings making a whooshing sound.

Mac felt the tears in his eyes, and he finally had to fumble a kerchief from his back pants pocket. "Damn, son you aren't that tenderfoot are you? You're a man, she's very fine looking woman, and only a fool could miss the looks you were shootin' at each other when you were loading the wagons on the ferry barge. I just put two plus two together and guessed."

Reuben shook his head, still looking somewhat shocked. "No, Mac, Rebecca and I really don't have a relationship. It's more like a cat and dog circling around one another in a yard. Sometimes our tongues are out, sometimes we're just growling."

Mac studied Reuben's face. *Wistful, maybe?* "Sorry if I offended you, Reuben. Didn't mean to intrude. Just doing some people math, that's all.

"Now, about stopping the train. We have to be mighty careful. We can't lose time, and we don't want to be vulnerable. We do have more females than typical. I think there's forty-six, counting youngsters. Maybe we will take five-minute stops midmorning, and midafternoon. I'll talk about that when we get together to eat that pig tonight." Mac glanced up at the sun beginning to fade into the gold of late day. "That's not all too far off. I want everyone knowing the rules, and I want to start getting their minds right about some unpleasantness that's likely to come our way and for that river crossing. It won't be the toughest that we do, but the first one's always the most interesting."

He pushed the edge of his hat back and scratched his forehead. "I'll call you forward when we stop and show you how to organize the train in a night circle without these pilgrims running each other over. Let everyone know that after they get set up for the night we will meet at the supply wagons for dinner and some talk."

He ran his thick, dirty fingers through his beard, thinking. "Probably have to split that hog into quarters over several roasting pits, otherwise we will be there all night. Tell everyone to come down about an hour after dark."

Reuben started to wheel Lahn around and Mac called out after him, "Tell the menfolk to bring their guns. We won't need 'em tonight, but I want folks building good habits early. It might keep them alive."

March 18, 1855

$\mathscr{A}$MONGST FRIENDS

THE FIRST PASTEL HINT OF EVENING COLORED THE CUMULUS CLOUDS
that hung suspended to the west. Reuben had made it a point to
spend a few minutes talking with the pioneers in each wagon. Those
of city origin were wondrous and wide-eyed, nervous and excited.
The country folks were more at ease, but obviously enthused with
the adventure of the moment. He was struck by the sense of shared
purpose, hope, and spirit that bound this wide array of personalities.
The powerful commonality was different than anything he had seen
or felt in Europe. The energy was manifested in the voice, manners,
and gestures of each and every person he talked to. He tried to
define it in his mind but could not.

The only negative interaction had been with the obnoxious Irishman, Jacob, earlier in the day. His curiosity about the how and why
of Sarah being with that burly, abrasive man grew steadily from the
moment of the first surprising sight of the *Edinburgh* shipmates—
together, no less—as he galloped by their rig in the early morning,
checking the line of wagons for Mac. Now he had again ridden up
alongside Jacob's side of their rig to let them know of the wagon
master's plans for the evening. Sarah smiled radiantly at him, over
Jacob's head, a definite blush in her cheeks, her eyes dancing. "Good
afternoon, Reuben."

He was reminded of the first times he had met each of them. Jacob and he had been oil and water from the moment of their first brief encounter on the wharf in Portsmouth as Jacob roughly shouldered his way past him and Johannes when boarding the *Edinburgh*. Johannes had been even more vehement in his instant dislike of the shady, belligerent immigrant from Ireland. *What was it Johannes had said when I commented that Jacob didn't seem like a nice fellow?* Reuben pondered, *Oh, Yes, "More than that, Reuben, he's far worse than that."*

Sarah had embarked in Portsmouth, too, as had Rebecca. The scene replayed in a flash in his mind. It was just several months ago, but it seemed like years, that he and Johannes had been aboard the *Edinburgh* since Bremen. They had returned from a leg-stretch down the wharf, had their encounter with Jacob, and Johannes had left him leaning on the rail, fascinated by the bustling wharf, the frantic commercial ship traffic, and the grand military might of Her Majesty's Royal Navy on display in the busy harbor.

As Sarah had begun to ascend the boarding ramp, her slim figure and red hair caught his attention. Their eyes had met, and she stumbled on the gangplank. Even from that distance, he could see the mortified scarlet bloom in her cheeks. During the voyage, he'd had short conversations with her at the rail along the bow of the *Edinburgh*, salt spray on their faces. And he could still remember her delicate touch on his arm when, days later, they found themselves together in the animated throng of passengers shouting and pointing at their first glimpse of America. "Oh, my, there it is," she had said, "the Harbor and Ellis Island!" How pretty she had looked at that moment, how unafraid.

He checked Lahn's gait, slowing to the speed of the wagon, and tipped his hat to her again. "Hello, Sarah," he said, smiling. He shifted his eyes to Jacob and he felt the involuntary tightening of his lips. He nodded curtly and heard the coldness in his own voice. Perhaps, he mused a twinge of jealousy too, "Jacob."

Sarah spoke again, with obvious enthusiasm. "Oh, Reuben, how nice of you to come visit us."

"Just want to tell you that we will be taking breaks twice a day, morning and afternoon, like the one a few hours ago for ladies and for stock, to check equipment, and stretch out just a bit. But they'll be short. We are going to camp a bit early this afternoon, learn how to circle up the wagons and get organized after this first day on the trail. Also, Mac is roasting a pig tonight at the supply wagons, and everyone is invited. He wants folks to meet one another, and he wants to talk to the group. We are all going to have to work together. It's a mighty long, hard way from here to there."

Jacob had a surly look on his face as he observed Sarah's smile and the way her big blue eyes fixed brightly on Reuben's face.

"What can we bring tonight?" Sarah inquired. Reuben watched Jacob's hands tighten on the lines.

Jacob leaned over the side of the wagon, and spat on Lahn's right fore-hoof. "I've got better things do go then go jabber with a bunch of goody-two-shoes and listen to that red-bearded bastard who thinks he's the King of England. I'd wager there's not a poker player in the lot of them. We will just stay at our wagon. We won't be missing much." Jacob glared at him with a nasty challenge in his eyes.

Reuben started to speak, but Sarah interrupted him. Her voice was tight, she had straightened her shoulders and sat stiffly, her pointed gaze directed at Jacob. "I am going down to the gathering, Jacob. You may do as you please." Reuben thought he detected a strain of fear and trepidation in her defiance, and he was sure she would not have said what she did had he not been present.

Jacob's lower lip curled in a sneer. "I say where and when we go anywhere, and what I say stands, woman." Reuben edged his horse closer to the wagon so that he was only feet from Jacob. Ignoring the man, he addressed Sarah. "Look forward to seeing you there, Sarah. If there are any problems, let us know."

Jacob clenched his hands around the lines so tightly his knuckles turned white. He didn't look at Reuben, but focused his attention on Sarah, his voice rising, "You'll do what I say." There was enough loud threat behind the words that Reuben noticed Dr. Leonard in the wagon ahead lean around his front canvas to see what the commotion was. Then the sudden sound of a horse approaching drew everyone's attention away.

Zeb reined in on Sarah's side of the wagon. Jacob fixed baleful eyes on the mountain man. His voice was bitter and malicious. "I seen you tailin' us for the last two hours, coonskin."

Zeb's lips compressed into a narrow slit below his mustache. He nodded his head at Sarah. "Good day, Miss Sarah. How are you feeling this afternoon?"

"Thank you for asking, Zeb. I feel much better."

"I suppose you'll be coming to the fixins tonight?" Those words were addressed to Sarah, but Reuben noticed Zeb's unwavering stare at Jacob.

Jacob gritted his teeth with such force that the muscles in his jaw trembled, but he said nothing. He lifted the lines and snapped them down hard on the backs of the team. The wagon lurched forward and both Zeb and Reuben had to spin their horses to stay abreast.

The momentary ruckus subsided and the wagon slowed. "Yes, I'll be there, Zeb." Sarah gave him a soft smile, then turned toward Reuben, her smile widening.

That ought to settle things for now. Pretty when she's angry, too, Reuben noted. "I need to ride up and talk to Johannes. I'm sure he's tired of rubbing against splinters all day and would like some saddle time."

The long scars on Zeb's cheek eased back toward his ear with a slight, forced relaxing of his lips. "I reckon I'll just drop back right to where I've been. Good view."

"See you tonight." Reuben tugged down on his hat brim and spun the large tan-yellow horse around.

Reuben spurred Lahn into a slow lope and wondered about Zeb's obvious attraction to Sarah. "What do you think, Lahn? Maybe it's just that I feel a need to protect her from that no-good Irishman?" Lahn did not offer an opinion. *Maybe I should make sure I don't interfere with whatever might develop between the redhead and Zeb. He's taciturn, but he's a good man. Felt it in the first minute we met back there at the livery in St. Louis.* Reuben laughed out loud, his chuckles blending with the cadence of Lahn's hooves. *There's no doubt Zeb is more than capable of standing up to the likes of Jacob O'Shanahan.*

Reuben was yanked from his thoughts by Mac's voice booming from up at the front. "Halt the wagons. Five-minute break. Reuben—where the hell are you?"

March 18, 1855

$\mathscr{C}$IRCULAR WAGONS

REUBEN GALLOPED UP TO MAC. HIS MARE, RED, WAS STANDING STILL but impatiently lifting her front foreleg, pawing the spring-softened ground.

"I figure we have about two hours of light left," Mac said, looking westward. Then he swung his gaze south. "See that rise up there? About two miles, no trees?"

"I do."

He watched Mac reach into his jacket and pull out a cylindrical brass tube an inch and a half in diameter and just under ten inches long. He raised the telescope to his right eye and extended its second section, taking a quick look before passing the glass to Reuben. "Take a gander."

Peering through the lens, he quickly picked up the hill, but found it impossible to hold the optical piece steady. Mac, watching him, laughed.

"Dances around, doesn't it? You can pull your hat down low and hold that forebrim to the top of the tube. That'll steady it some. But, if you really want to watch something for a while and study the details, you need to dismount and find a rest against a tree or rock. Over the saddle will do in a pinch, but the horses are none too steady, either."

Reuben nodded and handed the glass back to Mac, whose blue eyes peered intently from beneath his bushy, red eyebrows. "So tell me, why do you think we should camp there?"

"It's high ground. Better view. The lack of trees will make it difficult for anyone to sneak in on us. Looks like it has good grass for the stock, too."

Mac looked pleased. "Exactly."

He shut the telescope and shoved it back in his jacket. "But remember, you have to adapt to the country. There's plenty of water now but that becomes a critical consideration the further west we go. The Plains Indians, like the Pawnee, Comanche, Cheyenne, and the Kiowa almost always camp on top of a rise just for those reasons. If you hole up by a river, and that's going to happen often, look for a spot that is exactly the opposite of the location where you want to have a crossing like we talked about. The best is a big bend or oxbow in the river, concave to your position, with steep banks, and deep fast current. The Sioux are experts at choosing those types of set-ups. That gives you a natural defensive line on two sides. If you string the wagons out proper across the wide part of the bend, you position them so you could bring a crossfire if anyone is stupid enough to want to have a fracas."

Reuben looked out at the rise, holding his hat in front and above his head to break the brightness of the sinking sun. "How exactly do you get the circle established on terrain like that?"

"The lead wagon will follow me. We will just work our way around the contours. You take up the rear and just hold that last wagon in the spot that I turn back and wave to you as we are headed up the slope. I'll bring the lead and following wagons around 'til we meet up with your rear. Then we will have a circle around the hill on about the same contour, with the high point of the hill and grazing area for the stock in the center."

"Will do," Reuben nodded.

"One more thing, Reuben. As we move further west, particularly after we get into the Kansas Territories, many of these high spots will have a steep, rough, almost abrupt face on one side or the other.

On those hogbacks or buttes, put your back to the steep, and you can double your firepower on the only accessible downhill side. No man, white or red, much likes climbing a hill against rifle muzzles.

"Generally, the best fight is the one you avoid." Mac smiled grimly. "There are those that don't know that rule, though. Let's get set up. I want to get those pig quarters in the pit for tonight."

He paused. "I notice your man, Zeb, has been hanging out mostly in the same spot all day two-thirds the way back in the train. Have him go on ahead and scout that hill. I don't expect any trouble in these parts, but better safe than sorry. And, it's wasted time I reckon, but you can tell what women-folk you talk to there ain't no need to bother getting dressed up." He chuckled. "Course, I suspect that'll do about as much good as telling a cat not to eat fish. Go tell the wagons."

Reuben nodded then hesitated. "What gave you the notion Zeb was 'my man'?"

Mac leaned over, spit, and wiped his beard. "I got eyes."

Reuben wheeled Lahn around, moist clumps of earth flying from the palomino's hooves as he sped back down the line of wagons.

<hr />

INGA HAD BEEN LOOKING FORWARD TO THE EVENING DINNER FROM the moment Reuben told them the news. Lingering pangs of guilt about her decision on the train to not share her dark secret with Johannes mixed with the anticipation of a social event. But they were far from New York City and getting further with every passing stride of the horses. *There was no one on the train or in the remote area to which they were headed that could possibly know certain parts of her past,* she told herself. This was a new chapter. Johannes was the first man she had ever truly cared for. Out here, she would never run into any of her "men clients" again. That had been another life, before her work at the Mayor's mansion. Before Rebecca, visiting the Mayor, had asked that she accompany her west. Most particularly, before Johannes. And, as she had vowed, she would never again stoop to such behavior. Regardless of the circumstances.

She turned and looked at Johannes as they ascended diagonally across the shallow rise. He was concentrating on guiding the team over the uneven grounds. There was something very sensual about his intelligent, intent focus, and she felt an involuntary constriction in her breasts and warmth begin to spread in her hips. She smiled a satisfied inner smile. *I can't imagine anyone ever making my heart beat more quickly.*

Johannes felt her gaze and turned to her, taking his eyes momentarily from the team. He flashed her a smile. "What are you looking at, Inga?"

"My man," she whispered, and wrapped her arm around his, leaning into him as she did so.

"Damn right," Johannes made a comical show of pretending to look around as if to see if anyone was listening. "But, shhhhh...this could ruin my reputation."

Inga felt an odd twist in her stomach at the word "reputation." She let a few moments pass. "I wonder what I should wear?" she said somewhat to herself, but also to Johannes.

Rebecca turned to her. "We should dress as ladies do for an event. I am not sure I have time to change, but I certainly intend on tidying up, removing this infernal dust from my attire, fixing my hair, and perhaps changing my hat and jewelry."

The silent mirth on Johannes' face was evident. "This is not a ball at the Queen's palace, Rebecca. Comfortable, clean, with as little fuss as possible will do just fine."

Tilting her nose slightly upward, Rebecca ignored Johannes before directing her dialogue to Inga. "You and I can take some time and sort the wagon so that we have a little space to change and dress for tonight, or any other time." She sniffed, and glared at Johannes, "The men obviously gave no such thought to our needs when they loaded."

Her eyes returned to Inga. "We can also sort out how to arrange our beds, particularly since Reuben and Johannes will be sleeping under the wagon." She obviously found it impossible to keep the tinge of triumphant irony from that final portion of her pronouncement, and Inga caught the look of satisfaction in her eyes when Johannes pursed his lips.

"That sounds like a good plan, Milady Marx. I'm very much looking forward to meeting everybody else, and seeing who else from the *Edinburgh* is on the wagon train. Did you hear Reuben mention it?"

Rebecca sniffed again. "Given the typical passenger I saw on the *Edinburgh*, I doubt that will be of much interest."

March 18, 1855

$\mathcal{D}$OE HIDE &
BROWN SHOULDERS

WALKS WITH MOON LANGUISHED IN THE WARMTH OF THE BUFFALO robes after Eagle Talon left the tipi. Finally, she stirred, readying herself for a day that promised to be full.

The other younger women of the tribe would be meeting down at the water midmorning, when the sun climbed high enough to cast its warmth across the waters. Their rendezvous was always on the inside curve of a sandbar formed by a bend in the river. The coarse, red-gold sand tapered gradually into the streambed before disappearing beneath deeper currents. These shallow edges caught sun in the middle of the still-short days and were perfect for washing and bathing.

Walks with Moon enjoyed listening—though she did not partake—in the gossip thinly disguised as yesterday's news from different lodges, and the arguments over what the decisions of the Council would be. Each morning, as they talked at the river, the women would discretely bathe and clean a few items from their tipis, buffalo horn ladles and bowls, or dried roots that would be used for the noonday meal.

Inside the lodge, Walks with Moon smiled to herself. No doubt Talks with Shadows would have some prognostications about what was being decided by the men. She would make these statements with surety, in a most convincing, all-knowing tone. Invariably, she would be wrong. The other women teased Talks with Shadows unmercifully about her incorrect forecasts. She would always shrug off the jests, suggesting, "I would have been right, if ...." Most often, she would launch into a brand-new, intricately woven story of yet another vision that had come to her.

Pony Hoof would compare the size of her belly with those of every other pregnant woman, a select and revered club, to which Walks with Moon now belonged. Pony Hoof, who was but a moon from delivery, had the largest, roundest midriff, which she pointed out whenever the chance arose. Walks with Moon laughed quietly. *After the baby comes, Pony Hoof will no longer have the stature of biggest belly. Will she begin to feast and feast, attempting to maintain her elevated status?*

Walks with Moon lightly placed the palm of her hand just below her belly button. Happiness coursed through her spirit. *You will make your father proud, and I shall love you like no other.*

She straightened the buffalo robes and stirred the embers of the lodge fire. Adding tiny shavings to the glowing coals, she got down on her hands and knees and blew gently on the remnants of fire until the shavings ignited. She carefully added small twigs, then larger sticks until the little fire was blazing and warmth began to push the morning chill from the tipi.

With the fire crackling, smokeless, she stood close to the flames, slowly twirling around, letting the heat radiate off her still-naked figure. She looked down at herself, ran her fingers over her filling breasts, along her sides, over the flare of her hips, and, palms down, extended their reach lower, past her groin, and down the insides of her thighs. She closed her eyes, pretending her hands were Eagle Talon's powerful calloused fingers, and giggled.

She looked forward to their coming night of tender but intense passion, which they shared often. Their physical attraction had always been special, but it had reached new heights since she had conceived. *Perhaps being with child somehow makes things more pleasurable,* she wondered to herself as she slipped on her doeskin dress.

The soft suede caressed her face and sensitive flesh as it slid over her head and then below her waist and settled on her hips. Its bodice was cut high, with buckskin ties that began just above her breasts and rose in a crisscross almost to her throat to keep her warm in the months before and after summer. Its hem came to just above her knees, good for wading and washing, particularly this time of year when the water was still frigid. A single row of carefully polished elk ivory were stitched just under the collar, and the paints and stains she concocted from juniper, alder, black and other berries, and cactus cores added color just below the ivories.

She tied the waist with a beaded thong of buffalo hide, its ends split into finely painted leather threads. Only then did she fold down the upper edge of the tipi flap and peek outside. No snow blanketed the ground and the frost had disappeared other than a few patches where the sun's rays were blocked, and the ground was in shadow.

No need for moccasins. It is a short way to the river. Walks with Moon ran the shallow-toothed comb Eagle Talon had fashioned for her from the antlers of a mule deer buck through her shoulder length, shiny black hair. The comb had been a wedding gift from her husband, handed to her with a shy smile.

Still humming, she gathered a few items needed at the river, including two metal pots, among her most prized possessions. Eagle Talon had traded for the pots at her insistent urging when trapper LaBonte and his Arapaho woman, Lola, were in camp prior to the leaves falling from the trees. The pots cost Eagle Talon a good number of beaver and coyote pelts. To this day he complained that he had overpaid. "But, my husband," she always countered, "the pots were well worth it." Their teasing disagreement became a treasured matter between them and provided ongoing laughs. Remembering, she smiled.

Walks with Moon stepped from the tipi. Toward the center of the village she could see Talks with Shadows and several other women already on their way to the river. They were laughing and bobbing their heads. Anxious not to miss any of the discussion, she set down the pots, fastened back the flap to keep in the warmth, and then hurried with eager footsteps to the gathering of friends.

IT WAS JUST AFTER MIDDAY WHEN SHE RETURNED FROM THE RIVER. She had planned to sew and prepare the main meal with the ulterior motive of drawing the buffalo hides around her and her husband early.

She was surprised to see Eagle Talon already sitting cross-legged in front of the tipi, his shield leaning several feet from him against the skin walls of the lodge. The shield was decorated, like her dress, with paints from berries and plants. As was the sacred practice, Eagle Talon had fashioned the shield, measuring it slightly wider than his forearm, fingertips to elbow. He had painted the enemy side with two circles of black and white, the top and bottom of each design pointing toward the center and then the outer edge of the shield. Their white halves directed light and strong energy to the center for protection and surrounded a painted eagle feather with a superimposed image of an eagle talon. Though Eagle Talon had protested, Walks with Moon had painstakingly, and secretly—at her husband's resigned insistence—stitched a quarter-inch thick cross-section of buffalo horn almost five inches in diameter in the center of the talon. She was careful to work on the shield only inside the tipi, and though Eagle Talon again protested, she had sewn a second layer of tough buffalo hide behind the first. The shield's center was secured by thick leather strands through a hole she had laboriously fashioned with sharp granite. Tied in a buckskin knot, their ends dangled another six inches.

Eagle Talon had sized the handgrip in the center of the rear of the shield to fit over his upper arm, affording him added versatility in transport or use. The skins were stretched tightly with thick rawhide he tied around a single, almost one-inch diameter alder branch. It had taken him several days to soak and bend the alder until its ends overlapped, forming a circle. The ends were tightly wrapped by triple rawhide bands that he wove through small holes whittled through the wood.

Walks with Moon knew it was one of the finest shields in the tribe. Her husband was proud of it and rarely left the tipi without it. "Your gift has added strong medicine," he admitted privately to her, smiling, and she, too, felt a twinge of pride.

His unstrung bow rested against the sidewall of the tipi next to the shield, as did the supple leather quiver full of arrows, their fletching of black, white, and a mottled grey duck feathers, a lethal bouquet that extended approximately ten inches from the folded over, stitched lip of the quiver.

Eagle Talon looked somber. The sun was slipping behind the tipi and his lower body was in shade. He usually teased her with his eyes, but this day his lips were compressed and his features hard. There was not the usual appreciative flow of his gaze up and down her body.

She stood in front of him clutching the two pots that contained the small pile of gourds and wooden stirring spoons she had taken down to the river. He looked up at her, his wide eyes dark and serious, as stoic as the dark marks on the bark of an aspen. He said nothing.

They had shared the same fire for more than two winters now, and she had learned to allow him his silence, though these moods did not come often.

"We had a fine time at the river today. Some sand and current and my pots are shiny and clean," she set them down on the ground. "I think they are worth twice as many pelts as you traded." This type of gentle prod usually elicited a smile, and a good-natured retaliation, but Eagle Talon's face remained stony.

She stood quietly, waiting.

"Some of our scouts have reported back," Eagle Talon said in a firm, low voice. "There have been several attacks against white wagons. Our scouts are convinced it is the work of renegades, Crow, or perhaps Pawnee."

She sat down beside him, folding her legs beneath her, and leaned into his words.

"A French trapper they called Pierre, his entire party, and his Blackfoot woman were killed and scalped southeast of the soldiers' fort on the River of the Laramie. The white soldiers are blaming the Sioux. They are using these events as one of the excuses to not honor the treaty The People made with the representative of the White Father five winters ago. Other scouts have reported two lines of white wagons are headed to where the sun sets south of us. They're still on the lands of the Pawnee. One set of wagons seems to have medicine men who perform strange ceremonies, and it appears it will take the northerly route north of the Padouca River in the direction of the soldiers' fort along the Laramie. The other is not at the juncture yet where a decision must be made, but the scouts feel they will turn south toward the Mountain of the Little Beaver That Never Reached the Top, the mountain the hairy faces call Longs Peak. This is the earliest we've seen white wagons. It is possible they spent the winter at the soldiers' fort they call Kearney far toward the rising sun. We fear there will be more wagons, more hairy faces, more soldiers."

He paused and squinted at her face, which was still bright with the sunlight. "And more disregard for the agreements The People made with the White Father."

"What did the Council have to say of this news?"

"There are those, you know them, Turtle Walks and Horse's Leg who wish to paint for war and drive the white man out before they become strong. There are others who say we must form alliances with the other tribes, including the Crow." Eagle Talon grimaced, and shook his head. "Still others like Sitting Bull and Buffalo Hoof counsel patience. They believe there is little to fear, a few white men will not make a difference, and, in the end, the White Father will honor his word to The People. The Council dispersed, making no decisions other than Tracks on Rock has determined we should break camp, move the village, and follow the tatanka herds to the southeast this year rather than to the east or north. There remains much snow north of here and the tatanka are likely to migrate in that direction later than usual."

Walks with Moon felt a wave of unease, "My father thinks we should move southeast, nearer the white wagon trails?"

"Yes." It was obvious Eagle Talon did not agree.

"What if we run into white wagons?" Walks with Moon hoped she hid the anxiety from her voice. She wondered what the elder wives were telling their husbands right now.

"We shall watch and remain invisible. We will go around them, though we will try and learn as much as we can." Eagle Talon smiled for first time. "However, if we run into Crow or Pawnee, we will count coup and take their horses. I could use more horses."

Walks with Moon was relieved to see the smile on her husband's face and she baited him, though she knew what the answer would be, "You have sixteen horses, husband. You can only ride one at a time." She laughed when his response was as she suspected.

"A man can never have enough horses."

Eagle Talon stood, pulled her up beside him, put his hands on both her arms, and let his look wander slowly and lovingly down the length of her form, as if slipping the leather from her shoulders with his gaze.

She giggled up into his face. "I shall prepare supper for us."

"Supper can wait," Eagle Talon said, his eyes twinkling. He took her hand and turned. With his free hand he hastily undid the leather ties to the tipi flap. As she bent her knees and reached back for the pots, she saw Flying Arrow standing at the entrance to his lodge, his arms crossed over his chest. He caught her eye, smiled, and nodded his silver-haired head in approval.

Inside the lodge, Eagle Talon tossed several sticks on the cold embers, turned to her and took the pots from her hands. He untied the leather strings at the top of her dress where they tightened the soft doe hide across the base of her throat, and then slid the leather from her tan shoulders, this time with his forefingers rather than his eyes.

The supple suede lining of the dress slid down her body and landed in a dark golden heap around her feet. He took a step back and surveyed her, and then nodded almost imperceptibly at the buffalo robes. A minute later, he slipped under the heavy pelts with her.

Delighted with the strong warmth of her husband's naked body along her length, she sighed softly at the tingle of his lips on her breasts. She moved ever closer in his embrace, one hand now gently stroking his fullness. He throbbed in her fingers and she could feel the pulsing in her throat grow more rapid.

She exhaled slowly from parted lips with steady warm breath in his ear. Her fingers tightened gently around him, and she gasped, her hips involuntarily twitching, as his hands slowly smoothed over the shape of their child in her belly and then found the wetted, ready area between her thighs.

Eagle Talon slowly rolled her over to her side facing away from him, held her hips and pulled her to his. With several gentle thrusts he embedded himself deeply in her. She felt pleasantly stretched, completely full of the man she loved, and she breathed a groan that mingled with the sounds of river current kissing the edges of rocks outside the tipi.

Her moans became throaty. Their increasing tempo urged his ever quickening movements and he pulled her closer, tighter, molding her to him, one hand splayed out across her trembling belly. She could feel the muscles in his stomach rhythmically tighten each time he pushed his hips forward. Waves of heat floated through her body. The interior of the tipi seemed to float, suspended on the edge of flight, and then she felt herself contract and spasm around him, the sound of her pleasure driving him to thrust hard once more, their beings centered on the point of his contact deep within her, and she heard him grunt, felt him explode, and then the sensual sensations of their consummation, their flesh, became a shared thing, until she could not tell where her body ended and his began.

They lay still, their breathing slowly returning to normal, enjoying the gentle aftershock tremors of their coupling. A great horned owl hooted somewhere downstream. She held her breath, wondering about the meaning of this—an owl's call in early evening might cause some to feel a tremor of terror. But as she listened to the whisper of river current, she thought to herself that the owl's call had seemed gentle, languid like the river. Perhaps it was not a warning so much as a reminder. But a reminder of what? Had Eagle Talon heard the owl?

Eagle Talon raised himself up on one elbow. His chiseled face creased with the smile of a man who has shared with his woman. He began to slip out of her. She made a sound of quiet protest and shifted her hips to capture him for a while longer. She did not think he had heard the owl. She exhaled a deep, contented sigh and stroked his hand where it again rested on her belly. "Our people will be safe, won't we?" she whispered.

He hesitated, and then his hug tightened. "We will be safe, wife. More men are reasonable than not, and, hopefully, they all have a woman such as you, to talk sense into them when needed."

His arms tightened around her again, and she felt the softening still buried in her begin to thicken. Her husband's whisper filtered, husky, through his lips as he nuzzled her neck. "Perhaps we will wait for supper until morning, Walks with Moon."

12

March 18, 1855

$\mathcal{T}$HE DRESSING ROOM

THE WAGONS HAD FORMED THEIR CIRCLE, THE HEADS OF EACH TEAM twenty to thirty feet behind the tailgate of the wagon ahead. Rebecca watched Johannes set the brake and tie off the lines with enough slack so that he could remove the collars from the horses.

"It appears Mac will simply allow the stock to pasture in the center of the circle tonight," he said to her. "I'll get the team unhitched and watered." He rose, put one hand down on the side rail of the wagon seat, and lightly vaulted to the ground. Turning back to Inga and Rebecca, he held out his arms. "May I?"

"Thank you, Johannes." Inga, closest to him, rose and took the single step to the edge of the footboard, and bent down her outstretched arms toward him. His hands caught her under her armpits, and he effortlessly lowered her to the ground.

Johannes held up his arms again. "Rebecca?"

She had noted the intimacy between the two, how Johannes took care to ensure that the front of Inga's body rubbed lightly on his chest for the last few feet before her boots landed on the ground. It irritated her.

"I shall manage. Thank you, Johannes." Rebecca climbed down the opposite side of the wagon. She brushed off her sleeves and skirt with short, rapid, energetic strokes and looked at Inga through the space between the horse's rumps and wagon front, over the tongue. "Let's get this wagon organized, Inga. Time well spent now will result in far more comfort in the coming weeks."

Johannes, already working on the collars of the four horses, looked over the back of the big bay he was unhitching. "Mind you ladies, when you shift things around take care to keep the load even front and back, and side to side."

Rebecca walked to the rear, unlatched the tailgate, slid out the small, rough-sawn wooden ladder that had come with the prairie schooner, and set it against the lip of the tailgate. The two women clambered in.

Rebecca stood with her hands on her hips, surveying the interior jammed with her trunks, grain sacks, ammunition boxes, foodstuffs, tools, tack, and four bedding rolls. "This is a perfect example of why you never let men pack anything. Light that oil lamp then help me with these grain sacks, Inga."

In a half an hour, the two of them, struggling together with the heavier items, had the wagon organized. They created a small walk-way, perhaps a foot wide, which began at the tailgate and ended at a tiny space they had cleared in the center of the wagon, an approximately two-foot-square area devoid of baggage or cargo. The grain sacks had been laid on their sides and stacked, rather than in a row, on end along with the india-rubber sacks of flour and sugar. Inga's bed roll was spread out on top of them. On the other side of the wagon, toward the front, they fashioned another relatively level area on top of cargo, lighter, softer items on top, its surface elevated slightly above the rim of the wagon side. Rebecca's bedroll, much thicker than the others, rested atop that makeshift mattress, which included Reuben's old leather case, overly secured with four rawhide thongs, cross-tied and knotted. Rebecca tried to ignore her growing curiosity about its contents, and concentrated on their task.

Satisfied with the wagon's transformation, Rebecca stepped back to scrutinize their work. "I am certainly glad I insisted on bringing that eiderdown. I think we shall be quite comfortable given the barbarity of the conditions. At least we can now move around a bit, and...," she pointed at the small barren area in the center of the wagon, "...we have a dressing room." She laughed. "My poor mum would simply be wrought with all this," she said, shaking her head.

"But, it is an adventure, don't you think Milady Marx? Don't you feel it? I think we are doing something grand. This is a whole new life quite distinct from anything we've ever known."

Rebecca felt one eyebrow arch. Something deep inside of her agreed with Inga—but she was not about to admit it. She had her plan and was not about to let any stray thought undermine it. "Perhaps, Inga. But it is temporary for me. While I dread having to make this trip back to St. Louis, I suppose I shall be experienced by then. Perhaps the return shall be less tedious since I will be on my way back to England and civilization. Would you happen to know what's in that leather case of Reuben's?"

Inga looked at her closely. "No. But, what about Reuben?"

Rebecca had begun to rummage through a trunk and had just located the looking glass for which she was searching. Inga's question irked her. Still bent over, she snapped her eyes to Inga's. "Reuben? What on earth would Reuben have to do with my return to England?" As she said the words, she again was aware of a nagging feeling quite separate from her terse reply. It annoyed her further.

"Let's concentrate on the evening, shall we?" She looked slowly around the wagon interior, and sighed. "It will be a base existence, Inga. The one thing we can maintain is our femininity, and this is the first time we will meet the other travelers. First impressions are important. If you would be so kind as to brush off my clothes and help me with my hair and rouge, I will assist you in dressing. You really need to wear something else for the occasion. I'm sure Johannes will appreciate it, too," she added dryly. Rebecca smiled at the evident delight which illuminated Inga's features at the suggestion.

Engrossed over Inga's hair, Rebecca heard a horse ride up and the voices of Johannes and Reuben. It sounded as if they were discussing getting grain to the horses and complaining they would have to perform that chore in the dark since the ladies were "hogging the wagon," as Johannes put it.

With the back canvas flap of the wagon cover closed, the occasional sweet smell of molasses drifted in waves from the small wooden keg stored in an easily accessible position toward the wagon tailgate. Once in a while, the odor permeated Inga's nostrils prompting a faint stir of nausea. *I love the smell of molasses. Why would that make me feel sick now?* she thought as Rebecca fidgeted with her hair, using a brush handle and dampened cloth to curl it. Her handiwork completed, she stepped back and looked Inga up and down with an appraising stare, making minor adjustments to the fabric at her shoulders and waist.

"Ladies," Johannes impatient voice penetrated the canvas, "if you don't hurry up, we will be having what is left of that pig for breakfast." Reuben followed up with sympathetic laughter.

"Disregard them," commanded Rebecca, "we shall be ready when we are ready. Gentlemen wait for ladies."

Inga took a deep breath to calm her stomach as Rebecca stood back, her head slightly cocked to one side, and again appraised Inga's apparel. Inga followed her gaze as she studied the medium blue wool skirt and bodice, her eyes especially focused on the neckline's inward slope from the shoulders, which tapered and drew attention to Inga's hidden cleavage. *Too much so?* wondered Inga. She smoothed the skirt's narrow curve at her hips. Below the hips, the skirt flared in tiny pleats, buoyed by the four stiff, horsehair petticoats Inga wore beneath.

Rebecca looked up at Inga with satisfaction. "The blue nicely intensifies the color of your eyes, a stunning contrast to your golden hair. I think, my dear Inga, that we shall now make the proper impression!"

A few minutes later, the two women untied the rear canvas, Rebecca extinguished the oil lamp, and Reuben lowered the tailgate, which they had raised for privacy. In the fading light of coming dusk, Inga watched Rebecca descend the ladder then she followed. Johannes and Reuben stood transfixed. Johannes' mouth was slightly agape as he surveyed Inga, from the forelocks of her coiffed hair to the toes of her brown leather boots just visible below the hem of her skirt. She smoothed her palms down her thighs, a bit self-conscious.

Rebecca had done a superlative job given the conditions, and Inga felt beautiful. She had not donned clothes like this since she and Rebecca had lunched together in New York, the day Rebecca had surprised her with her request that Inga leave the mayor's employ at Gracie Mansion and accompany her west.

Rebecca turned to her with a smug look. "I told you, my dear, did I not? Now, let's be off."

Reuben and Johannes hastily fell in step beside the women, and they strolled toward the halo of flickering light partially obscured by the dark outline of the slope. As they neared, and rounded the hill, they could see a large fire, silhouetting the moving images of people.

CHAPTER

13

March 18, 1855

$\mathscr{T}$HE BULLWHIP

REBECCA GLANCED BEHIND HER AND SAW A COUPLE SOME DISTANCE back, also headed toward the campfire. In the gathering gloom she could not distinguish the features, but something seemed familiar in the small petite figure of the woman and the stocky shape of the man and his purposeful swaggering walk.

She walked beside Inga, with Johannes and Reuben abreast, and into the circle of light cast by the flames. Faces turned toward them. The eyes of most of the men widened and fixed on her and Inga without so much as a glance at Reuben and Johannes. The other women, Rebecca noticed quickly, for the most part were dressed in clean but simple calico or wool traveling dresses, some still wearing their sunbonnets. The expressions on their faces were split evenly between welcoming smiles and disapproving stares. Several looked at their menfolk, obviously displeased by the clandestine glances cast in Rebecca and Inga's direction.

Mac walked over to them with an athletic lumber. He smiled at Inga, swept off his hat and bowed slightly, the fire radiating his wavy red hair with golden highlights. "Ma'am." He lifted her hand and planted a clumsy kiss to her knuckles.

He turned to Rebecca and repeated the gesture. "Miss Rebecca, I believe? You two ladies have outdone yourselves tonight. Very pretty."

"Thank you, Captain, that is very gracious."

Mac had yet to turn loose her hand, and the narrow space between his beard and mustache split into a wide grin. "Well, it's true enough that some of these wagons are called prairie schooners, but I'm not a captain, ma'am. I am the wagon master. We'll talk more about that after supper with the entire outfit."

Johannes began to say, in a joking tone, "I think General would be more...," his voice trailed off. His eyes widened and his jaw slackened as he looked over the shoulders of Rebecca and Mac, arresting the women's attention. They turned and Reuben's gaze followed.

COMING INTO THE CIRCLE OF LIGHT WERE JACOB AND SARAH. JACOB had one large hand wrapped tightly around her upper arm. Even so, it was obvious Sarah was making every attempt to keep distance between them.

Reuben felt the pause in the chatter around the campfire. The surprise in Rebecca's expression was unmistakable. Inga's eyes flickered from the arriving couple to the faces of each of her friends, finally pausing at Reuben with a questioning stare.

Her puzzled look brought a sudden realization to Reuben. *That's right, Inga has never met Jacob or Sarah; she was not on the Edinburgh.* Jacob and Sarah paused, unable to ignore the tension in the group.

Jacob thrust his face slightly forward. "I am Jacob O'Shanahan and this is my betrothed, Sarah Bonney." Reuben caught sight of Zeb's shadowy form standing just at the outer circle of the fire's bright light. He stood impassively, his eyes seeming to move from Sarah to Jacob and then back again. His arms were crossed in front of his chest, his feet spread in a wide stance. Reuben glanced back at the ladies. Rebecca's look of surprise had become one of astonishment at the word *betrothed*. Her dark, perfectly formed eyebrows were elevated halfway up her forehead and her lips were parted.

Reuben galvanized in the uneasy silence. He took several steps over to Jacob and held out his hand. "Glad you decided to join us, Jacob."

After a moment's hesitation, Jacob slowly extended his hand and shook Reuben's, squeezing with all the considerable power in his thick wrist and fingers. His slightly glowering expression remained unchanged. Reuben squeezed back, maintaining the semblance of smile he had forced in concert with his greeting. He noted with satisfaction that though his hand was smaller, the power in the clasp between the two men was equal.

Then, the test of dominance was over but only after several extended seconds. Reuben turned to Sarah. The glow of fire deepened the color of her hair, and its flicker reflected seductively in the blue of her eyes. Reuben bent forward slightly, reached for her free hand and raised it to his lips, brushing the top of her wrist with a soft kiss.

Sarah's eyes widened slightly when Reuben's lips touched her skin. "The two of you are arriving at exactly the right time. I think everybody from the camp is here, and we were just about to make introductions."

He turned to Mac. "What do you think, Mac, maybe it would be good for all of us to introduce ourselves?"

"Good idea, Reuben. That's one of the things I want to get done tonight. Folks who know each other are more likely to cover one another's backs."

Mac's eyes moved coldly to Jacob. When they returned to Reuben the bushy red eyebrows relaxed somewhat. He raised his voice and spoke to the group. "I have one keg of ale. It won't be ice cold, but it's cool enough that it'll do. I figure there's enough for about one cup each. Don't want to see anyone having too much, but whatever does not get finished tonight gets thrown out. From here on in, it'll be a water keg. Going to need it."

Mac turned and motioned to the two herdsmen who were mounted uphill of the campfire, keeping watchful eyes on the milling stock above them. "Charlie, dismount down off that horse of yours, get the top off that keg, and grab a ladle to get folks started. John, go up there with the critters and keep an eye out. Charlie will stay you in a spell, and you can come down. We'll make sure we save you a cup."

Charlie nodded, dismounted, and began to walk over to one of the supply wagons. John raised his hand in a friendly half-salute, quarter-turned his horse and slowly made his way into the darkness in the direction of the occasional whinnies and brays of the horses and mules, and the soft wheezing grunts of the oxen. The rising half-moon, the first two stars, and the last thin band of disappearing sunlight silhouetted horse and rider.

Mac turned to those who had gathered. "I suspect you all know how to make introductions between one another. Don't be bashful. We're all in this together for quite a spell. And I would expect that many of you have interesting stories to tell your new neighbors, some more so than others."

Reuben noticed Mac's gaze again fixed on Jacob as his booming voice echoed across the campfire.

REBECCA SIMPLY COULD NOT BELIEVE THAT OF ALL THE PASSENGERS on the *Edinburgh*, that petite, attractive red head—who obviously had an interest in Reuben, and with whom she had traded sarcastic barbs on several occasions—was one of the other *Edinburgh* ship-mates on this wagon train. *And she is with that bastard?* Jacob's appearance was another surprise. She had deliberately never spoken to Jacob in the six-week crossing, very purposely avoiding his roving eyes and ignoring his lewd sardonic grins as he visually undressed her each time their paths met. The one time he had made a real effort to catch her attention, she lifted her nose and marched straight past him as if he was merely air. "Snotty, limey bitch," he had cursed behind her. *And now the two of them together?*

She was staring at him as she remembered, and suddenly realized that Jacob was returning her look, his lips turned in the same lewd sneer she had seen him cast her way aboard ship. She hastily averted her eyes, but not before she saw Sarah attempt to take a step forward. Jacob tightened his grip on her arm and pulled her back, only releasing her when Sarah sent an angry glance at his hand and then to his face. Free, the red head moved quickly to the clusters of people sipping ale and talking animatedly on the far side of the fire.

Inga stooped to whisper in Rebecca's ear, her lips no more than six inches from the side of Rebecca's head. "What was that all about, Milady Marx? Who are those people? They were your shipmates on the *Edinburgh*? Are they your friends?"

Rebecca turned to Inga, patted her arm and laughed. "That brute Irishman is not my friend. It would be a safe bet that he has no friends."

"The little red head is quite attractive," Inga said in a low voice. "She's his fiancée, so at least one person must like him."

Rebecca shook her head. "My dear Inga, Sarah is a commoner, although she dresses well enough. I understand from shipboard gossip she and her sister owned a ladies clothing shop in Liverpool and sewed their own designs."

Rebecca shifted her eyes across the fire where Sarah stood, her back to Rebecca and Inga, talking to a plump middle-aged lady dressed in a worn, heavy cotton traveling dress. A grey knit shawl was draped over the woman's ample shoulders. "I can't say that Sarah is my friend, though we have spoken on occasion, perhaps a bit pointedly. But, I think there's far more to this story than the unilateral pronouncement of the Irishman."

She was surprised to suddenly find Reuben standing close to her, a teasing look in his eyes. "I have never seen you quite so startled. I told you there were other *Edinburgh* travelers in the wagons."

"You certainly made a fool of yourself with the seamstress," she said under her breath. "Was that kiss to her wrist to impress all the other attendees, get under Jacob's skin, or...," she looked at him intently, "...to make me jealous?"

He laughed. "It was the gentlemanly thing to do, particularly since—and I know you caught it because I saw you staring at her—she was very uncomfortable. It wouldn't surprise me if there was a bruise on her arm where he was holding her."

Reuben moved closer to Rebecca so that just a foot separated them. She felt herself getting lost in those intense green eyes, a giddy feeling swirled in her stomach, and she realized she had unconsciously arched her back toward him.

Her eyes dropped to his lips. "I suppose now you're trying to kiss me, perhaps to impress all the other travelers again?" She hoped the comment flowed as sarcastically as she intended and that Reuben would not consider it an invitation. *Or was it?* She blinked at the thought.

Reuben shook his head slowly, his eyes fixed on hers, and stepped back. "You seem well practiced at spoiling moments, Milady Marx. There is not a jealous bone in your body when it comes to any man, including me."

Rebecca resisted a wild urge to reach out and touch his arm, tempted to say softly, "I'm sorry." But she didn't. Instead, she made a conscious effort to slightly relax her stance. "I did notice Sarah's discomfort. I have never really liked her."

"That, Rebecca, has been obvious since the *Edinburgh*," broke in Reuben tersely. "What has she ever done to you, or do you just regard her as beneath you, the same low esteem, I might add, you seem to project toward everyone with the occasional—very occasional— exception of Inga. But, in Inga's case her adoration of you feeds your ego just enough so you can afford to be nice once in a great while."

Rebecca was stunned by the harsh edge in Reuben's voice. This time she did reach out her hand apologetically, but he had turned abruptly away, headed toward a group of four or five men clustered around Mac and listening intently to the red-bearded wagon master.

Had anyone witnessed the exchange? she wondered. But she stood completely alone, unengaged in conversation with anyone. Only Jacob, in a solitary sulk by the ale keg, stood by himself.

She looked back to their wagon. The darkness was gathering rapidly, the land almost indistinguishable from the edge of the night sky. Beyond the firelight, the tops of the wagons rose like apparitions in the dark. She shivered and drew her shawl around her shoulders, returning her gaze to the campfire. Johannes lounged nonchalantly against the side of the second supply wagon, a tin cup in his hand. Inga and another couple stood in front of him talking. She saw Johannes watching her over their heads and her eyes caught his. Even in the dull firelight, his expression was one of amusement. Then his head swiveled as he watched Reuben make his way to the group gathered around Mac.

Rebecca sighed and sat down heavily on one of the crates Charlie and John had set out as makeshift seats. The inky night behind her seemed ominous, a wholly different energy than the soft, gay crackle of the fire. She lowered her head and stared at her thin, delicate fingers for a moment, then raised them to her temples and began to gently rub the hollow above her closed eyes in a circular motion.

She didn't hear the footsteps. But when she opened her eyes, a pair of scuffed and scarred brown, laced leather boots were planted directly in front of her. Her heart made a sickening thump as she looked up and into the eyes of Jacob O'Shanahan. He had positioned his bulky frame to block the fire so there was light on her face and shadow on his. She darted quick looks to either side of his hips to see if anyone was watching.

Thirty feet away, Reuben had his back to her, engaged in conversation. Johannes, further distanced, had taken his eyes off her, and was smiling and nodding at the couple who conversed with Inga and him. Jacob's stance effectually blocked her movement unless she made a concerted effort to stand and walk around him. And he knew it.

"Awww...princess," he scoffed, "that Prussian farm boy hurt your feelings?"

Rebecca glared at him, trying to gather her wits about her. Jacob spoke again, in a lowered voice.

"Maybe I can help? Bet I could put a smile on that pretty face of yours." He ran the tip of his tongue slowly out of his mouth and swiped it slowly, very deliberately, from one corner of his lips to the other, his face filled with a fierce, almost wild look.

Clearing her throat with as much disapproval as she could muster, "You have no manners, Mr. O'Shanahan. Be off with you. God only knows why the King has not untethered England and the Empire from the mantle of Irish filth and despair."

Jacob's leer stiffened. Rebecca knew she should go no further, but her anger at his intrusion into her space and his filthy insinuations was rising by the second. Before she could say more, he dropped swiftly to one knee, reached out a thick muscular hand, and gripped Rebecca's chin, roughly cradling her jaw between his fingers and thumb.

She tried to shake her head free, but he tightened his grip. She slapped his wrist with one hand as he lifted her face toward his. "Take your hands off me this instant," her words were slurred by the inability to fully open her mouth.

Jacob bared his teeth in a nasty sneer and exhaled a blast of bad breath almost causing her to gag. "Don't you ever talk to me that way you pompous..."

A sudden thump of colliding bodies knocked Rebecca backward off the crate. She struggled to one elbow and raised her head. Mac stood by the crate, a bullwhip coiled in his right hand, his face as red as his beard, his eyes glowing dangerously. Jacob, stunned, struggled to raise a shoulder from the ground.

"If I ever see you touch a woman on my wagon train inappropriately again," Mac raised his arm and expertly flicked his wrist, "I will tie you to a wagon wheel and give you fifty lashes with this." He snapped the end of the whip. A sound like a rifle report shot through the air. Dust flew into Jacob's face just inches from his ear. He pushed frantically with his feet, propelling his body backward along the ground and away from Mac, one hand desperately rubbing his eyes.

Mac advanced toward him, flicking the whip, its tapered leather tail hissing like a snake in the night air. "From one Irishman to another, you know that this is neither blarney nor bluff. Your back will look like you have been dragged ten miles by wild horses."

The crowd that had gathered in a semi-circle behind Mac stood silent, including Reuben and Johannes, who had turned the moment the whip cracked the air. The wagon master took a deep breath and studiously coiled the whip, obviously trying to calm himself down.

Jacob got to his feet, his face a mask of hateful menace. It was apparent that he could barely control himself. Several of the women helped Rebecca upright. Inga brushed off Rebecca's dress with worried motions. "Are you all right, Milady Marx?"

Rebecca inhaled, catching her breath. She looked down at her hands. They were shaking. She clasped them together so that no one would notice. "I'm quite fine, thank you."

She turned to the two women who had helped her to her feet. "Thank you very much for your kind assistance. I am Rebecca Marx." One woman, perhaps in her thirties who might have once been beautiful, had dark hair similar to Rebecca's, but shorter. The other was plump, florid and middle-aged with greying hair under her sunbonnet. She looked shocked. "I should say..." her voice trailed off. The younger lady spoke up, "I am Saley." She nodded slightly.

The older matron shook her head energetically, her heavy jowls jiggling with each movement. "That was quite surprising. My, my, my. I am Margaret, Margaret Johnson. That's my husband, Harris, and our children, Becky and Eleanor over there." She gestured to a large, kind-looking man in overalls with a large, heavy-set build, and the same pudgy, florid cheeks as she. His hands rested on the shoulders of two apple-cheeked little girls whose arms were clinging to their father's ample legs with eyes wide as silver dollars. "I'm sorry my children had to see this. Thank the Lord, Mac came to your aid."

Rebecca rubbed her jaws, trying to restore the circulation. "He did indeed." Mac was watching her intently. She smiled shakily at him, "Thank you, wagon master."

Mac smiled warmly back at her, the animal glare gone from his eyes. "Anytime, ma'am."

He turned to the people gathered around him. Reuben, Zeb and Johannes stood slightly behind the crowd, their eyes turned on Jacob, who lurked by himself in the shadows, outside the circle.

The murmurs of the group died instantly. "That incident was unfortunate," Mac said, "but it happens from time to time on these trips. Sometimes you could say things get worse the longer we go."

Relieved that she was no longer the center of attention, Rebecca stepped away but kept her eyes on Mac. "I planned to talk to all of you," he said, his voice booming, "when your bellies were full of pig and potatoes. But we have a prime example before us of one of the things about which I want to speak, and our supper needs another half-hour in the pits. So, since we are all gathered here now, we will get what needs to be said out of the way."

He looked slowly around the circle with a level, steady stare. "First, I am the wagon master. What I say goes. Anyone who does not do as I say *when* I say is endangering the families in the other wagons and the rest of the train. I won't tolerate it. I'll leave you to go it alone, and I will not stop to bury your buzzard-picked remains on the return trip."

The faces in the crowd exchanged quick looks. A night hawk flew over the group, it's grunting call and beating wings the only sound.

"I'll do my level best to get us all through safe, but I'm here to tell you now that the odds that we all make it healthy and alive are not too good. There are one hundred twenty-six men, women and children on this train. Five to ten percent of us probably won't make it." He paused to let his words sink in. "We're traveling into an unforgiving wilderness. If we see an army patrol, it will only be near Fort Kearney on the Platte, and then again, if we are lucky, we might run into troops along the South Platte east of Fort Laramie on the last leg to Cherry Creek. The only help we got is ourselves. If we don't stick and work together, even with folks you're not keen on, all our chances are diminished."

He paused again to let his words register.

"Charlie and John are my herdsman and drive the supply wagons. They will tend the critters at night, but as we go further west, we will be watched. Indians, half-breeds, renegades, and outlaws are all horse thieves. If we get stuck out here without stock, odds are we will die. Starting in a week, I'll detail three men from the wagon train to ride night duty with John and Charlie. I'll try to keep that chore even, but if it is your night, you do it. No lip, no guff. Everybody has to do their share. Five days from now we cross the Gasconade River. We will encounter far bigger and faster streams before we get to Cherry Creek, so pay close attention to my directions."

REUBEN SOUGHT REBECCA'S GAZE, BUT SHE SEEMED ABSENTLY transfixed by Mac's speech. His attempt to catch her eye was interrupted by the mention of his name.

Mac gestured toward Reuben. "Reuben is the assistant wagon master. We agreed on it today. Unless I say otherwise, his words are my words. Follow them. The night after we cross the Gasconade, we will camp a mite early. Reuben will muster all the men, and you all bring your long guns and pistols. I want to see how you shoot." He turned to Johannes, "John, I..."

Reuben chuckled when his friend, obviously unperturbed by Mac's dire warnings, interrupted the wagon master, correcting him in a friendly tone. "Johannes, Mac. The name is Johannes."

"Okay, Joohan. Where was your military at?"

Johannes looked momentarily surprised at the question. His face twitched and there was a tangible extended silence. "I don't recall ever saying I was in the military," he responded, smoothly sidestepping Mac's inquiry.

Mac looked at him hard then his intended reply dissolved into a partial grin. "Well, have it your way...you will assist me and Reuben in gauging the men's shooting skills, and helping them out of any bad habits they might have acquired along the way."

"I am at your service, Mac."

Mac turned back to the crowd. "We can't wait for no one. Better take good care of those wagons. Check wheels and axels each time we stop for breaks, which will be a few minutes each morning and afternoon, 'til we get further west. Then the schedule will change. And, check 'em at night. I hope you followed the lists I gave you all and have spare parts in your toolboxes. We will spend time weekly on regular repairs and maintenance. I have some spare parts and a forge in the supply wagons." His face became stern and serious. "I will not put the entire train at risk for one wagon.

"Next thing, only God knows if this will be a wet or dry spring. If it's wet, we'll be fighting mud, high rivers and sickness. If it's dry, good water will be scarce. If I have to, I will have all the water kegs on the supply wagons spiked shut, and it will be rationed. If we ration and I find anyone stealing, I will kill him, if it's a man. If it's a woman, you've doomed your family because your wagon won't be traveling with us as of that minute.

"Finally, if there's any fights, any bad behavior..." Reuben watched Mac's head swivel toward Jacob, "or the slightest untoward bothering of any women, anyone responsible will answer to me." He looked around the circle again, slowly, "Any questions?"

The only sound as Mac's words settled on the group was the crackle of the fire and the slight whisper of the night wind that swept with stealth through the grass, carrying the scent of the stock from uphill of the group.

"Good," Mac continued. "Let's show this pig how hungry we are. We will be moving at daybreak." He slapped his pants leg with the whip, half-smiled, and walked over to the roasting pits marked with iron stakes pounded in the ground halfway between the fire and the supply wagons. The gathered pioneers separated widely to let him pass, everyone's eyes following his movement.

Seizing the moment, Reuben moved over beside Rebecca, who was smiling at Mac's retreating back. "Are you sure you're all right?" he asked, aware of the concern in his voice.

"I'll be fine," she said. "I was just thinking that watching Mac part the crowd was almost like Moses without a staff." She sighed. "I am such a very long, long way from London."

"I'm sorry I didn't come to your aid, Rebecca. By the time I realized what was happening, Mac had things well under control."

"That's all right, Reuben," she said, mustering a smile that looked forced, almost too sugary sweet. "Yes, Mac certainly did."

"That he did," Reuben said, keeping his face impassive. "So I suppose *he* deserves the smile." He turned and walked away into the darkness.

March 18, 1855

ECISION MADE

SARAH HAD BEEN ENJOYING HERSELF IMMENSELY. THIS WAS THE FIRST time since that horrible day when Jacob induced her to travel west with him (in separate sleeping cars, which she realized too late had never been truly intended), that she had the opportunity to speak relatively freely to other people. She drifted from one small group to another introducing herself, smiling and chatting. Some people were warmer than others, but there was not a single person she met who she did not like.

Thelma and Arthur Leonard were among her favorites. He was a medical doctor, a lofty, thin man with closely cropped mustache, grey hair and an academic look. Thelma was also thin, with short grey hair, casually well-dressed, and vivacious. Mr. Leonard was pale and, in some indefinable way, did not look well. Sarah found herself wondering if Thelma's incessant wind of her arm through her husband's was for support or affection, or perhaps both.

The woman was fascinated with Sarah's brief rendition of her history, the death of her parents in 1852 and 1853, and the sewing shop established by her mother that she ran with her sister, Emily. They beamed when Sarah offered to mend the slight tear in the seam of Arthur's nappy brown wool pants where they extended over his boots.

"You're such a sweet child," Thelma said, pulling her arm. "And so young to be traveling all this way. It must be quite the adventure."

Sarah fought to keep the smile on her face. "More than an adventure, Thelma. I had originally planned to stay in New York and assist my aunt with her shop on West 47th Street. But it appears the talk of war that's circulating has dampened business at the same time the new Singer sewing machines have sped production. My Aunt Stella simply could not afford to keep me on."

Feeling a pang, Sarah swallowed and looked around. Jacob glared at her from a distance. "And, then I intended to stay in St. Louis, but other situations arose that resulted in my decision to go west. I hear Cherry Creek is growing. Perhaps I can open a shop there."

Thelma had followed her eyes when she looked at Jacob and was now carefully searching her face. "How did you and Mr. O'Shanahan meet?"

Sarah felt a tightness in her chest. "We met on the *Edinburgh* during the voyage across the Atlantic."

The older lady smiled, either not noticing, or pretending to ignore the terse texture of Sarah's answer. "How fortunate that you were able to become engaged and have a traveling companion on this journey."

The twinge of skepticism in Thelma's tone made it clear to Sarah the older woman was probing. Thelma did not believe that she and Jacob being together was fortuitous whatsoever. Sarah tried to smile disarmingly. "Jacob likes to proclaim that we are betrothed. But we are not."

Both Thelma's and Arthur's faces blanched. "He is your friend, then? Relative perhaps?" she asked, persistently.

An idea began to rapidly develop in Sarah's mind. She already had a plan; its careful formulation began the night after Jacob first raped her on the train. The plan germinated unexpectedly with the encounters between Jacob and Zeb on the barge, and between Reuben, Zeb, and Jacob just hours ago as the wagons trundled west. She felt a sudden burst of courage. *Why not begin telling a portion of the truth?*

She held Thelma's inquisitive stare. "No, he is not a friend and he is not relative. He is merely somebody that for now I am forced to travel with, unfortunately."

Thelma's eyebrows shot up. Arthur shook his head. Sarah could literally see the curiosity well up in their features but she did not

wish to overplay her hand. Behind the couple, she saw Reuben talking to three of the men, turning his pistol in his hands. The men's
heads were bobbing up and down, and each passed the Colt to the
next who examined it just as carefully. She desperately wanted to
talk to Reuben alone. It was the perfect excuse to disengage from
her conversation with the Leonards, which she did not wish to continue further. At least for now.

"If you'll excuse me, it has been such a great pleasure to meet
you. Please do bring those pants over to the wagon, and I will have
them looking brand new for you in no time. Right now there's somebody I really need to talk to."

She had moved only half the distance between herself and Reuben
when she felt a hand on her arm. In the same instant she thought it
was Jacob, she realized the touch was much smaller and lighter. She
turned, startled to see Rebecca. She was even more surprised at the
look in the brunette's face, particularly after their encounters on the
boat, which had been mostly sharp, traded barbs. However, now
Rebecca wore the empathetic, earnest expression that one woman
wears when she talks to another about serious female concerns.

Sarah smiled faintly, "That was a dreadful incident. Are you all
right?"

"Yes, of course. Thank you, Sarah, I'm fine." Rebecca paused,
studying her face intently. "I notice you didn't apologize for your
betrothed actions, and you seem rather unconcerned about him
accosting another woman."

Sarah felt her cheeks redden. "Jacob is not my fiancé, and nothing
he does would surprise me, especially when it comes to women,
money, or poker."

Rebecca obviously did not expect such a direct answer. Her look
of womanly concern deepened. "Has he hurt you? Why the dickens
are you with him?"

Her question and apparent sincerity flooded Sarah with a rush of
bitter, distasteful memories—Jacob's hands on her body, her torso
pressed defenseless against mattresses, the pain, hurt, indignity, the
searing burn of his vicious penetrations, his threats and bullying,

and the beatings. Rebecca's face grew blurry as tears came to Sarah's eyes. Her lower lip trembled. She bit down on it, averted her gaze, and took a deep ratcheting breath.

A look of horrible realization replaced the brunette's air of concern. She moved close, gently put one arm over Sarah's shoulders and leaned her forehead into Sarah's. "I am truly sorry for my demeanor toward you on the *Edinburgh*. May I call you Sarah? I had no way of knowing..."

Sarah's lips trembled as she attempted a smile. In a soft whisper, the words began to pour out, "Yes, of course. It was after that...it started on the train. We must have been just a day or two behind you. I was a naïve fool, Rebecca." She quivered, hoping she hadn't overstepped herself. She could feel the cool evaporation of the drying tears on her cheeks. She had so needed to tell someone.

Rebecca pulled their foreheads together more firmly. "Come stay in our wagon. Inga and I can make room."

"That's very kind, but it would be much too crowded with three of us, and besides...." The waves of humiliation, seething inside of her for weeks, rose up in anger. *That wagon and everything in it, will be mine. I shan't leave it to him. The last chapter of the story has not been written. I will have that gold map. He owes me and he shall pay.* She took a deep breath, which particularly caught in her throat. "Mr. O'Shanahan will not bully me away from what is mine."

Rebecca looked puzzled and pressed closer, almost whispering. "Then you be careful. I hope you change your mind. I will bring Inga to meet you. You will like her. We shall visit as often as possible and if anything happens, let us know and we will tell Johannes and Mac..." she lifted her head and smiled, "and Zeb. I have seen him looking at you. I think he would do anything for you..." Rebecca glanced behind her where Reuben and three of the men were still discussing the Colt, "and Reuben, too."

Sarah noticed a strange look flit across Rebecca's eyes as she said those last words.

"You be very careful, Sarah."

"You, too, Rebecca. I can't tell you how much I appreciate your thoughts. But, you're a beautiful woman and you have shamed him. Be very careful."

To Sarah's complete astonishment Rebecca leaned into her again and hugged her, but Sarah was suddenly pulled from the embrace by a hard, strong hand, which gripped her arm with indelicate force.

"Well isn't this lovely. My betrothed hugging a woman." Jacob looked Rebecca up and down, from her eyes to her boots. "Two pretty lassies in love, eh? How tender."

Rebecca stiffened and her face hardened, but she caught the imploring look in Sarah's eyes. *Not here, not another scene now, please!*

Jacob lowered his head close to Sarah's ear. "It's time for us to go. We have spent far too long with these pie-eyed sheep." Sarah looked up. Mac and Zeb stood side by side together watching the scene carefully. She yanked her arm away. Jacob, following her gaze, did not resist. He released his hold, but not his demands.

"Let's go, woman."

Sarah felt the stares of many as she and Jacob headed into the darkness back toward their wagon, including Reuben, who had turned from his discussion, his mouth a grim line as he watched their departure into the blackness beyond the reach of the fire.

March 18, 1855

ℛEDHEAD ASSERTION

SARAH AND JACOB WALKED BACK TOWARD THEIR WAGON, THE VOICES of the pioneers still gathered around the fire receding behind them. The darkness deepened as the flames grew more distant. Though they walked abreast of one another, Sarah was careful to keep at least a three-foot separation. Inga had looked worried when they left the gathering. Zeb frowned, and Reuben stared hard at Jacob.

"That's certainly an odd bunch of people," grumbled Jacob.

Emboldened by the support of the Leonards, Zeb, and her other *Edinburgh* shipmates, Sarah was forthright in her response. "I think they're very nice. Some may be simple, but all have a dream. There was more excitement and hope than I've heard in any discussion for a long, long time. This country, this land, seems to breed a sense of opportunity. Perhaps it is these open spaces. This never-ending wild land. I've been on these shores less than a month and I feel it. I don't understand it yet, and it is different than what I expected, but it's real."

Even in the darkness, Sarah felt Jacob's nasty glance.

"You are a naïve fool. Everybody's out for themselves in this world. These people just put on airs. You'll get to know them on this godforsaken trip. You'll see. I've been around. They can't fool Jacob O'Shanahan for a second."

"That, Jacob, is exactly what I would expect you'd think," she snapped back angrily.

Jacob pulled up short and turned his sturdy frame to face her. "Now, Sarah, you're my woman, and I'm your man. I was just telling you what I think."

She ignored him, kept walking, and quickened her pace.

He stood for a moment in surprise, and then hurried after her. Quickly closing the distance, he sidled up next to her when they were a few paces from their wagon and attempted to put his arm around her shoulders.

Sarah spun out of his grasp. In the dim flicker from the campfire, she stared at his wide, ruddy face and deep-set eyes. His mop of hair looked aflame from the red glare. "I'm not your woman, and you're not my man, Jacob. Never have been, never will be," she spat, an unmistakable venom in her tone.

Jacob recoiled. His face took on an ugly, menacing look, and the right corner of his upper lip twitched. "You redheaded bitch. After all I have done for you. Every woman needs a man. I bought you things. I have protected you, let you come on this journey with me. I even shared the secret of the map to the gold with you..." He paused. "A secret you promised to keep."

A steeled coldness gave Sarah's voice a rigid edge. "Jacob, from the time you first raped me on the train, and every time you raped me thereafter, you diminished my dignity. You have stolen my honor. You have treated me as a slave with threats, bullying, and vulgar manhandling."

She leaned forward, almost on her tiptoes, her hands clenched tightly at her sides, the freckles across the bridge of her petite, finely-formed nose highlighted by an angry flush. She took a deep uneven breath. "That is over as of right this minute. I will throw your bedding down to you. You may sleep under the wagon or wherever you choose."

Turning abruptly, Sarah unlatched the rear of the wagon, took out the ladder and set it against the lip of the extended gate, wedging its base into the earth. She climbed the first two wood rungs and was ready to step from the ladder onto the surface of the tailgate when she felt Jacob on the ladder behind her. He shoved her roughly, headlong into the wagon on her stomach, his heavy frame on top of her, his hand clamped tightly over her mouth and nose, his knee trying to force her legs apart.

She lay still, not struggling, something she had learned from countless attempts, and from the bruises and pain that resulted from trying to fight a brute man who outweighed her by more than a hundred pounds. But this time, she had a plan.

He fumbled with his free hand, trying to raise her dress. She turned her head to avoid the exhale of his dank, liquored-up breath. At the feel of his saliva dribbling down her neck, she felt the onset of nausea, something she'd been plagued by during the past two weeks. She closed her eyes, pressed her lips together, and suppressed the urge to retch.

"Nobody talks to me like that, you wench. You ungrateful redheaded English bitch. I bought this wagon for you, did I not? I brought flowers to your aunt's stinky little sewing shop in New York. I was a gentleman. You wanted it on the train. You would've never come with me if you didn't."

He mouthed her ear, his raspy wet tongue leaving a thick film on her cheek. "You want it now. I can tell when I take you, you like it more and more. We fit together good," he grunted.

He raised her skirt and single petticoat halfway up her legs. His hand reached under the hem and began to move up the inner part of her thigh. His grip over her mouth tightened. "I spent good money on this wagon so you wouldn't have to walk all the way to the damn mountains. I told you about the gold. I will not sleep on the stinking ground like a damn animal." His lips and tongue were now pressed against her right ear.

She shuddered, focusing on her left hand, which she had been quietly extending over the coarse covers of the grain storage bags.

"Ah, I knew you liked it, freckle-faced slut. You're my woman and I will take you when I want. You can pretend but I know different, Sarah Bonney of Liverpool. I know different."

Her fingers felt the leather underside of the satchel she and Emily had carefully sewed. She inched her hand up from the bottom, where she had hidden her money in the secret compartment since England, into the carryall. She had purposely left the handbag open and in a certain easily accessible spot in the wagon, exactly for this moment. The surprise of many of her *Edinburgh* shipmates being on this wagon train had merely accelerated the inevitable. She knew this time would come when she had made her plan and agreed to accompany Jacob to the Rockies.

Jacob had smuggled four jugs of whiskey onto the wagon in St. Louis. He was partially drunk, a nighttime ritual. His hand reached the tender, soft area where her inner thighs merged and where the tips of his thick fingers probed, intent on forcing their way into her. She did nothing to prevent his penetration. As one finger slid savagely into her, she concentrated on holding her shoulder still as her left hand fumbled carefully inside the satchel, willing herself to recognize the various objects as her fingers brushed against them.

She knew from the bitter experience of the last weeks that once he raised her petticoat and skirt up over her hips and forced her legs fully apart with his knees, he would straighten up to kneel behind her in order to pull his breeches down before lowering himself on her to rape her once again. Her thumb came into contact with a small piece of cold metal. Her heart jumped. Jacob now had both knees between her thighs. Her little fingers closed around the metal. She withdrew it quietly, slowly, and waited.

Jacobs harsh, threatening whispers transformed to heavy breaths and boarish grunts as he plunged two fingers in and out of her and ground his pelvis against her leg. "That's better woman, much better. You don't need to fight me—you and me, Sarah, we have plans."

He rose to his knees. She could hear him cursing as he fumbled with the buttons on his trousers.

Her face was free of his stranglehold, and her back released of his weight. In a quick, agile movement she had practiced one hundred times in her mind, she gathered her right arm under her upper body, raised and twisted her left shoulder and head back toward him, and extended her left hand almost to his face, cocking the hammer of the small, single-barrel .45-caliber Philadelphia Deringer as she did so.

The sound of the click of the gun's hammer within the canvas enclosure could not be mistaken. Jacob froze, his pants slightly below his hips, his eyes wide and focused on the muzzle of the three-inch barrel a foot from his face.

"Get off me right now, or I will pull the trigger. Don't move, except to backup. Don't say a word." Her voice was fierce, harsh, commanding, determined. She heard herself speak as if she was a spectator. She tightened her grip, ever so slightly, on the trigger.

Jacob came up off his knees, directly backward, sitting down heavily on the inside edge of the tailgate. His wide shoulders, with arms raised and palms facing her, were silhouetted by the dim light filtering through the open canvas from the campfire.

"You're crazy, you ungrateful skinny-assed tart. You can't do this to Jacob O'Shanahan. You're mine. This wagon is mine." His face was contorted, almost demonic in the dim light. Sarah knew he'd convinced himself that his position was invincible.

"So that's why you excused yourself when we was waiting to load on the barge?" he snarled. "To buy a pistol? What will you tell all these pilgrims? How will you explain your man lying here, his eyes shot out? These do-gooders would probably hang you or take you back St. Louis to be tried for my murder."

"Jacob, if you move one more inch, there will be a bullet in your sick brain."

He froze, startled by the deathly tone and unemotional ferocity in her voice.

"And while you're lying on the floor of this wagon bleeding," she added, "I will take that stiletto out of your boot, cut your throat, then sink it up to the hilt in your sick, evil heart."

She paused. Jacob stared at her, incredulous. Her voice continued in a deadly hiss.

"Yes, that is when I bought the pistol. You've not thought this through, you Irish bully. I am now among friends. People who know me. Reuben is decent and strong and actually respects me. Zeb seems attracted to me. He would like nothing better than to slice you up with that knife of his—you do remember the barge, don't you? These people from the *Edinburgh,* which the good Lord has thankfully reunited me with, *they know you, too.* You can see the way they stare at us. They are shocked that I am with you. They will believe my story. Remember, I have bruises to show—all over my body. And I'll have Dr. Leonard's wife examine me where you have ripped me apart time after time."

She could feel the scalding heat of tears flowing down her cheeks. Her right eyelid ticked. Her face felt like it was burning. There was a metallic taste in her mouth. She took a deep breath to steady herself.

"You will not touch me again. Ever. You will not sleep in this wagon with me. If you touch me, or threaten me, I will go to Mac, Zeb, Reuben, and Johannes. They despise you. I will tell them everything." She paused, to catch her breath and let her words sink in. "And I will tell them about your gold map with the bloodstain. You killed or maimed somebody for that map, Jacob. I know you. You always take what is not yours. You live without regard for others. You hurt people without remorse. As of this second, I am no longer one of those people."

Jacob's lower jaw trembled with rage. He began to speak, "You..."

Her face forward, teeth bared, Sarah interrupted him, her tone filled with hatred and contempt. "Not a word, Jacob. Not one single word. Never threaten me again. You will not gloat over how you would break my neck or throw me off the train."

Sarah took a third, steadying breath. "We are now in a small, tight-knit group. Everyone is watching. You saw how Rebecca came up to me. And Mac and Zeb. How Reuben came over to the wagon three times today, then Zeb. I know you noticed Zeb rode directly behind us for several hours. He could have been behind any of the forty-one wagons, Jacob. Why do you think he choose ours?"

A growing rage clutched her chest. "If anything happens to me, it will not be me that gets hanged by this group of brave men and women, Jacob. It will be you."

Jacob did not move. Sarah could tell he was carefully weighing her words, torn between his narcissist perceptions, and thinking of his own self-interest. After a minute his muscles relaxed and he sat back fully, no longer making any attempt to force himself on her again.

When he finally spoke, his voice was like thick, poisoned honey. "Well lassie, I am impressed. You've been scheming. You've led me on all this time. Here I was thinking you were liking me. And every minute you were planning this. What you really want is the gold map."

He shook his head and chortled an evil half-laugh. "I knew it, Sarah. You and I, redhead, are much alike. We are a team. Jacob O'Shanahan always recognizes and respects cunning and planning. You've done well." His voice grew more menacing. "My rules are like this: You don't threaten me again. If you breathe a word about anything, especially the gold map, I will kill you for the sport of it whether or not I hang." His eyes bored through the darkness into hers. "And you know I am not bluffing."

Sarah straightened her spine, the Deringer still extended, her forearms balanced on her knees, one hand holding the gun, the other wrapped around her shooting wrist. "Get out of the wagon, Jacob."

He hesitated, then edged backward. Reaching behind him, he found the ladder with one hand and without looking down, climbed to the ground, his eyes fixed balefully on hers.

Without taking her gaze off him, Sarah kept the pistol pointed at his head. She fumbled with her left hand for his bedroll. She found it, brought herself to her knees and then stood, never taking the ominous blue-black .45-caliber muzzle of the Deringer from his figure. She walked within a few feet of the open tailgate and kicked the bedroll out and into the dirt.

"Close and latch the tailgate, Jacob. Put the ladder inside the wagon, and then close off the bottom three ties of the canvas."

The last thing she saw as he sullenly obeyed her commands were his eyes staring malevolently at hers while he tied the last chord at the base of the canvas top. Then the fabric tightened, obscuring his face.

March 18, 1855

BLACK FEATHER'S BAND RODE EAST AWAY FROM THE MOUNTAINS AT a steady, ground-eating pace, roughly parallel with the Cache la Poudre River. Twenty miles from the last of the foothills, they veered northeast, away from the cottonwood trees that marked the river's turn to the south. He planned to meet the river again after it, too, had veered north and, fed by tributaries, merged with the Platte.

For the first several hours his men joked, comparing the bloody scalps they had taken and arguing over which was more valuable, blond, grey, or dark. Occasionally, the discussions became heated and the men lapsed into native tongues. Black Feather shook his head at the indistinguishable bragging and bickering behind him. At times, he craned his head around to see how the girl was riding, reaching behind him to tug her back into a centered position on the black stallion. Three times he asked, "You want to talk yet?" The thin blond girl would not reply or raise her eyes to his, but the grip of her thin arms tightened in their partial circle around his waist, and he could feel increased pressure where her forehead was buried in the army tunic's dark blue wool, halfway between his shoulder blades and belt.

They stopped late in the morning to rest and water the horses in Double Kettle Creek. Black Feather scanned the men until he found Pedro. He waved him over. "Pedro, I'm going to untie the lash. Lift her down from the saddle and bring her over to the shade behind those cottonwood trunks."

Black Feather loosed the rope that held her to him, and she slumped sideways into Pedro's thick, waiting arms. "Easy, you fool," he admonished Pedro, who then carefully set her feet down in the dry sandy soil. But her knees buckled, and she couldn't support her own weight.

Pedro looked up at Black Feather, trepidation clearly etched in his face. "Patron, what should I..."

Black Feather interrupted him, "Carry her over there if you have to." He gestured with his hand much as one would shoo a stray dog. Then, still mounted, he looked quickly around. "Hank, Snake, and Chief, you too, González, I don't want any blue-coated surprises. Gonzales, cross the creek and set up a scouting post a half-mile south. That's a high fold in the ground. Keep your eyes peeled to the southeast and west. Don't skyline yourself."

He turned to the other three. "You three spread out. Hank—go back downstream to that last oxbow we passed behind us—stay in the cottonwoods. Snake, get your ass a half-hour's ride up this creek bed and slightly north, and you, Chief, I want you a half-hour ride due north. When you see dust, you will know we're moving again. Keep your position as we move. Keep the same pace as this morning. I don't want to waste time, but we can't wear out the horses either."

The men started to pull on their reins but Black Feather stopped them. "Wait!" he barked. "No gunplay. Those blue coats will be all over you like dogs if there's any shots. If you can't handle any problem with your knife, sneak back here and tell me."

The outriders galloped off and Black Feather slid off the stallion. He stretched out one long leg, then the other. He snatched a water pouch from the clutch of one of the band and walked over to where the girl sat, her back against a tree, her knees to her chest, her face buried in her hands.

Black Feather knelt down slightly to the side and in front of her, careful not to be too close. *Skittish as a mustang foal that's lost her mama in a roundup,* he thought to himself. He held up the water pouch. "Thirsty?" The girl was silent. He reached into the side pocket of his tunic, pulled out a hardtack biscuit and took a small bite. "Good. This is a *good* biscuit." He extended his hand part-way toward her, the biscuit at the tip of his fingers. "Want some?" There was still no verbal or physical response of any kind. He withdrew the proffered food, and, to spell his increasing annoyance, shifted his position from kneeling to sitting cross-legged, still more than an arm's length from her. *Never crowd a cornered foal,* he reminded himself. "Well, this time, I will save you the biscuit. At some point, you will be hungry."

He relaxed, stretched out his bared arms behind him, and leaned back. He squinted up through the tree branches that stirred just slightly with the faint breeze of late morning. Wisps of clouds floated in and out of the limbed frame of the sky and moved lazily to the northeast, the same direction of travel as he and his band of outlaws.

Lulled by the changing pattern of blue and white, and perhaps influenced by the shocked, mute trauma of the girl, his mind faded back to his regression at the morning's ambush, a memory long suppressed.

His mother Sunray was Osage, a full-blood. She was beautiful, the tallest woman in a tribe, her athletic body proportioned perfectly. Her thin waist flared to hips made for childbearing. It was rare that her perfect white teeth were not displayed in a broad and friendly smile that complimented her wide, acorn-brown eyes. His father, Jonathan Harrison, was older, tall and lanky, with greying hair. He traded often with the Osages. He gave them milk, eggs from his chickens, and vegetables he set aside each harvest.

In return, he received tanned leather and several horses, including the family favorite—an aging grey mare. The Harrison farm was on the very outskirts of civilization, the edge of the frontier. There were few settlers west of the Mississippi in the 1830s. On his very occasional supply trips back to St. Louis, not yet a city, Jonathan would always return with five or six small wool blankets, which he gave as gifts to children of the tribe, asking nothing in return. It was this generosity, greatly respected by the Indians, which eventually led to his being given permission to marry Sunray, a very rare blessing for a non-Osage, from a tribe with tightly regimented marriage and breeding traditions.

His parents had met on one of these trips to the village, in the summer of 1822. He remembered his mother telling him the story many times, her face glowing, her eyes usually fixed on her husband, though she was speaking to their only son, whom they had named Samuel Raysun Harrison. "Love at first sight" his father had called it.

Unconsciously, still lost in his reverie, with the blond captive only a few feet away, Black Feather grunted in disdain. Love at first sight? After twenty bloody years on the outlaw trail, love was a foreign word from another world.

On the farm, he helped his father with the chores and his mother around the house. Several nights each week, his father gave him and his mother reading and writing lessons. They would sometimes fish together in the ponds, and he learned the skills of hunting, fishing, trapping, and self-reliance of both white and red, taking the best from each, eventually using those lessons to stay alive.

He was twelve when it happened.

Black Feather opened his eyes and stared at the huddled, unspeaking figure curled in a tight ball in front of him. He blinked. *I was just a few years younger than her, maybe that's why.* He pushed away the unwelcome thought.

There were nine men, all white, all bearded. It was just after the midday meal. They rode up to the farmhouse, drunk. His father was back in the fields on the other side of a dense stand of trees less than a half-mile away, farming the twenty-acre tract that Black Feather had helped him clear and cultivate. His father taught him respect for each tree felled, each root system pulled from the earth. Half the field was irrigated with the ingenious ditch system he had dug by his father's side.

Three of the men stumbled up to the front porch. Samuel was in the shadow of the barn interior, able to see and hear, picking up most of the words, but unseen himself.

His mother answered the door. Even at that distance he could see she was bobbing her head, gesturing happily, trusting visitors, which were few and far between and always welcome at the Harrison farm-house. Samuel saw two of the men suddenly grab her under her arms. She kicked at them, losing her balance, and fell backwards. The third man grabbed her feet. Her scream pierced the shadows where Samuel hid, like a knife to the heart. One man, his big burly form topped by an old round hat, two black feathers sticking up from its crown, raised a fist and struck her in the face. The men laughed, and the big man waved the other men off the horses and into the house.

Young Samuel, frozen and mute by her screams, walked in dazed circles inside the dark barn. He saw the pitchfork, with its sharp prongs imbedded in a bale of straw. He jerked it free and held it like a lance, but it was only a pitchfork. No good against guns. He stabbed the bale, again and again, wanting to fight, but not wanting to be seen, wanting his father, but afraid of what he knew would happen to this God-fearing man he loved. "Fighting is never the way to solve anything, son." Those words paled in the horrible reality of the afternoon.

His mother's screams went on for hours then fell to whimpers. Then she was silent. The shadows lengthened in the late afternoon sun. The burly man and one other walked out on the porch buttoning their britches. One went to the horses and returned with a whiskey jug. In turn, they slung it over their elbows and took long gulps, sometimes rubbing their crotches, thrusting their hips out and laughing as they guzzled.

Crouched in the shadows of the barn and still gripping the pitch-fork, Samuel heard the distant sound of a horse at an easy lope—his father on Dot, their now old, grey mare. The marauders heard it, too. They scurried back into the house and closed the door. The oil lamps were lit and their yellow light radiated invitingly from the windows. Samuel stood up numbly, despairing. He realized through his fog that they were making the house looked natural. They were setting a trap for his father. He wanted to run out to him, but somehow his legs would not move. The more he told himself he must warn his Pa, the less strength in his limbs, until finally the pitchfork fell to the dirt floor and he sank down to his knees, his other hand sliding along the vertical rough-sawn lumber frame of the barn door, driving a jagged splinter into his palm that went unnoticed.

The short white blaze on Dot's forehead shone in the dimming light. Samuel watched as his father paused, seeing the horses tied outside the house. *Company is always welcome, son.* How many times had he heard those words? A surge of nausea swept from his gut up to his throat. He pressed his nose against the doorframe, his right eye peering around the edge of the wood. His father dismounted, called a cheerful, "Hello there!" and began untying the saddlepack, his back to the front door. When he turned, four of them stood on the porch, two with rifles and two with pistols.

His father froze. The last words from out of his mouth before his voice was drowned out by the simultaneous roar of the guns was a despairing, questioning shout, *"Sun Raaaaaaaay...."* The volley knocked his father's body back into Dot. Several bullets either went through him or directly hit the aging, gentle mare that Samuel had known all his life and learned to ride on. Dot collapsed, screaming in pain and uncomprehending fear as the bullets pierced her, too. Samuel gagged.

The next moment was etched in Sam's mind and in every cell of his body. The burly man walked down to his father, who was weakly trying to raise his head, drew a second pistol, shouted, "Stinkin shit Injun lover," cocked the hammer and fired.

Dot, her grey coat splattered with bloody bits of his father's skull, waved her hooves frantically as she tried to regain her footing, but she couldn't. Her head and upper body rose and fell to the earth as she strained to rise, her terrified whinnies echoing off the side of the house directly at the barn door. The burly man pulled out a knife, and walked toward her head. He paused, re-sheathed the knife, and viciously kicked the mare. He turned with a wave of his hand as if dismissing trash, and walked back into the house, laughing.

Samuel clutched his belly and vomited. Then everything went dark.

When he finally regained his senses, he staggered to his feet and looked out toward the house. He heard an unearthly howl and realized it was rising from his own throat, his own clenched jaws. The charred remains of their home glowed and smoked. Here and there, still standing, larger upright beams canted in eerie angles toward the black sky. The acrid smell of burnt wood hung in the night air, along with another smell, that of burning hair, like singed hog's skin at butchering time. The odor was punctuated by the infrequent weak whinnies of Dot. It was the smell, and the mare, even more than his mother's screams or his father's head blown to bits, that sealed his vile hatred that night.

The men's horses were gone. Dot's great grey head moved weakly and one front leg pawed the dirt. Her breath came in a wheeze, stirring small puffs of dust near her nostrils. Samuel walked stiffly over and picked up the pitchfork. Holding it by the handle, he dragged it dejectedly behind him, as if in a dream, until he reached the mare. His father's body was gone, perhaps drug to the house before they torched it. He fell to his knees next to Dot and began to cry, great, ratcheting, heaving sounds he did not recognize as his own. One hand stroked the neck of the dying horse. A dull recognition of her terrible agony caused him to rise. He lifted the pitchfork and, through the blur of tears, aimed its pointed tines at the top of Dot's neck, just behind her jaw, before plunging down with all his might. She convulsed, shuddered, her eyes rolled white toward him, and then the mare, too, was gone from his world.

It took three years, but Samuel finally tracked down the heavy-set white man with the two black feathers in his hat. He had kept the blubbering hulk alive for two weeks, cutting off fingers and toes each day, finally castrating him and letting him bleed to death, savoring the pain and glazed fear in the man's eyes. He plucked the feathers from the fat man's hat and braided them into his hair, grown long and dark since the day at the farm. He raised the bloody knife to the sky and proclaimed, *From this day on, I am Black Feather, and I shall make the white men scream!*

Black Feather opened his eyes. He was sweating profusely. His throat burned as if he had thrown up. With a start, he realized the girl had taken her hands from her face and was staring at him with large green eyes, as if sensing a kindred pain.

The hand on his shoulder startled him. Catlike, he leapt to his feet, his knife extended. Snake jumped back, "Damn boss, that's the second time today you drew that blade on me. I was just comin' to tell you it was time to move out. We been here a half-hour. We thought you wanted to make Box Elder Draw by nightfall."

Black Feather straightened from his crouch, pulled the knife back in toward him and sneered, "If there's a third, I will cut your hand off. Don't ever sneak up on me again." He looked back at the girl. Her face was again buried behind her hands and she was trembling. He sheathed the knife blade and stood for moment looking down at her. *Very pretty girl. She's going to be a hell of a woman.* He bent down to her and leaned close, "It's time to go, can you walk?" Again there was no response.

He carefully slid one arm under her bent knees and worked the other behind her shoulders. He lifted her off the ground effortlessly, carried her over to his horse, and handed her to Pedro. "After I'm up, put her behind me and lash her again." Pedro nodded.

Black Feather opened his mouth but Pedro cut him off, "I know Patron, *gently.*" Black Feather nodded, and sprang into the saddle.

They rode steadily the rest of the day, taking only one quick break, and stopping long after dark when they reached Box Elder. Black Feather put out six picket sentries and two more on the horses.

"Gonzalez, Hank and Turtle Face, put up a half-faced bivouac over there in those trees for me and the girl. Use the branches from that cedar for the roof. I want the half-face toward the horses." Even in the darkness Black Feather could see the white flashes of teeth as they grinned at one another. Others in the band who had overheard his order slapped each other on the back. He knew what they were thinking, and he didn't care. "Pedro, grab my bed role and two extra blankets."

"But, Patron, there are no extra blankets in your bed role."

"I know that. Take two from the men."

Pedro scurried to gather up the bedding and followed Black Feather over to the simple, makeshift lean-to. Two thick, vertical, five-foot forked sticks had been pounded into the ground a foot deep. A single small log lay horizontal across the forks, two others descended at an angle to the ground, and the cedar boughs had been laid over that primitive frame.

Black Feather knelt, the girl in his arms and nodded his head at Pedro, "Lay out those blankets there." After Pedro had done so, he gently laid the young woman on top of them. She immediately turned away and curled into a fetal position, hiding her face in her hands.

Spreading out his own role, Black Feather delicately covered the figure of the girl with one of the blankets. "We could make a trade," he said. "That hardtack biscuit for your name?" There was no response, nothing but silence.

Fifty yards away, the small campfire the men had built was dying. Everyone had turned in after the long day. He looked at the form lying a few feet from him, his eyes traveling its length. She was not yet mature, but the coming curve of her hips was unmistakable and the angular shape of her upper body, even under the blanket, was provocative. For a moment he was tempted, but his mind flashed back to his recall of the afternoon. He half-sighed, half-grunted. He rolled over on the blanket, his back to her. He pulled the collar of the tunic up around his neck and shut his eyes.

A few seconds later Black Feather heard a small voice, almost a woman's but not quite, a single word spoken. *Dorothy.* His eyes snapped open. He was surprised as much at the bitter irony as he was to finally hear her speak. Not wanting to frighten her, he neither moved nor rolled over. "Dorothy? A full-grown woman's name. I shall call you Dot."

There was a long moment's silence, and the little voice said, "Okay."

March 23, 1855

$\mathcal{D}$ANGEROUS CURRENTS

As they descended into the shallow valley, the sounds of the river became more strident, the noise saturating the tree-covered slope both beckoning and warning.

The land rose in a series of shelves, alluvial plains eons old, and the vegetation became ever denser near the river. From above, Reuben saw Mac rein in Red and stand in the saddle. The glistening current wound serpentine below him, part of the river visible, other portions obscured by the growth of dense deciduous trees and wild undergrowth that had replaced the grassy meadows and scattered shrubs through which the wagons had been traveling.

Mac turned in the saddle and thundered, "Reuben! Zeb!" Buck and Zeb appeared from the timber on one side of the plateau, moving ghost-like toward Mac downslope. Reuben trotted in from the wagons, which were halted several hundred yards uphill of the wagon master.

When Zeb was alongside, Mac turned to him, "Why don't you mosey on down there, get yourself and your horse across and take a quick look-see on the other side. I doubt it, but let's make sure we don't have any company."

There was an almost imperceptible tip of the coonskin cap atop Zeb's intractable, rugged features. Reuben watched him reach down and shove the Sharps into the empty leather of the over-under belly scabbard. When it was secure, he reached down and withdrew the Enfield, held the musket up, and inspected the breech. Without a word or look at him or Mac, he whispered, "Down, Buck," and the big paint began to pick his way down the last of the slope, toward the edge of the river, Zeb's tall, slender form swaying in the saddle with each of the gelding's cautious steps.

Mac unfurled the telescope and carefully surveyed the stretches of river he could see, alternately cursing Red who seemed delighted to move each time her master had the lens to his eyes. Reuben chuckled, "I think that horse is teasing you." Mac moved the telescope several inches from his eye, didn't turn his head, but clicked his eyeballs at Reuben and then back to telescope. It was not an unfriendly glance, but it was serious, and Reuben felt his smile fade.

"I thought this was one of the easiest of the larger rivers we need to cross?"

"It can be. It's not the largest tributary of the Missouri, but did you notice the clouds gathering to the southwest last night? That's some of the highest country in the Ozarks, the San François Mountains." Mac pointed across the river, "See that rock, on the opposite bank, big, grey, with the point?"

Reuben picked it out immediately, "Yes, what's its significance?"

"You can gauge how much water is in this river by that rock. High as that waterline is, there was either a big rain upstream, or what's frozen up near its source is starting to melt."

Mac lowered the telescope and shoved it in his jacket. "Damn, I was hoping this was going to be easier, but the water is between us and where we want to go, so I guess the pilgrims are going to have some higher level training sooner than we all supposed."

Reuben watched him run his fingers through his beard, contemplating his next order. "Head back down the wagon line," he said. "Tell folks we are taking a short break. I want to see if Zeb finds anything on the other side. That trouble west of here between the slavers and the non-slavers has been creeping east. My gut tells me we need be a bit more careful. There's folks that get all riled up over their notion of right and wrong."

He spat a stream of brown juice off to the side. "Then there are those that just use the excuse to kill you. They'd blame it on the color of the sun if they couldn't come up with any other reason. Anyways, tell everyone to check their goods. Anything they can make watertight, do it. If they have to, they can shift things around so cargo that needs to stay drier is on top. But, tell 'em don't make the wagons top-heavy; keep the weight low as possible. And let them know any extra stock will be driven across separate in a few bunches."

"How deep you figure it is, Mac?"

Mac dug out out his telescope again and aimed it at the grey rock on the other side the river. "Normally not over the axles of the wagons, but I'm thinking it might be up pretty near the bottom of the wagon beds right now." He turned back to Reuben, "Well, assistant, how would you handle this?"

Reuben almost smiled. "You like testing me, don't you, Mac?"

"No, I like learning you, so that you and the folks that depend on you and me are still breathing when we get to Cherry Creek."

Reuben nodded his head. *Teaches much like my father—and he is right, of course.* "Well..." he spoke slowly, his eyes carefully searching various points in the river below them, "I'd ride down there along the bank and study the surface of the water until I found the most shallow spot, not too rocky, as gradual a descent into the water as possible where we enter the river, and a pull-out with the same characteristics, at least several hundred feet downstream."

"Not bad, but you left out two important points. First of all, you're in charge, you can't leave the wagons sitting up there by themselves with a bunch of greenhorns without somebody in command. Your idea is good but your choice of who does what is bad. Way better to send Charlie and John down there. They know what they're doing and that's what they're paid for. Second thing, you didn't figure anything about a place to gather the wagons without having an uproar on the other side. We get wagons jammed up on the other bank because there is no room for them to move, and the wagons that are in the river will stall, maybe get swept downstream of the exit point, and then we have a real problem."

I should've thought of that, Reuben chided himself, his eyes widening. *I ought to be taking notes.*

Mac must have read his mind, "You don't need to be taking notes. You just need to be using that common sense the good Lord gave you. What you need to do is clear as a bell if you think it through, and that's true of most things." Mac chuckled, more to himself than to Reuben, "but not all."

Reuben returned his gaze to the river, analyzing what Mac had said. He was startled when Mac boomed out, "Get moving. You can look at that damn river all you want, but it ain't going to change!"

Lifting his reins and wheeling Lahn around, Reuben urged the horse back up the slope to the wagons, their white canvases and rough wooden sides peeking through the tree trunks. He paused for a moment when he reached the rig that Inga, Rebecca, Johannes and he had called home for the past five days, and would for another two months, or so. Inga and Rebecca were in the driver's seat, the lines of the team in Inga's hands. She looked nervous. Rebecca, overdressed again, sat in her typical rigid posture, back slightly arched, shoulders squared back and chin elevated. Her hands rested demurely in her lap. Reuben could see by the points of her boots, just below the hem of her deep red traveling dress, that her ankles were properly crossed.

Johannes emerged from behind the wagon leading the big bay mare that stood almost seventeen hands. She suited Johannes' height well. She followed Johannes with her head slightly down, her stride just a tad clumsy, but Reuben knew from the mare's powerful shoulders and haunches that the horse was steady and fast when not loafing.

Johannes smiled up at Reuben, "I like this horse. I can't wait to get her out on some open flats and see what she'll do. I've named her, too."

Reuben's curiosity overcame his distraction, "You named her? So what's her name?"

Johannes laughed and rubbed the mare's shoulder lightly. Then with a straight face he answered, "Her name is Bente."

Reuben could tell he was trying to suppress a smile and couldn't wait for him to take the bait. He chuckled, "Okay, I'll bite. Where in hell did you get the name Bente?"

."Can't tell you," Johannes said, one eyelid closed in a half-wink that belied his enigmatic tone of voice. Then they both broke out in laughter. "I wish you could see your face, Reuben," he said.

Reuben leaned down closer to Johannes with a quick glance behind to make sure the women were out of earshot, and said in a low voice, "This will be more difficult than Mac thought. The river appears to be quite a bit higher than normal. Mac is concerned since this is our first crossing. You should drive the wagon. The women just don't have the skills to do it yet. It is far too early in this expedition to lose supplies, and I know neither of us...," he looked hard at Johannes, "want any harm to come to the ladies."

As he explained the situation, Johannes immediately understood the seriousness. "You're right Reuben," he said simply, and turned and walked Bente to the rear of the wagon.

Reuben backed Lahn, a maneuver the palomino had expertly learned over the past week. When he drew up even with Inga and Rebecca, he tried to keep any hint of concern or emotion from his voice. "Johannes will drive the wagon. We are stopped for about a half an hour. The two of you should probably go back and make sure anything you don't want to get wet is higher up off the wagon floor, but don't make the rig top-heavy. Johannes will help you."

Inga looked up at him, "But, I thought Johannes was going to ride Bente?"

Reuben felt his lips twitch, and decided a smile would probably be reassuring. "So he's already told you the mare's name, eh?"

She nodded and smiled in her typical radiant fashion, "He asked me my opinion before he made his final decision."

"Is that so?" Reuben chuckled.

He looked over at Rebecca. She was studying his face closely. Reuben knew she had deduced exactly what the situation was. "I need to go talk to Charlie and John and the rest of the wagons, so if I don't see you before, we will see each other on the far bank." He tipped his hat and spurred Lahn.

REBECCA TURNED TO INGA, "INGA LET'S SEE WHAT WE NEED TO DO in the wagon. There's only two ways things can get wet."

"What ways, Milady Marx?"

She really has no experience at this sort of thing at all, Rebecca thought. "The wagon tips over," she said aloud, "or the waters are high enough to come in the bed. If the wagon tips, it does not matter how you put things away, so it's my presumption that the men think the water might be high enough to come in the wagon."

Inga's eyes widened. "Milady Marx—I thought this was just a little stream?"

Rebecca shrugged. "So did I. Let's get busy."

The two ladies clambered down from the driver's seat as Johannes came around from behind the wagon. "Do you need some help?"

Rebecca shook her head, "We can manage, thank you. If we need you, we will call out."

"Good," he said, his eyebrows descending in a frown and his response absent the usual verbal sparring. "I want to check the collars and traces on the teams and make sure the lines and attachments are snug."

Rebecca felt a little butterfly in her stomach. *Reuben must've said something to him that he did not share with us.*

"Let's go, Inga, we don't have much time to do this." The two women walked swiftly to the back of the schooner, lowered the tailgate, slid out the ladder, and were quickly inside, discussing, pointing, and moving things.

"Inga, help me get these grain sacks off the floor, that ammunition, too. Let's wrap that up in these blankets and then over that we will wind the gutta-perchas Reuben got us. Get me some rope. We will lash these piles so they don't shift. Oh...and hand me Reuben's leather case. I'm sure he does not wish whatever is in it to get wet."

Inga straightened up. "You know how to tie knots?"

Without stopping her sorting Rebecca said a bit wistfully, "Remember, my father was a sea captain."

Inga struggled to place the sack of pemmican on top of Rebecca's locked trunk. Rebecca looked up from the floor of the wagon. "Hold on, Inga. There are some things in that trunk I must get out." Inga gratefully let the heavy bag sag to the floor.

"Help me open this." Rebecca lifted up her skirt and petticoats and reached down into her boot, which came several inches above her ankles. She knelt down and placed the key in one of the two large locks in the dome shaped steamer trunk, highlighted with polished oak ribs and silver scroll. The lock clicked and the top of the trunk opened. Inga leaned forward, holding it, while Rebecca rummaged through the contents, one hand emerging with a tightly rolled parchment, three feet long.

"What is that, Milady Marx?"

"A map, Inga."

"A map? To what?"

Still on her knees, Rebecca looked back over her shoulder and said, "It's a map my father gave me when he died. It marks some land that he apparently bought. I need to see it, ascertain its value, and then sell it before I return to England." She handed the map to Inga who continued holding the trunk lid with her free hand.

Rebecca's fingers searched, then closed on something solid, wrapped in a thin wool blanket extending corner to corner in the bottom of the trunk. She withdrew it and stood, admiring the .52-caliber Sharps rifle, a gift from her father. She realized now he had obtained the weapon during his prolonged journey to America, just several years before his death.

Inga instinctively took a step away, a startled, almost fearful expression on her face, as Rebecca turned the rifle in her hands. "Milady Marx, whatever do you need that for? Do you know how to use it?"

"Indeed I do, Inga." Rebecca gave her a stern look. "And I will trust you to say nothing of the rifle or the map."

Far down the line they heard Mac shout.

"I shall not breathe a word, Milady Marx."

Rebecca, still watching Inga, saw her eyes flutter, then her complexion turn pale, her fair skin blanching to a pasty white. She grimaced, placed her hand on her stomach, and swayed.

She reached out to steady her blond companion. "What's wrong, Inga? It's only Mac."

"I suddenly don't feel very well."

"We all ate the same thing last night, that pemmican stew—which you did a fine job of preparing, I might add—hardtack biscuits and dried fruit. Reuben and Johannes looked fit, and my stomach is not upset."

Inga eased herself down on one of the trunks and bent over slightly. "I have felt this way on and off for the last week. It usually passes in five or ten minutes."

Rebecca bent down, one hand on Inga's arm. "What is it? How do you feel?" Rebecca could hear the concern in her own voice though she had tried to keep her tone steady.

"Just cramps, and queasy," said Inga her head slightly lower.

Rebecca straightened up looking at the bowed locks of Inga's golden hair. She felt a sudden jolt as a thought struck her. *Can't be.* She shook her head, "Well, you just rest up and I'll finish what we have to here. Johannes can help me move those provisions boxes and the molasses keg. They are heavy. You need to have your wits about you on this crossing. Can I get you some water?"

Without lifting her face, Inga wagged her head, "No, no, Milady, I should be fine in a few minutes."

Rebecca stopped and turned back to Inga who was still partially doubled over. "Remember, not a word about the map or the rifle to anyone, Inga."

The tall blonde looked up weakly, "Of course, but why, Milady Marx?"

Rebecca laughed. "The men shall know about the rifle soon enough. Tonight I believe..." Her tone grew more serious, "... as to the map, I have my reasons."

Inga looked up. Some of the color was returning to her face. "Not a word, Milday Marx."

Clambering over gear to the front of the wagon, Rebecca poked her head from the canvas, "Johannes," she waved, "Johannes."

Up at the head of the team Johannes was carefully checking each horse, harness, and attachment. He looked up.

"We just have a few things that we need help with. When you're done, would you mind?"

"I'm just about through here. I'm glad I checked. The collar was loose on that sorrel."

Rebecca ducked back inside. Inga was on her feet but not completely steady. Johannes climbed in the back. The smile he flashed at Rebecca faded when his eyes moved to Inga. "Are you all right, Inga? You don't look well."

Inga opened her mouth to reply but Rebecca swiftly interjected, "She's fine, Johannes, just a momentary thing. Would you grab one end of that trunk for me?" She bent down and grasped one handle, catching from the corner of her eye Inga's silent look of appreciation.

———

SITTING ON RED, MAC HAD A BAD FEELING HE COULDN'T SHAKE. Reuben, Charlie, and John pulled their horses up alongside him. "Everybody told?" he asked the men.

"Yes," was the unified reply.

He turned to Charlie and John, "You boys go find a spot to put in. I don't want the wagons working down at too much of an angle. They'll be fine unless somebody panics and pulls on the brake, or spooks their stock. The one thing you have to watch is a pilgrim turning their wagon uphill before the river. This hill has just enough lean to it that could tip the wagon over. It's your job to make sure that doesn't happen."

He gave his head a toss but still couldn't shake the bad feeling. "Zeb already gave me the 'all clear' from the opposite bank right before you rode up. I waved to him to come back over. He can handle the wagons after they are out. Once you men are across, make sure each wagon gets out of the way of the next, without crowding. Last thing we'll do is come back across and bring the extra stock over."

He pointed. "See those chunks of ice in the water?"

Reuben, Charlie, and John craned their necks to see. Here and there floated large pieces of ice, perhaps several feet squared.

"That answers part of the puzzle on why the flow is so high," Mac said. "Steer clear of 'em—they're heavy and if they hit an animal or a wagon and catch the current, they could be mean."

Mac thought for a moment before giving instructions, "As the wagons get out, Zeb can get them organized and over to that meadow. Make sure people have their wits about them. I imagine it will take us an hour to get everything sorted out after we get across. Reuben and I will stay here and anchor this side of the river. That'll give us two horses on either side if things don't go smooth."

THE LEAD WAGON HAD NOW ALMOST REACHED THEM. MAC HELD UP his hand and turned to Charlie and John. "Ok, Charlie, head on over there. Check on the footings, and make some adjustments so we stay out of big rocks or soft bottom. Tie off this bandana to a tree over there so the wagons have a downstream marker. John, we have two big block and tackles back there in your wagon. Bring them across with you and grab two hundred feet of rope. Fasten them to the biggest damn tree you can find and get them rigged up, just in case you need to help the wagons coming out. Make sure each wagon gets out of the way quick and follows Zeb over to that field beyond the trees. I don't want them thinking about it while they're in the water, but remind the menfolk to get out their rifles as each rig gets out."

He turned to Zeb, who had ridden up from the downstream side, the Sharps slung across his back, and the Enfield in his hands. Buck was dripping and Zeb's leather fringed pants were wet almost up to his saddle seat.

"Did a complete sweep a quarter mile either side of where we are now," he said. "No sign. The river is pretty deep and mighty cold. Had to dodge a nice block or two of ice when we crossed. It's not moving all too fast, but that current is powerful with that heap of water."

Mac turned to Reuben. "Is Johannes mounted?"

"No, we decided he better handle the lines. The women are not experienced enough just yet."

Mac nodded and spit a ball of tobacco juice. "Yep, good idea."

He looked around. "Well, gentlemen, daylight's wastin'. We can't spend all day jawboning." Charlie, Reuben, Zeb, and John looked at each other and grinned. John took off at a gallop back to the supply wagons to fetch the rope, block and tackle. Zeb and Charlie nosed their horses into the current and began to splash across.

Mac watched them keenly. The water grew deeper as they rode into the center of the flow. The current crested high on the upstream side of the horses about six inches below the bottom of their saddle seats. The horses were not struggling, but working hard. The upstream flow around their shoulders and rumps formed a downstream pocket that gurgled below them. He watched Zeb rein in Buck to let a chunk of ice flow by the front of the horse. Another slab brushed the rear of Charlie's horse. It wasn't big, less than two feet around, but the extra force of current when the ice clipped the horse's rump was enough to knock its rear legs downstream. Charlie dug in his heels and leaned forward to get his mount re-pointed toward the exit point.

The riders clambered up the far bank. Charlie tied off the red bandana on the downstream side where he'd exited the river. John was now in the water, block and tackle dragging in the current pocket downstream of the horse. He checked up his mount twice to allow small masses of ice to flow by. When he reached the opposite side he, John, and Zeb quickly and expertly set the big pulleys and rigged them with rope, most of the heavy hemp coiled and ready for use.

Mac nodded, satisfied. He turned to Reuben. "Well, I think we've set things up best we can, other than actually doing. I'll lead the first wagon across. You hold the second wagon here until the first one is out of the water. They can start when I am halfway back. Don't think we want two wagons in the water at the same time before we see how this goes."

Spinning Red around, Mac trotted her back to the lead wagon, about sixty feet behind. It was driven by an elderly couple. The man was medium build, in his early fifties. The bald top of his head was pale where it emerged from underneath his black hat with its high-rounded crown and stiff, curved brim. He had a white shirt on, as always, with the western bowtie that seemed to be his trademark. A large silver crucifix hung from his neck from a beaded chain. His wife was smaller, frail looking, with short grey hair. Her face was wrinkled, but her light blue eyes were kind.

Mac tipped his own hat at the man. "Preacher Walling, would you say a few words for the wagon train that we get to the other side?"

The preacher smiled. "Hope you mean the other side of the river."

"Huh? Oh, yeah," Mac chuckled, "that's what I meant."

The preacher bowed his head, the lines held in the center of his clasped hands. Beside him, his wife raised her hands to her lips in silent prayer. She tipped her head and closed her eyes.

"Oh, great and powerful Lord, watch over your children as they cross this river. Keep them safe, and protect their wagons and stock from mishap. We thank you, Lord, and trust in your divine guidance and the wisdom and truth of Jesus Christ our Savior. Thy will be done. Amen."

Mrs. Walling softly echoed, "Amen."

Mac, figuring he needed all the help he could muster, breathed out the word *Amen* louder than he intended. Then, urging Red forward, he said, "Preacher, follow me. The trick here is to keep the oxen steady. You see that red bandana out there?" The couple nodded.

"What you want is to come in just upstream of that. Know that when the current hits the wagons it will feel like it's floating. Matter of fact, these Conestogas are built to double as a boat. When the oxen are moving, hold them real steady on course. That will straighten things out. Nothing to fret about. Reuben's behind us and Charlie, John, and Zeb are over on the other side. You will be just fine. Ready?"

The preacher and his wife nodded again. Mac noticed Preacher Walling's hands trembled slightly and the lines made a soft tap on his knees.

"Let's go."

Mac moved Red into the current. She was a prankster, but unflappable when need be. He turned back in his saddle. The preacher's lead and rear oxen were already up to their lower shoulders with the Conestoga just coming off the bank. The current touched the wagon wheels—first the front axle, then the rear—and the back end of the Conestoga swung slightly downstream. The preacher snapped the lines with just the right amount of force, the oxen strained, the wagon straightened, and then they were moving steadily behind Mac.

So far so good. A few minutes later, without mishap, the team scrambled up the opposite bank, the preacher shouting, "Pull, you beasts, pull!" The wagon followed Zeb toward the meadow visible through the trunks of the tree-lined water's edge. Mac saw him speak to the preacher. The preacher reached behind him, got out his musket and laid it across his knees. *Good man, that Zeb.*

Mac turned to Charlie and John. "One down, forty to go." He reached into his breast pocket where he had moved his timepiece. "Took nine minutes. We will have to hurry it up, or we will be here all damn day."

He spurred Red, plunged back in the river and headed across to the opposite bank where Reuben let loose the next wagon, a prairie schooner, driven by the ailing Dr. Leonard and his wife, Thelma. Mac met up with them when they were a third of the way across. He turned Red around twenty feet upstream of the two oxen. The mare, her rump to the current, protested at the momentary weightlessness and drift. Mac steadied her and began to move toward the opposite crossing point, parallel with the two oxen that pulled the schooner. A block of river ice floated by Red's shoulders and struck the upstream oxen in the front shoulder. It knocked the big beast into his downstream teammate for a moment. There was some splashing as the animals regained their footing. Mac's eyes flashed to Dr. Leonard. His face was tense, but he looked steady. The wagon crossed without mishap.

The next wagon was Johannes'. Red met them when they were one quarter the way across. Rebecca smiled and nodded at him. She seemed completely unconcerned. Mac chuckled to himself. *I do believe*

Milady Marx is enjoying this. Inga looked either ill or scared, Mac couldn't tell. Johannes was focused, but his usual self. He grinned as they moved past Mac on the far bank. "Looks like this river's better suited to tall people than short people, don't you think, Mac?"

Mac's eyes did not miss a step of the horses dragging the wagon up the incline of the bank, but he laughed. "Better to be compact and close to the ground than some skinny bean pole. That way when you fall, it ain't so far."

Johannes laughed without taking his attention from the team. The crossing of their wagon was the smoothest yet.

Mac, more confident now, turned Red back into the current and raised his hand at Reuben. "Hold up," he shouted above the river noise. He crossed over and Red climbed up to Lahn, the two riders abreast, their horses facing opposite directions. "Everything seems pretty good. The pilgrims are doing fine and though you can always make a mistake out there, I think we can pick up the pace. We will have two wagons in the water from here on in. Get the second wagon going when the first wagon is two-thirds of the way across. You and I will take turns leading the first wagon out the first third, and Charlie and John will take turns leading them the last third. They will be on their own in the middle, but one of us will be close enough to get to them quick if we need to. Take Lahn over. Get a feel for the crossing and the current. See what the teams are up against and let Lahn get his feet wet. Tell Charlie and John the plan."

Reuben and the palomino made their way across. After a short time they were back. "That water is freezing!" exclaimed Reuben. "No wonder there's ice."

Mac nodded. "Enough jabber. Let's get going."

Jacob and Sarah's wagon, the thirtieth in the bunch, made it without mishap, the only notable event the dark, spiteful snarl Jacob flashed at Reuben and Mac, offset by the glowing smile Sarah projected toward Reuben, and her friendly wave to the wagon master.

The plan worked well. There were just five wagons and the stock left to go. The next wagon was the family from Kentucky. The man, his sallow-faced wife, Saley, and their teenage son nodded and smiled as they left Mac's stewardship and moved through the current toward John, who waited for them mid-river. Their three little ones had run to the back of the wagon and were waving at Mac, fascinated with his red beard since the day the family walked into the livery stable back in St. Louis.

Mac started to wave back, but froze when he heard shouting. John was gesturing upstream. Behind him he heard the same loud warning from Reuben. He turned in the saddle and looked up river. "Jesus, Mary, Mother of Christ," he said out loud. An ice chunk, much larger than the others they had contended with—perhaps six feet across— rose and fell in the current's swells, making its way steadily on a collision course with the Kentucky wagon. Mac spurred Red to try and catch up to the family. From the corner of his eye, he saw John doing the same from the opposite side, shouting and pointing.

Too late, the driver realized the danger and frantically applied the lines to the mules pulling the modified schooner. The beasts picked up the pace but their shorter, squatter bodies had more difficulty than the taller horses or heavier oxen.

For a moment, Mac thought the ice would miss the rig but it caught the upstream, rear corner with a sickening thud. The schooner's downstream end slipped under water, its upstream side rising. The rear face of the slab caught the current like a frozen sail. The wagon groaned and started to spin sideways. The sudden wrenching threw one of the little girls, screaming, from the rear of the wagon into the cold waters.

Mac hesitated, torn between the floundering wagon and the child. Reuben shouted, "I'll get her." Mac turned Red into the rushing current toward the wagon, watching as John's horse, downstream of the lead mules, struggled to gain his footing. Nearly abreast of the team, John used his mount to steady the mules.

The wife screamed, "My baby, my baby!" The wagon's spinning rear wheels caught on a rock and the entire wagon tipped upstream, the water rushing through the canvas over the rim of the wagon box.

Mac reached the mules, and now he and John were on either side of the two leads. Yelling and coaxing, their hands on the harnesses, the spooked animals splashed forward. The wagon righted itself and began to move again. The little girl's mother was wailing, sickened by the sight of her daughter downstream, her head bobbing to the surface for a moment, then disappearing, then surfacing again.

Reuben was almost to the girl. Lahn lunged through the current, great sprays of water erupting with each surge of the palomino. Reuben leaned far down from the saddle in a desperate reach, the Sharps in the other hand pressed against the horn, his shoulder almost in the river. He straightened and dragged the little girl up over his lap.

Mac, still holding the harness to steady the animals, watched Lahn struggle in the strong current of the upstream approach as the wagon reached the other side. The Kentucky mother jumped off before the wheels were on dry ground, sinking into the river up to her knees, her soaked skirt clinging to her legs. She stretched out her arms toward Reuben. He reached the hysterical woman and handed the little girl down to her. The child, shivering, cried out, "Mama, Mama, I'm cold." Her mother looked up at Reuben, and Mac could see the tears in her eyes.

"Thank you, Mr. Frank," she said. Reuben pulled at the brim of his hat, and smiled. "It worked out, fine, ma'am. You better go get both of you warmed up and in dry clothes."

Reuben was a good choice, Mac silently complimented himself. He dismounted and looked inside the drenched wagon. They had lost a good portion of their foodstuffs. Flour sacks had been knocked off their perches. Some of the pemmican, dried fruit, beans, and biscuits were soaked through. The man and his son joined Mac as he surveyed the damage.

"I reckon we lost about half the food," said the father. "Our musket balls got wet too but that don't matter. Sure glad we tied the powder up." He pointed to several small leather sacks dangling from short strings of rope latched to the top of the bowed hardwood ribs that supported the canvas top. "Guess we can always kill what we need to eat."

Mac turned to him, "That was a fluke accident, and you are lucky. Damn good thing we were strung out the way we were, or you would have lost more than flour," he nodded over to the man's wife, who was drying off their daughter, making clucking sounds.

"Sure enough. I owe you and John. I surely owe Reuben," the father said.

Mac slapped him on the back, staggering the smaller man. "You owe us nothing. We are all Americans, and we're neighbors. We'll see if folks can spare some vittles and grub for you and get you reorganized. Head on out there with the other wagons, get dried off and laid out. We will be here at least an hour before we're moving again. Use the time wisely."

Mac walked over to Reuben, and laid a hand on his shoulder. "That was quick thinking, son."

"There was no thinking, Mac. Just had to be done."

Mac smiled, nodded, and bit off a large chunk of tobacco. "Go back over and get the rest of rigs and stock ready to cross. You tell Harris and Margaret in that back Conestoga to keep their kids up front with them and seated. We might not be so lucky a second time."

As Reuben headed across, Mac peered through the trees where the rigs were grouping. His eyes rested on Rebecca and Inga's wagon. Johannes had remounted his horse and Rebecca had taken over command of the driver's seat. She held the lines loosely in her left hand, but her stature was erect and at-the-ready.

March 23, 1855

$\mathscr{P}$ETTICOATS AND LEAD

Z EB'S HORSE, BUCK, LED THE WAY, ZEB'S THIN BUCKSKIN-CLAD PRO-file towering in the saddle, as the four men trotted out from the circled wagons. The rough bark of the trees sucked the clamor of the camp and the sound of the river from the air until only the thud of hooves and woodland noises remained.

Johannes admired the surefooted and fluid gait of Zeb's paint. The horse wove between trees, moving without any obvious commands. He noticed that Zeb wasn't the only one holding his rifle loosely, but at the ready. Mac and Reuben also moved cautiously among the long timbered shadows. As the day waned, birds chirped angrily at the intrusion and sortied between limbs, their wings flashing the dull brown of wood sparrows, the black and orange of the occasional oriole and the dull grey of red-breasted robins. In the distance, the muted, raucous call of a flock of crows rose from the woods.

Zeb pulled up and waited until the others reached him. "I figure this will do, Mac." He waved a finger lazily out to the side from where his forearm rested on his saddle horn.

Johannes quickly assessed the shooting range the mountain man had chosen to test the marksmanship skills of the men on the wagon train. He was impressed with Zeb, with his silent mannerisms, keen, deep-set eyes that missed nothing, and the frontiersman's air of quiet confidence. He smiled. "I'd say this works well, Zeb."

Mac turned to him with a piercing look, "What makes this so perfect, John?"

"The name is Johannes," he corrected. Then he laughed aloud, enjoying a memory that sifted into the moment and the pending question. There was much these three men had yet to learn about him. "What makes this so perfect, you ask?" he looked at Mac. *Should I tell them just how it is I came to be here?* The memory came suddenly alive, and he laughed again, unable to control his amusement at this very private recollection.

Mac looked puzzled. A hen pheasant hiding just a few feet from them, unnerved by Johannes' loud guffaws, took sudden flight. The frantic whistling noise of her wings startled the horses, except for Buck who merely cocked one ear and shook his head. Lahn jumped, but settled down quickly, as did Johannes' bay horse. Red, however, bucked in a circle at the startling explosion. Mac cursed, finally getting the mare under control.

He turned to Johannes, "What's so damn funny?"

Johannes saw a mental image of the Chief Magistrate of the Royal Danish Court and the judge's stern look belied by the laughter in his eyes as he rustled his papers, and peered down from the bench at him just months prior. Six ax-wielding guards had stood at attention on either side of the great double doors to the courtroom. "What have you to say for yourself?"

"She is a very beautiful woman," Johannes had responded.

The judge looked up sharply, amusement apparent in the twitch of his mouth. "She is that. You do know that sleeping with another man's wife is a crime?"

"Yes, your Honor."

"You know also that indiscretion may be punished in a number of ways. Certain physical changes can be made to your person to ensure you never again make such an error."

Johannes' knees trembled. The Magistrate continued, "Or the Court could sentence you to ten years hard labor, or both."

"Yes, your Honor."

"There's one other measure available to the Court. I see here you have a distinguished record as an officer in the King's Heavy Cavalry."

Johannes had said nothing.

"Twice awarded the Cross of Merit, correct?"

"Yes, your Honor."

Johannes remembered, as if it was yesterday, how the Magistrate leaned back in his chair, the high-backed purple velour all but engulfing his portly frame. He had clasped his hands across his protruding belly and regarded Johannes studiously. "Because of your past service to Denmark and the heroism you have shown in the defense of the Kingdom, I will not order you incarcerated or castrated. You are, however, hereby exiled."

He had paused, letting the finality of sentence settle. One of the guards shifted his ax.

"You are never to set foot on Danish soil again, or you will be subject to arrest and both of the alternative punishments. Is that understood? As one other condition of the sentencing, you will talk to no one concerning this case or any related matter, ever, whether within or outside of the country. You will have no contact with any public official, any relative of an official, the royal family, or any minister of the Kingdom at any time in the future. Is that understood?"

"Yes, your Honor."

The judge turned to the Captain of the Guard. "Captain, take the prisoner to the first available sea transportation to a non-Danish destination. He is not to leave your sight. He is not speak to anyone. You are not to return until his ship disappears on the horizon. Is that clear?"

The Captain of the Guard clicked his heels. The Magistrate's features were stern, but Johannes had clearly seen a slight wink. "That is all, Captain Svenson."

Mac's mare, still skittish from the pheasant, raised her head and snorted. "Dammit, Red," he said, giving the reins an impatient jerk. Then he turned his attention back to Johannes.

"What in tarnation is so funny?"

Johannes looked at his three companions. Mac was clearly irritated. Reuben wore a wondering expression and was watching him closely. Zeb's fingers thoughtfully stroked the tip of his long handlebar mustache. His face was impassive, as always, but Johannes could detect curiosity in his eyes.

"The hell with it. I will give you the short run of a long story." His eyes shifted to Mac. "Mac, you don't have to beat around the bush. If you wish an answer, ask the question direct. You are fishing as to *why* I knew this was a good spot for a shooting range. You didn't need me to explain the logistics of Zeb's selection."

Mac's eyes widened.

Johannes swiveled his head to each of them in turn. "We are all in this together for months. You need to know who you ride with and our trust in each other must be automatic..." his attention again focused on Mac, "just like in battle."

Mac nodded. Johannes knew the wagon master was congratulating himself on his correct supposition regarding Johannes' background. "One of my lady friends back in Denmark, a beautiful young creature, went by the name of Bente," he turned to Reuben and grinned, "that answers your question on how I came up with the name for this bay."

Johannes cleared his throat and continued, "Unfortunately for Bente, she was married to a diminutive, egotistical, self-absorbed little runt who, over eleven years of marriage, had been unable to satisfy her. I ask you, gentlemen, a beautiful woman in such distress, what's an officer and a gentleman to do?"

Reuben shook his head, chuckling, Mac burst out laughing, and even Zeb smiled.

"It was Bente's unfortunate circumstance that I was gallantly trying to alleviate. My predicament, even less fortunate, was that her husband was the First Minister to the King and I was merely a captain in the King's Heavy Cavalry. To make matters worse, we were caught in his own bed, and I was somewhat less respectful than the midget rooster thought proper. He had me hauled in front of the Chief Magistrate of the King's Court. In an ironic and lucky twist of events, the judge and I had shared some time in one of the high-end brothels on the outskirts of Copenhagen. To my benefit, he was married. He used my service and decorations as the pretext, but in reality he feared the wrath of his wife if the case became public as it certainly would've in the palace. I was exiled, a far better fate than the incarceration or castration called for by the law. One of the conditions of his leniency, however, was that I never tell the story to anyone, ever. I will therefore request of the three of you that this tale never be repeated."

Reuben, Mac, and Zeb looked each other and then back at Johannes. They nodded their agreements silently, but all had wide grins on their faces.

Johannes swung one long leg over the bay's ears and in a smooth motion slid off the saddle sideways, landing lightly on his feet. "This log is perfect as a shooting rest," he pointed. "It is my suggestion that we have each man fire two rounds from the rest and two rounds standing. That will tell us whether he knows how to shoot, and his standing shots will indicate how he'll be under pressure. Shooting at paper and firing at blood are two different things."

Johannes fell silent and looked out across the field. "There are three groups of trees out there across the field. I would judge the first cluster to be about one hundred meters, the second double that, and the third approximately three-hundred-fifty meters. I suggest we tack the cloth pieces Zeb brought out as targets, three in each clump of trees. Let each man pick the targets he wishes to shoot at. This will tell us his confidence in his own ability and with luck give us at least a few marksmen who can shoot at distance.

"For those men who will rely on a pistol as their primary weapon, we shall place a target at approximately fifty paces, over on that thick oak behind us," he gestured. "Each man will take three shots with their pistol. We should give them the latitude of shooting whichever style they wish—military, dueling, or American, which I understand is also referred to as 'from the hip'."

The other three men nodded their acceptance of the plan. Johannes continued, "I believe at the end of the session we will be able to determine who can shoot. Those men can go back to their wagons. Those who can't will break into four groups. Each of us will work with that group and help those men identify their bad habits so that they can at least begin to think about them. However, I would suggest we repeat this exercise several times over the next week with the men who need improvement. I have turned men who couldn't hit the broadside of a barn into semi-proficient marksmen rather quickly, but it takes time for them to get confident in their own new-found abilities. One will never make a shot that he does not believe he has the skill for." Johannes smiled, "Rather like life."

Mac looked at him with obvious respect. Zeb was rolling a smoke and nodded. Reuben was staring at him with his eyes wide and his mouth slightly open.

"What is it, Reuben?"

Reuben shook his head, "You named your horse after the First Minister of Denmark's wife?"

Johannes chortled, "I was rather fond of her." Everyone guffawed.

Mac turned in the saddle, "Zeb, if you don't mind, go back to the wagons and have the men follow you back here. We will tack up these targets."

"What if someone does not want to come?" Zeb asked laconically. Mac looked at him. Without hesitation, his voice grim, he answered, "If that son of a bitch O'Shanahan gives you any guff, you have my permission to do whatever it takes, but I want every man except the ten guarding the wagons out here. No ifs, no buts."

Zeb's smile indicated that he hoped Jacob would refuse to attend. He cupped a match to his cigarette and without a word, and without any apparent command, Buck trotted off in the direction of the wagons.

Johannes had just finished fastening the last target cloth to the widest trunks he could find in the furthest stand of trees when he heard the voices of the approaching group. He mounted Bente and trotted back across the field. The men dismounted. Those whose wagons only had oxen had doubled with those who had horses. Two men rode mules. He glanced toward the horizon to the west. They had little more than an hour of daylight left.

He turned to Mac. "May I?" Mac nodded.

"Gentleman, if you'd be so kind as to form a line. Shoulders one foot from the man on either side of you, facing me please, and hold your rifles by the barrel, stock down, buttplate on the ground."

There was some pushing, jostling, and confusion as the men began to line up.

The sound of horse hooves at a full gallop from the direction of the wagon train turned eyes and heads. The figure of a woman, sidesaddle, dark hair streaming from under her hat and what appeared to be a rifle draped over her hip, was riding toward them. With a start, he recognized the horse as being one from their own wagon, and the rider none other than Rebecca.

He glanced quickly at Reuben who radiated astonishment. Mac looked thoroughly surprised, and Zeb's fingers were working his mustache more industriously than normal, his eyebrows arched.

Rebecca galloped up, reined in to an abrupt stop, and in one motion smoothly and expertly dismounted, her Sharps rifle in one hand. There was a murmur up and down the line of men. Some men stepped forward, some back, to get a better view.

Johannes collected his thoughts. "Men, get back in line, please."

He looked on incredulously as Rebecca fell in on one side of the line and quickly mimicked the positioning of the other's rifles. There was a haughty amusement in her eyes as she returned Johannes' stare.

"Miss Marx, may I ask what you are doing here and where you got that rifle?"

Rebecca straightened her shoulders and smiled triumphantly at Johannes as she displayed the weapon. "This is a Model 1852 Berdon Sharps rifle, .52-caliber, slant-breech, levered, pellet primer feed, with Enfield adjustable ladder sights. When I was thirteen years old, my father brought it back to me from a trading mission to this very country. He taught me to shoot and ride and several other skills when I journeyed with him on his trading ships and during those infrequent times when he was home in England and not on the high seas."

The men exchanged looks up and down the line. "Thank you for that information, Miss Marx..."

Rebecca cut Johannes off with an icy voice, "... Milady Marx."

"Yes, of course. How could I forget? Well, Milady Marx, this was to be a gathering of the men of the wagon train. I'm quite sure you don't qualify in that regard."

Color crept into Rebecca's cheeks and she lifted her nose. "There might come a time in the next few months when an additional rifle and someone who knows how to use it could be important. I have every bit as much right as any man here to have my skills assessed if there's need for them in the future."

Johannes' eyes caught Mac's. He was struggling to suppress a smile. Mac nodded his assent. "Very well then, Milady Marx, we are honored to have you join us."

A number of the men snickered. Johannes' brow creased and his back stiffened. "There will be none of that. Whatever your thoughts, you will show respect to one another at all times. Your life might be saved by the man...," Johannes swiveled his head to Rebecca, "or woman, standing next to you. Please hold your weapons out directly in front of you, left hand on the forestock, and right hand below the trigger guard. No fingers on the triggers, please."

One of the men, younger, surly looking and, Johannes remembered from the campfire, from some city in New Jersey, blurted out, "I paid good money to come on this wagon train. I didn't sign-up for no military bands." Johannes walked over to him and stood with narrowed eyelids. The man held his glare for a few seconds then darted angry glares at the men on either side of him before looking down and raising his rifle as instructed.

Johannes walked down the line of men, periodically stopping to examine the unimaginable assortment of firearms. Several of the men had Sharps, others Enfields, one had a new Model 1855 .58-caliber minnie ball Springfield musket, and half had old muzzleloaders. The father and son from Kentucky each had very long, narrow-bore rifles with thick octagon barrels, and iron sighting systems Johannes had not seen before. They resembled the 1841 Mississippi Muskets, but small metal balls rested on top of the barrel at the muzzle, similar to the bead on a shotgun. The rear sight was an elevated circle of iron.

The buttstocks had deep curves. The firing mechanism required flintlock percussion caps, still in use, but rare.

"May I?" The father handed his rifle to Johannes who hefted it several times. Despite the extremely long barrel, it was perfectly balanced. He peered through the rear sight. As he suspected, the round rear aperture aligned perfectly with the ball at the front of the barrel. He handed it back to the man, who smiled.

"Has your daughter recovered from her time in the river today?"

"She has, thank you. I am Elijah. This is my son, Abraham. These here are squirrel guns. Had 'em made special. Shoots a .32-caliber ball. Not too awful heavy, but we can take squirrel out of a tree at three hundred yards," he paused, "and I can guarantee these little balls will drop anyone dead in their tracks if the hole is between their eyes."

Johannes turned to the boy. "How old are you?"

"Thirteen, Sir."

Johannes blinked. "Are you okay with your boy being here?"

"He's here, ain't he? He can handle himself. He's put food on the table since he was five, and he's kilt two big bear with that gun. I reckon he can handle whatever comes at us."

Johannes nodded, "Very well."

He stood back from the group. "Gentleman, and Milady Marx, each of you will advance to the log, fire two rounds using the log as a rest, reloading as quickly as you can. Then two rounds standing. Before your shots you will declare your target..." Johannes pointed out across the field toward the first set of targets, "we estimate the range to be one hundred meters, two hundred meters, and," he pointed off in the distance, "approximately three hundred and fifty meters. Those who can shoot with accuracy will go back to the wagon train and relieve the ten men standing guard. Certain others of you will stay here and work with me, Reuben, Mac and Zeb. Is this procedure understood?" Heads nodded up and down the line.

A memory sifted, fleeting but powerful, through Johannes' mind. Déjà vu. *A tree-ringed sunny European field, battle flags flying, the crump of cannons, his troops lined up smartly before mounting to form the columns for advance.* He blinked at the sudden thrill somewhere deep within him.

"All right then, who wishes to go first?"

No one moved other than to bend slightly forward to peer down the line for who would be a fool enough to volunteer. Rebecca stepped forward, "I shall go first."

Despite himself, Johannes was impressed." As you wish, Milady Marx."

Rebecca marched up to the log, and knelt down smoothly on one knee, layers of her petticoats showing under the pleats of her traveling dress. She laid out three rounds on top of the log. She planted her elbows solidly on top of the log, tucked the gun into her shoulder with a motion that comes with practice, and lowered her cheek firmly against the stock. "I shall shoot at the target on the left, at two hundred meters."

She snuggled her cheek back to the stock, took a deep breath and began to exhale. Fire belched from the muzzle of the Sharps, her shoulder jerked, and she brought the barrel back down and steady in follow-through. She lifted the long gun, levered in the next primer, expertly removed the cartridge, deftly shoved in another, closed the breech, and resumed her firing position. She stood and repeated the procedure on her third and fourth shots.

Mac had his brass timepiece out. He looked at Johannes', his eyes wide. "Thirty-six seconds." He reached into his jacket and walked over to Reuben. "See how she did."

Reuben moved to a tree, and using it as rest, peered through the telescope. He lowered the glass, blinked as if disbelieving, and raised the telescope again. He turned to the group, "I'll be damned. All four holes are within six inches of dead center. Three are grouped within two inches, slightly right. One is four inches low."

There was another murmur in the ranks. Several men looked panicked. Johannes knew they were thinking about what it would feel like to be outshot by a woman. Rebecca marched back to Johannes, threw him a quick glance, and flashed an indecipherable smile at Reuben, "I assume I shall not be required to take further lessons?"

Johannes gave her a silent look of respect. *Rebecca, you are quite something. Full of surprises.* "Milady, further instruction will apparently not be necessary."

"Then I shall return to the wagons. I would like to tidy up prior to supper and assist Inga with preparations."

Johannes nodded slowly, "If you would be so kind as to wait for the next man to get done, he will accompany you back to the wagons. Despite your proficiency with that weapon, I think it wise that you not ride unescorted."

"Very well." Rebecca turned, strode over to her horse, expertly mounted, draped the Sharps over her hip and waited.

Six of the men proved proficient marksmen. The father and son team from Kentucky both grouped their shots in one inch bull's-eye clusters at the furthest targets. Most of the others were passable. Five of the men could not group their shots at all, and missed the target with at least one round. One man, a previous postal inspector from Washington DC, did not hit the target. Reuben pronounced the three men, including a glowering Jacob, who had only pistols, "acceptable."

Johannes split the five into two groups and directed them to Mac and Reuben. The unfortunate former government worker was assigned to Zeb. The last group of ten men arrived and the procedure was repeated, more quickly this time because the sun was beginning to dip beneath the horizon. Johannes was pleased and surprised. Only one of this second set of riflemen did not know how to shoot.

Dusk was creeping through the trees when they finished. Each of the instructors had made tentative dates with the men, whom they would continue to instruct over the coming week. Reuben, Mac, Johannes, and Zeb mounted up and began their return to the circled wagons.

"Better than I expected," commented Mac.

Johannes' shook his head. "Far, far better than anything you'd see in Europe other than military. I'm beginning to see why the British couldn't keep these colonies."

Mac looked at him. "It's far more than the aim, Johannes. It's the spirit behind the trigger."

"Rebecca was quite something. I think she could outshoot ninety percent of the troops in my company. What do you think, Reuben?" Johannes' tone was teasing.

Reuben looked at him and grinned. "I say there's more to Milady Marx than meets the eye, though there's plenty of that, too."

Mac and Johannes laughed as the orange winking lights from the cooking fires became visible through the trees. Mac slapped his thigh. "Oh, yeah, Harris told me his wife Margaret is a respectable shot and can handle a gun, so there are at least two women on the train we can count on."

April 9, 1855

TENDER TRAIL

ZEB LOVED TO HUNT. IT WAS SECOND NATURE, SUBSISTENCE, AND something more. A link to the past. His mother, a schoolteacher before her murder, had taught him rudimentary reading, writing, and arithmetic. She also taught him to play chess. *Kinda like a game of chess between me and the critters, 'cept the land is the chessboard,* was the way he liked to think about it.

Mac had ridden out to Zeb's trailing position a half-mile southeast of the last wagon in the line of rigs that morning. "See if you can kill a deer or two. I plan on stopping tomorrow afternoon for wagon and wheel maintenance. There's several wagons with metal tire jackets working loose. Should be plenty of time to smoke the meat, and I have a bit of jerky seasoning in the supply wagons. Going to get more and more unfriendly as we get toward the border of the Kansas Territories. Chances to hunt, 'cept in a party, is gonna be scarce. You get the game down, and I'll send the Kentuckians back to help you. Just bone 'em out where they drop. They can pack the meat back in panniers."

Zeb had grinned. This was the type of chore he liked. "Sure enough, Mac. You partial to buck or doe?"

The wagon master had laughed. "Tender doe meat is tasty, but don't matter much since we'll be jerking the meat. Take the biggest, fattest, first thing that comes along."

That had been hours ago. Usually Zeb could pick up a trail right off and not lose it regardless of the tracking conditions. If the quarry was headed into the wind, then more often than not it would be in the pan by nightfall. But this humid spring morning with its smells of midwest woodlands stirred the memories. He walked through the timber along the Missouri River bottom, looking for sign in the heavy leaf cover, blown and disturbed by the winds of the previous night, his eyes fixed on his surroundings, his mind traveling backward in time.

He had fled Missouri almost twenty years ago, seeking solitude to dampen and escape the vicious cruelty that had befallen his family. At Fort Laramie he made the decision to drift north, driven by bits and pieces of information from other solo men and trappers he met on his journey. They had told him about the Holes, the places where mountain men congregated during the winter in valleys more sheltered from violent storms and wind. The Holes usually had open water, and far less snow than in the mountains that surrounded the secluded and secretive gathering places.

He had heard talk of the Grand Tetons, the *Great Teats*, as the French and Indians called the massive, towering walls of rocks that both red and white men held in mutual awe, and the Hole below them, Jackson's Hole.

Along the way, on the eastern edge of the Big Horn Mountains, he had run into a small band of Oglala Sioux. The war chief was named Flying Arrow, and the medicine man of the tribe was called Tracks on Rock.

He had stumbled into their camp, half-starved, a squirrel gun his only weapon, and sadly lacking in the survival skills critical to living in any season, much less the oncoming winter in the high plains and mountains of the West. He was sure they thought him a fool, but they took him in.

He didn't have much, an old farm horse, and an equally aging, no longer sure-footed mule, which reluctantly packed his meager belongings. He had stowed the old, ornately framed, six-by-three-inch, oval mirror his mother had loved. It had somehow miraculously escaped the fire. Little else had. Zeb had taken great pains to ensure it would not break. He had grown weary of the anxiety and checking to see if it had survived another day of travel each time he camped. He was certain it would not survive the journey that was growing ever more rugged.

Tracks on Rock's wife, Tree Dove, was more handsome than she was pretty, but she was certainly friendly. Her face carried scars of a battle with the smallpox. She had borne Tracks on Rock two children, a boy and a girl.

Zeb lifted his nose, sniffing at the damp air as he looked for sign. After a few more paces, he found what he was looking for— split-hoof, heart-shaped tracks, all does, maybe three or four, meandering along the river bottom, pawing at the oak leaves, searching for shoots and fallen acorns. He knelt, squinted at the story in the leaves, and shook his head, annoyed at his atypical difficulty following the trail. *Too distracted with memories*, he thought.

Leaning against the trunk of a massive oak, the Enfield musket across his lap, he shifted so his back scabbard didn't dig into his ribcage and began to roll a smoke. *I'll let those deer bed down. I'll give them a spell, and let my brain sort out.*

Zeb inhaled on the cigarette, rested his head on the tree and thought about the two Indian toddlers. The youngsters had been fascinated with him, especially the little girl. They liked to run their fingers on his wrist and the back of his hand, fascinated by the color of his skin, chattering to each other in Sioux made more indistinguishable—Zeb was certain—by gibberish occasioned by their age, which he estimated at slightly over two for the girl and three for the boy.

He squinted up at the hazy blue of the sky above the barren branches of the Missouri woodlands and tried to remember the daughter's name. *Something Moon.*

He had quickly learned that the Sioux referred to themselves as "The People." Their society was matriarchal. The men pronounced the big decisions, but no plan for significant action was ever arrived at without the counsel, scolding, and stern approval of their women. He had given his mother's mirror to Tree Dove as a thank you for the help of the tribe. The gift ingratiated him to that family, and he soon found himself on hunting excursions with Tracks on Rock and other young men of the tribe. It was from them he learned many of the skills that had kept him alive over the years. Tracks on Rock joked that he had turned into the second best tracker under the sky except for Tracks on Rock, of course. Zeb took another draw of the cigarette and smiled at the recollection.

He never became proficient in the Sioux language, but he learned enough to be able to generally follow the conversation, and—with sign language—get his major points across in a discussion.

There was a woman in the tribe, Horse's Mane, who often cast shy glances his way. According to the Sioux, she was one-quarter white. She had lost her husband, evidently a fearless brave whom the Sioux spoke of with great respect. He had died from a Pawnee arrow during an ill-fated raid by The People on their adversary's camp to steal horses.

One night, Tree Dove had come to the lodge Zeb shared with two other young unmarried braves and invited him to share supper with the family. To Zeb's surprise, Horse's Mane was there, and he noticed Tree Dove took special care to seat them together around the lodge fire as they ate. It worked.

After that evening, when Zeb was not out hunting, or getting instruction from Tracks on Rock, he and Horse's Mane took long walks. Between the bit of Sioux he knew and the smattering of English she spoke, they managed to talk, though neither of them, Zeb was sure, could understand much of what the other was saying. It didn't matter. The current of communication between them was far more than verbal and the physical attraction more than a rutting urge. She was four or five years older than him, Zeb reckoned—maybe twenty-three or twenty-four. Her skin was lighter than the deep brown of most of the rest of the tribe, and her hips a bit more rounded than the other young Sioux woman. *Must be that white blood,* Zeb had told himself. She had shown him how to stitch skins with sinew and an awl, but the lessons had continued long after he had become proficient. By the second pair of leggings, she no longer looked for an excuse to be with him.

It was a late afternoon in that seasonal hiatus between coming winter and departing fall. Virtually all the trees along the Powder River's south fork, where the tribe made its winter camp, were barren, except for a few stubborn leaves that clung to branches protected from the wind. They had been for a walk and stopped outside her lodge. Zeb was about to say goodbye, but Horse's Mane took a step toward him, her leather dress clinging to her thighs and rounded breasts, which were just inches from his lower ribs, her large brown, almost hazel, eyes fixed, questioning, up into his, "You do not need to return to your lodge."

Zeb didn't know quite what to make of that statement or what she was getting at, but he was uncomfortably aware her proximity heightened the energy between them. And that thought quickly manifested in an increased tightness in the crotch of his fringed leather pants. He must have shown his inexperienced embarrassment because Horse's Mane looked down at his middle and then back up into his eyes with a warm, teasing smile, her pale-tan face darkening slightly. She took his hand and nodded her head at her lodge. Like a newborn colt on his first trail following a bell mare, he followed her through the lodge flap noticing a single, definite nod of approval from Tree Dove, who watched the scene from the next lodge down toward the river.

Inside the tipi, he stood dumbly, not sure what to do, whether he should do anything, or whether he should leave. Outside, the river rushed by.

Zeb blinked and stared at the barren oak trees, wondering why the deer tracks triggered memories he'd rather push away. Hell, he embarrassed himself with these thoughts even now. Maybe it was the women on the wagon train, or the sparks flying between Johannes and Inga. And it was damn hard to miss the sexual tension running like lightning between Reuben and Rebecca. Odd thing, too, how loathing played into it all. It riled him to know Sarah had been manhandled by that deranged wolf, Jacob.

The smoke from the cigarette he had rolled a few minutes ago drifted upward, spiraling into the branches and disappearing. He ought to be paying more mind to staying downwind of the does, but the memories were a luxury, and an indulgence he didn't often allow. And remembering how Horse's Mane had smiled shyly at him that day was dang sure a pleasant one.

She had squatted down delicately, rekindling the embers of the lodge fire into small flames that cast moving shadows on the sloped walls of the tipi. Her leather dress drew up tightly against her buttocks, accentuating the flare of her hips and the long tapered shape of her thighs. His leather breeches became increasingly uncomfortable. He shoved his hands in his pockets trying to cover the growing bulge.

Horse's Mane stood, moved to him and placed one hand softly across his crotch, cupping him. With her other hand she untied his shirt's buckskin draws, leaned forward and tenderly kissed his chest. Zeb had heard men talk of moments like this, but he didn't feel prepared. Horse's Mane, sensing his inexperience, motioned to him to raise his arms, and she began to work the shirt up his middle, speaking to him in a low, alluring singsong. She gestured for him to finish the process, signing that he was too tall for her to reach over his head. His shirt stripped off, she stood back and slowly, seductively, one rawhide lace at a time, untied the top of her dress. Zeb's pulse was racing so loudly he could no longer hear the river. The single, throbbing, sensation rising from his groin was almost painful.

She crossed her arms in front of her and with each hand smoothed the dress from one shoulder, then the other, taking care that it fell slowly down across the fullness of her breasts, then the smooth flesh of her belly, then deep curve of her hips, until it lay in a crumpled heap surrounding her feet.

She had taken his hand and led him over to the buffalo robe bedding. Then, sensuously, delicately, her soft, full lips followed the descending line of the top of his pants, barely brushing his skin as she eased them over his hips and down to his knees. Her tongue flicked out slow, warm and gentle, lathing the tip of his hardness, its rigidity now almost purple. She pulled him down to the robes, still holding his hand and leaned back against the skins, her light tan flesh accented by the coarse grey-brown hair of the tatanka. She lowered his hand to the dark temple of hair where her legs joined. Zeb's fingers instinctively stoked the velvet wetness. She bit her lower lip and whimpered, pulling him to her, over her, on her. She bent her legs, pulling her knees back toward her sides, wrapping one arm around his back. With the other, she guided him into her.

"Damn!" Zeb dropped the cigarette butt, which had burned down enough to singe his fingertips. He spat on the small blisters that had already formed and reached down to field-strip the butt before it fired the dry leaves.

They had spent the winter together. In the spring, the tribe broke camp and headed east to follow the buffalo. Zeb moved on toward the Tetons. He never saw her again. *Hell, I ain't seen none of them again. Wonder how old Flying Arrow is now, and them kids of Tree Dove must be full grown.* He shook his head.

There had been a few other women through the years. A Ute half-breed, not much to look at, but the best cook he had ever met, died of fever just a few months after he had taken her into his cabin. Zeb laughed to himself as he recalled the wild, pretty, young blond daughter of the Army officer. His troop—on some "exploratory expedition" as the captain had explained—camped for four days down on the Uncompahgre River, a mile below his lowest cabin on the flanks of Las Montanas Rojas. He had taken an instant attraction to her, and she to him. Each night Zeb had stolen her silently out of the soldier's camp. *Easier than stealing ponies.* She had about the same level of experience as he. Their short-lived relationship had been fun, hot passion, laughs, tender giggles, and bathing nude in the cold waters of the river under the moon. That the squad of soldiers and her father slept just a quarter of a mile away, heightened the excitement and fire of their frequent unions.

Zeb started to roll another cigarette. There had been one other. *Might be the only one that got to me,* Zeb sighed, his exhale caught in the breeze of the river bottom and whisked away. He had taken the mules to Bent's Fort on the Arkansas for supplies. Melinda's family, along with other—in Zeb's opinion—overly pious pioneers, was headed west to the Salt Lake. She was beautiful, slender, with auburn hair and a coquettish, vibrant manner. Every move, every interaction, every sentence from her full lips was a *come hither* provocation.

The daughter of a preacher, Melinda had a rebellious streak against her father and his mores. Zeb had been speechless when they met at the bustling mercantile. He had bought a bath, visited a barber for the first time in a decade, and extended what he had planned to be a one-day supply trip to a week then two. They spent the afternoons together, walking, talking, holding hands. She stole his heart. He had picked wildflowers for her the day before her family, with the rest of the wagons, was to depart. Blushing furiously, with stammered words and the carefully picked wildflowers, he had proposed.

She had laughed, unkindly, batted her eyelashes and nimbly escaped his first attempt to kiss her. "Oh, Zeb, how nice. But we barely know each other. What would my father think? If you ever get to Salt Lake though, look me up. I am sure our farm will be the biggest in the valley. It should be no problem to find me."

With an odd laugh, almost triumphant in its tone, she had turned and walked back toward her wagon, leaving Zeb standing motionless, the flowers drooping in one hand, the ring he had purchased with the money he had intended from the sale of pelts to use for balls and powder in the other. She had stopped, turned, and waved. "If, of course, I am not already taken by then."

Zeb rose and began to cautiously follow the tracks of the camp meat, but his thoughts continued. Now, there was Sarah. An entirely different attraction than he'd known with any of the others. She made him feel like a man, a father, a protector, *and a spectator.*

Zeb cursed as half of the tobacco fell out of the partially rolled cigarette paper. He threw the rolling paper away, disgusted. She was with that Irishman, though Zeb noticed there had not been a single night the stocky bully was not camped uncomfortably underneath the wagon, the rig shut tight, and Sarah on the inside. *She is obviously attracted to Reuben. That's clear. And, you have to be at least twice her age, you old fool.* Try as he might, though, he couldn't get the image of the sun-streaked highlights in her red hair or the inviting bridge of freckles across her nose, from his mind. Each track he followed not only brought him closer to the does, but also to an unsettled feeling in the pit of his gut.

SITTING BY THE SMALL FIRE HE HAD BUILT, ZEB HELD AN AWL AND two strips of leather in his hands. The hobbled mules grazed contentedly about twenty feet away, and Buck rubbed his neck up and down against the smooth bark of a beech tree, scratching himself, the white portions of his hide shining dully in the firelight, the mottled darker brown pinto markings disappearing into the night behind him. The two big does had long since been skinned, butchered and cut into strips. The Kentuckians had packed the venison back to the wagon train.

Zeb looked up. He could see the fires of the train twinkling in the distance, forming a lonely, traveling circle of civilization in a black void of wilderness. He focused again on his project, and carefully worked the awl through the leather, drawing the rawhide thread tight. A few more stitches, and he held the elk hide leg moccasin up to the firelight, turning it in all directions, regarding his work critically.

He picked up the other one, held them side by side and then held them out toward Buck, "What do you think, horse? Not too bad, eh?" Buck stopped rubbing his neck on the tree, regarded Zeb and the moccasins, blew a soft snort from his nose, and went back to scratching.

"I'll take that as a yes. I think I'll finish these up tomorrow night. They ought to work just fine."

He wrapped the moccasins carefully in the extra blanket he was using as his pillow and propped the folded wool against his saddle. Zeb looked up at the stars and smiled. Then he wrapped himself in the other two wool blankets that constituted his bedroll and settled down for the night, the flames of the small fire leaping up as they caught the dry core of the small cedar log he had laid on top of the embers.

April 10, 1855

COMMISERATION

INGA BENT TO TIGHTEN THE LACES ON HER BOOTS THEN STRAIGHT-
ened and stretched, surveying the camp. To the east, the sky glowed,
the indigo blue of departing night absorbed by a spreading pink that
sifted upward, gilding the edges of several long wisps of clouds with
the crimson fire of dawn. Never before had she seen such a sunrise.

The countryside had been evolving over the past weeks. The familiar
stands of oak, beech, and elm were gradually yielding to wide open
spaces framed by the very occasional grey faces of intermittent, narrow
cottonwood stands with bushy eyebrows of alder and red willow concentrated around springs or along small creeks. Even Rebecca's attire
had evolved. At the beginning of the journey, her dress was better suited
to the courts, palaces, and gala events of Europe. Gradually, her clothing had become more sensible. Inga noticed, but said nothing.

She had become accustomed to the morning noises of the wagon
train, too—the sounds of creaking leather and jingling metal as men
led oxen, horses and mules to harness. The constant hum of voices
was punctuated by an occasional shout or curse when hitching up
teams was going less than smoothly—usually because of an unwilling
animal or an inexperienced pioneer.

Several small fires flickered, welcoming the day as mothers with
small children heated up a quick breakfast for the young ones and

coffee for their men. Inga saw Harris down on his hands and knees, his ponderous belly almost touching the ground, looking underneath the wagon bed at the rear left wheel. Elijah and Abraham were busy cleaning their Kentucky long rifles, alternately running swabs down the barrels, then holding the guns, muzzles to their eyes, so the bores would catch the brightening sky, and they could check their handiwork. The night before they had helped Zeb, the mountain man, bring the meat from two deer to camp, in part to repay the other wagons that had helped replenish their supplies after their close call in the Gasconade River. Fortunately, the next crossing of the larger Osage River had gone without mishap.

Inga smiled to herself thinking about the chatter and camaraderie of the previous evening. The entire camp had pitched in to prepare and preserve the meat. Some venison was cooked, preserved in salt and wrapped. Other portions were smoked and flavored as jerky. The camp worked together like a synchronized team. Several men started fires. Five women, including her and Milady Marx, had hauled large cast-iron boiling pots to the crackling flames. Zeb and the Kentucky family expertly carved thin strips of meat, trimmed from the larger chunks they had cut from the carcasses.

Some women supervised the pots as the venison boiled. Others tended the jerky fires, or took the lean cooked strips of venison and rolled them in salt, working the mineral into the tissue, and then dropped the slabs in a briny bath to chill. Later in the evening, when everyone agreed the meat had properly cooled, Mac produced a large role of paraffin paper from the supply wagon, proudly proclaiming he was "the completely prepared wagon master."

Virtually everyone participated in wrapping the salted meat—a quick double roll, fold the ends so they overlapped, and tie with a single, thin strand of rawhide. Mac made some comment about how easy a deer kill would seem after the camp contended with their first buffalo.

Inga recalled that other than the children, engrossed in taking turns at being the hunted or the hunter, the only person who had remained aloof was that man Jacob. He skulked in the shadows, moving and leaning against alternative wagons as he occasionally changed his vantage point of the activity around the fires. His leering, unsettling, almost intrusive fixation on her and Rebecca, mostly Rebecca, made Inga uncomfortable. He would alter his stares at them with predatory glares at the redheaded Sarah, casting venomous looks at the men—especially Mac, Reuben, and Johannes. At one point he seemed to be sharpening something, a small knife perhaps.

That unsettling memory yielded to an inner smile as more intimate and tender memories from last evening surfaced. Johannes truly was an explorer—his eyes and lips exploring every inch of her body, gently licking her, preparing her for consummation. She had never had that experience, and she felt a moist rush of warmth as she recalled the delicious spasms his tongue occasioned.

Inga pressed her thighs together involuntarily, casting embarrassed eyes side to side as she felt a flush rise from her throat to her cheeks. The temporary encampment was busy, preoccupied with getting back on the trail and heading evermore west.

She leaned back against the wagon and dreamily recalled Johannes' antics. He had proved most resourceful over the past weeks, devising private places and times where they could make love. She remembered her inner spark of anticipation when she noticed him walk over last night and then lean down to Reuben, who was wrapping meat. He whispered something in his friend's ear. Reuben had paused his wrapping and flashed Johannes a look of humorous exasperation. Then, he nodded. The two men spoke a few seconds longer. Johannes had laughed and ambled off to the side, apparently waiting.

Reuben tightened the rawhide tie on the package he was working on and smoothly moved over next to Rebecca. He engaged her in conversation quite obviously, taking the whole scene into account, with the purposeful motive of diverting her attention. Then Inga had suddenly felt Johannes' hand on her arm. He nodded his head back toward their wagon. With skillful nonchalance, he led their drift out of the direct light of the fire into the descending darkness. Holding her hand, he quickened their pace, almost pulling her along. He lifted her into the rear of the wagon and then vaulted in himself not bothering with the ladder. He quickly closed the tailgate and lashed the canvas flap. She had gone to light the oil lamp.

"No, my love, no lights. We might amuse the camp with some quite interesting shadows," he laughed softly.

He had pulled her to him, not roughly, but firmly. His lips found hers, a needy, passion-filled kiss that literally sucked the breath from her. He gently lowered her backward on her makeshift bed atop the quickly diminishing sacks of grain, lifted her dress, petticoats, and chemise up one inner thigh, then the other, alternatively using his hand and tongue until his mouth had been sweetly fastened to her, his tongue delicately lathing her turgid flesh.

Feeling terribly languid and indulgent at the vivid memory, Inga looked up at the clouds, just now fading from dawn colors to the tepid white of early morning. She closed her eyes and exhaled—a long, deep, contented sigh.

"What on earth was that for, Inga?"

Startled, her eyes popped open. Rebecca stood just feet away, looking at Inga oddly, her dark hair curled around the high neck of her gold-trimmed, fitted, grey jacket. She held a bucket of water in one hand and her Sharps rifle in the other.

Inga felt a blush warm her cheeks. She stammered, "I-I-I...I was just admiring the sunrise, Milady Marx." Inga did a mock curtsy and both women laughed.

Rebecca's face was tanned almost to the light brown of her eyes from weeks in the sun. With the water and rifle she looked every bit like an upscale image of the drawings of pioneer women that Inga had seen in stories in the New York papers as the movement west became more frequent news fodder.

"Yes, of course, Inga, what was I thinking? What else could it possibly be?" Rebecca said with a teasing tone.

There was a sudden twinge in Inga's abdomen, which she masked with a smile. She ignored the stab of pain, turned and swept her arm grandly toward the sun, which had just become visible on the eastern horizon. "Of course, Milady Marx, what else could it be?"

Rebecca's lips formed a suppressed smile. She set the bucket down, and reached out a hand. In her palm was Johannes' pocketknife. "You might tell Johannes to be a bit more careful. I found this in the wagon..." She looked at Inga with a definite twinkle in her eye, "he should take care to collect whatever drops from his pants."

Inga felt her blush deepen. Heat seeped through her cheeks. She took the folded blade from Rebecca and in a serious tone replied, "I shall definitely do that, Milady Marx. He must've somehow dropped it looking for supplies yesterday."

Rebecca stooped over to pick up the bucket. "I need to get this water into the kegs and organize my bedroll in the wagon." She straightened up, and looked directly into Inga's eyes with a warmth and concern that Inga did not expect, "Be careful."

Inga watched her turn and walk toward the rear of the wagon, her petite figure bent like a willow stick toward the weight of the water bucket.

The grumbles in Inga's belly were more insistent. The first small wave of nausea crept into her throat. The vacillating feeling of cold and clammy, sweat and surges of heat that she had grown accustomed to over the past week began to increase. She knew that, within moments, she would be sick. Slightly hunched forward, she looked around desperately. A short way from the circled wagons there was a small, dense stand of young trees, their leaves just beginning to bud, the base of their trunks hidden here and there by willows.

"Milady Marx," she called out to the rustles in the wagon. "I will be back shortly."

She looked around carefully to make sure no one observed, and walked as quickly as she could into the clump of trees, hunching her tall figure slightly forward, one hand on her stomach.

SARAH PULLED THE WOOL BLANKETS OVER HER HEAD. THE MUTED morning sounds of the camp preparing for the day filtered through the wagon's curved canvas cover. She lay on her side, her knees drawn up to her chest, as another wave of lightheadedness washed over her and the bitter taste of bile rose in her throat.

She did not want to be sick in bed. That had already happened once. She tentatively pulled the blankets down from over her eyes and looked apprehensively at the ties in the rear canvas flap, wondering if she could stave off the nausea long enough to get up, untie the lashes and make it to that group of thick mixed trees she had taken care to pick out the night before, just in case.

She had known for several weeks that she was pregnant. Jacob's child grew in her belly. The surreal thought disgusted and frightened her. Her time of the month had been regular and then, when she had anticipated it in the days immediately before their departure from St. Louis, it hadn't come. At first she had hoped, and prayed, that the stress of contending with Jacob, the trauma of the repeated rapes, and the whirlwind of events from the time she set foot on the train back in New York until the wagons began their great journey west from the Mississippi, had merely thrown her cycle off. But now the evidence was overwhelming. The tenderness in her breasts and belly, the daily nausea, the feeling of fullness in her middle, and the missed arrival of the monthly curse had removed all hopeful doubt. *An ungodly situation*, she thought grimly.

The flap seemed a long way away. Fortunately, she had been exhausted the night before. She had laid down fully dressed, with every good intention of rising and then disrobing for bed, but that had not happened. She sighed, carefully slipped off the covers, palmed the Deringer from under the grain sack, which was her makeshift pillow, and stumbled to the rear of the wagon.

She concentrated intensely on untying the flaps while trying to ignore the worsening nausea. She made it to the ground, resting momentarily against the open tailgate as the sweat on her face evaporated in the cool dawn air. She was relieved to see Jacob was not under the wagon. His blankets were rolled, tied, and leaned against one of the wagon wheels. He had learned not to poke his head inside the wagon for any reason unless invited. He finally took seriously Sarah's promise to blow it off his shoulders if he intruded upon her privacy in the least.

Sarah turned weakly toward the trees, measuring the distance. Then, not bothering to see who might be watching, she walked unsteadily toward the trees, both hands pressed to her middle. She staggered the last few steps to the trees almost doubled over. Edging behind the first trunk large enough to hide her still slight figure from the wagons, she turned sideways, sagged against the trunk, and collapsed to her knees, her shoulder bruised by the rough bark.

She groaned. Her upper body sank forward until it was supported by her hands spread wide on the ground in front of her. Her back bent as her stomach involuntarily spasmed, and she retched. She closed her eyes. The back of her throat burned. She tried to catch her breath and then retched a second time, her hands still spread in front of her, the rough ground cold on her knees even through the fabric of her blue dress.

When she opened her eyes, the sight of bile seeping over the dried grass and brown leaves brought another wave of nausea. She rolled partly back against the tree, leaned her head against the bark and took deep breaths. She felt better, though clammy from the previous sweat. She closed her eyes, and, partially propped up by the tree, spread one hand on her still upset but no longer queasy, stomach.

What am I to do? How can I hide this? I wonder if I will be showing by the time we reach Cherry Creek? Frightening snatches of thoughts tumbled through her mind. Her heart sank. She slowly wagged her head back and forth against the bark of the oak tree. "*Not fair, not fair, not fair. What will Reuben think?*"

Somewhere in front of her, leaves rustled. There was the snap of a twig. She froze. Carefully, without turning her head, her eyes searched the woods, looking for any movement in the visual alleyways between the tree trunks. She slipped one hand into the pocket she had sewn into her dress, and closed it around the Deringer. She let out a quiet gasp of surprise as a tall blond woman shuffled with a staggering gait into sight. The woman's shoulders were hunched forward, her head was down, and both her hands were pressed against her belly.

That's Inga! Why is she here?

Inga's eyes were fixed down. She barely looked up in front of her, and certainly did not glance left or right. *She hasn't seen me!* Sarah held herself very still, and let her pass. Inga stopped, reached out a long arm and steadied herself against an elm tree. She suddenly bent forward, her upper torso almost parallel with the ground, and threw up, her free hand attempting to keep her long blond hair out of her face. She groaned, and sank down on both knees, her hands folded in her lap, shoulders stooped, and began to sob.

Not caring any longer if she was discovered, Sarah rose shakily to her feet and walked slowly over to Inga. She knelt gingerly beside her. Inga's eyes were closed. She was still crying and, Sarah realized, still oblivious to Sarah's presence. She reached out her hand and lightly touched her shoulder. Inga's head snapped up, and she started so violently that she almost fell over. The look of surprise and embarrassment on her face was unmistakable and all-consuming.

Sarah reached out again and lightly grasped the taller woman's shoulder. "Are you all right?"

Inga's eyebrows lowered. She pressed her lips closed and nodded slowly. Her skin was blanched, with small beads of sweat across her forehead.

"You are Inga, Johannes and Reuben's friend, and you travel with Rebecca Marx?"

Inga nodded again, the furious red in her throat an obscene contrast with the pasty pallor of her face. "And you are Sarah? I've seen you, of course, and heard Milady Marx speak of you since the campfire the first night. I saw the two of you talking. Reuben and Johannes mention you often."

Sarah's heart simultaneously leapt at the news that Reuben talked about her, and beat faster with dread of what those discussions might have been about.

Inga began to cry quietly again. "I think I am sick, Sarah. This morning's sunrise was so beautiful. I was in such a good mood. I've been so looking forward to this adventure. A new life. I finally found a man I love. And now I fear I have some horrible illness. I have felt like this almost every day for more than a week."

"There, there. There, there," Sarah put one arm around Inga's shoulders.

"I certainly hope I didn't disturb your privacy, Sarah. We have so little of it as it is. If I'd known you were here I would have found somewhere else."

Sarah laughed softly, a bitter irony in her chuckle. "I've not been feeling well either, Inga. If you had seen me just a few minutes before I saw you, I would've been in the same condition." Sarah leaned her head toward Inga in a conspiratorial posture, but as she said the last words, a realization struck her. Her chin snapped up, and she felt her eyes widen at the thought.

Inga had eased back onto her heels. She was focused on her hands, which were smoothing the skirt over her thighs in repetitive motions. She did not notice Sarah's startled, pensive expression. "It is just as I feared..." she said in a low, sad voice. "I am sick and you have it, too. It's a strange illness. We will probably infect the entire train." She turned her head to look at Sarah, who had returned some control to her facial expression. Her large blue eyes were watery, and beseeching. "Do you think it is serious, Sarah? Do you think we will die? I have rarely felt so wretched and surely not for days on end. I think it's getting worse."

Sarah shifted her knees slightly so that she was closer to Inga. She tightened her arm around the tall woman's shoulder, which was at the level of Sarah's eyes. She rested her forehead against the heavy fabric of Inga's dress and tried to speak in a reassuring tone. "It's all right, Inga. I don't believe we have any strange illness, and I am quite sure we are not going to die, or infect anyone else."

"Why are you so sure?"

"Inga, can we be friends? Good friends? I think we both need someone to talk to. We can share secrets, and perhaps help each other deal with the journey and our conditions."

"Our conditions?" Inga was staring at her again, salty dried tracks of tears staining her cheeks. There was a small bit of saliva at the corner of her mouth. The muscles below her left eye quivered. Her jaw dropped and she stared wide-eyed at Sarah.

"Oh, Lord. How could I not have known? I feel so foolish. Of all people, I should have realized." She shook her head.

No doubt if I had had a looking glass, that would have been my exact expression when I realized I was with child, Sarah thought. "You have been with Johannes?" she asked.

"Have I been with Johannes?" Inga repeated slowly. Some color returned to her face and she looked down. "Yes, I have. But, it is different. I love him very much. I think I have since we first met on the train to St. Louis. I believe he loves me, too. He hasn't really said so, but I feel it."

Sarah wondered momentarily about Inga's words, "of all people," and "it is different. *Different than what?*

"Well, unfortunately," Sarah said bitterly, "loving has very little to do with pregnancy."

"What am I to tell Johannes? Or Milady Marx? Do you think they will know?"

"Before I saw you stumbling around in here like I had been minutes before, I was asking myself the same questions, Inga."

Inga's eyes widened further, an intake of breath clearly audible through her long fingers still covering her mouth. She shook her head in disbelief, took her hand from her mouth and placed it gently on Sarah's leg, "Do you mean you're pregnant?"

Sarah nodded slowly. Her teeth bit into her lower lip.

"Oh my," Inga shook her head slowly from side to side. "Oh my. Oh my."

The two women leaned their heads together. Inga pulled away, and her eyes searched Sarah's face. "But, but, I thought that Irishman you are traveling with was simply a traveling companion. During supper the other evening, Reuben had said something about how the two of you pooled your money to buy the wagon and were making the journey west together for pure convenience. Rebecca mentioned she enjoyed talking to you at the campfire and Reuben asked her for her opinion. Milady Marx said that she agreed with Reuben's assessment of your situation..." Inga's voice trailed off.

Despite the grip of their shared despair, Sarah felt a strange sensation. Since she had last seen her sister, Emily, tearfully waving farewell from the doorway of their Liverpool sewing shop as she clambered into the carriage to Portsmouth, and the *Edinburgh*, she had felt very much alone. There was no one to trust, even Aunt Stella. No doubt guilty about not being able to provide the job in New York she had promised Sarah in their trans-oceanic correspondence, her aunt had been more preoccupied with justifying her decision than in listening to her niece.

And then Jacob. His brutal rape of her the very first night in the train, the continued assaults, wrought changes in her that she did not quite yet understand. What a godsend to find out that Rebecca Marx of all people could be trusted, and now to make friends with a woman who was, by quirk of fate, in a position identical to her own. Then she heard Inga's voice and realized she had asked her a question.

"Is it the Irishman's baby?" Inga repeated.

"It could only be Jacob's child," Sarah said stiffly.

"Oh, I'm sorry. I did not mean..." Inga paused, "but, when did your relationship change? He did not appear at all respectable at the pig roast, and many people commented on his treatment of you and Milady Marx. Did you find yourself falling in love with him?"

The familiar rage welled inside her. She looked down momentarily and then back into Inga's eyes. "You and I are friends, Inga. For whatever reason God has put us in this place, at this time, in similar circumstances. I despise Jacob O'Shanahan."

Inga drew back, obviously stunned by Sarah's vehemence.

"Actually, that is not nearly a strong enough word," Sarah continued. "I hate him. He raped me—over and over again." Her chest tightened and her throat constricted. "He is a brutal man."

Inga looked shocked and appalled. She leaned forward, her long fingers wrapped around Sarah's upper arm, "He raped you? Will he force you to marry him? Does he know about the pregnancy?"

"I don't know exactly what I'm going to do, Inga. But I would kill him before I would refer to him as *husband*."

Inga put her arm over Sarah's shoulder. "I am so sorry, Sarah. I understand. Truly, I do."

Sarah felt her emotions turn cold and she pulled away. *How could she possibly understand?* Her voice was bitter. "You are in love with Johannes. Carrying the child of a man you love is quite different than being pregnant with the bastard child of a man you despise. Though you are kind enough to say you understand, I am not sure I can fully explain the pain this situation has caused my heart and my mind."

Inga leaned closer, put her hand on Sarah's leg, and squeezed, "I really do understand, Sarah," she whispered, "my parents died when their fishing boat capsized in the fjord below our home in Norway. I was only thirteen. I was devastated. My father's brother, a sloth of a man came, he said, to take care of me. It was my father's wishes, he told me." Inga shook her head sadly, tears again welling in her eyes.

"He sold our beautiful stone cottage, overlooking the brilliant blue fjord and the white foam of breaking waves on the rocks below it, the cries of seagulls, and the fishing boats going to and fro each morning and evening. It was my last connection with my parents...." She took a choking breath, "and my uncle sold it. He took all the money and dragged me off to New York City with him to a dirty, dingy, little more than one-bedroom flat in a filthy part of the city. I was a virtual prisoner. He drank more, grew more obese, more disgusting and..."

Inga took another deep breath. "And he... he...he molested me...." There was a deep tremor in her voice. "I obtained sleeping potions, and one night when he was in a drunken stupor I mixed them all into his whiskey while he snored like a pig on the couch. I don't know to this day if it killed him, but I hope it did."

Inga paused, a faraway look in her eyes, her grip on Sarah's leg viselike. Sarah waited, riveted to her story. "I left that night with a few meager possessions, the clothes on my back and my most treasured item, a silver handled hairbrush my father gave me when I was ten." She looked up, a sad, wistful smile on her face. "I use that brush every day. It is like my parents are there, brushing my hair."

Sarah put her hand over Inga's. "But you were only thirteen, and alone in New York City. How did you survive?"

Inga looked at her for a long moment, beginning a reply several times, and then simply said, as she loosened her grip on Sarah's thigh, "I did what I had to."

"We are the same in many ways," Sarah said, "each doing what we must do." She paused, "and it is a miracle that we would come together here, like this." She lifted her arm and swung it in a small circle that encompassed the stand of trees and the wagon train beyond.

Just then, Sarah heard a woman's raised voice, faintly but distinctly calling out, "Inga...Inga, where are you? We're almost ready to go." Seconds later, a man's deep, thick, accented baritone shouted, "Inga...the team is hitched."

"Rebecca and Johannes," Inga said, starting to rise. As they helped each other to their feet, in an intimate gesture, Sarah pressed her face into Inga's shoulder. Inga rested her chin on the top of Sarah's red hair, and they embraced.

Sarah stepped back. "You see, Inga, things are good for you. There are people who care about you and love you."

Inga hugged her again. "And now you have someone who cares about you as well."

Sarah nodded, "That I do, and be assured that you do, also. We shall help each other through this even though, in the end, our decisions might be quite different."

Inga nodded, then turned and started walking toward her wagon. *Quite different,* Sarah said to herself. She turned and headed toward her wagon but stopped after four or five steps. She turned around. Thirty feet away and framed between two trees, Inga had stopped, too. Her face lit up with a wide grin, and she waved. Sarah waved back.

CHAPTER

21

April 19, 1855

CONFESSION

SQUATTING NEXT TO THE RIVERBANK, SARAH SWISHED A CHEMISE IN the clear waters, pausing for a moment to look upriver where the flow of the North Fork of the Big Nemahaw River was obscured by the next bend. An assortment of garments lay on top of a canvas bag that sat beside her. Next to her, on either side, Inga and Margaret were engaged in the same ritual. After more than four weeks on the trail, the women felt like well-seasoned, though cautious, travelers. Only a few feet from them, Margaret's Enfield musket leaned against a thick alder tree.

The current chugged here and there around boulders. The deep, ice-blue of the water was enhanced by the dark, grey-brown bark of the stands of oaks and elm that intermittently lined the bank, here and there mingling with alder, willows, and wild rose. Several thick trunks had toppled from age or wind into the river, their roots exposed like gnarled fingers. The flow swirled and gurgled around the thick, round obstructions. Streaks of riffling gold shimmered, appearing and disappearing, as the water facets caught, and then lost, the afternoon sun.

"This water is the coldest yet!" Sarah exclaimed, extracting her hands from the river and briskly rubbing them together, then snatching the chemise as it began to drift away.

"It will get colder before it gets warmer," said Margaret. "Snowmelt hasn't started to the west yet. Mac says by the time we get to the other side of the Nebraska Territory and peel off south to Cherry Creek, those rivers will be two or three times as high from all that spring melt comin' off the Rockies."

"I like it," interjected Inga, her eyes focused on the legs of a pair of Johannes' britches she was vigorously scrubbing together. A smile was visible between the strands of blond hair, which hung from her head almost to the surface of the river. "Reminds me of the water in the fjord in Norway when I was a little girl."

Margaret rose heavily from her squatting position, wrung out a garment and tossed it on a wide, flat rock. She put one chubby hand behind her and rubbed her lower back. "I wish Harris and I had decided to do this ten years ago," she smiled. "I would have been only a bit older than you young ladies."

"There are times when I don't feel so young," Sarah said, looking up at her.

Margaret gave her a sharp glance, but Sarah had returned to the chemise in her hands and did not notice. Squeezing the delicate undergarment, she asked, "Do you mind if I share that rock with you, Margaret?"

"It's a good one, isn't it? Wide, flat, dark, and warm. Help yourself, Sarah."

Sarah stood and looked down at her pleated skirt. Uneven fingers of wetness worked their way up the calico fabric and extended more than a foot above the hem. She sighed, "I will have to change, or put up with being damp all evening. But, it's good to be back on a river. Mac says taking this trail rather than the main track will save a week or more, and I know he wanted to avoid Kansas City, and by-pass Independence, but those few days through the corner of the Kansas Territory before we turned north again—they were desolate and dusty."

"Yeah, that stretch of country didn't excite us much either." Margaret shook her head in agreement. "Did you notice how careful Mac was to not show the wagons anywhere near Kansas City? He seems very concerned about this slavery violence, though personally, I don't see the fuss. The government ought to stay out of folk's business. He has made sure we don't get within seventy miles of Independence or St. Joseph, either, and we got cousins there we was hopin' on see-ing. Been fifteen years since they moved there. Got a good farm and five darkies judgin' from their letters."

Sarah felt her brow furrow. She did not yet understand the slavery issue everyone talked about enough to say anything, but something about Margaret's words struck her wrong. *Aren't negroes people, too?*

Inga threw Johannes' pants on a rock near her, then cupped her hands in the river and splashed herself in the face. "Refreshing!" She looked up at Sarah and Margaret, and all three women burst out laughing.

"Margaret, you, Harris and the girls should really come down and have supper with us one night," said Inga. "We had a lovely get-together with Sarah, Zeb and Mac last Saturday." She paused and her brow furrowed. "Was it last Saturday? I am beginning to lose track with the ever-changing countryside and the surprises that seem to come with every turn. It has certainly been exciting." She caught Sarah's eye and the two exchanged a knowing smile.

"It might seem like a short time to you two young women, but this old body is quickly getting weary of the bouncing on that wagon seat. You'd think whoever designed those wagons could have thought of more than one front wheel spring." Sarah felt a twinge of compassion as the older woman moved one thick arm behind her and massaged her back again. "I am sure glad Mac stopped early today to inspect and repair all the wagons," Margaret continued. "Harris discovered one of our wheels was working loose, and I sure needed a break."

"I've heard several people in the Conestogas complaining about how rough the ride is," Inga said, drying her face. "Not that the jour-ney in the prairie schooner is much smoother." She turned to Sarah. "Did you overhear that discussion between Rebecca and Reuben after supper that night?"

"About the Jewish holidays? Or about whether or not Rebecca should be on a horse once in a while, rather than sitting in the wagon for the whole trip?"

Inga giggled. "I heard both. Honestly, I don't know from day-to-day if they will ever speak to one another again, or if I might find them embracing behind the wagon."

Sarah's lips drew taut at the thought of any embrace between Rebecca and Reuben. Inga quickly realized she had said the wrong thing and cast an apologetic look. Sarah grabbed the next article of clothing, squatted down again in the river, and busied herself with washing.

"I'm sorry, Sarah. Really. I wasn't thinking."

"It's all right, Inga. Things are the way they are." She looked up at Inga and smiled. "But, it is still a long way to Cherry Creek."

Inga chuckled and shook her head.

"I take it," Margaret said, standing with hands on hips, and a puzzled but bemused look on her face, "that there's two women who set their caps for Mr. Frank? He is a handsome fellow. If I was twenty years younger, and not married, and without children...," she laughed heartily. "I might throw my hat in that ring, and that would be 'woe' to any other woman."

The three women broke into gales of laughter, and Sarah almost fell as the clothing she was washing once again drifted just beyond her reach and she had to lunge for it.

"Did you mention something about Jewish? Mr. Frank is Jewish?" Margaret asked Inga.

"He is indeed. I haven't talked to him directly about it but from what I've heard from Johannes, or overheard, his family back in Prussia is rather devout."

Sarah watched Margaret closely. The heavy older woman hid it quickly but a definite look of surprise, and something else, flitted across her face.

"And Lady Marx is Jewish, too?"

Sarah stopped washing and looked over at Inga. She appeared uncomfortable. "I've never talked to the Milady Marx about the subject, but it would seem so. I was not sure until their discussion about some holiday that had just passed, or was coming up—I'm not sure which. Purim, I think it's called."

"Well, I'll be danged. That explains it," Margaret shook her head knowingly.

"Explains what, Margaret?"

"Well, we invited Reuben down for supper. He was interested in that old Betsy Ross circular flag that we fly, and he is certainly Becky and Eleanor's most favorite person on the wagon train. They just think he's wonderful. He will make a great father one day."

Sarah felt a sharp twist in her chest, but kept her eyes fixed on the garment in her hands.

"We was saying grace over the meal," continued Margaret, "and Mr. Frank didn't join in. He said, 'Amen' afterwards like he meant it, but Harris and I talked later about why he didn't say the prayer with us. That's what it explains. I've never known no Jewish folk before, have either of you?"

"I met many people of the Jewish faith when I worked for the mayor at his mansion back in New York," replied Inga.

Sarah nodded. "There were several customers who were Jewish at our shop in Liverpool. Those women were among our best customers, although I must say their attitudes were not very dissimilar from Rebecca's."

"Certainly can't be too many Jews this far west or headin' west either. I've always thought they liked the cities and such."

Sarah looked up at her. "Actually, I did not know this either... not so much in England, but over on the Continent many of the largest cattle farms are owned by Jewish families. Reuben told me just a bit about his family's farm, which was outside a little town. I believe the name is Villmar. He named his horse after the river that flows through their property, the Lahn."

She lowered her head and went back to her scrubbing, missing the quick look Margaret flashed at her, as if something had been confirmed in her mind. "If Lady Marx is Jewish, and Mr. Frank is Jewish, that might help explain whatever it is between them."

Sarah looked up. Margaret's eyes were fixed on her and she decided not to respond, but simply nod.

There was a splashing downstream and the distinct muffled clunk of horse hooves on rocks in water. Margaret hurriedly darted over to the alder and grabbed the musket. Sarah quickly wiped her hands and reached into the pocket of her skirt for her Deringer.

Fifty yards downstream where the river wound its way out of view, the shoulders of a brown and white mustang appeared, then the rider. Zeb's tall, lanky form, coonskin hat, and well-worn, fringed leather attire, with his Enfield musket comfortably cradled in the nook of one arm, could not be mistaken.

Margaret relaxed and leaned the musket back against the tree as Buck splashed toward them, sending sparkling droplets arcing over the water each time the horse pushed forward. He climbed out on the bank ten feet away. Zeb gave a friendly but somber nod to Margaret and Inga. "Afternoon, Miss Margaret. Afternoon, Miss Inga." His eyes moved to Sarah and he smiled. "And, Miss Sarah."

Inga and Margaret looked at her, and she could feel a slight heat rise in her cheeks. Zeb had not taken his eyes from hers. "Zeb, what a pleasant surprise," she said. "Do you have laundry you want us to do?"

They all chuckled. "No, these clothes just get better with use. Once in a while if they get too gamey I will tidy them up some. When they get too old and ragged, I just make me a new set."

He reached into the breast pocket of his leather jacket, pulled out a tobacco pouch and began to roll a smoke. Sarah felt Margaret and Inga exchange glances behind her back.

Margaret cleared her throat, stooped down, and began to pick her laundry off the rock. "I'm about done here. Can't get 'em any cleaner, so Harris and the girls will just have to put up with it."

Inga caught on quickly. "I just finished my last piece of clothing, too," she replied. "Shall we go back to the wagons, Margaret?"

Margaret had already risen, her laundry draped over one arm. "Let's do," she said, picking the musket back up with the easy grace of someone familiar with the weapon.

Inga smiled up at Zeb and then over to Sarah. "Would either of you like to join us for supper tonight? Johannes and Reuben said they would be done with the work on the wagons before dark."

More time around Reuben! The thought made Sarah smile. "I would love to. Jacob has thankfully found several men who play poker, so he is around very little. Not that it matters. Something other than my own cooking would be a delight."

Zeb shook his head. "Thank you kindly, Miss Inga, but Buck and I killed a rabbit this morning, I'm not ambitious enough to salt it, and if we don't eat it tonight, it'll spoil. Another upcoming evening, maybe."

Inga nodded and trailed Margaret into the trees, toward the distinct sounds of camp.

Zeb dismounted and knelt down on the riverbank a few feet from Sarah, leaning slightly on the Enfield, stock down on a lonely area of sand. The musket had not left his hand. "How are you today, Miss Sarah?"

"I'm just fine, Zeb. I'm so glad we ran into one another. We haven't talked for several days. Sometimes I look out from the camp at night, and I can see your fire far in the distance." A sudden shot echoed from up-river, followed by five very quick rounds. Sarah jerked in surprise, and she felt her heart jump.

"No need to be alarmed Miss Sarah. That's Reuben practicing with that Colt of his. I 'spect you have heard it several times over the past weeks, just further out."

"Oh my, that did startle me," Sarah could feel the rapid beat of her heart beneath the hand she had raised to her chest. "I didn't realize that was Reuben." She shook her head and took a deep breath. "I was about to ask you, Zeb, why don't you spend the nights with the wagons?"

Zeb chuckled. "Truth is, I'm not partial to being around people." He paused and a strange look passed over his face. The purple scars on his jaw seemed to twitch. "With very few exceptions, you being one of them. I...," his voice broke off and he looked down at the gravel at the edge of the river. He picked up a small, flat rock, turned it over in his hand and threw it sidearm. It skipped six times across the surface of the water before disappearing.

"Why, thank you, Zeb. That means a great deal to me. And though I said nothing at the time, when you told me the story about your farm being burned and your parents murdered by that evil half-breed, I knew how horrible it must have been for you, and surely not a story you shared often, if at all." She reached out a hand and lightly rested it on the mountain man's forearm.

He looked up, his stare penetrating her eyes, and smiled a resigned half-smile. "Well, I know you're young enough to be my daughter, but...," he broke off again, and stared down at the gravel.

"And what, Zeb?" asked Sarah, unable to overcome her curiosity.

Zeb raised his head. "And, and, I made you a pair of moccasins. Tough, good hide off a big bull elk I killed last year. Them boots of yours..." he nodded down to the round toed, heavy brown leather boots visible below the wet hem of her skirt, "are going to get mighty uncomfortable as we get further west, the weather warms up, and the going gets tougher."

Before Sarah could respond, he rose quickly, and walked over to Buck who had been standing patiently, watching them. *Perhaps with an air of amusement*, Sarah thought.

Zeb reached into one of the saddlebags and took out a pair of moccasins, the leggin' type that would rise to just below her knee. He shyly handed them to her. Her seamstress eye appreciated the work. They were beautifully, if roughly stitched, patterns of leather overlapped with rolled edges, the heavy diagonal rawhide threads more or less evenly spaced. *A bit like their maker*, she mused. Durable, yet soft, supple and smooth in her hands.

She was surprised, and knew she was blushing. "Why, why, thank you, Zeb," she stammered. "Do you think they will fit?"

Zeb nodded. "I 'spect they will. Hope you don't mind, but I had Reuben bring me one of your boots. I measured the leather off it."

Sarah felt a sudden flood of warmth toward the weathered, scarred, loner. "Zeb, I..."

He interrupted her. "You feeling okay?"

A small bolt of trepidation coursed through her. "Why, yes, Zeb, why would you ask?"

"I have seen you leave camp several mornings and come to talk to you, but it seems you've been sick." His concerned gaze was piercing.

She felt her blush heighten and her heart rate quicken again. She looked down, playing her thumbs across the dark, gold leather of the moccasins. "I think the food doesn't agree with me. It's a much different diet than I'm used to."

"Well, I didn't want to disturb you. Bein' sick is a private thing, I think."

He looked away and squinted at the sun. "If your chores is done, let me bring you back to the wagons."

Sarah decided saying nothing was best and simply nodded. She gathered up the laundry and stuffed it back into the canvas bag. The clangs and bangs of the maintenance on the wagons had ceased some time ago.

They silently made their way back to the edge of camp, Sarah walking slightly ahead of Zeb, who led Buck. As she stepped out of the trees, a pace in front, she turned around to say thank you, but the mountain man was gone. All she caught was a glimpse through the trees of Buck's brown and white rump and the swish of his tail, already many yards from her. She sighed. Then she looked down at the moccasins in her hands and smiled. The warm feeling toward Zeb stole over her again. *I can't wait to try these on.*

CHAPTER

22

April 19, 1855

$\mathcal{R}$EVELATIONS

SARAH BEGAN TO WALK BACK TO HER WAGON WITH THE MOCCASINS then stopped. *I really have no cause to hurry to the wagon. The later I get back, the better the chances are that Jacob will be out playing poker.* She did an about-face and ambled absent-mindedly toward Inga and Rebecca's prairie schooner, a number of wagons further up in the night circle.

Admiring Zeb's handiwork as she walked, she remembered his bashful bestowment of the gift. *What could he have been trying to say?* she wondered. It was evident that he was attracted to her and just as apparent that those kinds of feelings didn't overtake Zeb often, if ever. She had instinctively liked him since they first met under the unusual conditions on the barge. It began as gratitude for his coming to her rescue, then graduated to respect for the way he had faced down Jacob. Finally, when he held her gently as she retched over the side of the barge, she recognized a tenderness that she was sure he did not display often. Up until today she had thought of him as a guardian angel, perhaps a father figure and certainly a friend. She mused, *but yet....* She shook her head at the thought.

Up ahead, Inga, Johannes, and Rebecca stood by their wagon. Reuben was unsaddling Lahn. *Just getting back from his pistol prac-tice,* Sarah realized. Rebecca, watching her as she approached, w~

and as Sarah neared their fire, smiled a sincere, warm welcome—not her typical biting smile. "Why are you shaking your head to yourself as you walk, Sarah? Is this wilderness driving you daffy?"

Everyone laughed. Reuben winked at her, and she felt a thrilling stir but quickly averted her eyes. "Actually, Rebecca," she replied, "the further west we go, the more I see the country open up, the more convinced I become that this is the sanest, insane thing I've ever done."

Inga walked over and put her arm around Sarah's shoulders. Sarah looked up into the taller woman's face and smiled. "I feel the same, Sarah. I truly look forward to each day. I thought the excitement would wear off, but I think it's just the opposite."

Reuben looked at each of them, but his eyes lingered on Rebecca. "There is an energy to this land. That is certain. You would have to have armor over your heart not to feel it." Rebecca impassively returned his stare.

"I was really in no hurry to get back to my wagon..."

Rebecca turned her gaze back to Sarah. "And that nasty, maniac demon," she added.

Sarah nodded. "Certainly that, too. I thought I would help you prepare supper since Inga was kind enough to invite me."

Inga laughed and spread her arms wide toward the fire. "We've planned a very special repast. Pemmican stew, with pemmican stew on the side with hardtack biscuits. And then, we have hardtack biscuits and some beans."

"Now that sounds special, Inga!" laughed Johannes in a jovial tone tinged with sarcasm.

"We do have quite a bit of bacon left. It is going to spoil if we don't use it. When Rebecca and I bought it we didn't know that Reuben does not eat bacon." Inga turned to Reuben. "I'm sorry, Reuben, I should've realized it to begin with, and certainly after the campfire, when I noticed you had none of Mac's pig."

Reuben smiled good-naturedly. "It's difficult to keep customs on the trail, and I imagine it won't be much easier when we finally get west. If there are a few simple traditions I can adhere to, I will. But you folks chow down on the bacon. It does not bother me," he laughed, "and I love the smell!"

Inga turned to Rebecca. "Then let's make one batch of stew with bacon, and a smaller batch for Reuben without bacon. Rebecca, what would you prefer?"

There was an awkward silence between the five of them. Rebecca looked surprised by the question. Her eyes moved to Reuben who stood watching her, his arms crossed over his chest, the Colt dangling at an angle off his hip, and the brim of his hat set low enough so that his eyes were in shadow.

She opened her mouth but abruptly closed it, returning her gaze to Inga. "Well, Inga, the bacon has certainly been tasty up to this point. But I think I, too, shall forgo bacon for the rest of the journey."

Sarah felt a little knot in her gut. Her eyes darted from Rebecca to Reuben and back to Rebecca. There was no communication between them whatsoever, yet there was. Her thought was interrupted by Johannes' exclamation, "Where did you get those moccasins? I'm jealous. Exactly what I think we will all be needing."

He walked over to Sarah. Glad for the diversion, she held out her new footgear so he could see them better. "Would you like to take a look?"

Johannes reached out eagerly for the moccasins, turning them over in his hands, looking at the soles, running one of his long fingers along the stitching. He whistled. "Whoever made these knows what they're doing. Double-stitched, extra thick, double-soled, rolled edges. If these were a pair of horses, I'd call them a fine thoroughbred team!"

The others had come over to see the moccasins also, and they passed them around to one another with similar laudatory comments. Inga reached over and touched her arm, "Is this why Zeb came up to us at the river?" she asked, keeping her voice low. "To give you the moccasins?"

Sarah nodded. She knew that despite herself, her face had a slightly dreamy quality. Inga's smile seemed all-knowing. Johannes, still engrossed in the moccasins, completely missed the look that passed between the women. "That old devil," he said, "wonder if I can talk him into making me a pair?"

Reuben laughed. "I'm not sure you could talk him into making anything, Viking. But, if you suggested, and then threw something his way he might want to barter for, you might have a chance."

Johannes looked up at his friend with a grin, "Isn't that the truth."

Sarah realized Rebecca was keenly watching Reuben, who was staring at her. She thought quickly. "May I put my laundry canvas over by the wheel?"

Inga gestured, "If you want, Sarah, you can lay out your laundry on the other side of the wagon. That's what I did. Might as well get it started drying so it doesn't mildew in that bag."

Rebecca had detached herself from the group and was surveying the encampment. She sighed, and turned to Sarah and Inga. "If you don't mind my not helping with supper, I really would like some time to myself down by the water before it gets dark. I did not realize how I had taken being near to the river every day for granted until we spent the last three days in that waterless wasteland. After the last few days in those conditions, I need to freshen up and clear my nose from the smell of this afternoon and the dust of Kansas. Every time I moved today, the wind seemed to shift and along with it the smell of burning wood and red-hot iron."

"Please do, Milady Marx. Sarah and I can get the food prepared and if we are lucky, we might have some help from the men."

Rebecca's eyes moved to Johannes and then to Reuben. The two men exchanged a resigned glance. Reuben spoke up, "Would you like some company, Rebecca? I'm not sure it's completely safe to be down there on your own."

Reuben's arms had dropped from their fold over his chest to his sides, where they were suspended from his gun belt by two thumbs dug in behind the shiny row of metal capped cartridges.

Rebecca smiled, "That's kind of you, Reuben, but I would rather some time alone." She walked over to the wagon and plucked her Sharps rifle from its leaning position behind the front wheel. "Besides, I will not be completely alone. I should be utterly safe."

Reuben nodded and turned to Inga "You're in charge, Miss Norway. Tell me and the Viking what you would like us to do."

The exchange made Sarah a bit nervous, but she couldn't quite pinpoint the reason. She watched Rebecca tuck an embroidered handkerchief in the sleeve of her woolen dress, then turned to help Inga begin dinner preparations.

REBECCA SMILED TO HERSELF AS SHE WALKED AWAY FROM THE WAGON and entered the scattered trees that separated the circular encampment from the river. She reached the edge of the river, drew up the hem of her skirt, and shook her head at the tiny explosion of trail dust from the fabric. Leaning her Sharps against a cluster of boulders, she checked carefully for nettles before easing herself down in a small grassy nook between the rocks. The circle of wagons was not more than two hundred feet away, but she felt almost as if they did not exist. She was alone in a vast empty space on the edges of the Big Nemahaw, five thousand miles from the expansive city she called home. Or *had* called home. She furrowed her brow at the thought.

Above the gentle murmur of the river current where it caressed the shore, she heard the faint crackle of the campfires, occasional laughter, and the clang of stirring ladles chiming dully against interiors of the great iron pots suspended from tripods as supper was prepared. Every so often, muted male voices cursed softly in unison with snorts of horses and the low brays of oxen as men carried water buckets to the stock. Downriver, the diffused steel-grey curtain of dusk stole toward her like a phantom from the east, gradually swallowing the golden waves of the prairie grasses visible in breaks in the mixed deciduous cover. To the west, the last rim of retreating sun blazed in an orange glory, its rings of shallow red, then fading pink and pale yellow, bidding farewell to the day in concentric arcs of flaming color.

The vastness, the emptiness, the sheer space enveloped her. The promise of tomorrow, etched in the direction of the dying sun, stirred a feeling of excitement. She sighed almost reluctantly at the remnants of disappearing blue as the evening sky darkened. She tried to remember home—her bedroom, and the cobblestone street lined by similar stately row houses outside the great front door of their elegant London abode. *I wonder how you are, Mother?* She closed her eyes and lifted her face to the cooling breeze to focus on the memory of crowds, city noise and fine linens, but the images remained distant, as if from a long-ago dream.

Her mind drifted back to the conversation at the wagon a few minutes before. She had every intention of answering Inga's question in the affirmative until, her eyes on Reuben, she opened her mouth and what came out was not at all what she expected. *I shall forego bacon for the rest of the journey.* Was it Reuben's presence? Or, after all these years of ignoring it, did the realization that out here, in the middle of nowhere, she had only herself, her friends and her God? She shook her head. She would piece together the puzzle later. Right now, there was the evening, the river, the solitude, and the setting sun.

This place was not like anything she envisioned. The journey was not what she expected. Despite her initial wish to remain aloof, the bond between friends strengthened every day. The fast budding friendships between her and Sarah, and Sarah and Inga, had taken her by surprise. Just six months prior she had been caught up in the society, and the shallow give-and-take of the city, exchanges always underlain by business or personal ulterior motive, and the continual cacophony of the crowded urban environment. Despite her resistance, her respect for the commoners in the other wagons, their spirit and courage, was growing.

She had not even felt a twinge of remorse when Mac announced they would avoid Kansas City, St. Joseph, and Independence, instead sending Reuben, John, and Charlie into "KC," as Mac called it, for certain supplies and parts with a stern warning to not mention the wagon train.

At first, she had listened begrudgingly, unable to imagine silence like this. That it would now whisper to her soul with such insistence was a revelation, as was this completely different world she had never known existed. Nor had she cared.

She closed her eyes as the last flame of color faded from the sky and struggled to remember exactly what their wise, old, prescient, aborigine servant, Adam, had told her as she boarded the carriage for the *Edinburgh*. His tone had been so earnest that it had momentarily diverted her from her poor mum sobbing at the top of the steps. Despite her father's insistence that the aborigine had a gift for seeing the future, she had dismissed Adam's words as gibberish. "I assure you, Adam, I'll be back in London, my goals accomplished, by the late fall." She had not even thought about that moment until now. *What were they?*

His deep baritone voice, thick with the accent of his native land, suddenly swam back into her memory, and her eyes opened wide, staring unseeing into the first twinkle of stars to the east. *"It will be a different life, Mistress, but you shall prosper. The power of the land and the man will hold you."*

She rose, feeling a bit unsteady. Adam's serious face, knowing tone, and the conviction in his words swirled round and round in her head. She knelt at the water's edge and withdrew the handkerchief from her sleeve, then rolled both sleeves up to her elbows. Leaning over the water, she rinsed her hands, then splashed water on her face. Drying her eyes with the handkerchief, she looked down at her reflection, barely visible in the remaining light. The mirrors of her uneasy eyes danced back and forth across the moving current.

Rising, she bent over and picked up the Sharps, stood, and took one last look downstream, where the Nemahaw disappeared into the darkness toward the Missouri. She took a deep breath, shook her head, and headed back to the wagon.

Inga and Sarah greeted her with smiles as she walked into the light of the small fire, "Perfect timing, Milady Marx. We just began serving." Johannes and Reuben merely nodded, their attention buried in their plates. The coffee chugged in the tin kettle, and the faint bubble of the pemmican stew, mingling with the smell of frying bacon in one skillet, and extra desiccated onions in the other, stirred her hunger.

She leaned the Sharps against the inside of the wagon wheel and accepted a modestly piled plate from Inga, thanking her, then looked around for a place to sit. Reuben was perched on his bed roll, leaning against his saddle, which was separated from the ground by a blan-ket. She walked over and stood in front of him. "May I join you?"

His head snapped up at the request. His eyes fixed on the wide, warm smile Rebecca knew she was wearing, and he stopped chewing. There was a moment of silence before he scrambled to his feet and extended an arm toward his makeshift seat, "Yes...I...Yes, please do."

CHAPTER
23

April 25, 1855

Maps of Fate

THE AFTERNOON WAS WARM, SUNNY, AND ALMOST CLOUDLESS. THE wagons had circled. Children ran here and there through the camp chasing one another, laughing and shouting, sometimes drawing exasperated looks from adults busy with pre-evening chores. Rebecca stretched, trying to soothe her bones from the jarring, daylong ride in the wagon. Inga was inside the wagon, straightening their slightly disarrayed belongings.

For the past several weeks, with increasing frequency, Johannes and Reuben had entrusted the wagon driving to her and Inga. Having had experience, she was comfortable with control of the rig from the beginning, and Inga was becoming quite proficient. When the trail was a bit less bumpy, all relatively speaking, of course, Rebecca had enough faith in Inga's prowess to occasionally doze off, only to be inevitably awakened by a particularly vicious jounce of the springs.

They had crossed the Osage weeks ago, the Big Nemahaw, several days ago, and a number of smaller rivers without incident. Rebecca noticed that Mac usually stopped travel an hour or so early the day before a crossing to afford the pioneers more time to prepare. Reuben had mentioned that the next river, the Little Blue, was yet several days travel.

Before attempting to cross the deep, wide Osage weeks prior, Mac had ordered all the prairie schooners and Conestogas blocked up with large square pieces of wood, placed at each corner between the rockers and the wagon beds. She applauded his foresight for caching these blocks near the entry point on previous trips. During the day-long extensive preparations, he gave strict instructions to the men. "Detach the teams from the smaller wagons. Empty out all supplies, the water kegs, too. Lash those so their lower edges are at the bottom level of the wagon beds—four to each larger wagon."

The seven smaller, makeshift wagons in the train, including Sarah and Jacob's, were stripped of their canvas tops, which were coated with linseed oil. "It will save you this chore a few weeks from now," Mac had joked with the astonished group of small rig owners. He then divided the people between the larger wagons, and increased their teams with the animals from the smaller wagons. Pointing to six men, he instructed, "Wrap the oiled canvas around the exteriors of the smaller ones, loose ends in the wagon bed." Then he, Reuben, Johannes, Charlie, and John, with a number of other men, had lashed the canvas, along with six empty water kegs, on each.

Charlie and John swam their horses across with several long hemp ropes, their stiff, heavy-trailing ends tied off to trees at the entry points to the crossing. One rope was stretched taut about six feet above the current. The other was tied to the front of what had become wagon boats. Zeb's mule packs were placed in the eight smaller wagon barges with the other supplies needing protection.

Rebecca found herself fascinated by the process and impressed by Mac's ingenuity. Each wagon barge was accompanied by one man. *Just in case*, Rebecca presumed. She saw Zeb, Reuben, and Mac in a huddle by the barge containing Zeb's mule packs, talking conspiratorially. Reuben had his wool coat on one arm and the old leather case he seemed protective of, in the other. He was apparently insisting to Mac that he be the "captain" of the barge. She watched as he carefully rolled his coat and the case in a gutta-percha, tying it securely with rawhide. *Intriguing, I really have to find out more,* she thought. Charlie and John, joined by Zeb and his mules, towed the boats across from the opposite bank.

Eight men and two oxen anchored the rear of the wagons from the near bank with yet another thick, coarse, piece of two-hundred-foot hemp. Two loops of rope were bolted to the top of the same side of the wagon bed rims, which were reinforced with planking in and out. The guide ropes, as Mac called them, were looped over the dry elevated rope, which stretched like a golden thread across the muddy blue of the river. These kept the converted wagons from being swept downstream.

The supplies had made it safely to the other side and then the larger wagons and their fortified teams, driven by anxious drivers, Inga and herself included, had crossed one by one, sometimes bouncing on the stream bed, other times literally floating, buoyed by the water kegs, and pulled by the swimming teams with the assist of the men, beasts, and ropes on either side of the river.

Her aching joints reminded her how glad she was that crossing the Little Blue was yet several days travel. Reuben and Johannes rode up on Lahn and Bente, breaking her reverie. Johannes maneuvered his horse to the back of the wagon where he could see inside the open flap and called a cheerful hello to Inga. They engaged in conversation, their sing-song Scandinavian dialect punctuated by Inga's giggles and Johannes' laughter.

Rebecca couldn't understand the language, but Johannes' provocative tone and Inga's breathless replies, imported the gist of the conversation. She chuckled to herself and shook her head. Reuben dismounted at the front of the team, Lahn waiting patiently as he began the work of unharnessing for the night. Rebecca walked over to the horse, gently took his reins and stroked his neck. His warm, moist muzzle brushed her cheek, and his thick pink tongue lapped against her jaw.

Reuben had been watching from a crouching position by the lead horses. He laughed. "I think Lahn likes you."

"The feeling is mutual," Rebecca's hand ran down the palomino's shoulder, and the big horse responded with another kiss.

"I wish we had apples or carrots for some treats for the animals each night."

Reuben straightened up. "Well, we have the last of the grain and there is green coming to the grass. Why don't you give him an extra ration tonight? From then on out you will probably get double kisses."

"I'll do that, Reuben," she said, turning her attention from the horse to the man. She smiled and their eyes locked. In the momentary silence, she felt her pulse quicken and a slight heat come to her cheeks. A bit disarmed, she broke the spell.

"We've been discussing for a while now, Reuben, that I would really like to ride as often as possible, but at least a few times a week for portions of those traveling days would be nice. Inga is getting skilled with the lines. It would be an opportunity for her and Johannes to have some private time driving the wagon together and...," she paused and felt her eyes slide to the glisten of his lips within the coarse stubble on his face. "If you would not mind the company, perhaps we could spend part of that time riding together."

Reuben straightened up slowly and smiled. "A practical approach and very tempting."

Rebecca's heart jumped again, and she pretended to be absorbed by her hand on Lahn, but the feel of the horse's finely arched and muscled neck did little to slow her pulse.

"If, in your judgment, Inga's up to it and we don't have any special obstacles or crossing on a particular day, let's try it," Reuben said, turning his attention back to the harness. But Rebecca noticed he had to repeat a few simple steps several times and was making little progress. She smiled at Lahn and his big yellow head seemed to nod. *And what, my fine horse,* she whispered, *do you think Reuben would do if offered an extra ration one of these nights?*

CHARLIE TROTTED UP. HE TIPPED HIS HAT TO REBECCA AND NODDED at Reuben "Evenin', Mistress Marx, Reuben. Mac wants to have a quick get-together as soon as everyone is unhitched and the stock picketed for the night. Over at my supply wagon...," he pointed a third of the way across the circle of canvas tops, "going to go over the route he's taking and some other things. This is where the country starts to really change. Where's Johannes and his girlfriend?"

"In the wagon, organizing supplies," Rebecca cast an annoyed look at Reuben who had broken out laughing from where he bent between the legs of the second lead horse he was still unharnessing.

Charlie grinned. "Well, bring them along." He waved and trotted toward Dr. Leonard's wagon, next in line.

"Reuben...," Rebecca stomped a foot down and Lahn took a step backward, "Think of Inga's dignity!"

"Oh, Rebecca, everyone in the damn expedition knows about Johannes and Inga. They are not some palace secret."

"And what about my dignity?" They both turned to find Johannes laughing, obviously amused.

Rebecca pounded her foot again, "The two of you..."

Johannes cut her off. "I think she is very attractive when she does that foot stomp, don't you, Reuben?"

Reuben's eyes met Rebecca's. "Very." His tone was serious, and Rebecca felt her exasperation suddenly dissipate.

"Inga," Johannes called out to the canvas. "Mac has called a meeting." He looked back at Reuben. "You don't have them unhitched, yet?" His tone was incredulous, and then a knowing expression flitted across his face. His eyes darted from Reuben to Rebecca and then back to Reuben. "Let me help you, farm boy," he said with another laugh.

REBECCA ENJOYED MAC'S GOOD HUMOR, AND TONIGHT WAS NO DIF-ferent. He held up his big beefy arms to quiet the chatter of the assembled pioneers.

"We're camped tonight on the Nemahaw. Tomorrow night, with luck, we will hole up near the headwaters of the Lancaster River. The next river we hit a few days out will be the Little Blue. It should be low and has a cobble bed. The crossing should be easy. Then we will follow the Seward back toward the North Platte and Fort Kearney.

We are saving several days cutting off a big north bend in the Platte, and taking this far less traveled trail but after tomorrow we won't be near water again 'til three nights from now. If we hit weather, it could be longer. Make sure your water kegs are full."

"We will stop for a day at Fort Kearney. It's not much, but there is a general store of sorts, a barber shop—if Sam ain't hunting—and a small candy shop." He smacked his lips and everyone laughed, except, Rebecca noted, Jacob.

"You'll likely see your first army at the post and your first Indians. Might be some Choctaws and Delawares or Shawnees that have drifted west. Might be on their way to hire out with the fur companies up toward Montana and Oregon. They are friendly. Matter of fact, many scout for the army. But they do like to trade and some beg.

"There's just four companies of soldiers there. The enlisted are mostly Irish. It's a boring post, and they pick fights to stay amused. Damn Irish." Mac grinned and stroked his bushy red beard. The group broke into loud laughter, again Jacob scowled. "We might run into a Mormon wagon train at the fort or west of there. I hear two of 'em got holed up by winter somewheres. Them poor Mormons are headin' to the Utah Territories. They call it the Exodus. Started in '48. They ain't been treated too pretty back east. Don't know about you folks, but I take exception when someone tells me who to pray to." He leaned over and spat a wad of tobacco to the ground. "Anyways, they are good people, and I think we will all get along."

"What I really want to tell you, though, is that from here on out it will be a different world than the last four weeks. There will be winds, sudden ungodly weather, a fair chance of running into folks who will be none-too-friendly, and April and May are the sickness seasons. Except for buffalo chips, fuel will be scarce." He looked around slowly to make sure everyone was paying attention.

"From here on in, I want your weapons within reach, even when you're sleeping. Starting tonight, as you noticed, we are picketing or hobbling the stock, and we are tripling the night sentries. Elijah, Harris, Jacob, and William will assist Charlie first shift tonight. Don't skyline yourselves. Anything funny, fire a shot. I'd rather have a mistaken alarm than no warning. Course, Zeb's out there some-where, and I doubt anything will get past him, but don't doze off—you might not awaken. John, Preacher Walling, Samuel, Thomas, and Clay will relieve you around midnight. When you are approaching one another out there, don't be trigger happy. The password will be 'Mississippi'. Ain't seen an Indian yet that can say that word.

"If anyone begins to not feel well," his eyes fixed on Dr. Leonard, "I want to know immediately. It ain't fair to others if you hold out." The doctor and Thelma nodded somberly.

"Ladies—do not venture out alone." He looked directly at Rebecca and she felt the eyes of everyone shift her way. "I don't give a tinker's damn how good you think you are with a rifle. You don't want the fate that awaits you if the Indians make off with you." Embarrassed, Rebecca looked beyond the group and caught Jacob staring at her with an enigmatic, intrusive smirk. She turned away quickly. "All of you be alert for rattlesnakes. They will be out as it warms up. You'll hear them before you see them. Teach your young 'uns to be wary.

"This grass is greening, but it's still dry. Starting tonight, clear an extra wide area around your fire—at least six feet—and dig a fire pit every night. Don't go to sleep without smothering the coals, with a good three or four inches of dirt. We've come too far to burn the camp down now.

"Some of you are going to find your boots getting uncomfortable. Not all of us are lucky enough to have a guardian angel make us moc-casins." He swiveled his head to Sarah, and grinned. Sarah turned bright red and dropped her eyes to the elk hide, legging moccasins that Rebecca noticed she had already begun to wear every day. Sev-eral of the pioneers looked at Zeb, who shifted uncomfortably. Jacob's lips curled into a mean twist.

"For those of you who don't have one, we got extra awls in the supply wagons, rawhide stitching and four good cow elk hides. Not as tough as bull leather, but they'll do. Zeb has volunteered to show you how to sew up a pair tomorrow night after supper. I suggest, less you want to hobble the five hundred miles to Cherry Creek, you take him up on his offer." Mac slapped his leg and laughed. "Besides, it cost me three pounds of sugar." Zeb smiled, and nodded.

"One last thing. When the weather warms up we will be moving an hour before daylight—taking a three-hour break at midday to rest the stock and then moving until just before dark. That's all folks. Have a good night."

Although still miffed about the rifle comment, Rebecca found herself walking a bit more cautiously back to the wagon.

REUBEN WAS AWAKE EARLY THE NEXT MORNING. HE SAT UP TOO suddenly, forgetting the bed of the wagon above them, and bumped his head on a wooden strut. "Dammit, been sleeping under here for five weeks and I still can't remember not to sit up straight without looking?" He laughed out loud. *Okay, I will admit to myself I am preoccupied with riding with Rebecca today.*

There was a chuckle from under the double blankets a few feet from Reuben. The top of Johannes' blond hair, framed on either side by the trough of his saddle, peeked out from the edges of the blankets, and the long form under the wool stirred. The muffled, sleepy voice was part complaint and part tease, "What are you laughing about, Reuben? And why the hell are you up so early? It's not even half-light yet."

Reuben lay down on one elbow, still rubbing his head. "Johannes, I think you'll agree that I have been of great assistance to you when you want time alone with Inga."

"Ooohhh. I think I know what's coming," said the barely audible voice in the bedroll.

Reuben chuckled and dropped his voice low, unsure of how much sound might carry through the bottom of the wagon bed to the women sleeping above them. "Well, friend, it's time to repay the favor. And you will get some time with Inga without Rebecca playing chaperone—for all the good that's done!"

"True enough," came the Scandinavian accent from the blankets. "Rebecca's attempted supervision has been somewhat less than effective," Johannes muffled his laugh into the saddle. "If she knew how ineffective she has been, she would be stomping that foot of hers like a one-legged dancer."

It was Reuben's turn to chuckle. "There are times when I believe she sincerely wished it was my head under her heel."

"You're not alone in that observation, Reuben."

The two men laughed quietly, and Reuben cast a guilty glance up toward the planks that formed the wagon bed. "We can take turns, but you ride with Inga in the wagon a few days a week. I'll spell you from time to time. Maybe you could teach Inga to ride. That way, Rebecca and I could man the wagon..."

"You mean woman the wagon," Johannes was laughing, and though Reuben couldn't see his head he knew his friend had put his hand over his mouth to try and stifle the sound.

"Can you be serious about anything? Rebecca and I would like to ride this morning."

"Consider it done, Reuben, but if you decide to be alone, don't get too far away from the wagon train."

"Johannes you know damn good and well that Rebecca and I don't have the relationship you and Inga do. In fact," he paused, "I'm not even sure we have a relationship."

"Well then, you're the only one who isn't."

REUBEN WAS IMPRESSED WITH REBECCA'S EASE IN SADDLING JOHANNES' bay. Johannes had offered her the use of his horse, obviously taking his payback to Reuben seriously. Reuben helped her with lifting the heavy saddle over Bente's back, not so much that she lacked the strength, but the combination of weight and the height of the horse made it cumbersome. It also meant that their bodies touched a few times.

He was surprised that she hadn't asked for her sidesaddle. He had noticed her skirt did not have the usual petticoat flare below her hips and clung more closely below her waist and to her legs. Now he understood why. Each thinking their own thoughts, they finished saddling their horses, Reuben hoping the tinges of color in her cheek-bones and the silent current that seemed to hover around them were not from the morning air.

"You need some help mounting?" he asked, regretting the question the moment the words left his lips.

Rebecca flashed him an annoyed look, "Certainly not." Holding the reins against the horn with her one hand, she pulled her left knee up with her other, fitting the toe of her boot into the stirrup, and effortlessly swung into the saddle.

Rebecca was obviously amused and thoroughly enjoying his poorly hidden astonishment. She slipped her right foot into that stirrup and smiled at him in a teasing way. "I've always hated sidesaddle. Far less stable, and somehow seems to say that a woman is not as strong as a man. I always rode this way when my father and I went riding."

Reuben opened his mouth, but she cut him off. "You wish to know why have I been riding sidesaddle, and why I rode sidesaddle at a gallop to the target practice?"

Reuben nodded.

"Because, Reuben, I thought the shock value of my riding up and demonstrating that I could handle a Sharps rifle was enough excitement for the moment. There's no sense giving people too much to talk about at one time," she smiled coyly. "Besides a lady has to keep some surprises for future use." She reached into the small traveling bag that she had hung on the saddle horn, and pulled out a stiff wool hat Reuben had seen her wear before, and placed it at a jaunty angle over her dark waves.

Reuben was taken aback again. In addition to the visor in the front, the hat now sported a visor in the rear slightly longer than the protrusion of the forward cloth.

Rebecca smiled. "I had Sarah sew this on for me. It's not quite like yours," she nodded at his cowboy hat, "it doesn't have the side brims though I plan to get one of those when we reach Cherry Creek. Might make quite the fashion statement when I arrive back in England."

She studied his face closely, and Reuben fought to keep his features impassive at the mention of her return to Europe. "Yes, ma'am, follow me."

Up from the front of the wagons, they heard Mac's good-natured curses, and then his daily ritualistic shout, "Let's get rolling, straighten up the line!" Then, like an impatient timepiece that brought daily order in a patch of timelessness, "I said, move 'em out!"

Johannes flicked the lines and their prairie schooner lurched forward. He caught Reuben's eye. "Have fun," he called out. Inga smiled and waved.

Reuben and Rebecca looked at each other and laughed. "That Mac is the salt of the earth."

"He is quite something. I feel safe with him leading us, and if I may say, I think you're doing an exemplary job of assisting him. I'm quite proud of you!"

Reuben expected a teasing, even sarcastic look, but Rebecca's face told him that she was serious. He could feel his eyebrows rise. "Thank you, but I have much to learn."

Except for a distant faint line of clouds hovering on the northwestern edge, the sky was blue from horizon to horizon. The fiery sphere of the sun was completely above the rim of the earth, its pale spring glow adding a pleasant heat to the air. The wagons unwound their circle in the same curvilinear fashion as they had grouped the night before, each wagon maintaining its position in the train. In the distance, a pair of golden eagles circled ever higher on the warm, rising morning currents.

Reuben pointed. "See those eagles, Rebecca?"

Her eyes followed his outstretched finger. "Yes, aren't they magnificent?"

"Even before my father informed me that I was the brother selected...," Reuben paused, "entrusted, to establish the family future in the United States, I read everything I could on America and that included much material on the American West. Indians consider birds of prey strong medicine, and under certain situations, a good omen."

He turned slowly back in the saddle to look at Rebecca. Her eyes were still focused upward on the eagles, her profile silhouetted against the sun. *Truly beautiful.* "Perhaps it's a good omen there are two of them."

The gaze she returned was sharp but warm, the brown in her eyes softened. "Perhaps, Reuben."

He braced himself against the saddle horn and craned back behind them, looking at the wagons. "Let's ride out to the side a bit and see the sights. How's that Sharps doing?"

Rebecca looked back at her Sharps rifle, wrapped in a blanket securely lashed to the rear of the saddle, one rawhide through the trigger guard behind the trigger, and the other triple-looped around the barrel just forward of the forestock.

"Fine, thank you, Reuben. I appreciate you showing me how to do that. I shall have to obtain a scabbard." She smiled at him.

Yes, truly beautiful. Reuben had noticed some type of change in Rebecca since the supper they had shared with Sarah a week before. Though she had not lost her sharp tongue, her tone was less biting, there was something in the way she looked at him, and when she touched his arm, or their bodies momentarily brushed by happenstance of the endeavor at hand, she seemed to let her contact linger.

They rode out two hundred yards from the wagons, about two-thirds the way down the line. The rumble of the wheels, occasional bang of uneven ruts, the creak of wagon springs, the sounds of leather, animals and the faint snaps of lines applied by the wagon drivers to their teams drifted, diffused, out over the land. There was a sudden gust of wind from the west, then another. Rebecca quickly raised a hand to her hat and held it in place. Reuben crammed down the crown of his over his head. "Where did that come from?" she asked.

"From the northwest." Reuben gestured with his hands as if he was ushering her through the door to a formal gala event in a great ballroom, "Shall we?"

Rebecca laughed, their horses abreast of one another. "Yes, Mr. Frank, we shall." She gently dug her heels into the bay's side, and they began to move parallel with the wagons, her legs almost touching Reuben's.

They rode in silence, content in each other's company, and in the wide open spaces punctuated by the occasional rolling hill or abrupt rise of a butte, accented here and there with scraggly stands of scrub and occasional patches of trees. The startling blue of the sky above deepened. Ahead was an endless, undulating expanse of land, its brown-gold grasses rippling in the wind, which had become more constant. The grasses changed colors and reflected the sun as the currents of air stirred them, as if engendered by the stroke of some unseen hand. On the western horizon the line of white-edged clouds seemed to have grown, fading to a dull grey where they disappeared behind the curve of the earth.

Occasionally, Reuben would turn his eyes to Rebecca. Engrossed in the scenery, he noticed her occasional deep breaths, seeming to inhale the essence of the vastness, then hold it, before exhaling slowly.

REBECCA FELT CONSUMED, YET COMFORTABLE, LOST, BUT FOUND, IN the vastness. She puzzled over those paradoxes, acutely aware of the creak of leather, smooth and slightly cold, in the quiet of the morning, mixed with the occasional snorts and prances of Lahn and the bay mare she was riding.

Reuben had moved slightly ahead of her. Her eyes followed his silhouette. Straight back, muscled thighs, casually at ease, and confidently in control. His head moved imperceptibly back and forth, and she knew his eyes were sweeping their path, ever vigilant. His presence and demeanor made her feel safe, secure.

With a smooth motion and the calmest movement of his hand, he pointed to a distant band of animals. They were small, beige and white, and all facing the train, alert. *Deciding whether to watch or run,* she thought. She smiled to herself. *I well know that feeling.*

"Antelope. These are the first I have ever seen. I read about them back in Prussia. See that buck?" Reuben swung his finger, "the one with the horns? If you look close, you can see that the bucks have a black cheek patch that the females don't. They are members of the goat family rather than the deer family. Very fast runners. They are supposed to be good eating, though I read that if they are excited, they have huge hearts, and just a few seconds of fear and their muscle tissues fill with adrenaline. When that happens, my father's scout said, most dogs won't even eat the meat."

"I put them at about three hundred fifty meters, Reuben. Perhaps we should shoot one or two for food." Rebecca reached back for her Sharps.

"No, if Mac wanted camp meat, he would have already sent Zeb or the Kentuckians out there. Hell, Elijah and his son could shoot them from the wagons without moving," he chuckled. But Rebecca noticed when she mentioned the idea of hunting the antelope, his look had been one of mild surprise and respect.

"Reuben, if you don't mind me asking, I heard Johannes say something about maps that you have...." Her words froze in her throat as she was met with an intense stare; Reuben's eyes suddenly a fiery green, with a hue of steel grey, *and a measure of hurt, perhaps?*

"I should've known." Reuben wagged his head, his disgust evident. "If you wanted to know about the damn maps, why didn't you just ask me over supper one night, or back by the wagons some morning. You didn't have to go to all the trouble of building up to this ride together." He spat the last word out as if distasteful and spurred Lahn into a lope.

Rebecca reined in, shocked, her mind racing and a sinking feeling in her chest. "Damn," she muttered to herself and put her heels to the bay.

She caught up with Lahn shortly and slowed her horse to match his stride. Reuben stared straight ahead. "Reuben, I..."

Reuben's head remained fixed, but from the side of his mouth, in a cold tone jarred slightly by Lahn's gait, he said tersely, "Never mind, Rebecca. I'd be happy to tell you about maps. I ask only that you don't bring them up to anybody else. What do you want to know?" His voice was emotionless, and cold.

Rebecca moved the bay closer to Lahn, then reached for and grabbed Lahn's nearest rein between Reuben's hand and the hackamore and tugged slightly, slowing the palomino. Reuben looked at her hand as if it were an irritant. The two animals stopped. Rebecca rested her fingers on Reuben's thigh. She could feel the warmth in the muscles under her hand and was distracted for just a second. "Reuben, look at me. Please."

Reluctantly, he turned her way. His shoulders moved forward, and he rested his upper body on a forearm perched on his saddle horn. "What?" The word was a report, like a rifle shot.

"I understand why you are upset. And, it is true in the beginning I used my looks and wits as I always have, and your attraction to me..." Reuben's head snapped up, his eyes narrowing. She could see that they were shading more grey, and continued hastily, "and my attraction for you, Reuben. It is true. I have been attracted to you since first time I saw you on the deck of the *Edinburgh*, talking to Sarah. I didn't even know you, but I was jealous," she smiled. "And I noticed your eyes lingered on the tight wrap of my skirt when the wind blew it back against my legs."

Reuben's eyebrows arched in surprise. The steel grey in his eyes began to soften. She held his stare and continued. "I realize I can be difficult at times. I feel something in me changing," she sighed, "a large part of it is you," she swept her arms around at the rolling emptiness around them, "and this. I have no idea what will happen. I want to be honest with you. My plans are still to sell my father's inheritance and return to England, but I find myself with less and less resolve." Her hand tightened on his thigh, and he dropped his to cover hers. The calluses where his fingers met his palm were warm and somehow seemed to fit perfectly between her small-boned knuckles.

"I am worried about my Mum," Rebecca said quietly. "She was ailing when I left. The family finances are in tatters. My father lost all three trading ships shortly before his death. Someday, I shall tell you what one of our servants said to me. He is an aborigine, whom my dear father firmly maintained until his death, was clairvoyant. But now I want you to know that I'm earnest. And..."

She took a deep breath and was surprised to feel the wet trickle of a tear on her check. "I'm scared and confused. You're the first man I've ever been attracted to. I keep thinking about that kiss back on the train. It was my first kiss, ever," she dropped her eyes in embarrassment and squeezed his thigh again. "I'm so sorry I tried to slap you. I've been meaning to apologize since that night, but my pride wouldn't let me."

She looked up to find Reuben's upper body leaning into her, his face only inches from hers. She opened her mouth to speak but her words died as his lips covered hers, their tongues dancing a soft kiss within the kiss.

Lahn shook himself impatiently, separating them from each other, forcing Reuben to sit upright in his saddle. Rebecca knew her head was still slightly tilted, her lips partly open. Reuben laughed, "I think Lahn is jealous."

Rebecca giggled. "He should be." Their eyes locked again. She could see a reddish hue underneath Reuben's dark tan. She knew her features reciprocated his blush.

"I am honored, Rebecca, that I am the first and only man to have ever tasted your lips."

His words were nearly as evocative as his touch. She felt a strange, dreamy longing. She leaned over, putting one finger to his lips. "Kiss me again," she said, almost purring.

Their lips met, deep and searching, and she shuddered. Reuben drew his face away a few inches, "Rebecca I...do you think we..."

Rebecca was sure he could hear the rapid beating of her heart. She cleared her throat. "Reuben, I have a map, too. My father was given a Land Grant by King Ferdinand of Spain. I don't know all the details, but it was at a time prior to it being an American territory. That was only five or six years ago, before that place they call Texas threw out the Mexicans, I am told. My solicitors in England tell me it's a completely valid claim, which was verified by my father's attorney in New York. It appears to be quite large, approximately one thousand hectares."

She looked around, immediately feeling foolish for worrying about anybody overhearing. Harris and Margaret's Conestoga, the last wagon in the line, was already several hundred yards ahead and south of them. "My father was delirious on his deathbed, but he kept telling me there was gold. I don't know anything about land, Reuben.

I know about gold trading from my father's business, but I know nothing about mining, if by some wild chance the ravings of a dying old man prove to be miraculously true. If that is the case, I would be shirking my duty to my family by selling it."

Glancing off in the distance, her voice dropped to a whisper. "I have this feeling, this premonition I am going to love it regardless of its other values. I know you will be busy, very busy, setting up your ranch, and I have no idea how far your land is from my father's grant, but I would appreciate if I could rely on your honest advice as the situation unfolds and the facts become known."

Reuben nodded slowly. His expression was soft and warm and there was a tender look of concern on his face. Rebecca had a wild urge to kiss him again.

"I will help in any way I can, Rebecca. You know that I would help a friend, even if we weren't... weren't..." His voice trailed off. "The distances could be large. Where is the land grant?"

"I will show you on the map this evening if we can find time alone from prying eyes, although Inga knows about it—and I would trust Johannes, despite the hard times we give each other," she laughed. "It is on the western flank of a mountain range somewhere in an area in the southwest part of the Kansas Territories. I can't pronounce the name."

She saw a startled look rush across Reuben's face and his eyes widened. "The Uncompahgre, by any chance?"

Rebecca was surprised. "Yes, yes, I think that's the name. I didn't know how to say it."

"Un-com-pa-grey. What is the name of the mountain range?" Reuben had unconsciously shifted in his saddle to search her face, his brow furrowed, his eyes bright.

Rebecca, surprised at his extreme interest, watched him closely as she answered, "Las Montanas Rojas."

Reuben jerked Lahn's reins and the gelding tossed his head in protest, but complied with a grudging stop. "The Red Mountains."

"Yes, Reuben. What is it? How did you know that?"

Reuben shook his head slowly, half in disbelief, half in obvious wonder. "Do you believe in fate, Rebecca?"

Rebecca thought for moment. "Prior to coming to America, I believed that fate was something we each created for ourselves. I still believe that's partially true. But here, you, this place, the people we've met, all of these brave souls risking their lives, chancing everything to travel a thousand miles to a place they've never seen, filled with such hope, and some spirit I can't define, has changed my most basic perceptions. For the first time, I truly believe there is a God." She raised her eyes to his. "So yes, Reuben, I believe in fate."

A soft smile played over Reuben's lips. "So do I, Rebecca Marx, so do I. We will look at the maps together. You'll see that the maps my father's scout drew also detail lands in the Uncompahgre on the south and east flanks of some mountains..." he paused, "called Las Montanas Rojas."

Rebecca heard her own deep intake of breath and felt her eyes widen. "Really, Reuben? You're serious? This is not a joke? Was that old leather case you were so attentive to back when we crossed the Osage your map case?"

Reuben reached across the space between the horses, and put his hand on hers. "Yes, you are observant. That is my map case. It was my father's and his before him. It used to contain the maps to the family's cattle farms in Prussia—the old country." He smiled. "Now it contains maps to the family's future. It is true, Rebecca. Destinies and connections are shaped by forces far larger than any of us. Our charts..." he paused, thinking, "you might call them the maps of fate."

He straightened up and shook his head as if to clear it. "Even more unusual, is that we have two maps from the scout. There was to be a third. The scout said he had drawn it in his last letter. But he was killed by Indians, and his brother, who was supposed to have received the third map, disappeared in New York." His eyes looked intently into hers. "It was, though we've never seen it, supposedly a map showing potential gold deposits on the lands the scout recommended for the ranch."

Rebecca raised one hand over her mouth, an overwhelming flood of emotions, thoughts, questions and thrills avalanching through her in a jumble.

"There's one more thing you should know, Rebecca, if you don't already." She just looked at him, her mind numbly racing, her hands still over her lips. "You know that Inga and Sarah have become quite close." Reuben laughed, "And we are both well aware that Inga and Johannes couldn't be closer." Rebecca felt her lips move in a smile beneath her fingers.

"Sarah has confided in Inga that she and Jacob have a map. I have not seen it, nor has Inga, and Sarah is very closed mouth about it—understandably so given her horrible predicament with that son of a bitch Irishman. But, from the little that Inga has apparently been told by Sarah, and has dribbled to Johannes, the map is also a gold map. And, apparently, marks a place somewhere in the Uncompahgre."

CHAPTER

24

April 25, 1855

FFRONT

REUBEN'S MIND WAS SPINNING. THE JOINING OF THEIR LIPS HAD BEEN consuming. More than a kiss. The maps, and destinies somehow magically intertwined. *His father's words, 'There are no coincidences, none at all.'* He paused and glanced toward the wagon train to buy time to formulate the question in his heart. To his astonishment, the wagons were circling up. *Can't be much more than early afternoon*, he thought.

He was about to turn to Rebecca when he saw a rider galloping to intercept them from the head of the train. The wind had picked up noticeably. The billows of dust that exploded from the hooves of the approaching horse swirled, caught the air currents and hurtled past the two of them from several hundred yards away. Across the broad expense of landscape, stronger gusts of wind flattened the grasses, turning their brown stems and tender green undershoots into moving waves of silver-gold ribbons.

As the horse and rider drew near, Reuben recognized Mac. The wagon master reined in Red brusquely within a few feet in front of them and looked sharply at each of them. "You two all right?"

"We are, Mac. Why are we stopping so early?"

Mac turned his body in the saddle, and pointed to the northwest. The clouds that had been a thin distant strip, hugging the horizon when they started out that morning, now consumed a third of the sky. Their leading edges boiled in a misty tapestry of dull grey, transcended to a solid grey, and mutated finally to dark, angry grey-black which stretched solidly north to south across the entire northern and western skylines.

A strong gust of wind blew by them. Rebecca hunched her shoulders into it, and Mac almost lost his hat. "Damn hat. One of these days I'm going to put me a rawhide chinstrap on this thing." He pulled the felt down tight almost to his ears and turned up the collars of his coat. "I think we're in for a nasty blow. The spring storms can get vicious out in this flatter country. We're circling the wagons behind that hill. I think it's about the highest place around for miles. Might break the wind." He glanced back over his shoulder. "I got a funny feeling that when this one hits, if we're not ready, we ain't gonna have a chance to get so. Temperature is dropping too. Feel it?"

Reuben nodded. "What you need me to do?"

"Well, you won't be practicing with that Colt this evening," Mac grinned. Another bluster of wind churned around them, and Mac bowed his head into his neck and held his hat, his eyes fixed behind Reuben. Craning his head, Reuben could see Zeb a half-mile out, Buck and the three pack mules seemingly braced forward as they trotted in the direction of the wagon train, directly into the teeth of the increasing gales.

"Zeb knows it, too. If he didn't think this was going be a whopper, he wouldn't be coming to the train. Reuben, we're going to have to make a corral for all these critters, each rig within a few feet of the next, otherwise they will be scattered to hell and gone in the morning, or whenever this thing let's up. Hopefully, it will be short-lived. Help Charlie, John and the folks unhook the teams. I need eight men behind each wagon. Stick the wagon tongue of the rear wagon over the axles of the one in front. That will form a tight circle with the stock in the middle. Hopefully, it'll just be rain. If it's snow, it could take a week for things to dry out, and we'll be fighting mud between here and the Little Blue, maybe Fort Kearney. After everyone is unhitched, talk to Charlie and John, and help them with whatever they need. They've done this a time or two before, but it's been a few years."

Mac turned to Rebecca with a slight bow of his head, his hand still holding his hat in place. "Miss Rebecca, I like that rifle sheath ya got rigged up there. Where did you learn to do that?"

"Thank you, Mac. Reuben showed me how to do it this morning."

"That so?" Mac grinned and leaned over to spit. An air burst caught the gob of tobacco spittle and blew it back on his trousers. "Damn." Mac began to laugh.

Rebecca and Reuben exchanged glances. She blushed deeply and found sudden interest in her hands folded over the saddle horn, which Mac noticed with a smile in his eye. Still wiping his trousers with his hand, he suggested to her, "You might want to get down there, Mistress Marx, unsaddle, and set up your wagon. No sense to start fires with this wind, and there's little fuel."

It took several hours of grunting, groaning manpower to position the wagons into a closed circle, organize the stock, and get the animals in the center before pushing the last wagon into place, closing and completing the corral. The line of clouds was now directly overhead and the first precipitation was beginning to beat down on the pioneers as they made final preparations.

It began as grovel, little round, white, cold pellets—half rain, half snow, that hissed and tapped on the wagons' canvas tops. The wind roared incessantly. The animals inside the corral were nervous, drifting back and forth, horses nipping one another, and oxen rubbing shoulders. The mules had turned their heads way from the wind, their great grey muzzles lowered to their forelegs, and their tails flattened out over their rumps. Anything left outdoors weighing less than a few pounds rolled, bumped, and skidded along the ground, moving too quickly for the hapless pioneers to catch.

Reuben looked out to the west. Johannes stood shoulder to shoulder with Reuben, their backs to the increasing gales. A few miles out, the landscape disappeared, swallowed by a sinister, pulsating wall of grey that moved rapidly toward them. Reuben pointed and yelled, "Here it comes!"

He felt a tug on his jacket and turned around. It was Sarah, her hands clenched around the collar of the wool traveling jacket under her oilskin, the red locks of hair at her temples frozen by white flakes. She had replaced the moccasins with her boots.

"Reuben, that damn Jacob forgot to fill the water kegs last night. I assumed it was done, but he must've gotten liquored-up. I just went to fill the water pouch to have water in the wagon during the storm, and they are empty. Could you spare some water? We only need a bagful."

Over the howl of the wind, Johannes overheard the conversation. He smiled down at her. "Stand in front of us, Sarah, we'll break the wind a bit for you. Do you mean to say you plan to hunker out the storm in the wagon with that Irishman?"

Sarah looked up at them. Her eyes blinked rapidly, snowflakes and gravel falling from her eyelashes. Clearly, she had thought about it and didn't like the idea either. She opened her mouth to speak, but Reuben quickly interjected, "Why, don't you come down here and weather it out with us?"

"Thank you, Reuben, but I can't leave him alone in the wagon with my things. They're all I have."

Sarah's cheeks quivered and Reuben couldn't help but grimace. "It will be a bit cramped, but that would save lugging water back and forth. With you two, there'd be seven of us, including Zeb, in the wagon. With the oil lamps going, it will be half-way warm."

The relief on Sarah's features was unmistakable. "Are you sure Reuben? I don't want to put you to any bother."

Reuben and Johannes exchanged glances, and Johannes nodded a curt assent.

"We are sure, Sarah."

"I'll go back and get Jacob then. I don't want him alone near the wagon with my belongings even for a short time. Is Zeb here? I saw him ride in."

Johannes reached out and grabbed her arm, "No, get into our schooner. Zeb's inside. The storm will hit any second. I will go back and retrieve the son of a bitch."

The wagon ladder shook from the wind as Reuben helped Sarah up, his hands around her waist. He was surprised at the full curve of her hips, and the slight rounded feel of her belly, not fully distinguishable under the traveling garb, yet his thumbs and forefingers almost met as he lifted her up the rungs.

Rebecca, Inga, and Zeb were busy in the prairie schooner rearranging the contents to create seats as comfortable as possible. "We're going to have company. See what you can do to make room for two more."

Inga looked up sharply, her eyes moving back and forth between Reuben and Sarah, "*Two* more?"

"Yep, Sarah and Jacob."

Zeb stepped forward with a smile to help Sarah. Rebecca stopped what she was doing and looked over her shoulder at Reuben with a questioning scowl, "Are you saying that scoundrel Irishman will be in our wagon?"

"There's not much choice. I'll explain later."

Inga picked her way carefully across the wagon to Zeb and Sarah, put her arms around Sarah's shoulders and smiled. "This won't be the only storm we weather together, Sarah." Sarah squeezed her hand. Reuben noticed Rebecca looking at the two women with a strange expression on her face before he turned, climbed down the ladder, closed the tailgate and called out to Zeb, "Lash up this canvas. I will wait for Johannes and Jacob. We'll holler when we need in, and then be quick about it!"

The first wave of heavy snow hit Reuben with full force as he walked from the rear of the wagon. It propelled him several quick steps, and he had to catch himself from being blown over. Some of the stock was settling, bracing for the storm, other animals were making a racket, though it could barely be heard. Several horses ran panicked around the interior circle of the wagons, now and again bumping wagon sides with their shoulders. The shadowy forms of those who had not yet disappeared into their wagons could be seen clambering up, leaning out, and closing up the tailgates and canvas.

The snow blinded Reuben, whipping horizontally and so thick that he couldn't breathe without inhaling sharp particles of ice. He took the handkerchief from around his neck, and tied it over his face and nose, squinting up toward Dr. Leonard's wagon. In just minutes, several inches of snow blanketed the ground, sifting and simmering over the land, driven by sheets of wind. The encampment disappeared into shifting furls of snow that snaked and whistled between the wagons, forming drifts where the gusts whistled around the spokes of the wagon wheels. The circle became invisible in the opaque air, and flakes flew by Reuben, careening away before they could touch the ground.

The dim, barely discernible shapes of Thelma and the doctor could be seen as Thelma tried to pull the tall figure up the slick ladder. The frail physician was having difficulty keeping his footing. Reuben hunched his shoulders and walked, stooped, into the wind, one leather-gloved hand holding his hat on, the other scrunching the fabric of his coat collar. He made it to the lee of their wagon, crouched down, put his hands on the doctor's buttocks, and pushed. Thelma pulled on Dr. Leonard's arms and finally they got the lanky form in the wagon, gasping for air. He looked terrible, white and sallow.

"Thank you Reuben. Thank you so much," she shouted above the din of the wind. Reuben nodded, shut their tailgate, and stumbled back to the rear of the prairie schooner.

He searched for Johannes and Jacob, but found no figures moving through the snow. Wind forced snow inside the folds of his wool coat. He tried to remember exactly where Sarah's wagon was in the corral, but the blizzard was disorienting. *Should he continue to wait outside, or get in the wagon and wait there, or try and find them?* Suddenly, two shadowy forms moved toward him, hugging the sides of the nearest wagon bed, feeling their way like blind men. They were only twenty feet away but almost indistinguishable in the crescendo of weather that cascaded down upon the camp.

"Johannes!" he shouted at the top of his lungs. The figures stopped. Johannes was in the rear. He shoved Jacob, and they continued making their way to the schooner, stumbling the last few feet, leaning, breathing hard, with their backs to the tailgate.

"I've never seen anything like this," gasped Johannes. Jacob didn't say anything. His lower back and rump was pressed to the tailgate, and he was bent over, wheezing, his hands on his knees.

The storm intensified. The wagon to the rear disappeared from sight in a swirling, blowing, topsy-turvy whirlpool, and the tongue of their wagon vanished from view in a gusting snow dervish. Except for their prairie schooner, everything became ghostlike, invisible.

Reuben put his face to the canvas and yelled, "We're out here!" He and Johannes fumbled with the tailgate as Rebecca quickly undid the canvas flaps and the yellow light of the oil lamps appeared. She shoved the ladder out, holding her shawl tight around her chest at the invading squall. Johannes leapt, got one knee on the tailgate, and rolled into the wagon. Jacob stumbled unsteadily up the steps, followed by Reuben. They closed the tailgate as quickly as they could and sprawled over the uneven cargo as Inga and Rebecca hurriedly retied the flap.

The wagon rocked and creaked with the force of the wind, like a small boat in a heavy sea, the sounds of the animals indistinguishable from the muted scream of the tempest. It took several minutes for everyone to settle down, find their places, and for Jacob, Johannes and Reuben to doff their soaked coats and hang them in the rear of the wagon.

Jacob sat with his back to the corner where the side of the wagon met the tailgate, his face cast downward, his expression angry and malevolent.

Reuben turned to Johannes, "What in damnation took you so long?"

A slow, laconic smile spread across Johannes' face. He was propped up against India-rubber sacks of sugar and flour, and his long legs extended almost across the entire width of the wagon bed, his ankles crossed, and his arms folded across his chest. "It took us a few moments to agree on a course of action." He winked at Reuben.

Reuben turned his eyes to Jacob from the caddy-corner position he occupied and studied the blocky, glowering Irishman. His eyes lingered on a bruise that was beginning to form between his mouth and his chin, and a smear of blood on his lower lip.

Johannes was watching him. He shrugged, nonchalantly. "Well, there wasn't the time to have a long discussion." Reuben stifled the chuckle creeping up his throat. The rest of the group was silent, uneasy at being in close quarters with Jacob. Reuben watched Zeb stare at the stocky tow-head with an unflinching look, his fingers slowly running down the taper of his mustache, the hand resting on one knee, a clenched fist. Sarah's gaze was fixed on her boots. Inga looked anxious.

His look lingered on Rebecca. She gave him a glance that made it clear she thought none of this was a good idea. He sighed. Outside, the wind screamed, ravaging any nook and cranny between the wagons that dared to stand in its path.

Even though he wasn't hungry, Reuben attempted to lower the level of tension. "Rebecca, what type of food do we have that will be easy to pass around? I'm starved." She gave him a curt, short nod of understanding.

"Inga made some delicious biscuit bread yesterday. I believe the baking tin is still almost full. We have a bit of deer jerky left, and plenty of dried fruit I can reach without too much rearranging."

Jacob looked up suddenly. His eyes lewdly scanned Rebecca's figure. "I would think being a queen, there would be more than lowly commoner food in this wagon."

Reuben felt his teeth clench. Zeb stopped working on his mustache in mid-stroke. Inga looked at Rebecca, her eyes wide. Sarah cast rapid, embarrassed glances at them all.

Jacob laughed, reached behind him and withdrew a silver whiskey flask from his rear trouser pocket. Without offering it to anyone, he tipped his head back, gulped a long swig, and smacked his lips with an exaggerated sound. Then slowly, and deliberately, he screwed the cap back on and held it up, turning it in his hand and examining it. "I won it, I did, in a poker game on the *Edinburgh*." His eyes flitted, beady and piercing to each of the other occupants in the wagon. "Anyone here play poker?" He looked around at each of them again. "Didn't think so."

Rebecca had paused in gathering up the food. She shook her head in disgust and went back to her task. Johannes stared at Jacob through languid, slitted eyelids, but his gaze was hard. Zeb's scars seemed to be more pronounced against the deepened color of his face.

"How may I help, Rebecca?" Sarah asked, anxiously.

"If you get the tin plates out of that box to your right, Sarah, that would be of great assistance."

Reuben tried to make himself relax. *The storm can't last too long,* he thought, without much conviction.

———•••———

SEVERAL HOURS DRIFTED BY. SARAH AND REBECCA HAD PASSED OUT the tin plates, each with small helpings of biscuit bread, a short stick of jerky, and two pieces of fruit. Inga was upset by Jacob's perverted fixation with Milady Marx's every move and stretch as she had passed out the plates with long reaches of her arm. He had ceased looking at Rebecca only when she drew a blanket around herself and dozed off.

Except for Johannes' and Jacob's plates, which were empty, the others had been barely touched. There had been little conversation within the omnipotent silence, punctuated only by the incessant rattling of the wagon, and the snap of the canvas against the bow supports. The tempest outside showed no signs of abating.

Inga had been aware that for the last hour that Jacob had focused his abusive glare on her. Once in a while, his eyes shifted elsewhere, but his gaze always returned to her, or some part of her body. *He's trying to remember something,* Inga thought with a touch of panic, her old life rising up in her mind, as dangerous as the storm outside. *No, I'm sure he's never seen me before, nor I him, not until the first night on the wagon train.* She took a deep breath, smoothed her hands over her skirt, and tried to calm herself. But she couldn't shake the ominous feeling that held her in its clutches.

One of the two oil lamps flickered. Sarah jumped up, almost losing her balance when her foot caught on the molasses keg. She reached up, snuffed out the lamp and untied the rawhide thong, suspending it from the forward bow supporting the wagon top. "Do you have some oil, Inga?"

Glad for the diversion, Inga raised her eyes. *Sarah knew!* She managed a half-smile and pointed behind the redhead. "I believe it is over there next to the sidewall, underneath those bedrolls."

Sarah refilled, rehung, and relit the lamp. Inga purposely kept her attention on Sarah's movements to avoid Jacob's eyes. Now that the second oil lamp was back in action and casting its dim yellow glow, she darted a glance at the Irishman. He stared at her, his forehead furrowed in shadowed lines.

Time passed, impossible to measure. *It must be near morning,* Inga thought. The wind had died somewhat, the wagon shuddering but not shaking as fiercely. Rebecca slept curled up on her side. Johannes, next to her, had leaned his head back against the canvas, his hat in his lap. His mouth was open and he snored softly.

Inga noticed that Reuben had made sure he had easy access to the pearl grip of the Colt snuggled in the holster on his right hip. His knees were drawn, his arms wrapped around them. His head would start to slowly sink and then snap up, with a rapid blink of his eyes. *He doesn't want to sleep,* thought Inga. Zeb sat in another corner on top of one of Rebecca's trunks. His back was straight, but his shoulders slumped forward and his chin rested on his chest.

Jacob's voice was low and beguiling. "I heard you hail from New York by way of Norway."

Reuben's head jerked up, as did Zeb's. Rebecca continued her slumber. Inga's quick sideways glance at Johannes revealed his eyes were open, looking fixedly at Jacob.

"How old was you when you got to New York?"

Inga was so surprised at Jacob's question she responded immediately, without thinking. "I was thirteen."

Jacob nodded his head, "Quite the city, New York. Makes Dublin look like a village. Where did you work?" His voice was level and smooth, but his eyes glittered, almost reptilian, like a snake that has found a mouse.

"I worked for the mayor at Gracie Mansion." Inga did not want to create a scene nor exacerbate the tension that permeated the wagon. *That's an innocuous answer. Shouldn't do any damage.*

Jacob nodded. "You lived in the mayor's mansion?"

"Yes, Jacob, I did," Inga fought to keep her tone level, but the ominous feeling had returned, more strongly.

"You started working there when you were thirteen?"

Inga felt the constriction in her voice, and a wave of fear tumbled through her chest. "No, Jacob, I first lived with my uncle, and then I moved in with four older women. We were roommates. I worked at a tavern, the Carriage Restaurant, on West 42nd street. The patrons were almost all important businessmen."

"Roommates, eh? You know, it's a funny thing. I played in several poker games while I was in New York before me and Sarah got on the train to St. Louis." He threw a leering, nasty grin at Sarah, who returned his look with an expression of contempt.

"Did pretty well, too. One game, in particular. You might say I found my fortune." He cast another evil smile at Sarah, and she pursed her lips. "Anyways, Ms. Bonney and I were not an item then," a nasty chuckle rumbled from his throat. "To celebrate, I had me a whore that night."

Reuben was staring intently at Jacob, his face grim. Zeb stood up, "That's no way to talk in front of ladies."

Jacob, obviously pleased that he had everyone's attention, reached in his back pocket, took out the flask and took another long guzzle, again deliberately screwing the cap on and returning it back to his hip pocket. "Relax coonskin, we're all grownups here. Everyone knows that hand—'cept maybe the Queen—and everyone has a card hid." He peered intently at Inga who tried to fight the terrible, hollow feeling creeping into her gut. She could feel Johannes' eyes slide from her to Jacob and back again. *Oh God, God, please, no!*

"Her name was Mary..."

Inga jerked involuntarily.

"She was okay, a little old, maybe, but fun. She mentioned she lived with four roommates, too."

Despite herself, Inga was transfixed. Jacob's eyes narrowed. He stared straight at her, a mean, triumphant expression on his face.

"Between us having fun she mentioned that one of her roommates was a tall, beautiful, young blonde from Norway," Jacob sneered. "She laughed about how popular the Norwegian was with fat old businessmen, and how the young woman entertained such gentleman on occasion for money, but maintained her job was as a waitress, and she really wasn't a lady of the night."

Inga wanted to disappear, to hide, to wake up and find this a horrible dream. Her hands rested open, palms down on her thighs, cold and clammy. She could feel Johannes staring at her from the side. Rebecca wore an expression of shock. Sarah looked at her with pained sympathy.

Jacob cackled a laugh. "It's a small world, ain't it, Lassie? Just think, if it was another night, could've been you and me..." He sneered at Sarah, "You and the blonde could have had that pleasure in common..."

Zeb leapt at him from across the wagon, leading with his knee. He tripped on the corner of a trunk and lost his balance, but not before smashing his fist into Jacob's evil smile full-force as he fell, splitting the man's lip with a splatter of blood. The women scrambled to the top of the trunks, Rebecca helping Sarah and Inga to safety, their heads grazing the top of the wagon as they crouched.

With Zeb off-balance, the Irishman struggled to one knee and the two of them, with barely room to maneuver, locked in silent combat. Enraged, Zeb pulled one long arm free and with his hand against Jacob's forehead, pummeled his head against a canvas top brace. They battled to their feet.

Horrified, Inga watched as Jacob's powerful bulk coiled, then exploded, shoving Zeb and forcing him to take a half-step back. He tripped over a crate, sprawling rearward. Jacob swiftly bent and in one smooth motion, drew up a trouser leg, the flash of his boot-knife suddenly appearing in his thick hand. Zeb's hand reached behind his back and curled around the hilt of his own knife.

There was no mistaking the hammer's half-cock of Reuben's Colt. Zeb stopped mid-action. Jacob froze, the pistol pointed at his head, four feet from the muzzle, the barrel steady, not a millimeter of shake in Reuben's hand. The young Prussian's face was deathly, his voice low, cold, and matter-of-fact.

"Out."

Wide-eyed, Jacob managed a blustery sneer. "Farmer boy, no need to get yourself in a tizzy. I wasn't talking about your woman," his eyes shifted to Rebecca, and then immediately back to Reuben. "Though as fine a creature as she is, I suppose she has secrets, too."

Reuben pulled back the hammer of the Colt to full cock.

Jacob dropped the knife and raised his hands. "I'm unarmed, farmer boy. This would be cold-blooded murder."

"The worst of it, Irishman would be that more of your blood would be in our wagon. How about I lay down this Colt, you try and reach me with your blade, and we'll see what happens."

Jacob's eyes flickered. No doubt, Reuben really would pull the trigger.

Through clenched teeth, Reuben repeated, "Out!"

Jacob stood up. Reuben rose with him, the Colt now at his hip pointed at Jacob's chest. Inga watched, unable to breathe, Johannes, still staring at her with impassive eyes. *What was he thinking? What had he surmised? Would he believe Jacob?*

"Untie the flaps and let the tailgate down," Reuben motioned with the pistol barrel.

Blood flowed from Jacob's lip, staining his shirt. He shrugged with a false bravado, but obeyed the commands. As he bent down to lower the tailgate, Reuben took one step and kicked him hard between the legs. Jacob grunted, doubled over, and sagged down on the open tailgate. Reuben put the sole of his boot to Jacob's back and pushed the groaning Irishman into the snow, where he landed on his side with a *whoof*, his hands between his legs, his face contorted with pain, the snow around his mouth turning pink.

Inga watched as Reuben, standing on the tailgate, twirled his gun twice, then smoothly slipped it back in the holster. Zeb stood, sheathed his knife, and took a half-step to the tailgate. His hand brushed his moustache and his voice was firm when he said, "Thanks," before falling silent again, staring down at Jacob's writhing figure. Reuben glanced at Zeb. Then, ignoring Jacob, he turned back to Inga and the rest of the group.

A grey dawn was breaking, and the wind had died to occasional gusty whispers. Perhaps a foot of snow had fallen, Inga thought, drifting in deep, finely sculpted shapes and hollows that rose up behind every obstruction.

"Looks like the storm has broken," Reuben said. "Let's dig ourselves out, though I doubt we will be moving today or tomorrow."

His eyes came to rest on Johannes, and then Inga, with a sad, anxious look. She turned her head slowly toward Johannes who had not averted his gaze, even during most of the altercation. His pale blue eyes were wider than normal, his usual smile absent, an incredulous, pain-filled expression on his face that chilled Inga to the bone.

On the eve of April 25, 1855

$\mathcal{I}$NTO THE NIGHT

THE OLD LEATHER HINGES SQUEAKED IN PROTEST AS LUCY SWUNG open the door of the shack. Israel barely looked at her. He was bent over the table, spectacles and nose inches from a dirty paper on which he scratched laboriously with a pencil he raised to his mouth and licked after each word or two.

"Israel..."

Israel held up his left hand and, without looking up, mumbled into his writing sheet, "Hold on, one minute. Let me finish this thought. I have to redo the sharp in this pencil soon, anyway."

Lucy heard herself sigh. She walked over to the table and gently set down a small, worn canvas sack with two potatoes and half a cabbage Mistress Tara had smuggled to her from the root cellar at the main house. The sound of Israel's pencil was halting, but clearly audible in the silence of the small, confined shack, making a noise somewhere between the scratch of chalk on a blackboard, and the raspy complaint her stiff cleaning brush made when she was scrubbing pots after serving dinner at the main house.

She went over and stood by the wood burning cook stove. She could hear the gentle whoosh of warm air rising up the haphazard flue pipe, and there was the occasional crackle from the log pieces as they turned into embers in the stove's belly. Standing with her back to its radiating warmth, palms facing back toward the heated iron, she looked around the one room they called home, narrowing her eyes at two canvas gunny sacks, partially bulging with some unknown contents. *They weren't here when I left!* "Israel…"

"Hold on just a damn minute, Lucy, be done in seconds."

Israel leaned back in the chair, which groaned with his weight. He fumbled in his pants pocket, one leg extended to get his hand in, and withdrew a small pen-knife with which he proceeded to sharpen the pencil stub. He looked up at her and smiled. "Just making a list."

Lucy felt a wave of trepidation. "A list for what? And why are these two sacks over here in the corner? Them bags look like they come from the harvest barn, just about brand spanking new. Who said you could have them?"

Israel stayed focused on sharpening the pencil. Then, still not answering, he held up the writing tool to the window, twirling it in his fingers, checking the point. He laid it on the table and peeled the spectacles away from his ears. "I'm making a list for when we light outta here. You know—me, you, north, and then west to those big mountains I've been readin' to you about." He nodded at the two sacks, "and them is our packs."

Lucy felt queasy. She walked over to the table and sat down on the only other chair. It squeaked as she adjusted her weight. "Israel, what fool talk is that? You said we be going this summer when the weather's warm," she paused, "and that was the final decision the two of us made."

"Things have changed, wife. We are headed to freedom tomorrow night," he grinned, "and praise the Lord."

"You know what they would do to us if they found those sacks?" she questioned, as angry as she was fearful, "and Lord knows what you have in them! Ain't no way we can deny you took them when they be right here in our shanty!" Israel laughed, and reached his hand across the table to take hers, but she withdrew it and glowered at him.

"Wife, neither them sacks nor us gonna be here long 'nough for anybody to find 'em. And, once we is runaway slaves, don't think it's going to matter much that we borrowed a couple pieces of canvas from the harvest barn, do you? I kinda regard it as our first pay as free people."

Lucy felt a dull stab of pain in her right knee and began to rub it. "What's the all-fired hurry, Israel? You said the traveling is easier when it's warm, after spring weather. You do remember what spring weather can be like in these parts, don't you, husband? Or are you getting so old, that black, nappy head of yours is getting forgetful?"

Israel chuckled. "No, no, but spring weather can be our ally, too. Some snow will make it more difficult for the dogs, so long as new snow covers our tracks. If that don't take care of it, that pepper I've been having you bring back from the main house bit by bit, is almost a pound. Ever seen a hound on track breathe in a nose full of pepper?" He started to laugh, "Let me tell you, when that happens, last thing those dogs will be thinking 'bout is our scent. And, over the last two weeks I caught and cooked ten horned toads, then burned 'em to ashes. We can rub that in with some water on the bottom of our shoes, and there ain't no beast that can follow us."

Seeing she had not dented his mood, Lucy decided it was time to put her foot down. "Israel, I think we should wait for summer like we originally talked."

Israel's smile faded and his head shook adamantly. "Lucy, I overheard talk today while I was shoein' some mules down at the barn. Was measuring out the shoes back in the stalls. Wasn't using no tools so there was no noise. Two of the bosses was talking. They intend to ship half of us darkies south on April 28. You and me is two of them. They seemed right nervous about where this anti-slavery line may wind up, and they figure this place is way too near what could be the union boundary if war breaks out."

He laughed bitterly. "They said they don't want to lose none of their property. How do you feel about being somebody's property, Lucy?"

"Israel, I don't care what they think."

Israel leaned forward across the table and his eyes bored into hers. She noticed the whites around the brown irises were no longer bright, their dull hue streaked here and there with red veins, and there was a thin light ring around the brown of each iris.

"I don't give a damn what they think either, wife. But I do give a big damn about what I think, and you think. And, we ain't no one's property. We own us—no one else."

He leaned back in the chair and tapped the non-sharpened end of the pencil on the paper.

"There's another thing, too. Looks like maybe a storm comin' tomorrow night out of the west and north. Since we're talking freedom, I took the liberty of getting us two gutta-percha rain ponchos out of the supply shed, so we's got some protection against the wind and the wet. And them sacks is painted canvas. That will keep things from getting too soaked. I have already packed my clothes, and I got most of the things on this list in my bag. You need to pack yours. Make sure you bring all your sewing things you have, and especially those awls of yours. I got us twenty fishhooks I've collected over the years, and I got paid for them last two saddles I stitched up in town, so we got $9.75 for emergencies."

Lucy shook her head. "I can't be ready in that short a time, Israel." She knew her voice sounded pleading.

Israel sat forward. "Yes, you can. I'll take care of the list. All you have to worry about is your clothes, shoes, see if you can't grab a couple extra potatoes tomorrow, and that sewing gear. We ain't going to have money to buy clothes, so we have to keep what we's got in the best repair we can. I plan on you and I heading out maybe an hour right after dark tomorrow, after you get back from feeding them up at main house. We'll head north. The ground is pretty dry that route, and not too hilly. The main thing we got to do is get across that Kansas line. Then we are in free territory."

He shook his head grimly, "Not that that's gonna stop 'em from pursuing us. That's where a little bit of snow, a whole lot pepper, and a dash of horned toad ashes will come in. I cut four good limbs today. Stripped them about a foot on the ends. One is a walking stick and one for our bags," he started to laugh, "I mean our luggage— so we carry them over our shoulders. If we travel with those bags at the end of arms, our shoulders will fall off."

Then what? Lucy felt resigned. She knew that finality in Israel's voice, and there was no swaying him once he set his mind and got all worked up. "So then we will be in free territory, the middle of nowhere, with a couple of potatoes, the hounds of hell and a whole mess of angry white folks after us, in country where we don't know nobody, in the center of a snowstorm."

Israel slapped the table and chortled, "Don't go gettin' bogged down in all those details, woman, we will do just fine. We'll find ourselves shelter from the storms. Mistress Tara is going to try and delay them figurin' out we is gone for as long as she can..."

Lucy felt as if she'd been slapped in the face. "You told Mistress Tara?"

"Damn right. You think she would turn us in after teachin' me to read and write and smuggling me papers? You saved her life when she was born. If she's said to me once, she's told me one hundred times how her mama told her the story. They would both be dead without that mid-wifing of yours. She's not keen on slavery, but more than that she feels she owes us. I think she's doing it as much for her own peace of mind, as she is for us and her beliefs."

He reached into his pocket. "She got us this," he held out his hand and the brass rim of a compass glowed in the flicker of the tallow candle Israel had been writing by. "No matter if it's dark, no matter the weather, no matter if we can't find the North Star, we'll know exactly where we're going, and where we're going first is toward Lawrence, Kansas.

"I been reading on it. There's something in almost every paper, even if they is two months old. They all says you get to Lawrence, you're as good as free. It's the center of that Underground Railroad Liberty Line. I already know a couple places we can hole up. Mostly just a collection of people's homes and outbuildings owned by folks that believe in freedom, and that we are all equal. We'll go find one of them folks. They are all members of the Emigrant Aid Society. They is why Kansas is a Free Territory. There's a Dr. John Doorway, a Major James B. Abbott, and Reverend John Stewart, and others. They don't ask no questions, and they ain't scared of that Fugitive Slave Act. We will probably be sleeping outside a good bit of time before we make contact. Then we can hide out in places along the way, Darrell, Topeka, Holten, Hortun and Albany and then Nebraska. Not too many of us come up from the South. This all got established mostly cause of darkies from Missouri. These folks runnin' this trail they believe in the highest law, God's law."

"Though," he reached out both hands, covered hers and squeezed, "I won't soft-talk you, woman. Once we get to the Nebraska Territory we will be pretty much on our own. Most of our kind head north to Canada, not many to the Rockies. What I been reading says the Indians figure we are just as bad as the whites, so we won't get much help there. And once we are west of Kansas, there's no way to stop every white man that comes along and ask if they is a Jayhawker or a Bushwhacker. We'll be alone. It will be hard, and we mights not make it—but we just gots to try, Lucy, we gots to try. We owe it to God, each other, and to us."

Listening to her husband, Lucy found her anger at the shocking move-up in the date gone. She was still frightened, but it was hard not to catch his zeal, his determination. Maybe it could work after all. She raised one of his hands to her mouth and kissed it softly.

"I will get my belongin's together now, Israel, and you tell me anything else on that list I needs to bring. I don't know if we will make it or not—most likely we won't—but there's worse things than dying with the man I love." She raised her eyes to the ceiling of the shanty, "We shall place our trust in Him. His will shall be done."

Israel smiled softly, and returned the squeeze of her hand. "Amen."

———

ISRAEL TOOK A LAST LOOK AROUND THE HOVEL THAT HAD BEEN their only home for many years, and turned to Lucy, "Ready?"

Her hands tightened on his arm. The whites of her eyes were wide in the faint glow of the candle. Her voice was tremulous, "Oh Lordy...Yes."

There was a faint howl of wind through the exposed rafter tails on the exterior of the shack, and the night was opaque beyond the solitary window. Israel turned to the door.

"Wait, Israel!"

"What? What is it?"

"Let me blow out the candle."

Israel first felt incredulity at her worry over this detail, then he began to laugh. He leaned over and kissed her on the forehead. "Leave it burning, wife. We rarely snuff it out 'til about a few hours after dark. By the time that short piece of wax burns down it would be 'bout time to blow it out anyways. If we snuff it now, people's might wonder if somethin's wrong, and we don't wanna do nothing out of the ordinary..."

"'Cept become runaways," Lucy said almost inaudibly, her lower lip trembling.

Israel pulled her to him and hugged her. "We are runaways where we stand in this dirty shack they let us use." He pointed at the door, "Soon as we walk out that door and take one step, we be free men runnin' for our lives."

Israel pulled open the door a crack, then partially shut it, and turned back to her. "It's startin' to snow. Put on that gutta-percha. The good Lord is giving us perfect conditions."

He helped her on with the rain poncho. "Now grab your luggage," Israel grinned and pointed to the stick to which he had tied her canvas bag, "and that walkin' stick. I figure we can make Thompson's barn tonight. It's a ways off from the main house, and sits in the creek bottom. We need to be moving up that creek 'fore daylight and hope it's still snowin'!"

He looked Lucy up and down and then fixed his eyes on hers, "I feel like I'm fifteen again, wife. I want you to know one thing."

"Yes, Israel?"

"I love you as much now, as I did then." Israel opened the door and together, holding hands, they stepped out into the night.

April 25, 1855

*H*IDE OF THE TATANKA

EAGLE TALON SQUINTED INTO THE RISING SUN AS HE SURVEYED THE long, straggling line of women, children, dogs, horses, and mounted braves. The grasses and earth were still wet from the melt of the wild snowstorm that had gnawed the tribe with sharp winter teeth just two suns prior on the banks of Lodge Pole Creek, yet the endless undulations of the prairie already showed hints of spring green as the thirsty roots, soaked up the unexpected windfall of moisture.

The drifted remnants of the tempest lingered in deep hollows and on the lee sides of ridges, where the pummeling winds had swept the onslaught of flakes. The tribe lost several horses in the holocaust of weather. Those not staked near the tipis had sought shelter in the coulees, the bodies of some were found when the storm broke; small patches of red, brown, or mottled hair visible above the snow mounded around them. The rib cages had blown clear, like grave markers carved by the hands of the Great Spirit.

They did not get an early start on the first day of their post-storm move, as they had been unable to strike the tipis until the morning frost had evaporated from the hides. Once the lodge poles were lowered and the hides rolled, the travois could be latched and the packing begun. At the head of the column, Eagle Talon saw the frail shoulders of Flying Arrow sway uncertainly with the gait of the big, dark sorrel he rode, a gift to him from the soldiers of the Great White Father far to the east. The old chief's lance pointed proudly toward the sky.

Beside him, but one respectful pace behind, rode Tracks on Rock, his broad, bronze shoulders accentuated by the bright colors of his beaded vest. The two tribal leaders each wore several feathers in their hair. Eagle Talon smiled as he pictured their ornate war and ceremonial headdresses, carefully packed away in rawhide parfleches. Flying Arrow's had trails of feathers that hung to his thighs when he was mounted. The strings of feathers on the heavy buffalo horn headdress of Tracks on Rock were almost as long. Two ermine skins hung beneath the horns, accenting the medicine man's long, black hair. Eagle Talon unconsciously smoothed the eight eagle feathers that hung downward from the side of his hair, fastened to one braid with a round, flat section of elk antler painted by Walks with Moon. *I need many more coups*, he thought to himself with a sigh.

Behind Flying Arrow and Tracks on Rock rode the lesser chiefs and members of the Council. Following them was the long irregular line of women and children, and horses dragging travois, two shorter poles crossed and latched with rawhide at the horse's withers, then loaded with the family's possessions—rolled or folded tipis, parfleches filled with ceremonial items, food, utensils, and clothing. The heavier lodge poles, sometimes as many as twenty, were strapped to the family's extra horses and balanced equally on each side.

Eagle Talon looked toward Walks with Moon, who rode distant but parallel with him, her horse dragging their travois, her right hand holding the lead rope of another horse laden with their lodge poles. His other fourteen horses, mostly mustangs, spread in a trailing tether behind. One of the few women mounted in the band, Walks with Moon's smile was radiant as she nodded at him. Eagle Talon was fully aware this was a subject of tongue-wagging by some of the older women, but he didn't care. The horse she rode had been stolen from the Crows, and with more horses than all the other braves but one, his wife was not going to walk, particularly when with child.

Pony Hoof was horseback also, her two-week-old papoose swaddled in skins and wrapped in a cradleboard hanging from the saddle.

He watched Walks with Moon as she rode, her pelvis rocking slightly back and forth as the mustang paced in stride beneath her. The easy movement of her hips, and the tightening of the leather over her legs, stirred him. *We shall have to have a late supper again tonight,* he thought with a smile.

His eyes looked out beyond the moving throng of the tribe into the vast emptiness that seemed to swallow them. A goshawk hovered, almost stationary, wings a blur, then dove. *Enjoy your breakfast, my friend.* Eagle Talon smiled at the good omen. Far out in the gently contoured landscape, the occasional figure of a warrior could be seen dipping then emerging again, only to disappear in the next small draw. The near-guard. There were eight braves surrounding the tribe, riding three arrow-flights away. He looked further toward the horizon. Ten more warriors were out there somewhere, at least a half-sun's ride away at full gallop, like a great, extended, protective phalanx all around, behind, and in front of the moving village. Two parties of two braves each were far ahead of them, perhaps several suns' ride ahead, entrusted with locating potential danger and searching for the great beasts that the tribe depended on—meat, fat, bones for tools, hides for clothes, lodges, rawhide and leather, robes for bedding, horns for spoons, and carrying the fire—all these things the tatankas provided.

The Council had been meeting each night, and some concern was beginning to be expressed about the lack of buffalo. Tracks on Rock and Flying Arrow were unperturbed, or seemed so. Each meeting had ended like the last, with the pronouncement by Tracks on Rock, "When the sun rises, we shall move toward it."

They had only one brush with danger thus far. Just prior to the storm, one of the outlying scouts from the south had ridden into camp being hastily set up in the half-light of dust. "Flying Arrow, a large Crow village, with many warriors, is on the move south of us, also heading toward where the sun rises." A council meeting had been called, and, with the older women nodding approval, it had been decided that they would change their course slightly northward, in the direction of the Flat River, the flowing body of water the white eyes called the Platte. To avoid a confrontation with this larger group of long-time adversaries was a wise thing.

The sun was in the middle of its arc across the sky and the air noticeably warmer, when he saw Flying Arrow, far ahead, raise his gnarled hand. The tribe stopped, and children, freed from the drudgery of the march, began to shout and run, playing games. Women up and down the line hurriedly took out gourds. Walks with Moon and a few other women extracted tin pots or other white man's utensils gained in trading. Dried chunks of the dwindling supply of buffalo meat were carefully cut, then ground and softened by the women's energetic grinding with stone or bone pestles. Others merely ate pemmican, mixed with fat and stored in rawhide storage pouches. Several of the better cooks, including Walks with Moon, added spices they had gathered and dried before winter camp. Sage, wild onions, turnip, and rosemary, along with water, were mixed with the tenderized meat. The men, still mounted, were fed first. Here and there they grouped as they ate, talking across their ponies, gesturing, and nodding their heads.

Eagle Talon watched Walks with Moon stroll toward him, her movement lithe and seductive, even without exaggeration. She proudly reached up one of her tin pots to him with both hands, grinning up at him, "I'm not hungry, husband. Please eat it all."

He leaned closer to her and whispered suggestively, "Perhaps supper can wait for a while after we have the lodge fire going tonight." He was pleased at the way Walks with Moon's face lit up.

Glancing into the pot, he was surprised to see only a small portion of the cold, makeshift mix, the bit of buffalo meat punctuated with silver-green slivers of wild scallions and turnip. He was suddenly concerned. "Walks with Moon, there is not enough here for both of us."

"I am not hungry, husband, really."

Eagle Talon felt his brow crease, "Tell me, woman, are we low on supplies?"

Walks with Moon glanced down at her moccasins and then up into his eyes, "Yes, husband, we are—but really, I am not hungry."

Eagle Talon shook his head. "You are with child. Our child. You must eat." He handed the tin to her.

She reached up her hand and rested it on his knee, "I did not want to worry you, husband, and remember you spent three nights on outer guard. Tree Dove tells me that Tortoise Shell and Hard Hooves come back in from the east tomorrow at sunrise," she bit her lip, a look of anxiety flitting across her face, "and you go out to the advance scouts for three suns."

"This afternoon I shall ride out. Even rabbit meat will quiet the gnawing hunger," he sighed. "It is too early for snakes. I am concerned, wife. It is not often The People go this long without finding the herds of our great brothers. The entire village has only killed two deer since before the snow, and I've not heard of anyone who has seen antelope."

"I know, Eagle Talon. We women always find time to talk," she laughed, but without any humor. "But news travels fast, like smoke on a windy day. The big winter has forced the animals far south, and the great snow of two suns ago did not help. But to turn south? There is the danger of Pawnee or Crow." Looking ill at ease, she again cast her eyes upon her moccasins. "Yet turning north brings us closer to the main wagon trails of the hairy-faced ones."

Eagle Talon looked over her head out to the prairie. "This is our land, our world. It is the home of The People. It will remain so. I do not see why we should alter our course for others," he swept his shield arm fiercely in a broad semi-circle and looked back at her. "It is the land of The People," he repeated.

There were sudden shouts from the head of the column, and they both looked forward, Walks with Moon standing on her tiptoes to see better. To the southeast, a rider could be seen, still very distant, but coming at full gallop. *There is news!* thought Eagle Talon.

Eagle Talon handed the pot, which Walks with Moon had again placed in his hands during their discussion, back to his wife. "Eat, woman," he said in a serious tone. Then he smiled, "You will need your strength tonight." Walks with Moon smiled softly back at him and nodded, before directing anxious eyes toward the growing commotion near her father and Flying Arrow.

Eagle Talon dug his heels into the side of the mustang with a loud whoop, and the horse lunged ahead at full gallop to the head of the column. He reached the group of braves and lesser chiefs that had gathered around Flying Arrow and Tracks on Rock. The scout, Three Knives, well-known for his excellent eyesight and sense of smell, held his musket in one hand and pointed excitedly behind him to the southeast with the other.

As Eagle Talon rode up, along with several other braves coming from different directions, he heard scattered words, "Soldiers... tatankas...war party...Pawnee..."

Flying Arrow spoke. "How many soldiers?"

"Twenty-four."

The musket Three Knives held was one of only three rifles in the tribe, an old 1841 weapon named after the Father of Rivers rumored to lie far east. None of them had ever seen this mighty water, and no one could pronounce the name. Three Knives had traded several good horses for the musket six winters ago.

Eagle Talon chuckled to himself, though he kept his face serious. He remembered when Three Knives first shot the musket after the French trapper had taught him how to load it. There had been a huge roar, a belch of smoke, and the kick of the weapon had sent the barrel flying up into the air. The hammer and breech struck Three Knives in the forehead, knocking him backward to the ground, bleeding, much to the shouted amusement of the onlookers, which was most of the tribe. Since then, however, Three Knives had learned how to expertly use the weapon, and Eagle Talon had seen him kill antelope at least three times further than he could shoot an arrow, even in an arc.

His focus returned to Flying Arrow's voice, "So, the soldiers are headed east and north, also to the Flat River and the white man's fort they call Kearney?"

The scout nodded his head vigorously. "And the war party—how many men?" the chief inquired.

"I did not have a chance to count, I almost rode into them. They were very close. I was lucky to escape. Maybe fifty."

Flying Arrow and Tracks on Rock exchanged quick, startled glances. "That is many warriors. How big is the village?"

"I would say at least one hundred lodges."

"Any sign of white wagons?"

"There's tracks that indicates a group of wagons passed before the snow. But I think they're more than halfway to the fort along the River of the Laramie."

Flying Arrow's expression remained stoic. "At least one piece of good news. How many tatanka?"

Three Knives shook his head. "Not many. Perhaps one hundred and fifty. Perhaps a few more." He shook his head. "The Pawnee will surely intercept them. They are several suns closer than we," he added sadly.

Tracks on Rock nodded. "That is not enough tatanka for two villages. We would wind up with bloodshed and no meat."

The group fell respectfully silent as Flying Arrow and Tracks on Rock discussed the situation, occasionally asking opinions from other members of the Council, and glancing at their wives who huddled in a group just beyond the circle of horses, watching and listening intently. Talks with Shadows had worked her way up to the edge of the men's horses.

Finally Flying Arrow held up his hand, and the murmur subsided. He nodded to Tracks on Rock to speak. "We shall continue east and slightly north. The Pawnee will be delayed by the small herd of tatankas and will lose several suns. We shall get head of them, and, hopefully, the next, larger herd will be ours. We will double the forward scouts and increase the speed at which we move. I think, also, that Three Knives should shadow the Pawnee war party. Their scouts are maybe several suns ahead of ours. Perhaps they've seen something," he paused, "and I think we should avoid them. Now is the time for food and hides," he nodded back up toward the women and children. "The People can always fight the Pawnee another day."

Men nodded around the loose circle of horses. Tracks on Rock looked over at his wife, the slight assenting shift of her head barely visible to anyone but him before she turned away.

Eagle Talon craned behind him looking for Walks with Moon. She stood with their horses, her hand shading her eyes trying to see what was happening. *I shall tell her everything.*

He realized Flying Arrow had called his name and turned quickly to the war chief. "Yes?"

"You shall accompany Three Knives. We need our two best warriors to shadow the Pawnee. You will leave as soon as Three Knives has eaten." Flying Arrow's gaze lifted past him, and Eagle Talon knew the great warrior was looking at Walks with Moon further back in the strung out line of the tribe. "I cannot guarantee we can relieve you in three suns. You must follow the Pawnee until we do."

April 25, 1855

*T*HREAD THE NEEDLE

"BISCUIT?" THE WORD WAS BARELY MORE THAN A WHISPER.

Black Feather knelt down, keeping his voice low and level. "Didn't quite hear you, Dot, that fire is too loud." Black Feather motioned to the blaze of buffalo chips, crackling in the small, makeshift stone fireplace on the other side of the one-room ramshackle cabin.

"Biscuit," she said more loudly, her wide blue eyes staring up at him through stringy, matted, blond hair.

No life in them yet, Black Feather thought. "Oh, you want a biscuit?"

Dot nodded her head with the peculiar slow jerk Black Feather had noticed after the first week on the trail. She had filled out a bit over the last four weeks as they rode slowly northeast, and her face had tanned, the deathly pallor of the few days following the ambush of her parents all but gone.

Occasionally, she spoke a few words, but only to Black Feather. She cowered from the other men. Black Feather had caught several of them, when they thought his back was turned, making obscene gestures toward her. Hank's arm was in a makeshift sling, the result of Black Feather shoving him savagely into a cottonwood tree. And Chief was hobbling, the caked bloodstain around the gash in his trousers finally dried.

A few days after Dot had spoken her first words, *water* and *please*, Black Feather returned from a quick ride to the advanced scout five or six miles ahead of the band of outlaws, and found Chief standing in front of the lean-to Black Feather had insisted the men erect for Dot. The outlaw stood, pants pulled down, hairy buttocks exposed, fondling himself in front of the young woman. Without a word, Black Feather crept up behind him and plunged his knife into Chief's leg. Caught unaware, the crude renegade collapsed and writhed in pain. Black Feather grabbed the convulsing man's penis, now flaccid, and raised his knife. Only the outlaw's pleading and blubbering promises to never again go near the girl had saved him.

After that incident, the men cleared a wide berth around Dot, most of them trying hard to resist the temptation to even look her direction. But the brutal scene had pushed her back into her shell. Unless they were traveling and she was lashed to Black Feather atop his stallion, she had lay curled in a fetal position, her hands over her face.

Gradually, she had emerged from that shock, but there remained a vacant, cornered animal look in her eyes. Her words to Black Feather were sparse, never a full sentence. "Water, please," or "hungry" or "tired" or, like now, "biscuit."

He gazed down at her. "I'll be right back." Her sudden look of alarm was unmistakable. He knelt down again, "I'm just going to get your biscuit. I'll be right back. None of them...," he jerked his head toward the single window in the cabin, framing some of the band gathered outside, "have bothered you lately, have they?"

She shook her head "no" with that same stiff motion.

"And they won't. I won't let them." Black Feather resisted the urge to reach out his hand and place it on her knee. "I will not let anybody hurt you. One of these days you'll feel better," he swung his arm around. "This is big, beautiful country." He raised a hand toward the roof of the one-room cabin, "and the sun is shining. The air is clean after that big snow a day ago," he made an exaggerated inhaling motion and sound. "Try it. Breathe in deep. Smell that good air."

Dot blinked and then took a deep breath, and held it, before gradually exhaling. Black Feather chuckled, "See, when Black Feather tells you something, you can trust it. Just like that the air smelled good, nobody's ever going to hurt you. Now, I will be back with that biscuit."

He stood and strode toward the door, pausing to speak to Pedro in Spanish. "Watch over her." He began to open the door but swung back to his portly lieutenant. Lowering his voice, he said, "Tell three men to get those two bodies out of the barn. Bury them behind it. I don't want to take a chance on her seeing them."

Outside, he walked over to a few of the men gathered outside by the fire. "Throw me two of those biscuits we got outta that wagon on the Poudre."

Snake looked up, glanced at the cabin, started to say something, then obviously thought better of it. He tossed two biscuits to Black Feather. "When we gonna have some fun, boss? It's been four weeks since the Poudre and two since we knocked over that east-bound stage. That banker's wife was good for laughs but only for a few days. I think she particularly liked Tex."

The men all laughed raucously and turned their heads to look at Tex, a stocky, bald, round-faced man with a scar on his neck who had joined the band, along with others, shortly after they crossed the South Platte several weeks prior. "I shave my head," he had told the renegades, "so as the Indians won't be so apt to scalp me." It wasn't an original line, but still a good excuse for sordid laughter.

He had his horse's foreleg between his knees now, busy scraping stubborn clay dirt, still wet from snow melt, off the shoe. Listening to the others, he took one more careful scrape with his knife before he lowered the horse's hoof, patted the medium-sized bay on the shoulder, and turned to the group of twisted smiles around him.

"Yep, I reckon she was mighty juicy," his Texas drawl elongating almost every word. "When she stopped moving, it surely weren't no more fun." He grinned, his yellow teeth behind thick lips accented by a gaping black space, held up his knife and rotated the blade so that it caught the sun. He chuckled, "So I had to make her juicy again." The men laughed.

"Well, it was a damn good thing you were out front and found this cabin before that storm hit," said Black Feather. "Some of us woulda been done for sure out there in the flats without shelter. And good thinking, taking care of those settlers the way you did before we got here. Saved the girl from seeing it."

Tex grinned again, held up the knife, repeated the rotating motion and nodded at the small cabin. "Yep, it surely was a shame them settlers weren't more hospitable." He grimaced grotesquely and stuck his tongue against his top teeth so that a portion of rough flesh bulged through the space of the missing tooth.

Snake and Chief clapped him on the back. "Well, you made 'em hospitable, Tex. Never met more hospitable folks. When did you get so mean?" they joked. Tex's gruesome smile disappeared suddenly. He turned and stroked his bay. "Ever since my pa killed my ma," he said quietly.

Black Feather said nothing and began to walk inside the cabin, but Snake, though momentarily taken aback by Tex's abrupt mood change, was persistent, "Boss, when you suppose..." The question hung in the air, unfinished.

Their leader turned slowly and focused his eyes on the thin, wiry man. The group fell silent. "You men have never figured it out. It's like anything in life. Pigs are fat and happy and hogs get slaughtered. Why do you think we ain't been caught, killed, or even shot at, except we make the first move?"

The men glanced at one another uneasily, several of them looking down, scooping the toes of their boots at the sodden ground.

"That was a big take we made back on the Cache la Poudre. Enough food for several months, powder, ammunition, clothes," he reached out and tugged on the fine grey wool shirt worn by Chief, "some money, and those scalps will bring a good price. We did okay with the stage, too. That was just luck. Been seein' them coaches since in 1850. These damn fools thought they could make the run from Laramie to Independence without an escort." He shook his head disgustedly.

"When we strike, you know we always do it fast, then ride hard and long. You don't think what we leave behind goes unnoticed, do you? Why do you think I make sure we try and leave no sign, or tell-tale marks? About half the time, whoever finds our handiwork don't know it's us, and we're two hundred miles away by then anyway. Hard riding ghosts are tough to find and moving targets is almost impossible to hit."

Black Feather could sense the men were not satisfied. "González tells me there's big bunch of Pawnee on the move ahead of us, maybe two days. We're probably right behind their rear guard. I imagine they were slowed by the snow, as well. I'll tell you boys the plans just this once, then don't ask me again."

Black Feather narrowed his eyes. Snake looked down to the ground. "Gonna be wagons 'bout this time every year headed in some way, shape or form toward the Platte and Fort Childs...."

González broke in with a thick accent, "You mean Fort Kearney. They changed the name a few years back to Kearney." Black Feather threw a hard look at the Mexican, who fell silent.

"González is right. I forgot. It's been a while since I've been this far east. We are about two days ride from Fort Kearney. As I recall, they don't have many soldiers there usually, four companies at the most. They like to keep it guarded by two, sometimes three companies, that means there are only a hundred or so soldiers patrolling this whole area. They will stick pretty much close to the river and the main Mormon and Oregon tracks. First, we will try and find out where them patrols is. Second, we'll skirt the fort by a fair distance south—at least a day's ride—thread the needle between the Cavalry and Pawnee and head toward the Little Blue and Seward Rivers southeast of Kearney. Them larger trains usually stick to the bigger tracks, but some years back I had picked off some smaller groups trying to cut off that big north bend of the river before it links up with the Missouri."

Heads nodded, and the ruffians listened attentively.

"There's thirty-one of us now. That's the most ever. Depending on how many families are traveling in the smaller trains, I figure thirty-one of us could easy take on forty or more of them. A third of them are farmers and never killed nothin' in their life except a deer, and a third can't speak English or come from a big city and don't know the ass end of a gun."

Black Feather held his head high as he listened to himself spell out the plan. "Have some patience, boys, it'll be well worth it. Think about how much we took off those four wagons on the Poudre, and those six Mormon wagons west of Laramie last year. Now, think about thirty or forty rigs."

His eyes moved from one man to the other. "And, think about how many women might be on a train that size." The men grinned and the approving murmur was growing behind him as he went back to the cabin with the biscuits, one for Dot, and one for himself.

May 3, 1855

$\mathcal{T}$HE GIFT

REUBEN ADJUSTED THE LEATHER BUCKLE STRAP FROM WHICH HIS lariat hung, and then sat comfortably hunched over in the saddle, pencil in one hand, paper in the other. The saddle horn was both a writing surface and support for his crossed forearms. Mac had asked him to assess each wagon for signs of loosening spokes or failing metal tire rims around the wagon wheels. He had gladly accepted the chore, thankful for the excuse to remove himself from Inga's tearful outbreaks, Johannes' uncharacteristic strong silence, and Rebecca's incessant baleful glares each time—and there had been many—that she had put her arms around Inga's shoulders, gently comforting her. Even Sarah was without her usual smile when their paths crossed. *I might as well have brought the storm inside the wagon by allowing Jacob to join us*, he thought ruefully.

Sighing, Reuben forced himself to focus on the task. "The air is going to get drier and drier almost every day now," Mac had told him that morning. "As wagon wheels lose moisture they shrink, even those New Hampshire ones of white oak, and the trail only gets rougher from here. We're gonna have to stop every week or so, get that forge out of the second supply wagon, and refit tires and spokes, or we will start losing wheels."

Mac had stood, grim-faced, from his squatted stance by the morning fire, taken a last gulp of coffee from his tin cup, and thrown the rest into the embers. "I reckon we only have three days at most to Fort Kearney, and it would sure be good if all the rigs could make it that far so we don't have to stop. The damn mud of the past few days wasn't helpful. We can't wait for no crippled wagon. Best to prevent something bad before it occurs. Get to the front of the column and watch each wagon as it goes by. Then repeat that on the other side. Pay careful attention to the wheels—spokes you see loose, any snapping, popping or loose-fitting tires. Be mindful of spokes rattling, or grinding or squeaking. Next water is where we hit the Platte downstream of the fort, so we can't even soak the wheels for a temporary fix 'til then."

As the wagons rumbled by, their canvas tops rolling left and right with the uneven ground, Reuben smiled and nodded at each driver. He and Johannes exchanged cautious glances, but neither of the women sharing the driver's seat looked his direction. Rebecca, who sat stiffly in the middle, had become a silent buffer between the two tall blondes. Reuben was dismayed that Rebecca seemed to avoid him, especially after all that had transpired that day they had ridden together. *The day before the storm. Or storms,* he thought glumly.

Reuben shook his head to clear it and get back to business. He knew Mac was depending on him, and he didn't want to miss something crucial. He stared ahead as the line continued its slow trek.

Preacher Walling crossed himself, making the sign of a crucifix as he and his family passed, and Reuben mouthed a "thank-you," at the same time wondering what his father, Ludwig's, reaction would've been. He glanced quickly back at his wool coat, triple lashed behind the saddle, and patted it. *Don't worry, father—all is well—I will claim our land.*

Jacob and Sarah's wagon rattled by. The redhead's face was reserved as she directed a long and lingering look toward him. Jacob stared straight ahead, his countenance set in a dark scowl, his beefy frame tipped forward over the lines, not acknowledging Reuben's existence. Dr. and Mrs. Leonard plodded by, their Conestoga pulled by four troublesome oxen, one of them moving with a pronounced limp in the rear hip. The doctor's shoulders shook, and he convulsed with frequent coughing that was audible three or four wagons up or down the line. His face was pale and drawn, and Thelma wore a worried expression as she patted him on the back.

The last of the wagons moved slowly past him, flying the Johnson's heirloom American flag with the circular pattern of thirteen stars. Both Margaret and Harris beamed at him as they came abreast of Lahn, their plump hands raised in greeting. Becky and Eleanor poked their young, round faces out the rear of the wagon canvas, giggling. "Are you going to come over for dinner again and tell us more about Prussia, Mr. Frank?"

"Of course," hollered Reuben with a laugh. "I'll talk to your parents and decide which night." The youngsters shrilled, clapped their pudgy hands, and ducked back into the wagon bed.

Reuben trotted to the front of the train then repeated the process on the other side, carefully noting which wagons, by the names of their owners, showed need of repair and maintenance. Margaret and Harris' Conestoga had just passed again when he heard hooves cantering up behind him. He turned in the saddle to see Zeb approaching, his features inscrutable as always, though his jaw was set with a slight scowl.

"Afternoon, Reuben."

Reuben nodded. "How are you, Zeb?"

"From here on in things might go downhill," replied the frontiersman. He looked beyond Reuben. "For the last few days I've seen occasional dust to the southwest of us. Been keeping my eyes out and haven't seen nothing, but I'm suspicious that it's been the same direction and seems to move with the train. I aim to go have me a look-see. Be obliged if you'd let Mac know."

Wheeling Lahn around, Reuben studied the vast lands to the southwest. Shallow hills fondled the bases of low-lying, rocky rose and brown buttes. Stands of budding trees and brush worked their ways up the intermittent valleys. The vegetation lines were slightly higher on the northern aspect of the contours. The sun reflected dully off scattered patches of pale green, struggling spring grass valiantly trying to push its way through the still matted, brown, dry cover of winter. Here and there, patches of snowdrifts lingered where the ground remained shady, their brightness subdued by the gritty cloak of blown sand and dirt. He searched the undulations of horizon where they met bright blue sky, but saw nothing.

He turned back to Zeb. "You sure? I don't see anything."

"I'm sure," said Zeb tersely. He spurred Buck, and the horse took off in an easy lope. Reuben noticed he drew the Sharps from its scabbard and held the rifle securely in his left hand.

Reuben cantered toward the head of the train. As he drew even with Sarah's wagon, he slowed and tugged his hat brim. "How is your day going, Sarah?"

Sarah looked up, startled, but she held his eyes and reddened. "Just fine, Reuben." Her tone was not enthusiastic. Jacob shot a quick sideways leer toward Reuben, leaned over the near side of the wagon seat, and spat, just missing Lahn's hoof, which seemed to be his favorite target.

"Careful now Jacob, this country is going to get drier and drier. You might need all the spit you've got." Jacob neither replied nor looked up, but Reuben could see his jaw clench under the bruises on his face. Sarah glanced from one man to the other with an alarmed look.

"Good day to you too, Miss Sarah." Reuben gently spurred Lahn up toward his original destination, passing his own wagon without checking his horse's stride. Mac was in his usual position, fifty yards in front and slightly to the left of the lead rig. Reuben noticed he had his Musketoon rifle out, perched sideways between the saddle horn and his hips. The wagon master's head swiveled carefully to different points in the horizon. Reuben reined in Lahn and fell in step at Mac's side.

"Zeb wanted me to tell you he has spotted dust along the horizon to the southwest the last few days. He headed out that way just now to see what it is."

Mac nodded. Without taking his eyes off the distant points he was keenly searching, he replied, "I seen it, too. We're getting into different country now. The land will be different, the trail more rugged, and the weather more extreme." He paused. Without turning to look at Reuben, he added, "And we're gonna have to start contending with others."

Reuben surveyed the rolling terrain and uneven skyline. "It doesn't look that crowded to me."

The older man grunted, "It only takes a few to raise hell. This ground dries quick. Slow-moving and dust-stirring as we are, they will find us."

Mac ran his dirty fingernails through the long red strands of his beard, thinking. "We should reach the main track of the Mormon Trail and the Platte well before nightfall. I think we will circle up there and get the rest of the mud off the wagons since we'll have water. That damn storm cost us four or five days. I see by your list there's four outfits that could use some work. The water will swell the oak, tighten the spokes, and firm up the tire rims—might be enough to get those rigs to Kearney. We can do the repairs there. Should work out just right."

"I'd like to help with the work on the wheels and tires," said Reuben. "That's a skill I want to learn."

Mac shook his head negatively, reached into his pocket, pulled out a piece of chew and bit off a huge brown chunk. He extended his arm to Reuben, still not taking his eyes from the distance. "Want some?"

"No, thanks. Then what do you want me to do tomorrow?"

"I aim to have you and Johannes, and the four best riflemen from this motley crew of pioneers, start riding a defensive perimeter for a quarter-mile around the train. And from here on, when we do stop to work on the rigs, it will be the same. With the forge going, and wheels off the wagons we will be sitting ducks. I suspect Johannes will know what to do."

The beginnings of a reply died in Reuben's throat. Far out he saw a vortex of dust, whirling across the land. It could only be a horse at full gallop.

Mac raised one arm. "Halt the wagons!" he yelled. The lead Conestoga jolted to a stop as did the other wagons, one by one, behind it. There was a perceptible buzz of puzzlement and fear moving up and down the train as the settlers tried to understand what had caused the sudden delay.

Reaching inside the lapel of his coat, Mac brought out the spyglass and extended the brass sections to full-length. "Be still you damn critter," he commanded Red, who was fidgeting from foot to foot. "It's Zeb, and he ain't wasting no time getting back. Don't see nothin' behind him, yet."

He brought the glass down to his lap, his great bushy eyebrows furrowed in contemplation. "Reuben, if I tell you, you skedaddle on down the train, tell folks to get out their rifles and gather in every other wagon. Get five men on horses and hurry back up here. Tell the men to bring extra ammunition and pistols if they have 'em. I'd choose Johannes, Charlie, John, Harris, and that son of a bitch Jacob. He is always looking for a scrap."

Minutes later, Zeb reined in from a full gallop, just feet from them. Buck's momentum and the west wind enveloped them in billows of dust.

"Thirty or so. Renegades or an outlaw bunch, I suspect. Been shadowing us for at least two days. I'm thinking they saw my dust. By now they already know how many men, women, and children we got. Most likely they will ease down here, check out how solid we are, and make their move later."

"Recognize any of 'em?" asked Mac.

"I recognized one." Zeb's cold tone caught Reuben's attention, and he looked at his friend closely. Zeb's face was impassive, but there was a slight twitch in the muscles in one of his cheeks.

Mac raised the spyglass. "Looks like you hit the nail on the head, Zeb." He turned to Reuben, "Get those men up here and get everyone doubled up. Now!"

"Should we put the wagons in a circle?" asked Reuben.

"No time. Anyways, they'll figure out we have more firepower. These types hoot like Indians, but they are mostly cowards. They prefer to do their work in the dark against folks that can't fight back. We will ride out, see what they want, and make sure they get their murdering heads around the truth that it would be best to not tangle with us."

Reuben quickly gave directions down the line of wagons. Within minutes, the five horsemen clustered around Mac. Reuben sensed nervousness in both men and horses, and he noticed Jacob wetting his lips continuously. The dust of approaching horses was now visible to the naked eye. Johannes had strapped on the 1840 saber Reuben had lent him the money to buy in New York, and wore a red sash knotted around his waist. He was carefully checking the load in his Sharps 1852 Slanting Breech Carbine, which he insisted was better than the Sharps rifle for mounted warfare. The handle of his .44-caliber Army Colt protruded from his belt.

"What is that?" asked Reuben, indicating the sash.

Johannes eyes sparkled, and he smiled, completely at ease, almost eager, Reuben realized. "That, my dear friend Reuben, is a battle sash. Some say it brings luck."

Without waiting for a reply, Johannes turned to Mac. "I suggest I take one rider, Charlie—he seems to be pretty good with a long gun—and we will ride out several hundred yards to the left to get on their right flank, dismount, and have the rifles at the ready."

Mac's teeth shown through the mat of red hair around his lips. "A crossfire if needed, eh? An old Cavalry tactic, I believe." He gave Johannes a knowing look, "Good idea. Go!"

Johannes gestured to Charlie, and they detached themselves from the group at a canter. Mac turned to the men around him, "You boys rest easy. Be absolutely ready—have those hammers cocked, but you don't do nothing—not even move a muscle unless I tell you, or lead starts flying. We're aiming to avoid a fight, not have one. These scum are most likely cold killer outlaws, but they don't wanna die anymore then we do." He glanced down at the Navy Squareback Colt and holster on Reuben's hip. "I would take the thong off that hammer, son."

He turned back to the men. "We're gonna ride real slow and easy. Don't bunch up. Stay at least ten to fifteen feet from the rider on either side of you. No sense making a compact target for a lucky shot. I suspect they will break into two bunches. A half-dozen or ten of them will get right close to see what we're made of. The rest of them will hold back." He chuckled. "We will see if they know any Cavalry and attach a couple of hombres to flank Johannes, but I suspect they won't." His yellow teeth flashed again in the jumble of beard. "Let's go."

Reuben slid his Sharps from its scabbard. Spread out in a line, the men from the wagons advanced at a walk toward the oncoming riders.

———◆———

AS MAC HAD SPECULATED, THE MAIN BODY OF THEIR ADVERSARIES stopped well out of rifle range. Their general features were still visible, however, and several were pointing at Johannes and Charlie, who had by now dismounted and were kneeling with rifles resting on one knee.

The two groups of riders maintained their steady approach toward each other. Reuben's mouth was dry, but not from fear. He felt an exhilarating rush of adrenaline. The colors of the day seemed sharper. The air had a special clarity. The immense rolling country radiated energy. Lahn felt it, too. The horse moved forward almost at a prance, ears pricked, nostrils flared. More than any other moment since disembarking from the *Edinburgh*, Reuben felt American.

"Looks like they want to get close," Mac called out in a low voice to the men on either side of him. He sheathed his Musketoon and pulled out his 1855 Colt Revolving shotgun, checking the loads in each magazine of the five-shot cylinder.

"Hold up," he commanded. "Let 'em come to us."

Reuben gripped Lahn's reins in his left hand and extended the fingers on his right. Steady, no shake, no twitch. He felt detached, a spectator rather than a participant.

The other riders, eleven of them, drew closer, also spread out ten to fifteen feet apart. Several had wool coats; others wore leathers, some just filthy shirts. A few had feathers embedded in braided hair. All had rifles or muskets, either held warily across a saddle pommel, or perched stock butt down on one thigh, muzzle in the air, finger on the trigger.

Astride a broad, grey horse, an equally stocky man sat, his round meaty shoulders wrapped in the once colorful stripes of a serape. He looked Spanish and rode to the left of the man who was obviously the leader. He had a tall, powerfully angular figure, with dark swarthy features that were not quite fully Indian. His long, dark brown hair hung in strings down his back, his heavy, faded, red wool shirt was visible under an open, blue army jacket, which Reuben realized with a start had a hole in its lapel framed by a dark reddish stain. A woman's necklace dangled around the half-breed's neck. His eyes were narrow, and there was a scar above his lips that formed a thin line above a jutting, square jaw. Two black feathers, fastened by a silver concho, dangled from his headband. Their tips hung to his shoulder. He radiated a dark energy, a sinister malevolence.

The renegades stopped their advance fifty feet away. The leader's horse, a black stallion as muscular as its rider, pawed the earth impatiently as his master's eyes roved over each and every one of Reuben's party. They lingered on Zeb. Both men almost imperceptibly shifted the muzzles of their rifles toward one another. The leader urged his horse forward a few steps. Mac did the same.

They stared at each other in silence. Finally, the man on the black horse spoke. "I count forty-one wagons. Are there more?"

Reuben was surprised at the man's excellent English. The outlaw's rifle was now pointed squarely at Mac, and the seasoned wagon master moved his shotgun to return the favor. Mac leaned over and spit out a wad of chew, never taking his eyes off the man. "I suspect so. Thousands. They just ain't here yet."

The outlaw's swarthy features showed no reaction, but his eyes shifted to Zeb. "Do I know you? I am called Black Feather."

Zeb's voice was even. "Don't believe we've ever met, though we've come close."

Black Feather returned his attention to Mac with a sly, contrived half-smile, "We are low on food. Perhaps you have some extra that you could spare?"

"Don't think so. We have barely enough ourselves."

The thin corners of Black Feather's mouth twitched. Without taking his eyes of Mac, he nodded his head back toward his band. "Hungry men can get desperate."

"Better desperate than dead," was Mac's gruff response.

"We see many women and children. That is a big responsibility for a wagon master to keep them safe." Even from twenty feet away, Reuben could see Mac's complexion reddening, and he well knew the wagon master had a quick temper. For whatever reason, Black Feather was intent on goading him. The others in the renegade group had now obviously each picked out one of the men from the wagon train on whom to focus.

There was another long silence. Reuben instinctively felt Black Feather sizing up the odds. This was not going to end peacefully. He knew he had to have his feet on the ground for what was to come. "I'm getting off my horse," he called out in a clear and nonchalant tone. Involuntarily, everyone's eyes clicked to rest on him.

Black Feather looked amused. "Parting with your horse is not wise in this country. He could disappear forever."

Reuben ignored the taunt. "I banged up my leg the other day. Need to stretch, and so you don't get jittery, I am going to slide this rifle back into the scabbard." Careful to keep his tone level, movements steady, and Lahn between him and the renegades, Reuben slowly dismounted. There were several incredulous murmurs from the horsemen behind Black Feather.

Reuben made a great show of stretching his legs, each effort moving him a bit further to the right.

"Steady, Lahn." The palomino followed him with his eyes, his reins hanging to the ground. When Reuben was satisfied with his position, he squared his shoulders and faced the opposing horsemen. The slightly left angle offered a clear line of fire toward Black Feather and the four nearest outlaws. He felt the weight of the Colt on his hip. His hands dangled loosely at his sides. "I have had my stretch. Maybe you fellas ought to go do what you need to do, and we will get back to the wagon train."

As Reuben had intended, Black Feather dismissed him as a simpleton. His swarthy face turned back to Zeb. "Why are you familiar to me?" The gaze between the two men was locked and unwavering. Zeb's was full of hatred and contempt.

"The Taylor Farm, Missouri Basin."

Black Feather's eyes momentarily widened before narrowing again. There was an ominous stillness, and, at that moment, John cocked the hammer of his musket, the click echoing across the barren earth and between the horses. Black Feather's riders were now swinging their rifles, and, from the corner of his eye, Reuben saw Mac's shotgun muzzle rise. There was a flash from Black Feather's rifle barrel. Zeb cursed and jerked sideways in the saddle, his Sharps discharging at the same time.

The Navy Squareback was suddenly in Reuben's hand, mechanical, practiced, perfect, without thought. He could feel himself crouching, the outside edge of his left palm working the hammer of the smoking pistol. A rider screamed and fell, and then another toppled. A third renegade began to swing his rifle in Reuben's direction. Reuben felt the Colt buck, and there was a sudden red hole in the man's forehead, his eyes looked blankly at the sky, his mustang reared back, and he fell silently backwards off the horse. Black Feather unleashed a blood-curdling scream, Mac's shotgun roared, then again, and another renegade crumpled over the neck of his horse, blood streaming down the brown sides of the saddle. Jacob's horse began to buck wildly out of control in a circle, the Irishman dropped his pistol and hung desperately to the saddle horn with both hands, shouting curses. John cried out and slid sideways off his horse, clutching his leg.

Reuben had not moved. The grip of the sidearm was an extension of his hand. He felt the barrel of the Colt swing like a rattlesnake tracking a rat. He fired again, and one of Black Feather's men clasped his stomach, groaned with pain and flopped over his horse's neck. Black Feather raised his rifle over his head and shouted. Almost in unison, the opposing band wheeled their horses and retreated at full gallop. Far to his left, Reuben heard the report from Johannes' Sharps Carbine. Yet another outlaw toppled from his saddle.

Coolly, Reuben rose to full height. If he had counted right, he had one bullet remaining in the six-cylinder Colt. Steadying his right hand with his left fingers wrapped around his wrist, he cocked the hammer, aimed high center at a fleeing leather-clad back, and squeezed the trigger. The man's arms flew in the air, dropping his rifle as he slumped forward on his horse.

Shifting the revolver to his left hand, Reuben held out his right. No trembling. Slowly and coolly, he took one shell at a time from his cartridge belt and slipped it into an empty magazine of the cylinder of the revolver. When the reloading was complete, he looked up. Mac had ridden over. With a twirl, Reuben slid the Colt back into its holster.

"I'll be damned and go to hell." There was a note of wonder in Mac's voice. The red-bearded man's eyes were wide. "Jesus. Do you realize what the hell you done? Johannes got one, I cut one bastard in half with the scattergun, and you shot five of those killers face to face and another when they were on the run. Damn, son, I had no idea you could handle a Colt like that!"

"Neither did I, Mac. Guess it's just practice and some natural gift."

Zeb rode up, a stain spreading from a red crease across the buckskin sleeve of his upper left arm.

"Son of a bitch almost kilt me." He gazed down at Reuben with a look the younger man couldn't quite fathom. Partly respect, partly surprise, partly concern.

"You have a way with that pistol, Reuben, young as you are. No doubt about it. Never seen nothin' like it." He gestured at the now distant dust of the renegades and swept his arm toward the other men from the wagon train. "You can't keep this quiet. Word will spread, sure enough. Biggest thing you're gonna have to do from now on is make sure that gift doesn't turn into a curse."

"Let's get back to the wagons," said Mac. "I'm sure everybody's anxious back there. We can clean up that scratch Zeb got, do some fixing on John's leg and get him in a wagon bed. Doubt we will be having more trouble from that bunch. They lost too much with nothing to show. Reuben was a surprise, and I don't think they will want to get in range of that Colt again." He looked up at the sun. "We got several hours of daylight left. I want to get to the river and get set up before dark. We have a hard day of work tomorrow, and then we can rest at the fort."

———————

JOHANNES AND CHARLIE RODE IN. CHARLIE REACHED OUT AND grabbed John's arm to steady him in his saddle. Johannes urged Bente over to Reuben and Lahn. There was quiet admiration in Johannes' voice. "That was some show. I could have used you in the line against the French at Selkirk." There was also some unusual quality to Johannes' tone, and Reuben looked at him closely.

"What?"

Johannes hesitated. "How do you feel?"

Reuben shrugged. "Fine. I am sorry John got shot."

"That's all?"

He could feel constant glances from the other men as they cantered back to the wagons. Reuben felt himself getting annoyed. He did not like being the center of attention, and it was not like Johannes to talk in riddles. "That's all," he responded curtly as they neared the lead wagon.

The tight resentful knot in Reuben's chest began to unwind at the sight of a slight, female figure with long, dark hair carrying a Sharps rifle two-thirds as long as she was tall. She stood with an anxious air ahead of the lead wagon far at the front of the rest of the gathering pioneers. One hand was on her forehead to cut the glare from the lowering sun as she intently surveyed the incoming riders.

May 3, 1855

$\mathcal{M}$ORMON WAGONS

BLUE SKY, WARM WEATHER, AND THE DISTANT CHEERFUL SPARKLES from the Platte River, appearing and disappearing through the trunks of cottonwoods as the wagons passed, did nothing to lift Johannes' spirits.

Occasionally, despite himself, he glanced over Rebecca's head at Inga. Sometimes she returned his stare with a beseeching look, sometimes her eyes were fixed on her fingers, which seemed interminably busy smoothing the fabric of her dress over her thighs. *She is either going to wear out that fabric or rub the skin off her hands.* He found no humor in the thought.

Rebecca would occasionally try to make some type of small talk— doing her best, Johannes was sure—to build a bridge across the frozen gulf that had separated him and Inga since that stormy night in the wagon. Inga would occasionally chime in, no doubt in hopes that Rebecca's attempts would begin the thaw. Several times Johannes felt the urge to speak, to take one hesitating step on the ladder of repair, but he didn't.

Inside his head, two voices waged combative argument. The square-jawed, egotistical voice of devil-may-care male screamed, *First woman I have ever loved, truly loved. First woman I ever truly trusted, and now this. To hell with it all!*

The other voice, that of the heart, humanity, and reality, argued back. *What are you so high and mighty about? You're not some chaste widower hoping to replace the only woman you've ever known with an equally virginal new mate. You are a scoundrel, whoring around. You can't even remember the names of the women you have been with. Now the one woman you are truly in love with, for the first time in your sorry drifting life, is to be discarded? On a principle that you, yourself, has never followed?*

Johannes sighed as the inner voices of his soul argued back and forth. *I was an officer and a gentleman—of sorts. I merely did what men do. My mistresses were all willing. Most of them made the initial advance. I promised nothing other than pleasurable times, whether for a night or a month. I made it clear to Inga that I had not been an angel prior to meeting her.*

The argument, invariably, would reverse itself. *Who are you kidding? You broke up several families with your self-centered lust. You knew some of those women fell in love with you, yet you tossed them aside as you would a discharged weapon on the field of battle. Sure, stroke yourself, pretend to be the 'not quite an angel.' But did you tell her everything? How many hearts have you broken? A hundred? Two hundred? Are you so presumptuous as to maintain that every word from your mouth, as you lured them to your bed, was the absolute truth and nothing but the truth? This woman loves you. You love her. Think of how long it has taken to find this. Think of the blessing bestowed upon you, despite your entirely undeserving existence up to this point. You are in search of a sense of self, of place, of heart. And you would sacrifice it on the altar of hypocritical ego? Shame on you!*

But dammit, she could've told me. If she had said something up front, I would've understood. Of all people, I would've understood.

He glanced over at Inga. Her cheeks twitched, and a tear dripped from her chin into her hands, still busy in her lap. His ambivalent heart wrenched, ego and testosterone driven one moment, heartfelt and empathetic the next. *Say nothing until you figure this out, Johannes.* The other voice asserted itself. *Say something, say a little, at least smile at her—ease her pain, and yours, as you weigh these facts and circumstances to find truth.*

He felt his jaw clench and his lips purse. *Say and do nothing as you ponder this.*

"Look," said Rebecca pointing at Charlie up ahead and casting a quick glance at both Johannes and Inga, pausing, he could tell, to see if there would be a response from either of them. "There must be some news. Charlie is stopping at all the wagons."

Finishing his short visits with the two wagons ahead of them, Charlie trotted over, wheeled his horse, and moved along with them. "Wagons up ahead. Twenty or so of them, stopped. Mac says we will take a break, trade news, see if they need any help, then continue on toward Kearney."

Johannes said nothing, nor did Inga.

"Thank you, Charlie," Rebecca nodded her head and smiled. Charlie pulled on the brim of his hat and trotted to the wagon behind them.

There were twenty-two wagons in the other train. Mac dispatched several outriders to keep watch and halted his group parallel to the other, their line of rigs overlapping the smaller one by nine or ten wagons on either end. One hundred feet of wide wagon ruts from the previous decade separated the two groups.

Johannes swiftly surveyed the situation. The people of the other wagons were waving and smiling, obviously excited to link up with kindred spirits headed west into the unknown. *Curious,* he thought. The men seemed to have clean clothes on, a few of them in black suits. Several of the older men had wide, round black hats that appeared particularly well cared for.

He turned to Rebecca, "Look at them. It is like they are dressed up for Sunday church."

Rebecca's head snapped, the surprise at the first words Johannes had spoken to her in four days evident in her expression. "Well, Mr. Svenson, perhaps that is because this is indeed, Sunday. I believe these people are some of the Mormons Mac spoke of. According to what little I've read in the London papers, they are very devout."

Johannes absorbed her words. "Makes sense." He set the wagon brake, tied off the lines, and took one quick look out at the endless expanse of prairie. He could see the dust of the riders Mac had sent out to sentry. He was about to turn to Rebecca and Inga—to ask if they needed assistance—but Inga had already clambered to the ground, and Rebecca was in the process of doing so.

He shrugged to himself and, curious, ambled over alone to the other wagons. A young, pretty girl smiled at him and flicked her eyelashes. He grinned at her mechanically, without passion, and tipped his hat.

On the other side of the wagons he was surprised to see a group of the darkly clothed travelers gathering. To his left, Inga and Rebecca had been joined by Sarah. *Damn sure the three prettiest women between St. Louis and Cherry Creek,* he thought. They were engaged in animated conversation and continuous smiles with a plump woman who wore a bonnet and dark dress similar to the others. All up and down the line, people congregated, exchanging small things, talking, and pointing this way and that, though usually their gestures were to the west. Mac and a man equally as broad, with an air of command, stood up by the lead wagon of the Mormon train engaged in earnest discussion and gesturing. Johannes grinned inwardly at the contrast between Mac—his wild red beard, worn wool clothes overtopped by a dirty crumpled felt—and the trim, black, almost dapper attire, and clean-shaven face of the other wagon master.

He felt a tug on his arm. A well-built man about his own age, with an unusually long, pointed nose and thin face, but a genuine smile, stood next to him. "I am Joseph. Welcome, brother, we are absolutely delighted to have company on this day of God." His tone was warm and sincere. "Though the Good Lord knows any day would be a fine day for company on this long trail. From where do you hail?"

Johannes began speaking, realizing quickly that Joseph was surprised by his heavy Scandinavian accent. "I am Johannes Svenson. I guess you could say we started across the ocean, at least some of us, and then New York, St. Louis, and now, here, in the middle of this great city," Johannes waved his arm, laughing.

"Perhaps one day there will be a city here, where we stand. I understand that there are settlers on the way to build houses and stake their claims down by Fort Kearney. We are part of the Exodus bound for Zion."

"Zion?" Johannes could not remember a place with that name on Reuben's maps.

"The Cache Valley, north of the Great Salt Lake. These wagons transport just three families. We are from many locations, but primarily Ohio and Illinois. We are Mormons." He looked at Johannes expectantly, seemingly half-braced for some negative reaction or derogatory comment.

Twenty-two wagons for just three families? Johannes felt his eyebrows raise. The memory of the unrest in his own country, the brewing bitterness among the German populace, many of them *Schleswig-Holsteinism* liberals who wanted independence, crossed his mind.

"Our wagon master told us a bit about you folks," he said. "Seems you are good people fleeing narrow minds and establishing a colony of similar souls, where you can find the unfettered freedom to believe as you please."

Joseph's facial muscles relaxed, a smile creased his lips, and a relieved look flashed across his eyes. "My father, Charles, is an elder. They have much stature in our church. Our wagon master is, too, and those other three men, one of them being my wife's father...," he pointed to the heavier set, more dowdy of the now two women talking with Rebecca, Inga, and Sarah, "are also elders. They make many of our decisions. In many ways, our life is our religion, and our religion is our life."

"It is good for the soul to have a cause," said Johannes raising his hand to Joseph's shoulder. "In many ways I envy you."

Joseph smiled, "It's a shame you weren't here yesterday. My little sister got married." He pointed out a cute, very young girl, her arms draped around the arm of a tall, gangly, dark-clad lad. *They can't be more than fifteen.* She was glowing, a huge smile seemingly pasted on her face, and he noticed the boy constantly reached up one hand and patted hers where it wound around his arm. The two stood side by side, their legs touching, joined, and now apparently inseparable.

Johannes felt a strange twinge of sadness and took a deep breath. Averting Joseph's gaze, his eyes fell upon Rebecca, whose stare was also riveted on the young couple. *Joseph's wife must have told Rebecca the news.* Rebecca was smiling, but her face also wore a soft, pensive look. He realized the Mormon was speaking to him.

"I'm sorry, Joseph, would you say that again?"

"I was asking if you would like to join us for services. They begin in a few minutes. They won't be long, and I'm sure the elders would not mind, given these unusual circumstances," he lifted his hands and twirled them around indicating the nothingness surrounding the lines of wagons. "Normally we do not allow non-Mormons to enter the Temple, although we are pleased to have them, and they are most welcome at events outside the Holy Tabernacle."

"I'm not sure I've been to church of any type since my mother used to haul me down there on Sundays before she died. I was young, and I always protested. My father was military. Once in a great while, he and I might have had an unplanned meeting with someone of religious persuasion, but I can't remember when the last time was. Are you sure you wouldn't mind if I stand and listen?"

Jospeh shook his head, "Absolutely not, brother Johannes, absolutely not. I am delighted, and I'm sure the elders will be, as well. Anyone in your train is welcome to listen. We all share the same God, no matter what some may call him, and he holds all of us in his equal love." There was an angelic glow lighting the man's face. *Serious. I'll be damned. Good for him.*

The rest of the Mormons were now gathering in a circle. In the center were several of the elders, one with two thick, open books. A number of the people from Mac's train had joined those gathered. Some looked thirsty for a church-like ceremony, which they missed, others curious. All the men in the crowd took off their hats, and Johannes hurriedly mimicked them, with the instant flash of a dim memory of his mother's face smiling sweetly at him as he stood behind the polished pew in the Church of Our Lady in Copenhagen, *"Johannes, honey, remember—always take off your hat in church."*

He noticed Rebecca and Reuben leaning against a wagon, perhaps one hundred feet away. Their attention was on the group, but they did not join. Reuben had taken off his hat. Occasionally they would begin talking. Johannes could tell by the way they were moving their hands that there was some disagreement between them. Rebecca stomped her foot, and they lapsed back to silence for a few minutes and focused on the gathering group of worshipers. Then they resumed their discussion, and their arms started gesturing again, Rebecca's rather emphatically. *Doesn't look like Reuben's getting the best of whatever's going on,* Johannes chortled to himself.

He felt an inner surge when his eyes fixed on Inga on the opposite side of the crowd. Even from a distance, he could see her face was sad and drawn. Again, he felt that wrench in his heart. The elders gave the invocation, and they began reading from the book. Joseph had been joined by his wife who nodded and smiled at Johannes. The couple stood next to him, Joseph's wife holding the hand of their very young son. Joseph whispered in his ear, "Our church is also called the Church of Jesus Christ of Latter-Day Saints. We use the King James Version of the Bible. The other book is the Book of Mormon. It is an important adjunct to the Bible."

The elder stopped reading, looked up, and surveyed the crowd with a serious, but kind, look. "Today, we will talk about forgiveness, how our Lord, Jesus Christ, forgives us, and how and why we should forgive others so that we may bring happiness to ourselves and to the world." Johannes started, and knew his eyebrows were arched. He looked up at the sky. *What are the chances? What is that phrase Reuben always uses—oh yes—there are no coincidences.* He redirected his attention to the Mormon elder and listened attentively.

The elder's words were powerful, his voice strong, and Johannes knew half-way through the sermon which of the warring voices within him would win.

The service concluded. He saw Mac shaking hands with his counterpart, and then heard him shout, "All you folks in the red-bearded Irishman's wagon train, let's get back to your wagons. We have places to go, people to meet, and things to do."

A murmur of voices all around filled the air as people said goodbyes with smiles, handshakes, and hugs to their new friends. *Whom they are likely to never see again in this life. Threads meeting, then diverging,* the thought flashed through Johannes' mind, *but then again, who really knows?*

Joseph shook his hand warmly, and his wife smiled and nodded, her smile growing wider when Johannes swept off his hat, bent from the waist, and kissed her hand. "If you ever get out to the Cache Valley, which is supposed to be very pretty, please, Johannes, you be sure to stop by and visit."

"Won't we see you at Fort Kearney?"

"Perhaps, though we do not travel on Sundays, and the elders have determined we will halt only long enough to pick up a Dragoon Escort. They call them Cavalry now. Our wagons have only three families, so we are small enough to qualify."

Johannes smiled. "Not sure I will make it that far west, Joseph, but you can count on me stopping by and saying hello if I do. Who knows? Does the danger warrant a Cavalry escort?"

Joseph's eyes widened. "You have not heard of the Grattan Massacre?"

Johannes' interest was piqued. "No, tell me."

Joseph sighed. "A very sad example of men's lack of understanding of other men. A Mormon wagon train on the Oregon Trail passed through Fort Laramie last summer, less than a year ago, in August. One of their cows strayed. An Indian staying at a nearby Sioux camp, they say his name was High Forehead, happened upon the cow and killed it to feed his family. The Sioux sent a representative to the fort to settle the matter. The commander in charge wanted to ignore the incident, but his next in command, Lt. John Grattan, a young West Point graduate with delusions of grandeur, wanted to arrest the Indian. The next day, indulging in drink, the foolish Lieutenant took twenty-nine soldiers, two cannons, and an interpreter to the village. They were intoxicated by the time they reached the encampment— an encampment with over five thousand Indians, I might add!" Joseph raised his arm, extending his hand and spreading his fingers wide.

"The young lieutenant demanded that the Sioux turn over High Forehead. The interpreter called the warriors "women" and other slurs. The chief, Conquering Bear, his warriors surrounding Grattan and his men, offered to give the emigrants a horse or another cow as a replacement. A frightened soldier raised his weapon and shot a warrior." Joseph looked down, shaking his head.

"All of the soldiers—Grattan, the interpreter, and the chief, who was shot in the back—were killed."

Joseph shook his head sadly. "The tension along the trails is even greater now. But are we not all God's children?"

Johannes began the walk back to their wagon, mulling over this new information, his awareness of the dangers they faced heightened. He spotted Inga moving slowly in the same direction, looking dejected, her head slightly bowed. He went to her. She looked up into his face, her eyes widening with a mixture of doubt, joy, and trepidation.

"Inga, I...."

She leaned forward, anxious.

He continued, "I've been thinking...it was a shock, you know. Not something I expected at all."

"Johannes, I am so..."

He put a finger to her lips then turned his hand so that her chin was cupped in his fingers. He tenderly stroked one side of her jaw with this thumb. "I know you were. I know you are. I just have to sort some things out. Maybe what's happened is a good thing. This has made me realize something important about you, and me. I think, in the long run, we will look back on this and believe it made us stronger. But I won't talk about it just yet. I want to organize my thoughts so that we can put this to rest, get everything in the open, suffer the anguish that might cause, and see if it breaks us or strengthens us. I believe it will do the latter, but I'm not prepared just yet."

Johannes saw Inga's face brighten when he said *for the long-term*, and then become anxious again as he finished speaking. He squeezed her arm. "Come on, Inga, let me walk you back to the wagon. In the next week or so, when I have my thoughts firmly settled in my mind, we will spend some time together, alone."

"Johannes, there is something I must..."

"Shhh—we will have plenty of time for each of us to say what we need to."

Inga's throat moved as she swallowed, a feeble smile playing on her lips. She nodded.

May 5, 1855

$\mathcal{F}$ORT KEARNEY

"WEREN'T THOSE MORMONS FINE PEOPLE?" ASKED REBECCA.

Reuben, his back to Rebecca and engrossed with the team, replied, "Uh-huh."

"And that newlywed couple. So young, so cute...so much in love."

"Uh-huh...ouch—damn!" Reuben shook his hand rapidly, then bent to check the left hoof of one of the horses.

"I'm glad we had our talk when we stopped to visit them, Reuben."

Reuben straightened up from the horse, gave her a quick look, and then turned his attention to unharnessing, methodically unhooking the britchen from the back straps.

Rebecca watched the way his shoulders moved under his shirt and waited, but he said nothing further. She walked up to him, stood close, and laid her hand gently on his shoulder blade. She could feel the muscles move beneath her finger as his arms and hands worked on detaching the collar.

"Reuben," she said, "if I did not make it clear when we were discussing the situation, I understand you did what you thought right. And it was certainly the best thing for Sarah. There was no option, really. I can't blame Sarah for not wanting that monster alone with her things in the wagon overnight. She certainly could not have spent the night in the wagon with him. Either she would've been brutalized, her screams silenced by the storm, or he would've been dead. Or both. A very dangerous situation, and... and..."

Reuben turned, "And what?"

"And I know you didn't want what happened in that wagon, especially between Inga and Johannes, to happen. It was not intentional. Sometimes the best heartfelt intentions go terribly wrong."

She saw his facial muscles relax, and there was a hint of a smile in his eyes.

"I might have to write these words down," he said, "and press them in a book for someone to read one hundred years from now. The day Rebecca Marx half-apologized."

"I did not apologize," she stomped her foot. His shoulders shifted back to the horse.

"Okay," she reached her hand out to his arm, "I suppose it was... at least, a partial apology."

He turned part way back to her, and her hand fell back to her side. She continued hastily, "You did the right thing. Unfortunately, it had a terribly wrong outcome. I would've done the same had I been you. And...," she cleared her throat, "this is an apology. I'm very sorry we have not been speaking much the last few days. That was my fault." She sighed, "It was just very traumatic. You have no idea how hurt Inga is. Her heart is broken and she is terrified."

Reuben's expression became puzzled. "Terrified? Johannes would never lay a hand on her. He's wildly in love with her—even though he is too... too set in his ways to get it through his own thick Viking skull."

"Yes, and she longs for Johannes. She prays that he will forgive her, and they can move on. She is very much in love with him."

"So what is she terrified of?"

Rebecca reached up again, squeezed his arm, and looked away, her gaze scanning the circle of wagons. She replied, without turning toward him, though her hand remained on his arm. "Something else. I shall tell you later."

"Well, then, let's kiss and make up."

Her eyes snapped back. Reuben grinned, teasing, his eyes twinkling. "Mr. Frank, I shall not kiss you in front of the entire wagon train!" she smiled coyly. "However, we could ride and make up. We're supposed to be getting into Fort Kearney sometime later tomorrow. Perhaps we could join Mac at the head of the train."

She tilted her head and batted her eyelashes at him. "Of course, when we ride into the fort, they will think that I am the wagon mistress, and the two of you are just my assistants."

Reuben burst out laughing. "Rebecca, you are certainly one of a kind! I'm sure Mac would love the company."

MAC ADMIRED HOW EASILY THE BEAUTIFUL BRUNETTE SAT HER SADDLE. "It's not often we have somebody as pretty as you ride at the head of the wagons, Miss Marx." Mac grinned at her as he spoke the words. "We saw you standing out there front of the wagons and the rest of the pilgrims, when your man there..."

The brunette quickly glanced at Reuben, and, Mac noticed, blushed scarlet. He laughed. "As I was saying, your man here saved the day. Would've been in quite a pickle if he hadn't turned the odds so quick and surprised 'em."

Reuben's eyes were studiously fixed on some point between Lahn's ears that only he knew, looking embarrassed, too, Mac observed.

"Yes." said Rebecca, talking more to Reuben than to him, not taking her eyes off the young man. "Yes, I think Mr. Frank did indeed save some pioneer lives."

The clear pride in her voice was obvious, and Mac smiled again. "So, Miss Rebecca, you're out there in front of everybody and God, with no cover, and your Sharps rifle, marching toward the fracas. What exactly did you think you were going to do?"

Rebecca returned his teasing look, but he was more than half serious. There was some laughter in her eyes, but a steely cold, too. It impressed Mac.

"Whatever I needed to," she answered.

Mac leaned over, spat a wad down into the trail, wiped his mustache with the back of his sleeve, and nodded. "I suspect you would've, Miss Rebecca, I suspect you would've."

Reuben shifted his attention, pointing up ahead of them. "What is that?"

Mac stood in the stirrups to see better, then sat down heavily. Red let out a disgruntled snort, and flicked her nose in the air, annoyed at the sudden cascade of weight on the saddle.

"Sorry about that, Red. Guess I got excited. That there is Fort Kearney. You can just make out the corner of the stockade, out there where there's a bend in the trees on the river in front of us. The fort sits pretty much in open, flat ground, a distance from and opposite some islands. They ain't ever going to complete it. Got some defensive bulwarks dug out on some sides, but they're always adding stockades. I doubt there will ever be a full fence around the place. Ten years ago, when we started this back and forth between Cherry Creek and St. Louis, there was just a couple of lonely buildings stuck next of the wagon track. The two-story you'll see is the commander's house. I hear the current colonel is a fella named Philip St. George Cooke. Rumor has it, he's planning to teach the Brule Sioux some respect for that Grattan Massacre. Nevermind, of course, that would break the treaty we signed with 'em in 1851. The Army don't care."

"What else is at the fort, Mac?" asked Rebecca, her interest evident.

"Now they got themselves a little central parade ground of sorts. When we came through here last fall, they had three buildings built and the fourth going up around it. There's a tall flagpole in the middle." He leaned over and spat again. "Interesting place. Used to be called Fort Childs. They changed it to Kearney on account of that military man, Stephen Kearney. I think the middle name was Watts, but I don't rightly recollect. Quite the soldier. War of 1812, headed up the Yellowstone expedition back in 1819. Big map man. If you folks get some maps in Cherry Creek, most likely the rivers—least the major ones—were mapped by that fellow. They've named forts and buildings for him about everywhere. There's one up southeast of the Big Horns, too."

He paused to spit again, then carried on. "Funny thing is, he found the spot for this fort but from what I hear tell, he's never been here since it was built. He figured if there was an attack the troops probably couldn't get to the river, so he has that Table Creek going through it so they always have water. Pretty damn smart. Made quite a name for himself designing other forts, too. He's somewhere down the southwest now. Hear tell he's leading expeditions to map all that territory we picked up from the Mexicans back in '48, if he is still alive. Now that's a pile of ground. One of these days, I'm going down to take a look. Rumor has it they get cactus trees twice as high as a man sets on a horse, and big rock formations that only God himself could sculpt," he sighed, thinking about his brother.

"But my brother Randy, at the Mercantile in Cherry Creek, is not too keen on the idea. Fact is, he told me he'd shoot me if I left him to run things alone."

Rebecca gave him a sharp look, a strange expression on her face, "Is there, by chance, a post office?"

The question surprised Mac. He stroked his beard in thought, "I think there might be. Matter fact, I think they put it in five or six years ago, maybe 1849. Never had no use for it myself, but now that you mention it, I have seen folks off the stage lines, carrying letters, and I heard a name," he paused, eyes up at the sky, brow creased, trying to remember, "oh yeah, John Heth. He's the sutler."

"Sutler?"

"Postmaster. Works for the outfit that runs the mercantile, too." He fixed his eyes on Rebecca, who was looking ahead at the still far distant and indistinguishable buildings with a hopeful look, "Why?" He noticed Reuben was also watching the brunette attentively.

She sighed, "I've written three letters to my mum. One I got posted in St. Louis before we left, but the others I've finished since we started our expedition. I would just like to get them headed to England."

"Well, Miss Rebecca..."

Rebecca broke into his words, interrupting. "Mac, I really would like you to call me Rebecca." Her voice was soft and sincere, and her eyes were smiling.

Mac grinned widely. "Well, thank you, Rebecca. I'd be honored. And I surely hope I'm right on that post office for you. Make sure you tell the folks you're writin' that you are posting from the very center of the United States of America. Folks say that Fort Kearney is just about smack dab in the center between the Pacific and the Atlantic. Them two railroads are killing themselves trying to get to this point first before they link up. That's a racket. The government is giving them every other section of land for the track they buy, and what else the good Lord only knows."

He reached into his pocket and took out his chew, bit off a chunk, and moved it around in his mouth, like a squirrel with an acorn. He smacked his lips. "I think the boys coming from the west is going to lose. That would be the Central Pacific. They have to fight mountains. Leavenworth, Pawnee and Western Railroad's coming from the east, and they got their own problems, but at least the land is fairly flat."

"Governments are like that, Mac," said Reuben with an edge in his voice. "They take from some, give to others, and get power in return. My family has had to put up with that for years back in the old country. In our case it is disguised with religion, but from what you're saying, it's the same everywhere, even in America."

Mac shot a sharp look at Reuben. The young man's jaw was set. Mac decided to say nothing.

"So what's the procedure in a place like this, Mac?" asked Reuben. "Do we circle the wagons, or is it okay to leave them strung out with the soldiers there?"

"Good question, Reuben. With the Army, I am not too worried. They usually have two or three companies, some infantry, some dragoons. Guess they just started callin' 'em Cavalry. Add the guns of this train, and that's three hundred or more rifles. Have to be an awful large crowd of fools to tackle it." Red flicked her head again, gaining slack in her reins, so she could drop her nose to the grass. *Impatient with all this chatter*, thought Mac.

"No," he answered Reuben, "what we'll do is just make sure folks are close and together, and line up the wagons side by side, in three lines maybe keeping fifty feet apart for room and privacy. When we get going we'll just pull out in the same order. Makin' these wheel repairs will be easier, too, rather than running up and down a third-mile of rigs. Fort's got a blacksmith for what work we don't have tools for. We'll get settled in, get John and Doc Leonard into the Army doctor, then get the Harris, Walling, Leonard, and the Kentucky wagons fixed up. Might be another wagon train come in while we are there, though the Mormon wagon master says they are stopping just long enough to get a platoon of Cavalry as an escort. Guess most outfits under thirty wagons are getting escorts now with things heating up with some of the tribes." He eased Red's head up, working the slack in the reins back through his hand.

"This is a big junction of the Mormon and Emigrant Trails and the Oregon, too. They all run together for a spell. That usually means we will run into someone. That Mormon Trail starts north. Most outfits like to jump off at St. Joseph or Independence. We like St. Louis. Don't have to put up with loading and unloading the paddle wheelers going up to Missouri and faster. Least I think so. I know it's cheaper."

He raised up in the saddle and looked back at the wagon strung along behind them. "People's tired, after that run-in with those bandits, and that storm was vicious, too. Been on the trail for six weeks. A good rest will help. We can make sure water kegs get filled, replenish ammo, and let folks just relax tonight. We're about two-thirds of the way to Cherry Creek, but this next four hundred miles is way tougher than where we've been."

"How many come through here, Mac?" Reuben asked.

"Almost fifteen thousand wagons have gone by Kearney since 1850, Reuben. But, 'cept for the Mormons headed down to Salt Lake, almost all were taking the northern route to California."

Rebecca's head jerked up. "Oh, I read about that in the London Times. Gold was discovered at a mill, Sutter's Mill."

Mac chuckled, "You impress me more and more, Miss... Rebecca. That's exactly right. Went crazy for a few years after 1848, but it was pretty well overplayed. Folks that made money were the folks that sold supplies to the fools chasing the gold. Bunch of damn...," he looked quickly at Rebecca, "Excuse me, Rebecca. Very few that chased the yellow, ever found any. They followed the Oregon Trail— it splits off from the Mormon and from where we're headed. Never been to California, but from what I hear there's places right settled up already." He shook his head. "Seems there's people on both sides the country and nobody in the middle, though it's starting. You folks are part of the vanguard."

REUBEN, CHARLIE, AND MAC QUICKLY HAD THE WAGONS ORGANIZED into two lines of thirteen rigs and one of fifteen. Rebecca was fascinated with the fort. It was quite unlike anything she had ever seen or imagined. Built on a slight elevation a few miles from the Platte, with Table Creek running next to and through it, it boasted five unpainted, weathered, but sturdy looking, single-story wood houses grouped around the central parade ground. Atop a tall pole in the middle was the American flag, flying proudly in the slight breeze from the west. The red and white stripes contrasted sharply, and the blue field blended perfectly, with the deep blue of the sky.

She tried for a moment to imagine a Union Jack on the pole. *It could never fit here.* The heavy cloth made a slight whooshing sound as the flag's furls brushed against one another in the wind. *The colors send a message*, she thought, *like a defiant shout into the void of nothing.* A strange feeling overcame her and she looked west, where the wide expanse of well-worn wagon tracks wound past the fort, disappearing in shimmers of ground-reflected sun.

"What are you looking at, Milady Marx?"

Inga and Sarah were smiling at her, though pain still clouded Inga's face. Rebecca immediately felt sorry for her again.

"I was just looking down where all those wagon tracks are heading, and thinking about the souls who have been here before us." She shook her head. "Mac tells us not too far down the well-used wagon track that we've been on for the last two days, the main road splits to the north and once again we will be on a much lesser used route. If the Mississippi was the edge of the wilderness, I have this strange feeling that this place, this fort, is the edge of the frontier."

Inga and Sarah exchanged glances, then all three turned their heads as an Army officer marched by, pulling on the brim of his hat. "Good day, ladies. A pleasure to have you at Fort Kearney."

Behind him a barrel-chested man with a blue field hat and black visor, chinstrap tight around the point of his jaw, and sergeant stripes on his sleeve, shouted cadence for eight marching men. *Obviously new enlisted recruits,* thought Rebecca, *by the way they stumble.* Their rifles held stiffly in their right hands, forestocks resting upward at a sharp angle on their shoulders. Several of the men ogled at her and the other women, but snapped their faces forward and stiffened when the sergeant barked, the words bouncing with his Irish brogue. "Look forward now, you mongrels. There will be none of that less you want twenty lashes and a day locked in the brig." The sergeant's face stayed rigidly forward, but his eyes clicked right to them. "Apologies from the troops, ladies."

Rebecca's head nodded involuntarily, as did Inga's and Sarah's. The men marched by, the cadence call receding in the distance. Another squad was mounted up, running through Cavalry drills on the other side of two dozen long, low buildings that appeared to be built out of grey, textured mud or clay, the roofs made of sod. The military horses pranced smartly, their red or dark brown hides contrasting with the light blue trousers and dark blue coats of the cavalryman, and the dark blue saddle blankets with yellow-gold trim. The squad flashed back and forth between the buildings in obvious exercise.

Here and there wispy, immature trees had been planted in an attempt at ordered landscaping around the crude parade ground. The two-story house of the commanding officer, Colonel Cooke, sat off to the side very close to the wagon track. *Not quite the grandiose military headquarters of England, she smiled to herself.* Beyond the fort, the land was flat, level, and barren except for grass. In the distance, a few straggly trees could be seen as they followed the wide meanders of the Platte.

She turned to Inga and Sarah. "How are you doing, Inga?" Inga's lower lip trembled. She looked down hastily and wiped a tear with her forefinger from her right eye. She sighed, "Johannes drove the wagon this morning. I sat next to him, but... but..."

Sarah finished the sentence for her. "But the big oaf barely said a word to her. Treated her almost like she didn't exist." Rebecca watched as Sarah reached out a hand and rubbed Inga's arm.

"We talked...," Inga continued, "after the Mormon prayer meeting. He said he would talk to me soon, but not until he is ready. I... I don't think he likes me anymore. I've tried to talk to him, to tell him I'm...." Her eyes raised up quickly to Rebecca, and she looked down again, embarrassed.

Rebecca took a step forward, put her arm around her shoulder, and hugged her. She'd always prided herself on facing problems full on. "And you're pregnant," she said.

Inga's head snapped up, mouth open, a look of total dismay in her eyes. Sarah did not look surprised at all. Inga's head bowed, and Sarah met the next question in Rebecca's eyes. *I'm right*, Rebecca knew instantly. The answer passed between them without words. *We women are all connected by our unspoken emotions, our thoughts, our common predicaments, bound by an invisible thread.*

She looked at Sarah, amazed at how calm her voice sounded. "And so you, too, are pregnant?"

Sarah's blue eyes never wavered. "Yes, Rebecca. We both are."

Rebecca reached out her free arm. Without hesitation Sarah stepped forward, and the three women hugged. Rebecca stepped back, keeping a hand on each of their arms. "I shan't say a word. I'm sure the three of us, if we put our brains together, can figure out a plan to calm down Johannes." She looked at Inga and shook her shoulder. "I, for one, am convinced he's in love with you."

Inga looked up teary-eyed, "Oh, Rebecca..."

"No, I truly believe that."

Sarah looked at Inga with earnest eyes. "I believe Rebecca is right, Inga. The way Johannes looks at you, touches you, interacts with you, is just like my father did with my mother, God rest their souls. And I often see him looking at you when you're not watching. I agree with Rebecca. It's time to let him know that you're carrying his child, that you love him with all your heart, and that whatever happened in the past is just that." She paused. "I don't believe Johannes was a virgin when you met."

Rebecca felt a laugh bubble up and bit her lip, but it spilled out anyway. Within a moment all three were laughing, their arms around each other again, the questioning stares coming from soldiers and pioneers, alike, merely fueling their mirth.

Rebecca reached into her sleeve, pulled out her handkerchief, and dabbed their eyes. "Oh my," she gasped, "oh my. I have not laughed that hard in months. No, Sarah, I believe it's a safe bet that Mr. Svenson has not been a virgin for quite some time." And that, of course, started the laughter all over again.

Rebecca returned the hanky to her sleeve. "Well ladies, let's visit the mercantile, and find that little candy shop that Mac was talking about. I hear it is one room in one of these huts that is sometimes staffed by a soldier whose hobby is confections. I will buy us all treats, and perhaps we can find the post office so I can post two letters."

She waved the envelopes in her hand. "To my mum. I've tried to write about what this is like, this land, this country," she looked around, "these people, and I have written about the two of you too, my friends, Sarah and Inga." The other women smiled broadly.

"Let's be off then," she said, and, as they set out for the mercantile, Rebecca noticed that they were followed by virtually every pair of male eyes in the fort.

———————

JACOB AVOIDED THE SMALL GROUPS AND FAMILIES OF PIONEERS that flowed in all directions from the wagons—to John Heth the sutler, to Dryer and Company Mercantile, and other various parts of the fort. He uneasily watched small troops of blue-coated soldiers drilling on foot and horseback. *Uniforms is trouble, whether coppers or the Army.*

He pulled the two decks of cards from his jacket pocket and smiled to himself. He smoothly, expertly, fanned them to be sure they were both marked, shoved them back into his pocket, patted them with a smug feeling, and looked across the parade ground toward the barracks. *Soldier boys get paid, and I bet there's not too many places to spend the money out here. Maybe I can have me one serious poker game on this trail, and stuff some money in my money pouch.*

Some distance away he saw Sarah, Rebecca, and Inga in a small circle hugging each other. "Bitches!" he spat the word into the air. Without further looks at them, he set off at a fast walk across the parade ground, whistling. He was impressed by the cannons, and counted them as he walked. Twenty-one of various types, sixteen block-house guns, two field pieces, two Mountain Howitzers, and one Prairie Piece, all set on either side of the parade area, and all pointing outwards from the fort.

He strode up to the first door. "C-Company—2nd Dragoons" was the name on the barracks. The door was closed. He knocked on it, but there was no answer.

A voice from behind him with a thick Irish brogue spoke up, "Eh, mate, that would be C Company. Dems poor darlings are out on patrol."

Jacob turned around. The man had corporal stripes on his uniform, medium build, towheaded like himself, with freckles, a ruddy complexion, and blue eyes that looked impish. "Damn me! Was that Irish brogue I hear?"

At the sound of Jacob's heavy Dublin accent, the soldier's face spread into a broad grin. "Aye—in fact, it's the most often you will run into on this godforsaken place, except for the officer-gentleman, of course." He spat on the ground.

Jacob grinned. He hoped it wasn't too eager a smile. "What company might be in? Any poker players amongst you soldiers?" He walked down the steps from the barracks and stood facing the corporal, who had not lost his wide grin.

"Poker is it, eh? I bet we could rustle up a game. We love fleecing you poor souls heading west."

A surge of excitement shot through Jacob, but he kept his face impassive, and tried to make his voice sound genuine. "Well, I just like to play cards. Just for fun you know. A pastime," he sighed and began to turn away, "sounds like you boys are too serious for me. Me fiancée and I," he paused, "we got enough to build our house and she would never talk to me again if I lost all that money." *Perfect inflection on the 'all'*, he congratulated himself.

Jacob smiled inwardly when the soldier took the bait, the tell-tale flicker in his eyes indicating a greed that gave him away. He was obviously taken with the notion—another sucker pioneer with lots of money had wandered into their midst. He reached out his hand and introduced himself. "The name is Sean."

Jacob shook his hand. "Jacob."

Sean slapped him roughly on the back, and put his arm around his shoulders. "I was just kidding. We don't play often, we don't play for much, and my sister could beat the pants off virtually any soldier in the fort, and she's never picked up a deck of cards in her life. It's just for fun. Same as you."

"You're sure?" Jacob was pleased with the perfect, tepid tone of his query.

"Sure I'm sure. I have been on clean-up detail. My squad's back from drill here shortly." He pointed across the parade ground where troopers were putting horses through paces along the low mud buildings. The corporal looked around furtively and lowered his lips to Jacob's ear, "And we got a wee taste of moonshine that no one knows. I hear your wagons are in all night, doing some repairs or some such. Come over here after dark. It will be great to talk to somebody from the old country. Did you come over recent?"

Jacob nodded. "Just three months ago."

"Good, then the news will be current. By the time we get a paper out here, the world could've ended." He laughed, "Not that any of us can read."

"After dark it will be then, Sean—and I thank you for your most kind invitation."

Sean slapped him hard on the back again. "It will be our honor, Jacob. Just a bunch of friendly Irishmen."

Jacob smiled, turned, and walked back toward the wagons humming loudly to himself.

May 8, 1855

PROPHECY

REBECCA'S MIND KEPT RETURNING TO THE SIMPLE, YET BEAUTIFUL, Mormon sermon, and the newly married young couple. She smiled to herself. *So in love. Such passion.*

She snapped back to the present when she heard the horses. "Rebecca, are you ready?" Reuben stood there, the reins of Lahn in one hand, and Bente's in the other. "Looks like we have three or four hours 'til sunset. Mac said it will take that long to help the Smiths and Johnsons repair the wheel axles on their wagons."

"Poor Harris has had problems with that wagon since we began. Every time we stop, he is on his back or belly underneath that thing, fixing or tinkering with something."

"Mac noticed it, too. Everyone has. They thought they had it fixed at the fort. He figures this time around they will fix it right and be done with it. Where do you want to ride? We had that brushup with the renegades little more than a week ago, and Zeb tells me he has cut track of unshod ponies several times. I don't think it's wise to go too far."

Rebecca's eyes strayed to Bente, and she gasped, "Reuben, is that a scabbard?"

Reuben's mouth worked like a fish out of water. Finally, he simply said, "Yes."

"How nice of you to lend that to me. That makeshift blanket wrap you taught me to do works fine, but it was certainly a bother to take on and off the horse. If I ever had to get to the rifle quickly, well..."

"It's not a loan, Rebecca. It's yours. Johannes and I bought an extra one in New York. It's been in my duffel this whole time. We are getting into more dangerous country, and you mentioned a scabbard on that ride we took before the snowstorm, and..." Reuben's voice broke off, and a look of enamored shyness flashed across his face. "Anyway, I thought you should have it."

"Oh, Reuben..." She walked over to the big bay and ran her hands slowly and delicately down the oiled leather. She tried to wiggle the stock of her Sharps, but it was firm. "Beautiful practicality," she said softly, looking into Reuben's eyes, her fingertips still lightly stroking the leather.

Reuben seemed suddenly shy again. She could see the muscles in his throat constricting. "Well, Johannes and I both have Sharps," he said quickly, "and since you do, too, I thought it might fit well, and it does."

Rebecca broke off her stare, pretending to further investigate the scabbard, but really to mask the intense desire that had suddenly welled up inside her. She wanted Reuben to hold her in his arms and kiss her again like the day before the blizzard. Or back on the train. She could feel the pulse in her throat. Swallowing hard, she turned around and looked off in the distance. A half-mile away was a thin line of intermittent cottonwoods that wound their way through a serpentine lower area, sometimes just the top half of their budding branches visible with the soft, pale green of unfurling leaves.

"Looks like a small creek up there. I think that's close enough to be safe, don't you?" she said, looking back at Reuben. His eyes were focused on the pulsing in her neck. She resisted the urge to lift her hand to cover the tell-tale movement of the delicate skin at her throat, but then he raised his eyes to her lips before letting them slowly meander down to her hips. She wasn't sure if he even realized that his gaze had wandered.

"Sure, that creek sounds good," he answered, seeming somehow absent from his speech, as if simply mouthing the words, his thoughts elsewhere.

"Are you feeling all right, Reuben?"

"Yes. I feel fine." He handed her Bente's reins, and opened his mouth, about to ask her if she wanted some assistance mounting. She threw him a teasing, yet stern look of warning. He closed his mouth without a sound, shook his head, laughed, and swung easily into the saddle on Lahn.

The day was warm, the warmest by far since they had left St. Louis. They rode in shirts. The sun was hot, the air dry, the grass half green now as far as the eye could see, and, in certain places, where it had received just the right mixture of sun and water, it had matured to almost early summer. A slight wind, and the movement of air from simply riding, should have cooled her, but Rebecca felt fevered. She realized she was perspiring. There was a certain but unreal quality to the ride. Birds flitted here and there from one occasional small bush or sage brush to another. Ground nesting birds scurried and hopped through the grass, their heads appearing and disappearing, almost comical in their antics. At the approach of the horses, they chirped angry protests and flashed away, dipping and weaving in an erratic flight of defense.

She rode slightly behind Reuben. Somehow she couldn't take her gaze off the taper of his shoulders to his waist, and the easy movement of his buttocks and hips as Lahn moved steadily toward the tree line. She ran her tongue over her upper lip, and, with her fingers, wiped the thin film of perspiration at her hairline. She couldn't pull her eyes from Reuben's back. She gave Bente a gentle spur and rode up alongside of him. *Can't be distracted by what I can't see!*

He threw her an easy glance, the fiery green of his eyes lingering in her mind long after his head turned, and he continued his careful scan of the land around them. She noticed the thong was off the hammer of his Colt.

Reuben reined in Lahn and pointed, "See where the trees are sparse up there? Be tough for anyone to sneak in on us, and, with a couple of quick steps, we would be visible to the wagon train, and they to us."

Rebecca leaned forward slightly, patted the small canvas bag suspended from her saddle horn, then nodded back at the blanket rolled and lashed behind her saddle. "As long as there's a level spot where we can roll out this blanket and have lunch, that is fine with me, Reuben."

Reuben's head jerked in surprise. "I thought we were just going for a ride. Did you bring food?"

Those green eyes. Rebecca forced her stare from his eyes and was distressed when her gaze merely went to his lips. "Yes, I'm hungry!" *Hungry for what?* an inner voice called out.

Reuben laughed, "Well, truth is, my stomach's been growling for an hour. What did you bring?"

"I brought some pemmican..."

"Now, that's a surprise," Reuben chuckled.

She laughed in return. "Yes. While our meals are filling and nourishing, one could hardly call the menus equal to the high epicurean standards of Europe," she said dryly. "And some dried fruit...and...," she reached into the canvas bag, drew out a small bottle of red wine, and held it up proudly, "French, I brought it all the way from England. Alas, in my frantic preparations to leave London, I forgot the obvious. A corkscrew."

Reuben was looking at her with his eyebrows raised and a slight, astonished smile. "I'm sure I have something we can get it open with, but aren't you saving it for a special occasion? You have brought it all this way."

"This is a special occasion, Reuben," she said softly. *What exactly do I mean by that?* she chided herself.

Reuben looked puzzled, but nodded.

"We survived the blizzard, over six weeks on the trail, an unsavory encounter with ruffians, and we are only three or four weeks from Cherry Creek."

He bobbed his head. "Then I suppose you could say this is an occasion." His eyes were again fixed on the pulsing in her neck, which seemed to have been increasing in intensity as they drew close to the little creek.

"And this land, Reuben, this glorious expanse of earth. Other than the few farmers we saw as we were leaving the Mississippi, and that dreadful Black Feather group, the people in Fort Kearney, and, of course, the Mormons, we've traveled over six hundred miles without seeing another soul. If I started on one coast of England and went that distance, I would have already walked into the sea on the other side, and I would have had to avoid millions of people along the way."

She laid the reins across the saddle horn, raised her arms, and spread them toward the sky. "And the sunshine. Absolutely glorious. Do you remember the weather in Europe? Damp and rainy half the time. No skyline. No horizon. The city smell of too many people in one place." She swept her arm around, "I am breathing air nobody's ever breathed. I'm seeing things quite possibly no one has ever seen. Every moment of every day is like a different painting, never the same."

She opened her mouth to say more, but stopped when she saw the look on Reuben's face. Strangely excited, softly intense, knowing but wondering. "Rebecca, is that the way you truly feel? You are not just saying it, not simply caught up in the moment?"

"I've never been more serious, Reuben, and I have never felt more free."

There was a mysterious smile on Reuben's lips. He said nothing. They entered the tree line of the scattered cottonwoods, some besieged by age, others, their time already passed, toppled, young shoots of growing trees reaching upward, eager for their share of the sun, the mature trees, coarsely barked, standing tall and proud.

A tiny stream wound back and forth through the thin stand of trees. It gurgled and tinkled. *Almost a wind chime*, thought Rebecca. Sparkles glittered off tiny rivulets where the water ran over small rocks and descended in miniscule waterfalls to a frothing reunion with the current. "Oh, Reuben, this is delightful."

Reuben nodded but continued to look carefully around. She knew he was gauging the safety of the place. "This'll do. But let's keep our rifles handy," he said, dismounting.

Still astride Bente, Rebecca reached forward for the canvas bag. One of the straps had somehow wound around the saddle horn. As she tugged at it, she felt strong hands on her waist. Reuben lifted her out of the saddle effortlessly and lowered her gently to the ground, the length of the front of her body sliding sensuously against his, their eyes fixed on each other. She felt as if her throat would explode. Breathing was deliciously difficult.

Reuben tenderly put two fingers under her chin, raised her face, and then lowered his lips to hers. The kiss built in intensity as her fingers wound tightly through the fabric of his shirt. Gripping his shoulder, she pulled him down to her until she could feel the muscles of his chest against her breasts, his hardness pressing into her belly above her hips. The kiss was more than the kiss on the train, more than the kisses the day before the snowstorm. The depth of it sucked the air out of her, replacing her breath with an equally weightless essence, as if she were breathing in a part of his soul. She felt light-headed, almost dizzy. Panting, her mind pleasantly hazy, she pushed him gently away, trailing her fingertips down his arm and across his partially outstretched hand. She took a half-step back, and took a deep breath.

"That creek looks so inviting. I want to wash the dust from my face and clean a bit. Then we could have lunch. Can you get that bag off the horn, Reuben?"

He nodded absently, a dreamy look in his face, but she noticed that before he fetched the lunch bag, he smoothly slid both rifles from their scabbards and placed them, ready for action, in easy reach against the trunk of the nearest Cottonwood, just a few feet away.

One small, curved part of the stream bubbled merrily in the sun, as if a beacon of light had found its way through the cracks of the floor of heaven. She walked toward it, unaware she was moving, oblivious to her own steps, fixated on a singular purpose, splashing water on her face from that mystical point of flowing creek. She knelt down, not realizing how the water had undercut the bank. As she lowered her hands and face to the creek, the slight edge gave way, and she tipped, headfirst, into the current, so narrow that her head was almost on the other bank.

With her front sopping wet, she giggled to herself, and awkwardly regained her balance. *Rebecca Marx, get yourself straightened out. How clumsy.* She didn't feel cold. The water was soothing as she splashed her face, rubbed her eyes, and then rose to walk back to where Reuben and the horses stood just twenty feet away. He had spread the blanket out and was reaching into the canvas bag to extract lunch when he saw her approach. He stopped, his mouth parted, and a strange expression stole across his face, along with, she thought, a rather hungry glow in his eyes.

"What's wrong?" she asked, following his gaze to where the creek water had soaked her chemise and the white cotton shirt she wore. Her body and breasts were perfectly revealed through the wet, cling-ing cloth, her nipples involuntarily erect and pushing pink against the fabric.

Reuben rose.

She looked at him and then down at herself again. "Oh, oh my."

She crossed her arms in front of her breasts. Her cheeks burned. Reuben stood directly in front of her, and she could feel his intensity. He reached up slowly, and gently, and uncrossed her arms, devouring her with his eyes before gathering her in his arms and kissing her. The world spun. She felt his fingers fumbling with the buttons on her blouse. *Oh my God. Oh my God. Oh my God.* She wondered if she was saying it out loud, or was it just a frantic, strident echo some-where in her mind?

Reuben peeled the shirt off one shoulder and arm, and slipped off the shoulder strap of the chemise. His lips were gently fastened to her neck, sucking, lathing, and she clung to him, afraid she would fall down without leaning into his strength. His lips sank slowly from her neck, to the seductive hollow of her collarbone, and then down the smooth expanse of her upper chest. She could feel the heat of the sun on her exposed skin, and then she felt his tongue on her nip-ple. Current shot through her. Her lower abdomen felt empty, yet filled with a desperate, primal need for satiation.

Slowly, he lowered her to the blanket. Her mind was whirling, her upper, inner thighs, quivering out of control. One of his hands slid up her legs, raising the loose folds of her riding dress. His burning, calloused touch reached the top of her pantaloons, and she felt his fingers slide beneath the waistband, then down her abdomen. *Oh my God, oh my God, oh my God.* He touched her, a light, delicate searing touch. She heard a groan and realized it had risen from her. Waves of pleasure washed over her. The empty yearning in her belly became a desperate want.

He tenderly slid off her riding dress and pantaloons as his hands touched her everywhere, each contact sending waves around, across, and through her trembling body. He knelt and raised the chemise over her breasts, and then fastened his lips to one, then the other.

She tried to cover herself, but he caught her arms and pinned them gently back against the blanket. "You are so beautiful," he whispered.

Rebecca could not remember how, but his shirt was off and the fine rich muscles of his chest were against her skin. There was a dark, wide, swath of curly hair that ran down the center of his chest and abdomen and disappeared mysteriously at his belt line. She wanted to know where that trail of masculinity led.

Her question was answered as he fumbled with one hand at his belt, unbuttoned his breeches and slipped them down to his knees. She looked down at his tumescence and, fascinated, reached out a small hand and held him. Her fingers couldn't circle his girth. He was hot against her palm, and she could feel the insistent pulse, the involuntary tightening of muscles. She felt herself drip deliciously down her upper thigh, and felt the fire in the smooth caresses of his fingertips as they traced again across her breast, savored her erect nipples, then continued down her hips and came to rest lightly, long-ingly on the smooth, pulsating valley between her hips.

The smell of him, and of them, mingled with the fragrance of the sunbaked sage and spring grass. Her heart pounded, the unfamiliar warm tingling permeating her loins, and she felt the blushing in her face. This was a feeling she'd never known, could never imagine, could barely absorb on so many levels. She swept a soft, fluttering palm over the chorded muscles in his arm. Consumed by a desperate yearning, a deep primal need, which overrode her fear of the unknown, she gasped, her hips writhing involuntarily as he lowered himself gently onto her. A momentary stab of pain and then overwhelming pleasure mixed, enveloping her as he slowly, carefully, began to sink into her.

She groaned, a muffled cry equally grounded in passion, trepidation, and wanting. He stopped, gently brushed a callused thumb leisurely across her forehead and down her cheek, and looked deep into her eyes. "Am I hurting you?"

She felt the tears welling in the corner of her eyes. She bit her lip and shook her head, her full answer to the question an ever-tightening wrap of her arms around his shoulders, the increasing instinctive bend of her knees, and the firm plant of her heels against the muscular flesh of his buttocks, drawing him in. *"Please, Reuben, please,"* she moaned.

He lowered his lips sensuously to hers, his tongue running over her inner upper lip and then her lower lip, all the while gently, tenderly, but inexorably sinking deeper and deeper into her until finally she could feel his pelvis mold to hers, his complete fullness lodged in her center, the stretching and small stabs of pressure she felt lost in avalanches of sensual sensations.

He pulled part way out and then slid slowly back in. Every square inch of her body tingled. The sun felt hot where her neck was out of the shade of his body. He pulled back slowly again and she desperately tightened her legs, raising her pelvis instinctively to keep him deep. Then he thrust forward, harder this time, her fingernails digging into his back. His hips bucked again, and another wave of pleasure swept her, enveloping her. Again his pelvis moved, this time harder, and the wave turned into a tidal flow of passion. He was moving faster, their hips rocking in undulating rhythm, synchronous in every give and take of movement. He drew almost his entire length from her and then plunged forward again. Bright lights exploded in her brain, mingling somehow with the rays of the sun above them. She felt her eyes roll back, and again he drew himself almost fully out, only to sink rapidly back in once more. Her lower body spasmed around his length, and then she was floating. They were one as he pulsed again and again and a hot, white searing heat erupted and spread through every inner pore, firing every molecule deep inside her. She felt herself contracting at that moment, and they groaned in unison.

They remained fastened tightly and completely, her body quivering, twitching, muscles spasming involuntarily, her nipples so hard they were delightfully painful. She struggled to regain her breath, felt the heat of the sun on her closed eyelids, and then he grunted, twitched, and pulsed one more time deep in her belly, that tiny movement sending her spinning off the edge again, his sun-warmed back, powerful and smooth beneath the press of her fingers.

He raised himself partially up, and, with a throaty whimper, she pulled him back down on top of her, squeezing her legs around his hips, savoring his weight.

He moved his lips to her ear and nibbled her lobe. "I love you, Rebecca Marx," he said in a warm breath in her ear. She said nothing, and he could not see the tears that formed in her eyes.

THEY HELD HANDS AS THEY RODE BACK TOWARD THE CIRCLED WAGONS, letting go of each other only when they were within several hundred yards of the men working on Johnson's Conestoga. Rebecca could smell him on her skin and on her body where he had dripped warm and milky on her thigh, and she delighted in it.

They rode up to their wagon, tying Lahn and Bente off at the rear, pressing their hips and outside thighs together as they lashed the reins.

Hearing them, Inga poked her head from the rear canvas and started to speak, but her eyes fixed on Rebecca's disheveled wet, transparent upper clothing only partially hidden by Reuben's shirt. Her eyes flicked to Reuben, the open coat revealing his undershirt. Her mouth shut. She looked from one to the other several times, and then she smiled, her face a soft, equal mixture of sad and happy.

"I'll take care of the saddles, Rebecca." He glanced up at the sky. "It will be dark soon. You better go see Inga. It looks like she wants to say something."

Rebecca stretched out her hand, which found its way into Reuben's coat and rested on his chest. He flushed, wrapped his arms around her, and drew her lips to his. The world began to spin again. His tongue probed her mouth, this time with an all-knowing energy. She was dimly aware that the flow of him, *of them*, was now halfway down her thigh. She shuddered.

Reuben slowly broke off the kiss, and she laid her cheek against his chest. *So warm, strong, so quick the beat.* Her hands stroked his back, and she sighed, the words of the aborigine's premonition repeating in the echo chamber of her mind, "*...the power of the land... and the man...will hold you.*"

Reuben stepped slowly back. His head turned slightly, and for a long moment he appeared to intently study a small patch of brush several hundred feet from the wagon.

She opened her mouth, "Reuben, I..." but his eyes returned to hers, and he raised his finger to her lips. "I understand. You must return to England." His jaw was tight. He bent down slowly and kissed her again, this time softly on the lips. "Rebecca Marx, I love you. I have for some time. But I will never stand in your way. Each must choose their own path." He turned, slid the saddle off Lahn, and began to walk to the head of the wagon.

Rebecca stood dumbfounded. *I was not going to say that at all.*

May 9, 1855

*U*NSHOD HORSES

THEY HAD JUST SETTLED DOWN TO SUPPER, REUBEN AND REBECCA sharing his saddle, casting evocative, shy, sensuous glances at one another. Sarah, much to Reuben's delight, was chatting animatedly with Zeb. The tall mountain man's eyes were fixed on the smiling features of the petite redhead. Once in a while, he noisily scraped a mouthful of beans and pemmican from the tin plate that he clumsily held, saying little himself, but nodding at virtually everything Sarah said. Reuben grinned into his food. *I shall ask Johannes to give Zeb some coaching. In fact, maybe that's the trade for the moccasins he wants.* The thought made him laugh and he almost tipped his plate.

"What is so funny, Mr. Frank?" Rebecca's voice sounded petulantly sarcastic, but, when he looked at her, her eyes glowed softly and the fire-lit sheen of her lips framed a flirtatious smile.

Reuben shook his head. "I decided on the perfect trade Johannes could make for those moccasins he wants so badly."

At the mention of Johannes' name, Rebecca's eyes flicked in the direction of the two blondes. Reuben followed her gaze. They sat side by side, but with perhaps a foot separating them, not molded to one another as before the storm. They glanced at each other occasionally with tentative smiles, but Reuben was sure they had not traded a word since supper started.

That afternoon, Reuben had ridden out to invite Zeb to join them for supper. When the mountain man repeatedly declined, Reuben tactfully demanded that he come. He thought Zeb had been preoccupied, and there was an aura of uneasy concern that seemed to shadow him and Buck. *Quite unusual*, Reuben thought, but chalked up his friend's unsettled energy to the length of the trip or perhaps the mountain man's frustration with his inability to express his feelings for Sarah. *Little does he know, it's evident to everyone, including Sarah.*

Finally, Zeb had insisted he would only come in to dinner if two men replaced him at his position for the few hours he would be at the wagons. "Why two men, Zeb? One of the Kentuckians or Charlie could come out and relieve you just fine during dinner."

The sharp green eyes underneath the bushy eyebrows had fixed on his with a strange look. "Nope, better be two. You need eyes in the back of your head out here, and there's been times over the past few nights I wished someone else was watching my back, and that's a rare thing."

Reuben puzzled over that comment on the ride back in, but the thought had evaporated with the sight of Rebecca, her smile, and the powerful, sensual energy between them.

From across the circled wagons, they heard Jacob's loud, bellicose voice, the words slightly slurred. "That's ten pots in a row—now if you bastards only had some money, I'd be having fun." Rebecca exchanged a glance with Reuben. They both shook their heads in disgust, smiling at their shared opinion of the obnoxious Irishman.

The sound of horse hooves at a lope permeated the darkness of the new-moon night outside the circled wagons. Reuben was surprised to see Mac and Charlie illuminated in the firelight where it filtered across the tongue of the wagon. The horses were impatient, and the flame-hued features of the wagon master had a look of concern. *Or was it just the shadows?* Mac's voice was calm, though. "Reuben, Zeb, Johannes—I hate to interrupt your supper, my apologies. But when you're done, could you come down to the supply wagons?"

Zeb stopped chewing. Johannes threw Mac a startled glance, then they both looked at Reuben, who nodded. "You bet, Mac. Say fifteen to twenty minutes?"

"That would be fine, Reuben."

They finished supper hurriedly, Reuben scraping the tin with fast motions, swallowing half-chewed bites. He knew Rebecca was watching, but pretended not to notice.

"What is it Reuben? What's going on?"

Reuben turned his head and looked into Rebecca's concerned, soft brown eyes. "I don't know, Rebecca. Maybe it is just to make some plans for the upcoming days," he shrugged and looked back at his plate, "or maybe it's something else."

"Reuben...," the touch of her hand on his arm sent a current of their connection flowing along the entire side of his body.

He quickly cut her off. "I promise you, my love, I will tell you everything when I return. I really don't know."

Rebecca blinked and a slow, wide smile spread across her face. "That's the first time you've called me 'my love.' A woman could get rather used to that." Reuben swallowed a mouthful of pemmican and beans without chewing at all and almost choked. He put down his plate, coughed to clear his throat, and leaned over to her. She drew back a bit, casting furtive glances at the rest of their friends around the fire. "They know, Rebecca. They've known from the minute we rode in from those cottonwoods yesterday."

Her eyes fell demurely to her lap. She leaned into him, lips parted, and they exchanged a long kiss. The flush in her cheeks was evident in the firelight.

Reuben pulled away at the sound of Johannes' voice. "Okay, might have to put 'Romeo' in front of 'farm boy'. Reuben Romeo Farm Boy." While not quite his usual pre-storm humor, it was the first chuckle Reuben had heard from his friend in more than a week. He looked up into the tall, partially shadowed face that towered over him. "Okay, Viking, we're going."

He reached out, squeezed Rebecca's hand, and scrambled to his feet. Zeb joined them, and they walked into the clinging darkness toward the supply wagons.

They found Charlie and Mac gathered around a small buffalo chip fire as they had expected, but also Harris, the Kentuckians, and two other men, Henry and Alex. Reuben had spoken to the latter two fellows before but had never grown to be friends with them, though he knew that they were among the better riflemen in the train.

Mac's eyes were on them as they approached the fire. The coffee pot bubbled and rocked in its precarious perch between two rocks. "Sorry to drag you men from your wagons after supper, so I'll get right to it. Zeb has been cuttin' track of unshod ponies, just four or five of 'em, from time to time. That's a pretty small band of Indians, particularly this far east. When we get out toward the South Platte, they will be right plentiful. I seen dust, and so has Zeb up to the southwest. Just occasional, might be the wind, but I trust my gut, and my gut tells me it ain't wind.

"We need to be extra sharp. I'm sending Charlie and Zeb out to the southwest tomorrow morning before light, so they can get across most of the flats while they can't be seen. I'm going to push the outriders out another half-mile. Zeb talked to me about this yesterday, and we agree except he thinks we ought to be working in teams. No more riding alone. Sometimes we all need an extra pair of eyes, and I think we're at one of those times."

Reuben was curious. "Zeb, how close do you think they've been to the wagons and how many do you think there are?"

Zeb pulled slowly on his mustache and rotated his jaw a bit while he thought, "Five ponies in that track I've cut twice. I think that's what there are of that bunch, but that dust further out ain't just five horses. This small group looks to be Sioux, though two sets of pony tracks is Crow. Most probably stole. They could be watching whatever the other is, and us. They have been within two hundred feet of the wagons."

Everyone's heads jerked up, eyes wide, and Mac exclaimed "I'll be damned!"

Reuben had an odd feeling. "The other evening when I came back from a ride with Rebecca," he looked over at Mac, "while you were working on Harris' wagon, we were behind our wagon and we were...." He broke off and cast an embarrassed glance around the circle of men, most of whom laughed, knowing full well what he was trying not to say. "Anyway, before I led Lahn back up toward the front, I had this feeling I was being watched, from some low bitter and scrub brush out about two or three hundred feet. I even stared at it for a minute and thought to myself about how animals turn around after you've looked at them for too long. They can feel it."

Zeb nodded his head slowly. "Yep, you open yourself to what's out there, and you'll feel it, too." He looked at Reuben sharply. "And when you feel that energy, son, never doubt it."

Mac stood up abruptly. "Harris and Elijah, tomorrow morning when we get going, I want you about a mile to the south. Henry and Alex, you stay between us and the river—that would be about half-mile. Reuben, you and Johannes ride drag. Stay about a mile behind us."

Reuben opened his mouth to speak but Mac cut him off brusquely. "Your ladies will be fine. I will watch 'em. I think they handle the wagon better than you and Johannes." Everyone chuckled, but without enthusiasm. "Zeb and Charlie, I want you up front of the train, five, six miles out in those low hills where we seen the dust. Try not to get out of sight of one another."

He cast a somber look around the circle of faces. "If any of you see anything, anything at all, fire a shot, if you can, and hightail it back here. This ain't hero work. This is smart work. I wish we had John here, but that Army surgeon was pretty clear if we moved him, he'd most likely lose that leg. We'll fetch him when we are back this way with pelts, but we sure could use his quarter-Cherokee savvy right now."

May 10, 1855

*U*NSPOKEN

In the early morning darkness, long before daylight, Johannes stood from buckling the cinch below Bente's girth. A few feet away, Reuben had just finished securing his saddle on Lahn. Mac's instructions to the men had been no fires or oil lamps. Trying not to disturb the women, including Sarah, who had spent the night in the wagon at Rebecca's insistence, Reuben and Johannes had been as quiet as possible.

Ten feet from the wagon, Johannes had just finished shoving his Sharps carbine into the scabbard and fastening his lariat to the saddle when he heard a rustling at the rear canvas of the prairie schooner. Inga, still in her sleeping robe but with Johannes's light wool jacket over it, eased the tailgate open. Without using the ladder, she let herself down gently to the ground. In the faint, pale blue light just beginning to show on the eastern horizon, she looked apparitional. He handed Bente's reins to Reuben, saying quietly, "Be right back, Reuben." He turned and went to Inga.

"What are you doing up? I'm sorry if we woke you."

"I was already awake, Johannes. I couldn't sleep. I have had minimal sleep the last week, but last night I couldn't sleep at all." She sniffled, took a quick step forward, and wrapped her arms round him.

He struggled for a moment with his emotions, hesitating. *Let it go,* he reminded himself. *Just let it go.* She was visibly trembling. He wrapped his arms around her, bent down, and kissed the top of her head, then raised her face with one hand and kissed her quickly on the lips.

"Johannes, there is something I must tell you..."

"We're even then, woman, because there is something I must tell you, too. I'm done thinking." He smiled, "May I have the honor of a date after supper tonight, just you and me? We can take a walk around the wagons, say what needs to be said, and I bet that we both feel on top of the world when that conversation is done. At least I hope so."

"Johannes, please, I..."

He put his finger to her lips, "Tonight, Inga, tonight. Tomorrow will be a bright, sunny day, I promise you. Now get back in the wagon and get ready to move out. The rest of camp will be stirring shortly. Remember, no lamps!"

REUBEN WATCHED THE EMBRACE BETWEEN THE TWO BLONDES, thinking how surreal Inga looked with the full skirt of her soft white sleeping robe flowing around her ankles, with her light hair and pale eyes. Her skin was almost translucent in the last glimmers of starlight. The only thing seemingly grounding her was Johannes' jacket. Reuben was silent as he handed Bente's reins back to Johannes, stepped up into his stirrup, and slung a leg over Lahn's saddle.

As they spurred Bente and Lahn from the wagon, Reuben glanced back at Inga. She was standing almost ghost-like, her attire and features gathering in the first vestiges of light sifting through the darkness. He studied Johannes from the side as the two men rode out of the circle of wagons to what would be the rear of the line. "I couldn't help but overhear, Johannes," he said. "What is the revelation that you intend to share with Inga?"

Johannes shot him a hard glance. "Reuben, how do you feel about Rebecca? You're in love with her, aren't you?"

Reuben hoped Johannes could not see his surprise in the dark. "Yes, Johannes, matter of fact, I am."

"Have you told her?"

"Matter of fact, I have."

A soft laugh, tinged with irony, escaped Johannes's mouth. "See, my friend, you've always thought that I had a way with women. But the truth is, you know more about them and about yourself relative to them, than I do. Or should I say, until last week. Like you, I am in love. Unlike you, I have not yet told that to the woman I love. I mean to tell Inga tonight."

Reuben reached across the long distance between the horses and slapped Johannes' thigh. "Congratulations. I suspect you will have one happy, very beautiful, glowing Norwegian blonde on your hands."

Johannes laughed. "Well, whatever shall Johannes Svenson do with a beautiful, lanky, golden-haired Norwegian woman—and she with him? I'm sure I can come up with something."

They pulled the lapels of their coats up over their mouths to muffle the sound of their laughter.

May 10, 1855

*B*UCK'S RUN

From her perch on the wagon between Rebecca and Inga, Sarah shielded her eyes against the sun, calculating its zenith in the sky. Suspended over them like a giant blue dome, the sky stretched as far as one could see, until it finally fell into the uneven edge of the earth. Here and there, bright, small cumulus clouds floated with unhurried nonchalance. About twenty yards ahead of them were sickly Dr. Leonard and his wife Thelma, in their oxen-pulled wagon and, beyond that, the lead rig.

She turned to Inga, "I really should've been riding with the two of you much more often. What was I thinking?"

Rebecca, driving the team and paying close attention to the lines, gave Sarah a quick sideways look. "You weren't!"

All three women laughed. Inga hugged her. "It's a pleasure to have you with us, Sarah. Johannes told me that he will be horseback far more often on this homestretch to Cherry Creek."

Rebecca leaned forward to see Inga better, "Pray tell. Mr. Svenson actually lowered himself to speak to you?"

Inga smiled, the first genuine smile Sarah had seen on her friend's lips since the blizzard, but there was a reserve in her eyes. *Obviously in better spirits, but she is still unsure.*

Inga smoothed the light green wool of her traveling dress over her legs as Rebecca leaned forward again. "So, what did he say?"

"He said that we will take a walk tonight, just the two of us, to talk things through, and that he has something to tell me, which he believes will make me happy."

"Have you told him yet?"

Inga looked down at her hands, then back at Sarah, then her eyes shifted to Rebecca. She glanced down at her hands again then raised her eyes.

"No, I... I have not told him yet. I've tried. God knows I've tried, several times when he walked me back from the ceremony at the Mormon wagons. And once last night, and then this morning. I felt sure this morning he would take a moment to listen, but he put his hand on my lips with the promise that we would settle things tonight."

"What I think," Rebecca said, adjusting the lines, "is that after Mr. Svenson gets over the shock of knowing he will be a father, he will be the happiest, tallest blond-haired man on the wagon train."

Sarah sighed with a mock serious air. "But he's the only tall, blond-haired man on the wagon train."

Rebecca shot her a look then smiled, "Right you are." Up ahead, a small river stretched across the land, its rapid, shallow current flowing golden-silver in the sun. The land was flat, a dry spring green. To the southwest, five or six miles, were low rolling hills that rose from the flats like the rough grain of heavy leather. Sarah could see Mac on Red, at the head of the train, trotting toward the crossing.

Inga mimicked the pseudo-serious tones of the two women next to her and, Sarah noticed, tried to change the subject. "I am glad that we dressed up today. It's been weeks since we have had on stylish clothes."

Rebecca looked at the two of them, bringing the conversation right back. "When are the two of you expecting?"

Sarah looked at Inga and smiled. "Honestly, Rebecca, we haven't figured that out, but given the circumstances, I'm sure the due dates are very close together."

Maybe I had better change the subject, Sarah thought. She pointed at the river ahead, which the Leonard wagon had just entered. "What is the name of that little stream we are crossing today?"

"I think it's Two Otters Creek," Rebecca answered. "Mac told me there's not much to it. Fairly fast current but shallow, maybe knee-deep."

"How are you and Reuben getting along?"

"We are...oh, damn!"

Up ahead, the wagon driven by the Leonards was having some type of problem in the water. The right rear wheel canted at an odd angle, and the rear corner of the wagon was tipped to a level just above the current of the rushing stream. Their team of oxen, which had rapidly gained a reputation around the wagon train as being "better for meat than for pulling," in Reuben's words, was obstinately refusing to move.

Rebecca pulled on the lines, and their prairie schooner creaked to a stop several feet from the water. Mac and Red splashed back across the creek, the big red-haired Irishman stopping for a moment to talk to the Leonards.

"He does not look like a happy wagon master," commented Rebecca.

Inga shook her head, "Uh-oh."

They could hear Mac's raised voice. "If I told you once, I told you one hundred times, Doc. You simply must keep these wagons in excellent repair."

Red came through the stream toward them, and, when Mac came abreast of their driving seat, he took off his hat, nodding his head quickly at each of three women in turn, before replacing it. "Good morning, ladies. We have a little accident, as you can see, that we will have to contend with, but, I don't want the train spread out in a single line like this for long, not in this territory. Hold up here for just a few minutes. I will be right back." He spurred Red toward the end of the column of wagons behind them.

Sarah felt Rebecca's anxiety. "This morning has not started out well," complained the brunette. "First we're awakened far too early by Johannes and Reuben, then we were not allowed to use the oil lamps, which almost ruined our plans to dress up today, and now this."

Inga looked over Sarah's head at Rebecca and said quietly, "Yes, and Johannes and Reuben are somewhere far behind us, just the two of them in country Mac obviously feels is dangerous."

Rebecca pursed her lips, opening her mouth and surely intending—Sarah was convinced—to proclaim some snappy thought, but then her mouth shut. To Sarah's dismay, Rebecca's lower lip trembled, and she took a deep breath. "You're right Inga, that's what's really set me off this morning. I don't feel good at all about the two of them back there. That is Zeb's usual position to the rear and out on one of the flanks. I'm quite sure that's where Zeb rides because it is the most dangerous and requires the most experience."

A sudden thought struck Sarah. She looked closely at Rebecca, who had now suppressed the quivers in her lip, her facial features partially restored to their usual alert but aloof status.

"May I ask a personal question, Rebecca?"

Rebecca looked at her, eyes wider than normal, surprised at Sarah's lead-in. "Of course, Sarah, we are all friends."

Sarah took a deep breath. Afraid of the answer but already knowing what it would be, she blurted out, "Have you been *with* Reuben?" She realized her hands were clenched tightly in her lap.

Rebecca was obviously shocked at the question. She took her eyes off the lines and looked into Sarah's. There was no annoyance in her gaze, just a soft understanding. She colored almost scarlet, took a deep breath, swallowed, and said, "Yes." And then she snapped the lines across the backs of the horses, who began moving toward the creek.

"Wait, Rebecca, wait! Mac told us to wait!" Inga exclaimed.

Rebecca drew hastily back on the lines, and the horses stopped their forward movement, shaking their heads from side to side, confused.

"I forgot."

Sarah felt a wave of deep disappointment wash over her, but something else, too. This news moved her away from an uncertain path, a dream perhaps, and clarified her direction. She reached her hand, rested it affectionately on Rebecca's thigh for a moment, and squeezed. Rebecca glanced at her quickly and they exchanged smiles.

"I'm happy for you, Rebecca. Truly. A bit jealous, yes, I'll admit. But very happy." A thought struck her and she laughed.

The two women looked at her, eyebrows raised. "And, what is so humorous?" asked Rebecca.

Sarah smiled, "I was just thinking about the three of us, here in the middle of nowhere, we are quite unique you know..."

SIX MILES TO THE SOUTHWEST OF THE WOMEN CHATTING IN THE prairie schooner, the hair on the back of Zeb's neck felt prickly. Buck felt the energy, too, his ears alert and rigid, nostrils widely flared, palpitating as they sniffed the air, a slight quiver in the tobiano's front right shoulder.

Zeb wrapped the reins, one loose loop over the horn, swung one long, fringed, buckskin-clad leg over the horse's head and slipped silently from the side of the saddle, the Enfield in his hands, at the ready. He paused, half crouching, and looked carefully in all directions. Then he straightened, reached into his pocket, and brought out a ball of rawhide string. He quickly knotted each end to the swivels on the Enfield musket, one on the forestock, one halfway toward the butt on the rifle, and slung it over his neck and shoulder, careful it did not overlap his back scabbard. He looked down at the Colt and, cap and ball pistols jammed tight in his belt, paused, his eyes searching every rock, swale, and contour of the rolling hills around him, his ears straining for any sound. He carefully withdrew the Sharps from its scabbard, checked the load, and, with a look at Buck, accompanied by a motion of his hand, signaled for the horse to stay put.

Hunched slightly forward, he crept silently up the little bowl-shaped draw toward where its rim disappeared into the startling blue sky, dulled only by the lazy movement of a few scattered puffs of clouds. He moved just a few steps at a time, careful to stay on the hill's slope, halfway up the north side from the tiny creek that gurgled through the bottom, but close enough to the shallow edge above him to duck over the top, or, if a crucial moment called for it, to make for the brush cover along the water. Each few steps he paused, listening, his eyes searching the rim above the spring where the little creek originated, and the ground around him, keenly searching for any sign. *I feel 'em. They've been here.*

His thick, elk hide moccasins moved silently. He was so intent that he missed a small prickly pear cactus hidden under a tuft of blue grama grass. The sharp spines dug into his heel and he bit his lip. Keeping the weight off his foot so as not to drive the tough, barbed needles in further, he eased himself to the ground, his eyes continuing to rove. He pulled the spines out one at a time then lightly pressed the heel of the moccasin down to his skin to make sure none of the cactus were still under the leather. Satisfied, he rose again, crouched for a moment, and then continued his silent stalk.

A warm breeze swirled lazily through the little draw, just enough to stir the early morning air. Slender wheat stalk and needle grasses wavered in the breeze, setting the low hillsides above him in subtle motion. He knelt by the spring, cupped his hand, and raised it to his lips twice, his eyes never leaving the area around him, continually glancing behind him at Buck, now about a hundred yards away. The mustang stood patiently watching. *That's a good sign. Ain't nothin' else got his attention. Best rearguard I've ever had.* He took four steps above the spring and stopped. *Good Lord.*

The tracks were plain, and they were fresh, very fresh. He knelt down, lightly running a dirty forefinger in the slivers of shade formed by the edge of the impressions, granules of dirt working under his nail. The tracks were dry. *Made this morning. Just hours ago. After the dew had dried.* He quickly counted, as best he could, the numbers of unshod ponies that had moved above the spring a short time before. Several moccasin tracks lead from the hoof prints to the water. *I ain't the only one this morning to taste this sweet water.*

He narrowed his eyes, concentrated on the count, deciphering— as taught to him long ago by Tracks on Rock—each different print by size, shape, drag, and depth of indentation. *At least forty, maybe more.* He knelt on one knee, leaning on the Sharps, its butt in the grass, and stroked his mustache, thinking hard. They were moving west, parallel with the train, just five or six miles away.

He heard Buck snort, sensed a disturbance in the air behind him, and instinctively rolled to the ground, dropping the Sharps, the blow from the tomahawk glancing off his shoulder ineffectually. The short, stocky, powerfully built brave, his face painted for war, leapt at him. Zeb rolled again, and the warrior landed with a heavy thud next to him, quickly pushing his upper body up from the ground with one thick arm and rapidly raising his war hatchet with the other. Zeb's pistols were scrunched into his stomach. *Would take too long.* The Sharps lay three or four feet away, and their eyes were locked only two feet apart, the Warrior's dark, angry, and intent as he launched himself sideways at Zeb, the tomahawk blurring the air as he swung it.

Zeb reached over his shoulder, felt the hilt of his knife in his hand, and desperately drew the blade, slashing at the hatchet , parrying the blow, the sharp blade slicing the warrior's upper arm as he did so.

Both men sprang to coiled crouches—two badgers gathered for attack—eyes fastened in a stare of deadly enmity. *Four feet between them,* Zeb gauged. The brave's look darted to the Sharps. Zeb followed his gaze. The Indian sprang from his crouch, like the strike of a rattlesnake. Zeb rose to meet him, his left hand catching the warrior's wrist just below the clench of the deadly hatchet, the warrior's free hand vise-like on the mountain man's forearm below his knife. The momentum of the man's powerful body drove Zeb backward, the brave on top of him. The warrior's weight pushed him against the ground with a thud. The Enfield at his back seared Zeb's side. Two ribs popped, separating from his spine. The pain jarred him, lent him strength. He broke the strong defensive grip below his knife hand and thrust the fourteen-inch blade straight up into the Indian's chest, then twisted it savagely. A look of disbelief flashed across the warrior's face. His eyes, dimming, fastened on Zeb's. Zeb twisted the knife again, driving it to the hilt. The brave coughed, splattering blood on Zeb's face. His chest convulsed and his eyes glazed over, lifeless.

Zeb shoved the body off of him quickly. He withdrew his blade and wiped it on the Indian's leather shirt, took two quick steps to the Sharps, and paused in a half-crouch, both knees bent, one leg extended forward, the quiet, close-in weapon still dripping from its blood groove in one outstretched arm, the long-range weapon ready in the other. Like an eagle guarding its kill, he rotated his shoulders, searching. He saw no other Indians. He sank down to one knee, the pain in his side sharp and biting, the taste of blood on his lips. *Might have punctured a lung.*

Zeb glanced quickly back at the inert form, thick red seeping down into the coarse, sandy soil. The grasses downhill of the body were oddly discolored. *Pawnee. Must be rearguard.* With each breath, pain stabbed his chest. He spat. The spittle was a frothy pink where it clung viscously to blades of grass—*lungs, sure enough. Charlie must have seen 'em—he will warn the train—but what if he doesn't, or can't? Reuben, Johannes, Mac—my friends. Sarah—SARAH!*

He rose and leapt down the little draw, a full frantic downhill run toward Buck, each contact with the ground driving pain into his chest and back like a dagger. The Enfield, still on its sling, bounced wildly against him as he ran. Buck shook his head and trotted to meet him.

He waved his hand in the air in a circular motion. Buck stopped, and turned his rump toward him. With a wheezing grunt, Zeb vaulted up over his back into the saddle and, without taking time to stirrup, dug his heels into the mustang's sides. "Go, Buck, go!" With a whinny, the mustang lunged forward at full gallop, Zeb's mind racing. *Poor Charlie, sure as hell hope he ain't been kilt. Sarah!* Buck bounded up several low hills and careened down their backside, barely braking.

Once in the lower, rolling country, which tapered off to the flats, Zeb hunched low over the saddle, his face almost in the horse's mane. Buck's powerful muscles rippled and worked below him. He gripped the Sharps tightly in his left hand, casting painful, furtive backward glances low over both sides of his shoulders as they sped in the direction of the wagons.

He heard a faint shrill, terrible, far off scream of pain and surprise—its dull, muted echo lost in the frantic sound of Buck's pounding hooves and heavy breathing. In flatter country now, the mustang fairly flew, gaining speed. Far, far in the distance, he could make out the barely visible white canvas wagon tops that marked his unaware friends. *Good God, they're stopped. Damn.* He dug his heels into Buck's flanks again. "By the Lord, if you have ever run boy, you run now—go, Buck, go."

Incredibly, the mustang sped up, his hooves a blur underneath Zeb's buckskin-clad form, his neck fully extended, his nose pointed toward the distant wagons, his tail straightened behind him.

Zeb looked over his shoulder and his blood ran cold. Indians were pouring over the nearest ridge, maybe two miles out. He could faintly hear their whoops and cries. *They had been spotted!* "Buck, run. Run!" He leaned down, grimacing with pain, and shoved the Sharps back into its scabbard. He wrenched the Colt Army revolver from his belt, raised the pistol in the air, and fired. "Dammit, listen up!" he shouted into the wind. He fired again. Behind him—at full gallop on his trail with a cloud of dust swirling in their wake—was the wall of Indians, bent over their ponies and mustangs, their rifles, bows, and lances held high, coming like the angry boil of a swarm of enraged hornets.

NEITHER INGA NOR REBECCA HAD LOST THEIR PUZZLED EXPRESSIONS. "Okay, so here we are, but what's so unique as to be funny, Sarah?"

"Well, I was just thinking. We are, three fairly good-looking women..."

"If we do say so ourselves," said Rebecca with a dry chortle, her laughter joined by both of the other two women.

"Oh my," Sarah laughed harder. "Fine, I will share my thought. I would wager Jacob a thousand dollars that we are the only three single women above the age of eighteen on this entire trail from St. Louis to Cherry Creek..." She paused dramatically and looked at the two of them.

"And...?" demanded Rebecca.

"And...?" echoed Inga.

"Who are neither virgins, nor widows, nor married."

There was a momentary silence as Inga and Rebecca stared at her from either side, their mouths open, and absorbed her observation. Then, suddenly, all three women broke into simultaneous gales of laughter so loud and cackling that the horses jerked forward and Rebecca had to haul back on the lines.

"Whoa, horses, whoa," she gasped for air between laughs. Sarah could not stop laughing. She felt a huge release. Inga was holding her sides.

Sarah's laughter subsided, and she became more serious, "However, the two of you are with men you love and who love you. I have not been so fortunate." Anger welled up in her again as she thought of the injustice of the whole situation.

Rebecca leaned over and put her arms around her shoulders, Inga did the same from the other side, and Sarah was squeezed from both directions. "Sarah, you've certainly had horrible misfortune. But you are beautiful," said Rebecca.

"And Zeb is smitten with you!" added Inga.

Crack! All three of their heads jerked up.

"What was that?" asked Inga, the anxiety in her voice clear.

"That was a shot, Inga, somewhere way out in front of us, I think," said Rebecca tersely.

The second shot was more distinct but still distant. The three women exchanged worried looks.

"What do you suppose...," began Inga.

Suddenly Mac rode by them, at full gallop, his voice booming. "Get those wagons across the Creek. Gather up on the other side. Circle up!"

THREE MILES TO THE SOUTHWEST OF THE DEADLY CLOUD OF DUST and fate hurtling toward the wagon train, Eagle Talon squatted next to the lifeless form of Charlie. The bloody handprints around the broken shaft of the arrow were evidence of the hairy-faced one's last struggle before he went to meet the Spirit. Eagle Talon's gaze searched the ground around the body for sign.

He nodded his head and looked up at Three Knives, then turned his glance to Turtle Shield, Brave Pony, and Pointed Lance. "They ambushed him here. The Pawnee warrior that loosed the arrow was hidden there," he pointed to a small patch of brush one hundred feet away, its spiny branches rising barely two feet above the grass. "White Eyes fell heavily from his horse... tried to remove the arrow." Eagle Talon rolled the body over, revealing a horrible gash to Charlie's throat that almost severed his head from his torso, and a raw and bleeding three-inch wound just above his forehead where the flesh and hair had been cut away. "They cut his throat, and one of them rides with scalp."

He rose. Three Knives pointed with his musket. "They are chasing the trapper and headed toward the white wagons."

Eagle Talon nodded. He sprang on the back of his mustang, carefully fitting his war shield over his arm. He took his bow from around his neck and shoulder and turned to the other four warriors. At the sound of a far-off shot, every head jerked up. A moment passed, and then there was another report.

"The trapper is warning the wagons," said Brave Pony. The men nodded their heads in silent agreement.

Eagle Talon looked at each in turn. "We have been trailing the Pawnee for sixteen suns. They have been trailing the white wagons for two suns. If it were soldiers, or just white men, I would not interfere. Three Knives, two sunsets ago, when we crept close to the white wagons, how many women and papoose did you count?"

Three Knives held up his hands, all ten fingers spread, and flashed them four times. "Over forty... but Eagle Talon, our instructions were to track the Pawnee for protection of The People. It is bad enough you called the other advance scouts to this place with smoke. We should be spread out at least one-half sun apart." The warrior's face was uneasy.

Eagle Talon lifted his chin and raised his hand. "You speak truly, Three Knives, but Brave Pony and Three Cougars have located the tatanka. Three Cougars has gone back to inform the village of the location of buffalo and to tell the Council of the movements of the Pawnee war party. The Council is fully informed. The Pawnee may win this day, but they will be bloody.

"This war party will no longer be a threat to The People. They will bring their wounded back to their column. They will move slowly if they have captured any white eyes. We are not far from the white man's fort, maybe four suns at the speed the wagons travel. Soldiers may come. We have done our job. The Pawnee are no longer a threat except to the hairy faces. If the tribe has moved at the same pace, they may have already intercepted the tatanka. There are over fifteen hundred of our brothers in the herd. There will be plenty of meat and hides. We are alone. We must make our own decisions..."

Eagle Talon thought back two evenings, how the white man behind the wagon that night gathered the small, dark-haired woman in his arms. The man wore a wide-brimmed, dark brown hat and a pearl-handled pistol slung low on his hip. The intensity of their kiss as Eagle Talon watched, the way she laid her head against the man's chest afterward, her hand lightly stroking his back, reminded him of Walks with Moon. Though he did not know the man, Eagle Talon had felt a kindred energy that night. He had heard Spirit whisper, *Friend. Strength. Honor.*

Eagle Talon blinked at the thud of another distant shot. His eyes bored into those of the other braves. "Imagine if we were five hairy-faced ones, and we were watching the Pawnee sweep down on our village, knowing women and children were there. What would you want us as white eyes to do then? Those hairy-faced ones are not our enemies. The Pawnee are our enemies." He raised his bow. "I go to count Pawnee coup this day. Who rides with me?"

The other braves exchange glances. Brave Pony smiled, raised his lance high above his head, shook it, and let out a wild scream. "I go with you Eagle Talon to count Pawnee coup, and I shall count more than you!" With a whoop, he launched his mustang down the hill, Eagle Talon's horse directly behind. The other three braves, after a moment's hesitation, launched their horses down the rise, screaming war cries.

SARAH TURNED TO REBECCA, WHO WAS ALREADY SNAPPING THE LINES. "Move, you horses, move!" she yelled and snapped the lines hard again across the team. They lunged into the water, throwing Sarah against the backrest.

The wagon jerked forward, pulled by the panicked team across the stream's rugged bottom. Spray from the horse hooves splashed the women as the wagon bounced onto the far shore. Rebecca slapped the reins again, urging the horses further on.

Fearful, Inga shouted at her, "Where you going, Rebecca?"

Rebecca didn't take her eyes off the horses. "We need to get far enough from the stream so the other wagons can form around us," she shouted. "Otherwise, we will all get boxed in, in the water!"

Rebecca stood, her small strong body literally leaning backward to bring the horses to an abrupt stop. Sarah watched as she set the brake and tied off the lines. "I'm going to grab my Sharps. Sarah, do you have your pistol?"

Sarah patted her dress pocket, nodded, and drew out the Philadelphia Deringer.

"Do you have reloads for it?"

Sarah bit her lip. "No. They're in my wagon."

Rebecca paused a moment, looked at Sarah, then turned to Inga. "Inga, you know where my ammunition is. Bring it all up front here, and lay it on the footboard."

Inga was uncomprehending, a petrified expression on her face.

"Inga, do it now!"

Still, Inga did not move. Rebecca rose, leaned over Sarah's head, and lightly slapped Inga, once with her palm, and once backhanded. Inga blinked. "Inga, I'm sorry. You must move quickly!"

Jarred back to reality, Inga scrambled over the back of the seat into the wagon. Sarah could hear her frantically moving cargo to get to Rebecca's ammunition. Rebecca jumped down from the driver's seat and took a position behind the tongue of the wagon, checking the load in her Sharps, her back to the creek two hundred feet distant. More wagons rumbled across the water, forming up haphazardly around the prairie schooner, their occupants scrambling down to the ground, virtually all armed except for panic-stricken mothers ushering their children into the backs of the wagons before hastily shutting the canvases.

One wagon, Sarah could not tell whose, had its rear wheel lodged against the Leonard's crippled rig. Now, both wagons were immobilized in the middle of the current, while still others tried frantically to cross. She could see Thelma trying to help the doctor into the back of their prairie schooner, but he looked too weak to climb over the seat. The Kentuckians, though much further back in the wagon line, had somehow managed to pull in next to them. Elijah and Abraham worked methodically, Elijah's wife laying out powder and ball, the young Abraham filling their powder horns, Elijah checking the primer in their muskets. He looked over at the women and called out, "We got ourselves an extra Enfield musket, if ya know how to use it, come get it."

Rebecca sent Sarah to retrieve the Enfield. Sarah held up her dress, cursing at herself for the foolish clothing. As she ran over to the Kentucky wagon, she shot a look out to the expanse to the southwest but saw only distant dust.

"Abraham," Sarah asked, "where's the Enfield?"

The Kentuckian didn't say a word, just nodded his head sideways. She saw the musket perched, butt down, behind the rear wheel. She ran over and grabbed it.

"Hold on, Sarah! Ma, pass Sarah the loads for that gun." Abraham's mother ducked back in the wagon, appeared a second later, and handed two canvas bags down to Sarah. Sarah reached up, their eyes met, and the other woman smiled, her facial muscles twitching with fear, and then she ducked back in the wagon. Sarah heard her talking to her children. "Help Mother get these bags up against the sides. They will stop the bullets. Lie down here flat on the floor, and I will tell you a story."

Sarah ran back through the commotion to their wagon with the Enfield. Rebecca had laid out a neat row of eight cartridges for the Sharps. She had wedged the ladder between the tongue and driver's seat as a shooting rest. Rebecca was practicing her firing position. She turned her head over the stock of the Sharps and spoke, "Sarah, you and Inga will reload. I can reload the Sharps quickly with these first eight rounds. When they are gone, I'll start handing the Sharps back to you. In the meantime, I'll take a shot from the Enfield, and then hand that to Inga so that we have one rifle employed at all times. Do you know how to load these?"

Sarah and Inga looked each other, "Not really."

Rebecca sighed, set the Sharps down, picked up the Enfield, and quickly gave instructions. "The key is powder and wad first, ramrod down, then the shot, again the ramrod. It is very important for the packing to be tight or it could misfire and be out of action. Better to take your time, be a little bit slower, and do it right."

She handed the Enfield to Inga. "Quick, Inga, practice. Say the steps out loud to yourself."

She turned to Sarah, thrust the Sharps into her hands. "Okay Sarah, here's how you load the Sharps." She snapped open the breech and ran through the steps twice. "With practice you can load a round in about eight seconds." Sarah practiced unloading and loading the rifle several times. Rebecca flashed a somewhat shaky smile at her. "We will be just fine."

The brunette's brown eyes, alert and wide, moved back across the creek where the last of the wagons were finally making their way across the current pulled by panicked animals, their drivers wide-eyed and shouting. Sarah followed her gaze past the two crippled rigs trapped in the stream. "Reuben and Johannes will be fine," she said.

There's more than a little worry in her voice, thought Sarah. She reached out her hand and put it on Rebecca's arm. "They will be okay, Rebecca, don't you worry." Rebecca smiled, put her hand over Sarah's and squeezed. "Thank you, Sarah." Then she whirled with the Sharps in her hands and laid it over the shooting rest, pointing at the ever-growing cloud of advancing dust.

Mac galloped up, jumping off Red before the mare had slowed to a stop. He lashed the horse quickly to the rear wagon wheel on the creek side of the schooner, wrenching his brass spyglass from the inside of his jacket. "I see Zeb comin' like hell's on fire, and behind him dust," he said to Rebecca, "a pile of it. Whatever it is, it's still a long ways out." Out in front of them, they heard another shot, this time much louder. Sarah was sure she could hear very faint cries or screams. *Maybe it's just the wind.* She looked over at Inga. Her tall blonde frame was leaning back against the wagon, her eyes closed, her face toward the sky, her lips moving silently. Sarah was certain she was praying.

Mac lifted the telescope again, this time resting it firm against the edge of the seat. Peering through the glass, he inhaled, then exhaled slowly, as if firing a rifle. Suddenly, he sucked in his breath. "Jesus, Mary, Mother of Christ. God help us."

CHAPTER

35

May 10, 1855

$\mathcal{S}$URPRISE

Mac turned to Sarah and Rebecca, his eyes wide, one meaty hand pulling at his beard. "It's Zeb, riding like the wind. Don't see Charlie, but behind Zeb, a mile, maybe two, there's a war party of Indians bigger than I've seen in a long time."

At the sound of whinnying and loud splashing, they looked up to see Johannes and Reuben riding in at a gallop, spray rising in silver arcs from the driving hooves of Lahn and Bente. Like Mac, they leapt off their horses, tying them quickly to the same rear wagon wheel.

Johannes strode directly to Inga and put his hands on her shoulders. Her face remained pointed skyward, her lips moving. He shook her. "Inga." She opened her eyes, dropped her head, recognized Johannes, and threw her arms around him. Johannes hugged her back then gently pushed her away. "Inga," Sarah heard him say, "listen to me carefully. Inga, are you listening?" She nodded her head but said nothing. Her eyes were blinking rapidly. "Get in the wagon, go into my duffel, bring me my saber, and there's a red sash that's wrapped around it. Bring it, too. And two boxes each of .36 and .44 pistol ammunition." Inga ran around the horses to the back of the wagon, and Sarah could hear the tailgate opening.

Reuben had his Colt Navy out, spinning the cylinder, checking the loads, as was Johannes with his Colt Army. Inga ran to him with the saber and pistol ammunition.

Reuben walked up to Mac and smiled at Sarah. He looked long and hard into Rebecca's eyes, then turned to the wagon master. "We heard the shots and came running. There's nothing happening behind us that we could see. What's going on?"

Mac grabbed Reuben's arm, "Step over here for a minute."

Reuben pulled away. "The women have every right to hear."

Mac stopped short, looked at Reuben, Sarah, and then Rebecca. His eyes fell to Rebecca's Sharps, went back up to her face, and he turned to Reuben, "I 'spect you're right. These women can handle it. What we got is Zeb coming at a dead run for his life. Damn good thing that Buck is one of the fastest horses I ever seen. He's at an all-out gallop. Ain't never seen nothing like it. Zeb must've been getting those rounds off from his pistol, cause from what I could tell, he ain't holding a rifle. Behind Zeb, one mile, maybe two, is a line of Indians a quarter-mile wide. Don't know what's behind them, but I would estimate there's at least fifty, maybe more, and they are comin' like they mean it."

He gestured around the wagons haphazardly scattered in a rough semi-circle, the creek at their back. "We didn't have time to set up a full circle, so this'll have to do. Johannes, grab four good men, bring 'em back here and reinforce them two wagons stuck in the stream. Those two brothers in that one wagon can fight, but Thelma and the doc won't be any good at all. Them two wagons might just be a saving grace for us. Any Indians trying to flank us will be slowed enough by the current so that six good riflemen can pick 'em off using those wagons as their station."

Harris, running over from his family's wagon halfway to the creek in the unorganized arc of rigs that had been formed, joined them, out of breath. Sarah could see Margaret jamming loads into their muskets, every once in a while raising her head, obviously scolding Becky and Eleanor to stay in the wagon and get down.

"What do you want us to do?" Harris huffed.

The wagon master looked at him and smiled. "You go back there with Margaret and your kids, Harris. You'll do just fine, though I would take that flag down. You're just callin' attention to yourselves.

Harris' eyes narrowed and he straightened his back, "I ain't takin' that flag down for no one, and for nothing. It's flown against the British in two wars. It ain't never been taken down, and I'm not about to start now." He shifted his glance to Reuben, "You understand, Mr. Frank, I told you about this flag."

Reuben nodded slowly, "I understand, Harris."

Without another word, Harris turned and lumbered back toward his rig. Mac raised the telescope, which had never left his hand, again using the corner of the wagon as a rest. "Zeb's about quarter-mile out now, ridin' like the wind." He turned and cupped both hands to his mouth. His voice boomed up and down the uneven line of wagons. "Have your ammunition ready. Set up a reloading team. Pick your targets. One good shot is better than three wild ones. The key is to keep them outside these wagons. Zeb's comin' in, so don't shoot."

Behind Sarah, Johannes was giving directions to four men as the group sprinted for the wagons in the creek, water up around their knees as they ran. Johannes was obviously pointing out positions he wanted them to take even while running, his red sash and saber clearly visible, his Sharps carbine in one hand and Colt Army in the other.

Mac followed her gaze. "He's all military, that one. No hesitation. Pure instinct and training. Better than most officers we got, for sure. Good luck, Sarah. Good luck, Rebecca." He tugged on the brim of his hat. "Reuben, follow me."

Reuben turned, then wheeled back to Rebecca, wrapped his free arm around her, and pulled her roughly to him. Sarah's heart raced as she watched him quickly, and deeply, kiss the brunette. Then he turned and followed the running, bulky form of the wagon master down the line of wagons.

OUT BEYOND THE WAGONS, SARAH COULD NOW SEE ZEB CLEARLY, Buck a beautiful blur of speed underneath him, the mountain man hunched over the horse's neck, pistol in one hand. Seconds later, several wagons down the line, they vaulted over the tongue of a wagon and, with a cloud of swirling dust, Zeb slid off the mustang, doubling over as his feet hit the ground, sinking to one knee, and holding his side.

"Oh my God!" Without thinking, Sarah ran to him as he stood slowly erect, one hand clutching his ribs. *He's been shot!* Her heart was in her throat as she ran up to him and looked up into his face. "Zeb, Zeb, have you been shot? Are you all right?"

Zeb smiled slowly at her. "I think lookin' into your big blue eyes, seein' them freckles, and the way that sunlight is bouncin' off your hair, makes every bit of that ride worth it." He chuckled, winced, and Sarah noticed a slight pink bubbling on his lips. She reached up her hands and grabbed his leather shirt with clenched fists. "Dammit, Zeb, have you been shot?"

"No. Just ribs. I'll be fine. You get back up there behind the wagon with Rebecca and Inga."

"But, Zeb..."

"I'll be fine. You get, quick. They're gonna be here any second." He ran over to Buck, murmured in the horse's ear, and drew the Sharps and Enfield from their scabbards. Sprinting to the Leonard's wagon, he knelt down, holding his side, and rested the Sharps on its tongue. Buck trotted behind him and, to Sarah's dismay, the horse flattened itself sideways against the creek side of the Conestoga, his muzzle toward his master.

She heard distant, wild screams and looked up to see the furious horde of Indians, terrible cries coming from their lips like demons descending on heaven. She gathered up her dress and ran back to their wagon. Rebecca was in firing position—the Sharps snug into her shoulder and firm against her cheek, the barrel steady on the wooden ladder rest.

Sarah took a deep breath, leaned back against the wagon, and closed her eyes. Her lids jerked open with the loud report of Rebecca's Sharps just feet from her. Rebecca did not look up. "One down," she said. The petite woman's tone was steady and level. The wagon train was alive now with the scattered thumps of rifles and musket fire. Sarah peaked around the corner of the wagon. The Indians were coming full bore. Several horses were without riders. She heard the report of their guns, saw flashes of fire over the tops of their horses, and the air filled with the deadly sigh of lead. She heard a scream and turned her head quickly. The boy from the Kentucky wagon, Abraham, was down on the ground holding his knee. His father scrambled over and dragged him by the collar, almost throwing him under their wagon. He picked up the boy's musket and tossed it to him, pointing. The boy nodded his head and, lying on his back, began to reload. She looked down the other line of wagons. Harris was still in the wagon seat directly under the flag, settled between the driver's bench and using the sideboard for cover. He took a shot then reached back for a reloaded musket from Margaret.

There was a sickening "thwak" nearby and one of their lead horses collapsed into the traces. The other horses tried to rear but couldn't, hobbled by the tangled harness weight holding them down.

She peaked around the wagon again as Rebecca fired and could clearly see the war paint on the faces of the advancing braves, who had not slowed whatsoever. They were coming closer. Her hand slipped into her dress pocket and closed around the Deringer.

Rebecca shot again. In front of them, Sarah heard another scream. Reuben and Mac were down at the end by the farthest three wagons, rigs driven by older couples, one of them the retired government man from DC. Reuben and Johannes had remarked he couldn't hit the target. She blinked when she saw Jacob at their wagon, his pistol out, taking careful aim, then firing, then taking careful aim again. An arrow lodged itself in the corner of the wood frame above his head. He ducked, then reached up, yanked the arrow from the wood, and, with a furtive glance around him, stowed it quickly, but carefully, in the footwell of the wagon seat. *Strange,* flashed across Sarah's mind.

Rebecca's Sharps barked again. *The eighth round.* Sure enough, Rebecca turned from her crouched position and handed Sarah the Sharps. "Reload. Be quick about it. Inga, give me the Enfield." Rebecca grabbed the musket from Inga's trembling outstretched arm, and again set herself up in her shooting position. In the same instant, three Indians and their mustangs vaulted over wagon tongues at various points in the curve of wagons, quickly followed by four more. Several more horses screamed and dropped in their harnesses. An oxen brayed in terror and fell slowly on its side, kicking its legs. More shots rang out and several Indians, who had breached the line, toppled from their horses. One loosed an arrow and four wagons away one of the pioneers rose to full height, clawing at the wooden shaft protruding from his chest, then sank to his knees, and rolled over into the dust.

There were more and more Indians now inside their circle, splitting the pioneer firepower from the outside of their shield of wagons. The two wagons in the river were burning. Johannes and another man were dragging Thelma and the doctor through the creek. The corpses of two pioneers and two warriors drifted downstream bobbing in the current like lifeless logs. Sarah stood stupefied. Her knees trembled. The sweat of heat and fear ran down her temples in grimy streaks. Smoke from the burning canvases, dust, and grey puffs of gunpowder rendered everything surreal, softening the apparitional shapes of the wounded and bodies strewn in grotesque positions. The guttural whoops of the attackers, screams of petrified and dying animals, and moans of pain echoed amongst the wagons and the sharp sounds of gunshots.

Sarah held the Sharps in one hand, breech open, ready for loading, frozen in shocked disbelief. The scene was incomprehensible. Through the haze of the battle raging around the wagons, she saw the shadowy figures of Mac, Reuben, and Johannes sprinting to a breach where the Indians had pulled over one of the smaller rigs. In that gap, Zeb, a knife in each hand, and two other men from the train, struggled in mortal combat with an increasing number of lance and tomahawk wielding invaders. Reuben and Mac each carried two rifles. Johannes had his carbine in one grip, pistol in the other. His saber scabbard slapped against his leg as he ran.

Sarah saw him look over his shoulder and could barely make out his shout. "Behind us!"

Johannes wheeled, ghostlike in the brownish grey cloud that enveloped the conflict, and stood calmly erect, his pistol extended.

He fired once from the Colt. The rider of the horse bearing down on the three jerked violently from the impact of the .44-caliber slug, then somersaulted backward over the rear of his steed. He lay unmoving, barely discernible in the groundswell of dust.

Sarah's eyes quickly searched the nearby wagons. Jacob had disappeared. Her mouth fell open when she saw Harris wrestling with a much smaller Indian who was obviously after that heirloom American flag, hanging ripped, tattered, and limp in the semi-opaque heat. Disbelief knifed through her numb detachment. *What type of people are these who risk their life for a piece of old cloth?* Below Harris, Margaret wielded her musket like a club, keeping another attacker at bay. Two men ran through the din to assist her.

"Sarah, load the damn rifle!" came Rebecca's frantic shout.

Sarah jolted back to reality. Trying to control the trembling that had overtaken her body, she jammed the cartridge into the Sharps with shaking fingers, then handed the long gun to Rebecca who, in turn, gave her the Enfield she had just discharged. Rebecca turned, rested the receiver and forestock over the lip of the wagon, and swung the muzzle as she found another target.

Without looking back, Rebecca commanded in a loud voice, "Inga, reload that Enfield. Quickly!"

Pressed against the side of the wagon box, Sarah fumbled in the saddle bag Rebecca had draped over the wagon wheel for the next round. She heard a whisper in the air, like the sound a small bird makes on a calm, peaceful evening in the stillness just before dark. And then a sudden, hollow, resounding *thud*. A woman's voice cried out in pain.

"Sarah, get the Enfield from Inga," Rebecca almost screamed. The urgency in Rebecca's voice made Sarah peer around the corner of the wagon, the next load for the Sharps in her hand. Headed at a gallop right for them were three Indians, no more than a few hundred feet away.

"Oh my God, Inga, the Enfield!" shouted Sarah as she turned to her friend, expecting to grab the musket and give it to Rebecca. She gasped, her breath caught in her throat, her mind suddenly blank.

Inga lay on the ground writhing, both her hands pressed to her belly. Between her shaking fingers was the shaft of an arrow, its fletching wobbling grotesquely as her body spasmed. Her head was partially lifted off the ground, her eyes wide she looked down at her wound.

"Sarah, Sarah, I've been hit. Oh Lord Jesus. Oh my God," she whimpered. Her voice rose, "*Johannes, Johannes.*"

"Sarah, dammit," Rebecca panicked, "The rifle. Quick!"

Sarah ran the few steps to Inga's prostrate form. Her skin was the pallor of dirty linen. Her pupils were dilated, and she was breathing shallowly in short rapid breaths, her eyes staring, eyelids blinking rapidly. A wide swath of red was spreading, staining her green traveling dress. Sarah knelt down, "I will be right back, Inga." Inga clawed feebly at Sarah's dress. "Sarah, the baby. Do you think the baby is all right?" Sarah fought the urge to vomit, patted Inga's bloody hand, grabbed the dropped Enfield, and sprinted toward the head of the wagon. The three braves had dismounted and were advancing on foot. "Sarah, throw me the gun!"

Rebecca caught the musket, juggled it into position, and turned, the first brave just feet away. Sarah reached for the Deringer in her dress pocket. Rebecca brought the musket level, just above her waist, cocked the hammer, and pulled the trigger. Click. Nothing. *Inga had not reloaded!* The first warrior reached across the wagon tongue and grabbed Rebecca, his hand quickly around her throat as he tried to drag her toward him, his other arm rising, holding a knife. She struggled, fighting him off, the other two braves close behind.

Sarah stepped up into the wagon seat, leaned over the front, cocked the hammer of the Deringer and, from two feet away, fired. The top of the man's head disappeared. He sank to his knees, his hand still clasped around Rebecca's throat, dragging her down with him. She struggled and finally freed herself from his death grip, but, by that time, the other two braves were almost on them. Sarah cocked her arm and threw the pistol with all the force she could muster. One Indian staggered back, blood spurting from between his fingers, his hand clamped to his forehead just above his eye where the pistol had found its mark. His lips curled, baring his teeth in a sneering smile, and he lunged forward again. Rebecca had the Enfield up, holding it by the barrel like a club.

From behind them came an unearthly half-scream, half-shout, boiling with anger and anguish—Johannes—his eyes fixed on them. Further down the line of wagons, Reuben was already running toward them; he threw down his rifle and pulled the Colt, his sprinting form drifting in and out of the smoke and haze.

Johannes wheeled to face a mounted Indian brave with a lance. The tall blonde fenced with his saber, ducked the man's lance, then ran the sword through the brave, lifting the body off the horse with the blade and throwing it to the ground. He raised the saber, and it flashed again as it disappeared in a downward arc into the dust toward the ground. He swung on top of the vanquished brave's mustang, issuing a bloodcurdling cry, his bloody saber raised and glinting dully in the sun and haze, and bore down on them at a gallop.

Sarah jerked, the Indian she had hit with the thrown Deringer had his hand on her wrist, trying to pull her down off the wagon. His eyes glittered black under the bloody split in his eyebrow from the pistol. Red and black paint in alternating wavy lines down his scowl accentuated his hawkish face. Sarah lowered her mouth and sank her teeth into his hand. He shouted in a strange, guttural tongue and let go, jerking his hand away. The other Indian, thick-necked and shouldered, lashed out viciously with his shield, catching Rebecca on the side of the head. She slumped to the ground. He grabbed her by the hair and began dragging her back to his pony. Blood trickled from her mouth as she feebly resisted.

There was a swish, a flash of steel, and the brave's arm and hand, which once again had been trying to drag Sarah down from the wagon, was suddenly not attached to his body. Towering above them on the Indian pony was Johannes. Again, his saber flashed. The Indian screamed, holding his throat. The saber dipped, and Sarah watched the Indian fall, gurgling, with a thud to the ground.

Johannes glanced quickly at Inga, his face ashen, and then at Rebecca, now dragged halfway to the fleeing warrior's horse. He dug his heels into the mustang, vaulted the tongue, and bore down on the marauding kidnapper, shouting Danish battle cries. Three other Indians on ponies charged out of the swirl of smoky dust, intent on joining the fray. The Indian let go of Rebecca and raised his lance, holding it at the ready as Johannes bore down on him. As Johannes neared the Indian, he lunged with the spear. Johannes parried smoothly with the saber and, as he raised it, twisted it deftly to the side. The headless torso of the brave did a grotesque dance of death before it toppled sideways to the ground.

Sarah tried to scream, "Johannes, Johannes, behind you," but no words came out, just a raspy croak. The soldier in Johannes already knew. He wheeled, spurring the mustang. The horse reared up, its forehooves pawing the air, and came back to the ground on the dead run. Johannes charged forward, saber held angled in front of him, his deep baritone voice shouting words Sarah couldn't recognize, but a challenge that she was sure echoed back to the dawn of man. He rode directly into the three charging Indians, his horse's momentum knocking one of the other horses over, his saber slashing, moving rapidly, wide swings, thrusts, parries. In a minute, it was over. The three warriors were dead and one of their horses was on the ground, struggling but unable to rise. Johannes shot the wounded animal with his Colt, turned his own horse back at a gallop toward their wagon, and was on the ground running long before he reached the rig. He leapt over the tongue, throwing a quick sideways glance at Sarah, a look that she would remember on her deathbed.

He knelt down next to Inga and reached for her hand, delicately taking her other hand from her abdomen. He spoke to her and she answered weakly in Norwegian. Tears trickled from her eyes. He let go of her hands and lifted his own. They hovered around the shaft of the arrow, as if unsure whether to extract it. One of Inga's hands clutched desperately at his sleeve. She tried to raise her head, but he eased her gently back down, leaning over to whisper to her.

Sarah tore her eyes from the couple and began sobbing uncontrollably. Several shots rang out and a strange type of whooping, different than what their attackers had surprised them with, filled the dusty mist. The Indians still around the wagons were suddenly talking excitedly, shouting back and forth at one another. They wheeled their horses and galloped out. Another shot. Then another. More cries echoed from out there in the opaque space. So strange. What was happening? Through her blurred vision, she saw Rebecca roll to her knees sixty feet outside the circle of wagons, her head on the ground. She ran to her. "Rebecca, Rebecca, are you all right?"

Rebecca shook her head slowly, obviously dazed, blood steadily dripping from her lip where the shield had caught her. Still crying, Sarah frantically helped Rebecca stagger to her feet and back toward the cover of the prairie schooner. *I have to go help Johannes with Inga.*

Grabbing one of Rebecca's arms, she put it over her shoulders, and half walked, half dragged the brunette the last twenty-five feet to the wagon. She helped her stuporous friend get under the driving seat, propping her up against the inside of the front wheel. "I'll be right back, Rebecca." Rebecca stared vacantly at her and nodded her head, indicating some degree of comprehension. Sarah tried to jump the wagon tongue but her dress caught and she fell, skinning both hands. She pushed herself up, skidded around the corner of the wagon, and then leaned back against the side, her hand involuntarily covering her mouth. *Oh no, oh no. Please no.*

Reuben stood with his hand on the small of Johannes' back. The tall blonde man was on his knees, hunched over, his face buried in Inga's neck, holding one of her bloody hands. Inga's eyes stared skyward to the side of Johannes' buried face, unseeing.

Reuben looked up at Sarah, his face contorted with pain, and wagged his head slowly side to side. He mouthed the question, "Rebecca?" Sarah gestured behind her. He patted Johannes one more time, straightened up, and ran around the corner of the wagon. He knelt by Rebecca, and with his kerchief tenderly wiped the blood from her mouth and chin.

May 10, 1855

*T*HE BOND

ZEB STAGGERED OUT OF THE SMOKE HOLDING HIS SIDE. HE PULLED up short, the tragic scene of Johannes and Inga spread before him. His eyes caught Sarah's. He walked quickly to her, gathering her in one arm and pulling her close. She sobbed uncontrollably into his buckskin. A wounded Indian lay about a hundred feet beyond the wagons. He fought to rise to his knees, trying to stand, then toppled over.

Mac showed up, one arm hanging limply, the broken shaft of an arrow protruding from just below his shoulder. Blood dripped from his fingers onto his dusty boot, each droplet raising a tiny puff of dirt. His shotgun was in the other hand, perched on his hip. With him was Elijah, with his Kentucky long gun, asking Mac, "Where in hell do you think they went?"

"I don't know. Strange they broke it off. I was pretty sure we were holding our own, but I figured they would make off with a few of us. Can't explain it. Never seen nothing like it."

A tremor ran through Sarah as another shot rang out, several hundred yards from beyond the wagons to the southwest. Then, through the wavering, sifting battle cloud that was beginning to settle, she saw dim figures moving toward them. Five Indians materialized, as if a mirage, the haze of the fight and wavy ground reflections of sun-heat distorting their figures. They rode slowly, with their backs straight, no war paint, no screams. *Taller than those who had attacked the wagons,* Sarah felt other subtle differences, too, *perhaps in their clothing.*

Elijah raised his rifle, but Zeb knocked the barrel down toward the ground. "Hold yer horses. They ain't Pawnee," he glanced at the Indian lying just a hundred feet from them, then back at the approaching riders. "I'll be damned, they be Sioux."

Reuben straightened up from Rebecca and picked up the Colt, which he had laid down on the ground when he knelt down next to her. Where he stood, outside the wagons, he was the closest to the approaching band of warriors.

Mac turned to Zeb, "You don't suppose..."

Zeb nodded. "Yep, them Sioux is what turned them Pawnee around. They must of hit 'em from the rear. Ain't often one Indian goes against another for a white man, leastways unless they were Army scouts."

REUBEN FELT NUMB—THE SHOCK OF INGA'S DEATH, THE SEETHING anger, tinged with guilt and worry he felt at Rebecca's near kidnapping, her injury, the heart-wrenching empathy he felt for Johannes—it gripped his gut like the tight vise of a blacksmith's tongs. He fought to get some measure of control back into his breathing.

He was unsure of the intent of the approaching braves, but he could hear Mac and Zeb's conversation behind him. Eight feathers hung from the lead warrior's long black hair. He sat rigidly athletic, graceful, and proud on his mustang, a bow hanging around his neck and shoulder, an ornate shield painted with the claw of a raptor fastened high on one arm, its rounded top slightly higher than his shoulder. He held a bloodied lance in his right hand. Reuben quickly counted the arrows in his quiver—only three. He glanced behind him at Rebecca. Peering through the wagon wheel spokes, her eyes were fixed apprehensively ahead.

The man rode steadily and deliberately. The four warriors behind him looked wary, and one clutched a bloody side, swaying a bit on top of his horse.

They rode up to the wounded Pawnee. Still alive, the enemy warrior tried to rise to his feet, one knee bent, one foot planted. The

Sioux brave in the lead urged his horse forward and without hesitation, ran his lance through the man's chest, then wrenched it savagely backward. The Pawnee fell in a heap, no longer moving. A warrior behind him leaped from his horse, pulled the dead Pawnee's head up by his hair, and with two quick circular motions of his knife, took his scalp.

"Oh, oh my God," came Rebecca's low, horrified voice from behind the wagon wheel.

Reuben watched as the Sioux leader silently raised the point of the lance to the sky. Then he urged his horse forward, and, fifty feet from Reuben, stopped, raising his free hand, fingers to the sky, palm to Reuben. Their eyes met over the short distance. There was a long silence. The tightness in his chest released slightly. He lowered his Colt, twirled it twice, and dropped it in its holster. He rose from his slight crouch.

"Reuben..." hissed Rebecca, alarm in her voice. Without breaking eye contact with the warrior, he replied in a low voice, "It is fine, Rebecca. He is a friend. I feel it." He slowly raised his arm, fingers up, open palm. The Indian's mustang pawed the ground, the brave's lips parted in the hint of a smile, and, speaking without words, their energies spanned cultures and a bond was formed.

Zeb was suddenly at Reuben's side. The Indian spoke in a resonant voice, and Zeb, without taking his eyes off the brave, said, from the side of his mouth, "His name is Eagle Talon. He wants to know yours."

Reuben looked at Eagle Talon. "Reuben Frank."

The Indian repeated slowly, "Roo-bin Frank," then nodded his head. His eyes moved to Rebecca, and he spoke again.

"He wants to know if she's your wife," Zeb translated.

The question made Reuben smile. He glanced at Rebecca. "Not yet," he replied.

Zeb repeated the words, also moving his hands and fingers in sign. The Indian nodded, smiled, and spoke again.

"He says she reminds him of his wife, and he says he understands, 'Not yet'."

Reuben nodded, as did the Sioux. "Ask him his wife's name, Zeb."

Zeb spoke and signed. The regal look on the brave's face softened. A deep breath filled his chest. When he spoke, his tone was almost reverent.

"Well, I'll be damned and go to hell." Reuben turned to look at Zeb. The mountain man's eyes were wide, and his face wore a look of total surprise. Reuben could not have known his friend was remembering a Sioux village almost twenty years prior, and the delicate touch of a little Indian girl on his wrist. "What is it, Zeb, what did he say?"

"I know this tribe, Reuben. They are Oglala Sioux. He says his wife's name is Walks with Moon."

"Tell him that is a beautiful name, and tell him Rebecca's name."

It was obvious Zeb was lost in thought and it took a moment for him to start speaking. The brave smiled at Reuben's compliment toward his wife, and nodded when Zeb motioned to Rebecca and told him hers.

"Ray-bec-ka." He nodded his head vigorously, "Ray-bec-ka."

Zeb asked him something that Reuben couldn't understand. The brave's eyes clearly widened in amazement. He nodded his head and said one sharp word. Reuben did not need a translator to understand the emphatic, "Yes."

Zeb spoke again. The Indian looked serious and nodded. He shifted his eyes back to Reuben, lifted his lance, and said, "*Toksa, Kola.*"

Reuben heard Zeb's whisper to the side of his ear, "That means, 'Until I see you again, friend'."

The warrior's eyes moved to Rebecca. "Ray-bec-ka."

The five warriors wheeled their horses and cantered toward the northwest, their shadows fading in the quickly settling dust of the retreating Pawnee.

CHAPTER

37

May 10, 1855

ℒETTING GO

REUBEN WATCHED THE SIOUX UNTIL THEY WERE SWALLOWED BY THE land. He walked back the several steps to the wagon and bent down next to Rebecca. The gash above her lip was jagged. The blood had mostly coagulated, though a thin trickle still seeped from the corner of her mouth, ending at her trembling chin. He took the kerchief from her listless grasp and gently tried to wipe the red streak from her face. She stared dully at his face.

"Is everyone all right?" she asked.

Reuben kept his eyes fixed on the handkerchief and rubbed the stubborn blotches of caked blood from her jaw. He raised the hand-kerchief to his mouth, licked it, and tenderly wiped the last remnant. He looked closely at her lip. "We need to get that sewed up."

She sat forward with effort, stretched out one hand, and clutched his sleeve. "Reuben, is everyone all right?" A vein of anxious panic laced her question.

Reuben looked down at the ground, traced absently in the dirt with his finger, reached up one hand, took hers from his arm and wrapped his hand around hers, giving it a gentle squeeze. "No, Rebecca, everyone is not all right." He sighed, once more awash in that bitter helplessness that had clutched him prior to his encounter with the Sioux.

"Johannes?"

"Johannes is fine. Well, he's uninjured."

Her eyes widened and tears welled in her lower eyelids. Her lips trembled. "Inga?" she asked, her voice an unsettling blend of hope, despair, and knowing. *She's beginning to shake.* Reuben sat down next to her, put his arm around her, and hugged her. Her voice rose, "Tell me, Reuben, is Inga all right?"

He pulled her shoulder tighter to him and squeezed her more tightly. "Inga's dead, Rebecca."

He could feel the shock radiate through her body. She turned her head into his chest and began to sob, "It's my fault, Reuben, my fault. I asked her to accompany me west, thinking only of myself. I needed a companion, someone to take care of the basic chores. I had no right." Her shoulders shook violently and she clung to him. "No right. Oh my God, that kind, beautiful woman is dead."

"It wasn't your fault, Rebecca. Inga loved the adventure. You did not trick her, she knew..." he paused and drew a deep breath, "she knew you were going back to England. She met her man, she saw the land, she felt a kinship with it, and she was a fine lady."

Rebecca's anguished sobs intensified, "You don't understand, Reuben, you don't understand. I didn't just kill her, I killed them. I killed *them*."

"Rebecca, you didn't cause her death or anyone else's," he rested his cheek on her head and wrapped his other arm around her.

"What am I going to tell Johannes, Reuben?"

Her body was shaking. Reuben lowered his head and kissed her soft, dark brown hair. "There's nothing you need to tell Johannes. He has a strong soul. He will be grief stricken for a long time, but he will emerge from it. I think Inga taught him much about himself, about life...and about love." *Did he have a chance to tell her before she died? Did she know at the end that he loved her?* Reuben felt a tear trickle down his cheek, and his throat felt tight. *Get ahold of yourself. This will not help Rebecca. Or Johannes.*

In between Rebecca's deep, ragged breaths were great heaving gasps. "I killed them...I didn't know...I was around the front of the wagon and should've helped...I knew something was wrong...I heard the scream, saw Sarah's face, but they were coming...Oh, Reuben, I wish I'd never left England..."

Reuben cradled her heaving shoulders and patted her on the back. Her sobs subsided, but only slightly. "Who else?" she asked, her voice muffled by his shirt.

Reuben took a deep breath. "Sarah's fine. Mac took an arrow in his upper arm and is bleeding badly. Johannes tells me that Dr. Leonard, though he wasn't injured, is very sick and having trouble breathing. Johannes had to drag him across the stream when the Indians torched the stranded wagons. Both of the Thompson brothers were killed, though they fought bravely. Abraham took a bullet in his knee. With Dr. Leonard incapacitated, we really have no medical person on the wagons other than Thelma, and her experience only comes from watching her husband over the years."

The government man from Washington is dead, too." Reuben shook his head, remembering as he spoke, "I was standing right there, reloading the Sharps. One moment he was talking to me, the next moment there was an arrow through his neck. That man Livingston, with the four children, four wagons down from ours, took an arrow through the chest. He's dead. Harris was shot in the leg. I think he will be fine. There are others wounded. That's all I know. I'm going to have a look around, check in with everybody, try and find Johannes and Zeb, and see what Mac wants to do."

Her hysteria had lessened, relegated to narrowly spaced, heaving, rasping breaths. "Sarah? I must talk to Sarah. I don't know what to do."

"Do about what, Rebecca? There's nothing you can do. What's done is done. None of it was your fault. You didn't will any of this to happen."

She shook her head, still leaning into his chest. "No, Reuben. You don't understand. I must talk to Sarah so that we can decide what to do."

She is tired, Reuben guessed, *delirious, might even have a concussion from that blow.* "Rebecca, let me help you into the wagon. It's going to take at least a day to sort out this mess and..." his voice caught, "and to bury the dead."

He stood and half dragged her from behind the wagon wheel. She was unsteady, her face pale, her lip was bleeding again, and her magnetic brown eyes were red and puffy, and brimming with tears. The bodice of her dress was stained with blood, and there was a large tear in the fabric where the Indian had dragged her. She sagged against him and he reached down and scooped up her small form, one arm under her knees, the other around her back. Her arms were wrapped around his neck and her head buried in his shoulder. She shook and wept.

"I killed two men today. Oh God, forgive me."

"You had no choice, Rebecca. They picked the fight."

Holding her, Reuben stepped over the tongue of the wagon. The flow of Two Otters Creek seemed unperturbed by the tragedy on its banks. Zeb stood nearby, clenching and unclenching his coonskin cap in one hand, comforting Sarah with the other. It was the first time Reuben had seen the mountain man without his headgear in broad daylight, and the amount of grey in his hair stunned him. Both of Sarah's arms were wrapped around Zeb's waist, her head reaching just below his shoulder. Her dress was ripped and tattered, and a large blood stain marked one entire side of the fabric. She was crying, her sobs and Rebecca's mingling with the sounds of the other pioneers in a low wail of grief and shock that blended eerily with the strangely cheerful rush of the creek's current.

He exchanged looks with the mountain man, their eyes saying everything, yet nothing.

"I am going to lay Rebecca out in the wagon. She needs rest. She may have a concussion. Do you know anything about stitching up wounds?"

Zeb's eyes dropped to Rebecca. "Her lip?"

"Yes."

"I can stitch her up, but she's probably gonna have a scar."

Reuben was shocked when Sarah looked up from the depths of Zeb's buckskin shirt. A wide smear of blood marred the side of her face, the blue of her eyes almost indistinguishable beneath swollen eyelids and a heavy film of tears. Her usually fair complexion was devoid of color, other than the freckles across the bridge of her nose, which seemed out of place and somehow diminished.

"Zeb, bring Sarah to the wagon, too," he said, looking down at Rebecca in his arms. "Let's stretch them out. They could use some time together. Wish we had a shot of whiskey—they could use that, too."

"Yeah, they need some whiskey, and I'd like to clean that lip off before stitching it up. Let's find that bastard Irishman. He always has whiskey...if he survived," he added, a hopeful tone in his voice as he helped Sarah.

Back at the wagon, Zeb opened the tailgate, leaned down, and kissed Sarah on the head. "Hang onto Reuben for a moment, Sarah. Let me get up in there." He handed Sarah off to Reuben, and she leaned against him for support while Zeb clambered onto the tailgate. "Reuben, this wagon's in shambles."

"Inga was looking for ammo and Johannes' saber."

Zeb straightened a few things around and laid out Sarah's and Rebecca's bedrolls. Reuben lifted Rebecca's form up to the mountain man. Zeb turned and laid her gently down on her bedroll. Then Reuben scooped up Sarah in his arms and lifted her to Zeb.

Zeb was about to jump down when Sarah's pleading voice drifted over to the men. "Zeb, Zeb, I can't lie here in these horrible clothes with Inga's blood. Help me get them off, please."

Zeb and Reuben exchanged glances. Reuben climbed up into the wagon and together the two men gently took her dress off, removed the stiff, blood-soaked crinoline, and then her three stiff horsehair petticoats. The blood had seeped all the way through to her chemise.

She looked down at herself. "Oh, God!" Her voice was shrill. "Cut it off, Zeb. Cut it off me!" she said, her voice rising. "Get this blood off me."

"Well...Sarah...I..."

"Get it off me, Zeb, please!" Her voice was frantic as she tried to rip the fabric away from her skin.

Zeb looked at Reuben, his deep-set eyes helpless. He took out his belt knife, "Turn away from me, Sarah." He carefully inserted the blade between her skin and the material, and ran it down the length of the chemise, peeling the fabric away as his knife hand moved.

Her pale, smooth flesh was bare upward from the waistband of her pantaloons, her small full breasts visible from the side. She was breathing deeply and trembling, somewhere between shock and sobs. Reuben's eyes widened at the definite roundness of her belly. Zeb noticed it, too, and again the two men exchanged glances. Zeb threw Sarah's blood-soaked clothing out of the back of the wagon. They pulled the blankets up over her and turned.

"Wait!" Rebecca was looking at them, her eyes blinking rapidly. "Reuben, please, take my dress off, too. Take it somewhere. Burn it." Her voice was strident, her upper body shaking. Reuben looked into her beseeching, teary eyes. He sat down next to her, helping her roll to her side. Then he undid the buttons and drawstrings down her back, sliding the dress over her shoulders and down her legs before throwing it out back to the tailgate.

She had not worn a rigid crinoline dome to give her dress a ballooning shape as Sarah had. A realization flashed through his mind, *Sarah is trying to conceal.* Instead, there were four sets of horsehair petticoats. He clumsily stripped the last layers from her until she was clad only in the chemise, the sheer silk revealing every curve of her body in filmy detail.

Zeb, obviously embarrassed, looked at Reuben and said, "I'll wait outside."

Reuben nodded. He bent down and pulled the wool blankets over Rebecca. She had curled into a fetal position, her eyes tightly closed. He bent down and gently kissed her on the cheek, then moved his lips to her ear and whispered, "Remember, Rebecca Marx, I love you. Now get some rest." As he was standing, she reached out and grabbed his hand, squeezing hard. "Thank you," she coughed.

Then, as he was about to leave, she called him back. He sat down again, leaning his head close so he could hear her. "Reuben, I'm proud of you. You were brave, very brave today."

He kissed her cheek. "No, Rebecca. It is you who showed courage today. Close your eyes," he whispered. "We will be back shortly." Then he rose, jumped down from the wagon, closed the tailgate, and partially tied the canvas before turning to Zeb.

Zeb shook his head. "A pile of sadness in one place," he said, "for such a short spell of time."

Reuben looked up at his friend, noticing for the first time the thin, pink film of blood bubbling on Zeb's lips. "Damn, Zeb, you hit, too?"

"No, just cracked some ribs. Got jumped by a Pawnee warrior up in the hills. Strong son of a bitch. Thought I was in trouble there for a moment. Broke my own ribs on the Enfield when I fell." He chuckled. "Damn fool thing to do."

"Have you seen Johannes?"

Zeb's lips tightened and a pained look crept into his eyes. "Nope. Last I saw him he was carrying Inga's body, a shovel, and his Sharps down river. I suspect he does not want to be found."

"Let's swing around the wagons and see exactly what the casualties and damages are. I'm sure there's many folks who need help. Then we will report to Mac." Reuben took a step, stopped, and straightened up. "We ought to have riders out. Maybe those Pawnee have left—maybe they haven't."

Zeb smiled, "Already got 'em out, Reuben. Figured you needed time alone with your woman, and Mac looked mighty peaked when he headed over to the supply wagons, so I just took things in my own hands. Hope you don't mind."

"Mind? Hell, no, Zeb. Thanks." He looked up at his friend, "But she's not my woman."

Zeb's eyebrows raised. "Well, whatever she might tell you, son, she thinks she's your woman. And while we're checking things, let's find that bastard Jacob and get that whiskey."

JACOB SAT IN HIS AND SARAH'S WAGON ON TOP OF A HALF-DIMIN-ished bag of beans—the cries and moans of the stupefied, wounded pioneers, the occasional pain-filled whinnies of horses and grunts of wounded oxen, usually followed by a shot—filtering though the canvas.

He examined the arrow carefully, running his large stubby fingers up and down the shaft in a thoughtful caress, turning it his hands, every once in a while testing the sharpness of the point with his index finger. Thinking hard, he reached into his pocket and drew out his Frontier Army short-barreled .44 revolver, grabbed a handful of shells from the small canvas sack where he carried his ammunition, and reloaded.

Moments later, directly outside the wagon, he heard movement, and he hurriedly shoved the pistol back in his belt.

"Jacob? You in there?" It was that damn Reuben Frank. "Zeb and I want to talk with you."

May 10, 1855

*T*HEN THERE WERE THREE

JACOB THOUGHT QUICKLY. *GIVEN THE BIGGER PLAN, WHAT IS THE best way to handle this? I despise both of these men, and Reuben is on my short list of four. With the confusion after the attack, I might never have a better chance.*

He looked around the interior of the wagon. *Wish that redheaded bitch hadn't moved her stuff to the queen's wagon. I was so looking forward to rifling through it.*

"Jacob are you in there?"

The impatience in the Prussian voice of the goody-two-shoes was unmistakable. Jacob took a deep breath, let it out, and, in a level voice, replied, "I...I...I'm in here. Pretty shaken up. Take me a minute or two, but I'll be out."

He stood, paused for what he thought would be a plausible long moment, and walked to the back of the wagon, stowing the arrow carefully under his bedroll. As he untied the canvas, the wooden tailgate was pulled open by Zeb, and it fell with a thud once he released it.

Zeb stepped two paces back.

Jacob smiled at them, careful not to be overly friendly. *Has to be just right.* He willed his face into a pained expression, put one hand down on the tailgate, and sprang to the ground. His eyes dropped to Reuben's Colt and then to the hilt of Zeb's back blade, barely visible behind the angle where the mountain man's shoulder met his neck.

"Bloody, nasty day. Simply a horrible day. Just about outta ammunition, you know. I got me two of them buggers, but this pistol has no range to it."

Jacob surveyed the scene around them quickly—people crying as they found their loved ones or helped wounded to the wagons. *Chaos. Good.* "Did anyone from the *Edinburgh* crew get hurt?"

Reuben and Zeb exchanged glances, their jaws tight, and a noticeable pain in their eyes. *Good,* Jacob pondered, *maybe it was that tall, blond son of a bitch who likes to pretend he's not a soldier boy what got hurt.* He concentrated on keeping a touch of concern in his voice. "Who?"

"Inga."

Jacob looked down at the ground, shook his head slowly. *One sweet thing I will never taste, but there are others.* He raised his head with his best poker eyes and said, "I'm sorry to hear that. I stepped out of bounds in the wagon the night of the storm. I meant to apologize." He swung his arm around the disorganized camp. "Never expected something like this. I'm sorry."

The eyes of the other two men bore into him, trying to gauge his authenticity, he guessed. He blinked rapidly and ran the back of his forefinger across one eye, as if arresting a tear. "I know we were none too friendly, but this is terrible. Except for that poor woman, we were all shipmates from Europe. That counts for something."

Zeb and Reuben exchanged glances, and Jacob picked up the slightest relaxation in their postures. *Good.*

"We need some of your whiskey, Jacob," said Zeb gruffly. "Several wounded need some doctoring."

Perfect. He nodded his head up and down energetically "Of course. Of course. How much do you need?" He turned to the wagon, stretched himself over the tailgate, fumbled under some supplies, and pulled two earthenware gallon jugs toward him, sliding them over the surface of the tailgate. "This 'ere one's about three-quarters full, and the other ain't even been touched. Was saving it until we got to Cherry Creek. You're welcome to it all." *Better not be going overboard.* "Let me just fill my flask, and if there's one left, I'd sure appreciate you bringing it back."

Reuben looked surprised. "Thank you, Jacob. That means a lot." Zeb's eyes were narrowed. A furrow of suspicion lurked in his eyebrows. Reuben turned. "Zeb, the Patricks down there need help. Looks like the Kirbys do too."

Jacob followed their gaze. Figures were huddled over several prostrate forms on the ground. At a further wagon three men carried someone— he couldn't tell man or woman—back toward one of the wagons.

"Jacob, if you wouldn't mind, just put those right inside the tailgate. We'll pick them up when we come back."

"Aye, whatever works. Let me...let me get myself organized, and I will come down and help you."

Zeb and Reuben exchanged glances again. "We appreciate that. I'm sure the others will, too." The two men turned and jogged toward the wagons further down the line, Zeb holding his side and gingerly jumping over the body of a dead Pawnee.

Jacob watched them go. *Not my best performance, but it worked. There was some blood on coonskin's lips. I should find out more about that. Could be useful.* He looked around the camp, and his eyes fixed on the two supply wagons. He jumped back onto the tailgate and closed it, taking care that no one from a distant point was peeking inside through the open canvas. He reached under the bedroll, picked up the arrow and broke it in half over his knee, hiding the two broken shafts in his shirt under his arm. *Too warm for a jacket— would make folks wonder.*

He lowered the tailgate, jumped down, reached back and pulled the two whiskey jugs just to the edge of the wagon bed—visible for someone who knew to look for them. With a glance in all directions, he stepped outside the circle of wagons and began walking toward the supply rigs, stopping at the end of each wagon and team to take a quick peek through the gap where he might be seen. But everyone was engrossed in dealing with the aftermath of the attack. *As I thought.* He reached the supply wagons and stood for moment, quietly looking at each. There was a creak in one, some heavy moving. Only silence from the other.

Jacob took care to stay hidden from the interior of the camp's semi-circle. He looked behind him to the west. Not a soul to be seen. He cast a furtive look around and called out, "Mac, wagon master, it's Jacob O'Shanahan. I—we need your help, or leastways your advice." He reached into his shirt, felt carefully, and withdrew the half-arrow with the sharp stone broadhead. He held it behind him, tight to his leg and buttocks.

The wagon creaked as Mac came to the open tailgate and peered around the edge of the canvas.

Mac's voice had an annoyed tone. "What do you want? Be quick about it. They're good people that need my help, and I was just getting ready to go. Soon as I wrap a bandage round this arm."

The wagon master's eyes were cold. His face was pale behind the bushy red eyebrows and beard. He clutched a piece of bloody cloth high on his arm. Every once in a while there was a flicker in his blue eyes. *Must be a little pain in that shoulder. Too bad for you, you bastard.*

"I'm sorry to bother you. There's something very strange going on out there," Jacob pointed behind him to the west. Mac raised his head and squinted. "I don't see nothing."

"No, come down here so you can follow my point. I don't know if it's more Indians or what. But I thought you ought to know. We may not like each other much, but you do what needs to be done." Jacob inwardly winced as he said the words. *Hope I ain't overplayed my hand.*

Mac eased himself down on his rump on the open tailgate, then pushed himself off gingerly with his good hand. Jacob tightened his grip on the shaft of the arrow, the arrowhead pressing against his leg. He moved slightly so he stood almost at the center of the wagon, the most concealed position from the other pioneers. "Over here, Mac, figure you best see from here." He pretended to point, his left hand extended and forefinger straight off into the distance, as if at something ominous. The wagon master stopped. "Let me get my telescope."

"No, you don't need it. Take a look first."

Mac had turned back to the tailgate, but instead took the final few steps to Jacob and cocked his head so his eye could follow the direction of Jacob's extended arm.

Jacob's grip closed even more tightly on the shaft of the arrow. With a sudden violent sideways swing of his right arm underneath his outstretched left, he plunged the arrow into Mac's chest. Mac staggered back against the wagon, one hand closed around the shaft of the arrow, the other reaching for Jacob's face, his bushy eyebrows contorted, a terrible look of shock and rage on his face. With the wagon master's back against the wagon, Jacob had leverage. He drove the arrow in further. There was a groan, and Mac's hand, which had slipped to his throat, slid weakly down his chest. Jacob pushed again. He felt the point pierce something firm inside the stocky man's chest. Blood came from both corners of his mouth, and he began to sag, his back slowly sliding down the canvas and the wooden side of the wagon.

Jacob stood up and looked around quickly. *One down, three to go.* He took the other, fletched half of the broken shaft from his shirt, and laid it on Mac's chest, still quivering with death spasms. He grabbed the big man's hands and soaked their palms in the bloody shirt, closing one hand around the half-shaft of the imbedded arrow, and one around its broken brother. He stood and surveyed the scene. "Guess you snapped it off when you tried to pull it out of you." *You pompous ass. Thought you could push me around since all the way back in the livery in St. Louis, eh? You won't be using that bullwhip ever again, either.*

Jacob looked down at his own bloody hands. One sleeve was wet and stained. He scrubbed out his boot tracks and snuck down the line of wagons to the creek to wash his hands. He ripped the stained sleeve off, wadding it up, and letting it drift away in the current. He stood and walked swiftly back up the outside edge of the wagons, taking extra precautions to make sure no one noticed. Or, if they did, would recognize him only as another figure in the anguished confusion.

He made it back to his wagon, climbing in through the front, and examined his clothes carefully. He made sure to change them and his boots. He checked the inside pocket of his jacket, his stubby fingers closing on the textured parchment of the gold map. He smiled. He folded it and carefully hid it under the last of the flour and beans.

"Jacob." He started, his hand jerking away. It was the Prussian farmer. *Timing couldn't be better.* "We're taking one of the whisky jugs and we could use your help."

Jacob walked the few steps to tailgate. "I think I am settled down enough now. What do you need me to do?"

"We have some bodies we need to move," answered Reuben grimly.

REUBEN WAS FOCUSED ON THE GRISLY TASK AT HAND. *WHERE THE hell is Mac?* He, Zeb, and Jacob went first to those wagons and groups most obviously needing assistance. They moved four wounded to their rigs. None of them appeared seriously injured. "They ain't going to die," was the way Zeb put it.

More difficult was moving the bodies of six pioneers, four men, a woman, and one child, the youngest of four children of a couple from Ohio. He and Zeb usually had the help of Jacob and several other pioneers as they moved the corpses. Zeb was quiet. Jacob seemed detached, untouched. One of the other pioneers was usually a friend or a relative of the dead. They were all emotional. Reuben simply felt numb.

The child's mother, Virginia, was beside herself with grief and guilt. Her husband and Reuben tried to console her, but to no avail. "I did everything I could," she said in a broken voice. "The flour sacks and beans and the kegs against the wagon wall. I had the little ones lie down and I spread myself on top of them." She clung to Reuben's hand when they tried to lift the little body. "I told them to get up, it was over, and they all got up, but she was gone. My little Lizabeth. I don't know how she got out of the wagon or why. Then I looked out and there she lay. I ran to her, shook her, but," her voice dropped and cracked, "she didn't move." Her head sank to her chest and she whispered, "*I shook her, but she didn't move.*"

Reuben looked up at her husband, "You might want to get Virginia back to the wagon—let her get some rest." He glanced back over his shoulder at the two brothers and sister of the dead little girl. *Oldest can't be eight or nine.* They were staring wide-eyed at their sister's small, twisted form lying motionless on the ground.

The man nodded, helped his wife rise, and, with an arm around her hunched-over figure, began walking back to their Conestoga. Reuben watched them, thinking of the deep jagged gash in Rebecca's lip. *Not too important, everything is relative.*

With the help of other pioneers, they resumed the sad job of lifting and moving bodies, laying them in a peaceful row in the middle of the semi-circle of wagons and covering them with wool blankets, the corners held down by rocks. Four men followed the creek and found the bodies of the two brothers who had died defending their wagon, stranded in the current.

Once the last corpse had been moved, Reuben straightened up and turned to Jacob. "That help was appreciated, Jacob. Let's see if we can't keep things smooth from here to Cherry Creek. We don't have all that much longer to go."

The stocky Irishman flashed an enigmatic grin. "Was no problem on my part, I assure you." He shook his head. "Tragic." They watched him as he walked back to his wagon. Reuben turned to Zeb, "Guess there's a little good in everybody, Zeb."

The mountain man's eyes fixed on Reuben's. "A scorpion doesn't lose its sting. Just bides its time, is all."

They went around to various wagons, checking stock, helping remove dead animals from harnesses, and reassuring the shaken pioneers. Reuben looked around, "We've been out here a spell. I'm surprised we haven't seen Mac yet. I wonder if he's okay?"

"Let's get back and stitch up that woman of yours before that wound binds up too much. Then we will go get Mac."

Reuben looked up, set to speak, but Zeb cut him off with a smile, "I know. I know, son. She ain't your woman."

They detoured by Jacob's wagon to the get a second jug of whiskey. The Irishman called out to them, "Should you be needing me again, you know where to find me." As they walked quickly to the prairie schooner and knocked on the tailgate, Sarah's voice came from inside the canvas, "Zeb, is that you? Reuben?"

The low, soft tone in the mountain man's voice when he answered made Reuben look over his shoulder at his friend. "It's me, Sarah," Zeb said, "and Reuben."

Reuben turned to hide his smile. They clambered into the wagon. Rebecca still lay curled in the fetal position, blankets pulled up over her. Sarah sat upright, a wool blanket wrapped around her, covering all but her bare shoulders. Obviously, she had not yet donned any clothes.

Zeb straightened up, looked at her, and smiled. "I'm sorry, Sarah, to disturb your privacy, but you were so distraught and..."

Sarah lifted a finger to the soft smile that played on her lips. Some of the color had returned to her face, but her eyes were still raw and swollen. "It's quite okay, Zebarriah Taylor. I'm sure it's nothing you haven't seen before..." she blushed and looked down, then raised her eyes and smiled. "This place strips you of modesty—the false pretenses people think are proper back in the cities. They don't exist here. There's just land, our spirit, and each moment. I simply had to have those clothes off me." She looked directly into Zeb's eyes with an unflinching stare, "I understand you better now, Zeb. Your quiet ways."

Reuben cleared his throat and turned to Rebecca.

She was no longer crying, but her eyes were wide and red, her pupils dilated. A corner of the blanket she had gathered under her head as a pillow was stained with spots of blood from her torn lip. She still wore the chemise, which hugged her body, almost transparent. Reuben pulled the blankets carefully back to just below her shoulder and looked anxiously at Zeb. "What do you think?"

Zeb pulled over a keg and slowly turned her face, intently examining the gash from several angles. "Reuben, light those two oil lamps and bring 'em over here close so I got some light," he said, pulling out a small leather pouch. "Went by Buck and got the sewing needles. Only got two. Generally use an awl cause these little things are worthless for leather. But, an awl surely won't work for a pretty woman's lips." He smiled at Rebecca, obviously trying to elicit a response. She simply looked at him, and then her eyes shifted to Reuben, tears welling in them again.

Zeb held the pouch up to the light, rummaged through it, and held up a small notched wood square around which was wound green thread. "This thread is going to look awful, but in the end it won't matter. Once the edges of that cut bind, I'll pull out the stitches."

Reuben looked at Rebecca. "She'll be beautiful, Zeb, even with green thread in her lips."

Zeb craned his head around. "Reuben, I ain't exactly sure that's what you say to a lady."

Rebecca's lips curled in the slightest hint of smile as Zeb uncorked the whiskey, washed his hands and then the needles, gently wiping her face and lips with whiskey after giving her a fortifying drink, taking every precaution.

Reuben winced each time Zeb gently worked the needle through the sensitive tissue around Rebecca's lip. Her hands were clenched in the wool blanket, which had slipped from her shoulders. The top half of her breasts and one darker pink areola shone vaguely through the thin uncovered chemise. She seemed completely immodest. Each stitch of the needle brought tears to her eyes, which trickled silently down her cheekbones.

Zeb finished the last stitch, tied it off, and she let out a long half-sigh. She started to raise her hand but Zeb reached out and grabbed it, "You don't want to get that infected." She looked down at herself, blushed, and hurriedly pulled the blanket up and around her chin.

The injured side of her lips had swollen to at least three times its normal size and her speech was thick. "I guess I don't have many secrets from you two anymore." She attempted a smile and winced.

Sarah giggled from the other side of the wagon. "Nor I," Sarah said, a hint of humor in her voice as she sat forward. Zeb and Reuben looked at each other and laughed.

"There's no part of a woman that ain't a secret," said Zeb matter-of-factly. "Reuben, let's go over and check on Mac. I'm getting a mite worried."

"Wait," Rebecca reached out, one hand holding the blanket over what had already been revealed and the other pointing at the whiskey jug. Zeb's eyebrows raised. He looked at Reuben, then handed her the jug. She tipped her head back, pressed the spout to her lips gingerly, and guzzled three large gulps. She set the jug down on her lap, some of it sloshing on the blanket, and began to cough.

"A bit much, Rebecca?" asked Sarah, wide-eyed.

Rebecca emphatically nodded her head and the men laughed.

"Well, give me some anyway," said Sarah. Zeb handed the redhead the jug and she mimicked Rebecca's actions, though partly through the second swig she coughed uncontrollably, almost dropped the jug, spraying whiskey all over the blanket.

Zeb retrieved the jug and shook his head from side to side as he stepped back, "You ladies need a good sleep, and I 'spect you'll get one now." The two women looked at each other and smiled, their necks and cheeks already flushed. "When will we be moving?" demanded Rebecca in a thick voice. "The sooner we get away from this place, the better."

Reuben began to speak, but Rebecca cut him off. "Go check on Mac," she ordered. "We'll be all right."

Reuben's last image of the interior of the prairie schooner was Sarah rising, wrapping the blanket around her, and sitting next to Rebecca, the two of them leaning into each other, their hands touching, their bare feet visible beneath the blanket.

He turned to Zeb and took a deep breath. Zeb nodded. "Them two saw more in one day than most see in a lifetime." He paused and looked vacantly somewhere to the west. "Course, that's what happens when you set out to do big things." His eyes dropped to Reuben, "Let's go."

THEY WALKED UP TO THE SUPPLY WAGONS AND PAUSED, UNSURE which one Mac was in. *I got a bad feeling*, Zeb thought to himself, his eyes roving the ground around each wagon. "Mighty quiet," he said to Reuben.

He raised his voice, "Mac?" There was no response. They looked at one another. "I'll check this one, Reuben, you check the other." Zeb walked around the back end of the second supply wagon. The tailgate was open. The rear canvas flapped slightly in the breeze.

He looked around the outside corner of the wagon and froze. Mac lay on his back, sightless eyes staring at the sky, his lips blue and curled back in a snarl, his head held slightly off the ground by a spoke of the front wagon wheel, one leg bent and curled under the other, his toe pointing toward the rear of the wagon. His right hand clasped the broken shaft of an arrow, sunk dead center in his chest. His left arm lay to his side in a pool of half-coagulated blood, his left hand holding the other half of the arrow's broken shaft.

Zeb leaned forward against the front of the rig, looking at the ground. He took a deep breath and shook his head. *Damn shame. One of the few I'll miss.*

He straightened up, "Reuben come on over here."

Reuben came around the camp-side corner of the wagon. "He's not in..."

He stopped when he saw Zeb's face. Zeb nodded to the west side of the wagon.

Reuben stepped over the tongue, walked around the corner, and came back quickly, one corner of his mouth twitching, his face pale and his eyes screwed down tight like he was fighting tears. "What the hell, Zeb?"

"I suppose he got killed by that arrow. The question is how."

They walked carefully around the body, Zeb searching the ground for sign, bending down once in a while to study things more closely. *That's right strange.* He stood and walked over to Reuben.

Reuben's eyes were fixed on the body of the tough, jovial wagon master. He asked in a low voice, "Well, what the hell? What do you think?"

"It's a Pawnee arrow, but I don't reckon a Pawnee put it in his chest." Reuben lifted his widening eyes. "You mean...?"

Zeb nodded and pointed out various indications on the ground, "See that scrape mark there? Somebody was covering track. If a brave looses an arrow forty or fifty yards away, he ain't comin' in to check what happened when he can see the arrow sticking out of the chest—not unless he aims to scalp."

Zeb looked up at the sky. *No weather coming. Doesn't feel like the wind will kick up.* He dropped his eyes to Reuben. His young friend's face was taut, his eyes shaded to grey. "I will take me a walk out there. I'm bettin' there's no horse tracks." He looked down toward the creek, "And I'm thinking that down there by the creek will be signs of somebody getting the blood off their hands."

Reuben's eyes had narrowed. Through clenched lips, he muttered, "And who might that be?"

Zeb looked at him, reached out a hand and shook his shoulder. "Reuben, you're the wagon master now. We'll figure out who done this and," he fought to keep the snarl from his lips, "I know ways to teach some justice—ways most never heard of."

He shook Reuben's shoulder again. "Reuben, we got wounded people, grieving families, we're in dangerous country. There's men, women, and children depending on you."

Reuben raised his eyes and Zeb instinctively pulled back from the sadness and pure, bitter anger that glowed in the younger man's eyes. He watched him take a deep breath, gathering himself up before speaking.

"Zeb, it's only right that people get to decide. If they choose me, I'll do it." He began to walk away and then turned back sharply. "And Zeb, it's best that we keep folks calm for now. Everyone is pretty damn rattled. We will just say Mac was killed by a Pawnee arrow, which is true enough. Let's keep the circumstances of how the arrow may have got into his chest to ourselves, and sort that out later."

Zeb nodded. "I'll get this arrow out of poor Mac and meet up with you shortly," he said, thinking to himself, *Reuben's going to do just fine.*

REUBEN MADE THE ROUNDS, VISITING THE MOURNING PIONEERS, informing them there would be a general meeting at dusk, just several hours away. To those who inquired, he merely replied, "To discuss some decisions that will have to be made between here and Cherry Creek."

He was on his way to check on Rebecca and Sarah when he spied Johannes' tall, lonely figure several hundred yards upstream from the last wagon, headed back to the encampment. Walking slowly, without energy, he carried only a shovel and his Sharps Carbine.

Reuben pulled up short. *Should I leave him alone? Go meet him? Let him initiate communications? But he is your friend...*

He turned away from the prairie schooner and walked out to meet Johannes, stopping and waiting halfway. Johannes did not increase his pace. His eyes seemed fixed on the ground and, as he approached, Reuben was taken aback by the blond man's ghastly lack of color and the sorrowful quivers around his mouth where so often in the past there had only been smiles.

Johannes almost walked into Reuben, stopping only at the last moment, his head snapping up with a startled expression.

For a long moment, the two men simply looked at one another then Johannes spoke. "I told her, Reuben. I told her...," a tear rolled down his cheek, "but I think she was already dead." He sank slowly to his knees, one hand supported by the barrel of his rifle, the other leaning on the handle of the shovel. He bowed his head. "I don't know if she heard." He took a deep, uneven breath and looked up at Reuben, pain etched in his face, "I raised my head to look at her, to make sure she'd understood...and...and...she was gone."

Reuben squatted down in front of him. "Johannes, she knew. Whether she was still alive at the moment you said those words, or had just departed, she knew." *Should I tell him about Mac? Should I add to the shock...or perhaps it would help get his mind elsewhere— away from the guilt.* "Johannes, I need your help..."

Johannes looked slowly up from where he knelt in the sand and cobble along the shores of the creek. He nodded numbly.

Reuben was not sure if his words registered. "Looks like we lost, besides poor Inga, eight from the train," Reuben sighed, "including one child who somehow got out of her mother's wagon during the fight. We have a total of eight wounded, none seriously, but four of them are incapacitated. We will need to figure out who can drive the wagons. Zeb thinks Charlie is dead," Reuben paused, "and so is Mac."

Johannes blinked, his eyes regaining their focus. "Mac?" Reuben nodded. "But it was only an arrow to the arm. What happened?"

He does need something else to think about. He told Johannes the rest of the story, leaving nothing out. As he spoke, he noticed Johannes' posture straightening and some color returned to his face. *Anger perhaps? The soldier in him, certainly.*

"So, someone needs to figure out who will drive the supply wagons, and what women in wagons with wounded men are capable of driving, and..." Reuben continued, "I have called a meeting. We need to vote on a new wagon master. I need your help." He watched his friend's eyes closely. *He understood.*

"I can be most effective, Reuben, in organizing the defense, guard, and outriders for the wagons. I am a soldier. My skills are at your disposition." Johannes' expression changed as if remembering something, "How is Rebecca? Sarah?" The question was sincere and anxious.

"They are shaken up. Rebecca was...hysterical. Thank you, Johannes for coming to Rebecca's rescue. I was too far down the line of wagons."

"There's no sense both of us losing the women we love," Johannes replied in a low voice, his lips pursed, "and certainly not on the same day."

Reuben extended his hand and squeezed his shoulder. They rose and walked silently back to the wagons.

As the sun dipped to the west, Johannes rode out to check on the outriders, his saber dangling at his side for the first time in a non-battle situation, his shoulders once again erect. *Thankful for a task,* thought Reuben, *an officer off to review the troops.*

Reuben had asked Johannes to tell the pioneers to gather at the supply wagons, and, as the setting sun's red hue cast a beautiful but grisly reminder of the bloodshed of the ending day, Reuben joined the assembling group. Zeb had covered Mac's body with a blanket, but had not moved it. There was a slight murmur of voices as Reuben walked up, standing in front with his back to the supply rigs.

"It's been a terrible day. We've all lost friends." Far in the back of the crowd a woman began to cry quietly. "Others have been wounded, though thankfully it appears they will recover. You all fought valiantly."

Everyone's eyes were fixed on him. Zeb's words ran through Reuben's mind. *There is no one else.*

"I wish I had an easy way to say this," he continued, "but there is one more piece of bad news. Mac is dead." His blunt announcement was met by startled looks. Several women broke into tears. The men exchanged glances. A current, like a wave of fear, swept through the crowd, a palpable tide of uncertainty.

Reuben held up both hands, saying nothing. The murmur died off slowly. "He was a good man and our friend, just like everyone else we lost today. Some of you lost loved ones. Mac told us that not everybody would make it. Even in death, he spoke the truth." There was no sound as the darkness drew around them save the distant howl of coyotes, the gentle flap of the open canvas of the supply wagons, and the creek's rushing waters.

"We need to elect a new wagon master. I think the fair way to do this is for anyone to call out the name of a person they want to take over. Speak out, then we'll have a simple vote."

A number of heads nodded, several people looked at one another, but most simply stared at him, a few seeming less anxious than when they just learned of Mac's death.

"Okay, let's have some nominations. We need somebody to head things up, do his best to keep us organized and get us through the next two or so weeks."

Nobody spoke. All eyes were glued on him. There was a voice behind and to his right, and he turned. It was Zeb, leaning relaxed against the corner of the wagon, one shoulder into the bow support of the canvas, rifle under one arm, rolling a smoke. *Like the day I met him at the livery stable*, thought Reuben.

"I got a nomination to make," he said, putting the rolled cigarette to his lips, licking, and sealing it. "I nominate Reuben."

Virtually everyone's heads nodded, other than Jacob who stood slightly apart at the outer band of the semi-circle of people, a strange glitter in his eye. When he realized Reuben was looking at him, he looked away.

"Surely there are more nominations?"

Still not a sound.

"Well then, let's vote. Yes or no, I won't take it personal. All those who don't want me to be wagon master, raise your hands."

No hands went up.

"Anyone who wants me to be the wagon master to Cherry Creek, please raise your hands."

Everyone's hands rose, some only halfway up to their shoulders, others enthusiastically stretched into the air. He noticed Jacob hesitate, give a quick glance around, then raise his hand, looking down at the ground as he did so.

"I accept. I'll do the very best I can. Mac gave you the speech two months ago. Keep his words in mind. I'm always open for suggestions. Just five months ago, I was a farm boy in Prussia. I don't pretend to have all the answers. I intend to rely on Zeb to be our eyes and ears. Johannes will keep our defenses, front, rear, and flank guards, organized. Since we've lost stock, we will need to sort out the teams. It's getting warmer—with less stock and dryer country. Mac told me that it would be wise to travel early and late, and rest midday. So that's what we'll start doing as soon as we cross Beaver Creek in the next few days."

The crowd was absolutely silent. "Tomorrow morning, we will bury the dead. Preacher Walling, would you be so kind as to do the service?" The preacher nodded somberly and patted his wife's hands, which were wrapped around his arm, her head leaning against his shoulder.

"If you would tell the wounded folks who aren't here, and the outriders when they come back, that would be good. Johannes will assign the guard shifts when he gets back. If all the menfolk could bring shovels tomorrow morning, I would appreciate it. And those of you ladies who wish to participate as well." He felt the catch in his throat.

"They were all our friends. I think they would like to be buried by friends. I will need two men in two shifts to stand watch over the bodies tonight and keep the animals away." Several pairs of eyes turned upward to a dozen turkey vultures flying in lazy circles, their black forms silhouetted against the darkening sky.

One of the men raised his hand, "Are we gonna do anything about those poor redskins?" he gestured out at the crumpled forms beyond the wagons, and the neat row of six braves that they had dragged outside the half-circle.

Reuben shook his head, "No." He looked across the circled wagons and, from the rear canvas of their prairie schooner, he saw Rebecca and Sarah watching, only their faces showing. "The next sizeable stream after Beaver Creek is Badger Creek. After we cross, we will take a half-day for wagon repairs."

A voice spoke out of the crowd, "I think we have several people getting sick. Poor Dr. Leonard, he's been sick since the get-go but that's consumption. Just in the last day before all this, Thelma complained to me about not feeling well. I checked on her on the way down here. Doc is not doing good, and she's running a high fever."

Another hand went up, "That Tommy, the boy that lost his Pa today, he has the same. Just started last night."

Reuben sighed inwardly. *On top of everything, now this.* He glanced back at Zeb. The mountain man shifted his gaze from Jacob where it had been fastened, and his deep-set green eyes locked on his. He could almost feel the mountain man's thoughts, *You're in charge. Make a decision.*

"To be safe, we'll need to put all the sick in one wagon. It appears that these particular folks who are ill have no one to tend to them. If it's cholera," there was a gasp from the crowd, eyes widened and nervous glances were exchanged, "it's very contagious. We can't take a chance on more people getting sick. We will need a volunteer to drive that wagon."

One man raised his hand. "I'll drive it. My wife can handle ours." A voice from between the supply wagons to his rear spoke up.

Reuben turned. It was Johannes on Bente, leaning on the saddle horn. "I'll bring them supplies and water."

Reuben could see Johannes' facial muscles twitching as he looked out over the group. "Preacher, after the service tomorrow, I would like you to come down and say a few words over Inga. I..." Johannes cleared his throat, "I buried her on the rise next to creek. She grew up on the water, you know, and...and I figured she would be happy resting by it."

Preacher Walling nodded. "It would be a privilege, Johannes." Next to him, his wife took out a delicate white handkerchief, held it to her eyes and buried her forehead in her husband's arm.

May 15, 1855

THE PATROL

REUBEN WAS CONCERNED. HE DIDN'T LIKE WASTING HOURS IN THE unseasonable midday heat to give the stock a break, but Mac's advice had stayed with him. *And, with many of the wagons now being pulled by less than full teams after the Indian attack, there really is no choice.*

He ate in silence, aware of the numerous darting looks—part wondering, part worry—that Rebecca threw at him across the small, wavering cookfire, the light of its dying flames no match for the brightness of the sun outside the shade of the wagon.

"What's wrong, Reuben?"

He sighed, set down the tin plate too forcefully, and watched his meal mingle with the dirt dug out for the fire pit.

"Nothing to do with you, Rebecca. It's Johannes. He disappears for long periods of time. He volunteers for the most solitary, dangerous, and remote tasks. I have been told by others in the train that he insists on taking their place on night guard. He volunteers to ride the flank where terrain, elevation, or vegetation creates situations more likely for attack or ambush. He's become quieter than Zeb."

Rebecca moved to him, leaned over, and kissed his shoulder. "I know, Reuben. His smiles are infrequent and the laughter gone from his eyes. There is a deep sadness in them. He is far too eager to stand in for Zeb, who has been joining us—and Sarah—for dinner." She smiled, then grew serious again. "He has eaten with us only twice since the Pawnee attack, and on both occasions he excused himself, took his food, and went off somewhere."

Reuben's glum mood deepened. "I followed him those two nights and found him sitting in the grass several hundred feet outside the circle of wagons—Sharps carbine either propped within easy reach or laying across his lap. He had that damn saber in his hands, slowly rotating the blade toward him and then away, fixated on the steel as if it held some answer, some truth, some relief. Tried to joke with him—*Johannes you need to eat something. You're turning into a scarecrow*—sometimes he just nods or gestures, but he flatly refuses to engage in discussion or conversation."

Reuben stretched out his legs toward the fire, drawing Rebecca to him with one arm. The warmth of the coals seeped faintly through the soles of his boots. "One time his elbows were just resting on the saber, its blade spanning the space between his knees, while he slowly turned that lock of Inga's hair he cut before he buried her."

Reuben leaned back into the shade of the wagon, positioning his back so the spokes ran up and down on either side of his spine, and took a sip of coffee. "For a tea drinking English lady, you are sure getting the hang of brewing good coffee."

Rebecca smiled, pleased at the compliment.

Reuben shifted and peered out around the back of the wagon. "That sun will be off its peak soon. In an hour or so we will start moving again."

"It's amazing how the weather warmed up," said Rebecca. "It seems like yesterday we were buried in the blizzard, and now I'm not sure I have clothes light enough so as not to perspire. That sun is brutally hot."

"You could go naked," Reuben teased, happy to have his mind pleasantly diverted. Rebecca feigned a shocked look and slapped him on the knee. "Reuben Frank..." Her words died in the press of his lips.

"That's why we stop midday." He grinned, picked up a small pebble and threw it lazily. It made a tiny track as it rolled through the sandy soil until its progress was halted by tuft of grass.

Rebecca cocked her head, "You don't mind kissing scarred lips?"

A joking tone, but a serious question. Reuben pulled her to him and kissed her again, this time letting his tongue play gently over the raised skin of the rapidly healing injury to her upper lip.

"Thank you, Reuben," she said softly. She laid her hand on top of his, "Johannes will be all right. His heart is broken. Imagine if..." her voice trailed off, she looked unseeing into the distance and a tear slid slowly down her cheek, leaving an uneven salty trail.

"I try and put myself in his position. But I can't—maybe don't want to—imagine," he paused, picked up another pebble, threw it out in the sun and watched it roll, "something happening to you."

Rebecca squeezed his hand, "Nothing is going to happen to me, Reuben, nor you. You're doing a great job of leading the train. People comment to me all the time. They respect you a great deal," she squeezed his hand again, "and they trust you—as do I."

Reuben heard himself laugh, his voice tinged with bitterness. "Well, I can't get Johannes out of his bad humor, and I can't seem to do anything about poor Thelma and that poor lad, Tommy, and their cholera. By my reckoning, we are about two hundred and fifty miles northeast of Cherry Creek and at least a week behind schedule. I'll know more exactly when we cross Beaver Creek in the next few days."

"That's not your fault, Reuben. We lost a number of days in the blizzard—the Osage was high and took extra time to cross." She looked down to the ground and, with a slight catch in her breath, continued, "And it took several days to sort out from the attack and... and...and bury the dead...I so miss Inga." She bit her lower lip, "I climb into the wagon at the end of the day and expect to see her smiling at me."

"I know," he sighed morosely.

There were several minutes of silence between the two.

"And, as to the rest," he said, searching for another pebble to throw, "well, all true. But we should've been to Cherry Creek by now, and, as I see it, we are still at least two weeks out, give or take a few days. That assumes we have to take at least a day, maybe two, for wagon repairs. Based on what Mac told me, it's late enough now that some of the rivers between here and there will be rising. He said the snowmelt usually started mid to late May." He threw another pebble. "I miss that big, red-bearded cantankerous beef, too."

"I do, also, Reuben. But, this land is timeless. We're young. So are most in the other wagons. These events were outside of your control—if they cost us a week or two, it makes no difference. You can start your ranch as easily on June first as on May sixteenth."

He watched as Rebecca moistened her lips, her tongue lingering at the forming scar. *I love kissing her.* "Have you thought anymore about what you're going to do?" he asked, and took a deep breath, "are you going back to England?"

She looked at him, her eyes steady. There was a long silence, and Reuben knew she was thinking carefully about her response, but before she could answer him, they were interrupted by an excited shout. "Cavalry! Cavalry! There's a cavalry patrol."

Reuben held her gaze for a few seconds longer and then, using the wagon wheel, lifted himself to his feet. "Soldiers. This will be a first. I was beginning to think the American Army didn't exist except back in the barracks at Fort Kearney. Squinting in the bright sunlight, he looked out past the wagons and saw the telltale dusty sign of riders moving slow but steady. The deep blue of the distant uniforms, juxtaposed with the brown swirl of dust behind the riders, was unmistakable. He walked over to Lahn, already saddled and tied in the shade of the wagon, gathered the reins, and lifted one foot into the stirrup.

"Reuben, who is that riding out there?"

He turned, mid-mount, and craned over his shoulder at the rough, hilly contours to the south. A lone horseman cantered toward the approaching cavalry patrol. Johannes—a tall figure in the saddle, his blond hair growing long, no longer caring a great deal, it appeared, about his appearance.

Reuben swung into the saddle, looked down at Rebecca, and smiled. Sarah, who had been napping in the wagon, poked her head out of the front of the canvas. "Might want to put a new kettle of coffee on the fire," he said. "Maybe they will want to ride in. Come on, Lahn, let's go meet the Army."

JOHANNES MOVED AT A STEADY CANTER TOWARD THE INCOMING troops. He straightened his shoulders and looked down to make sure his saber was in proper position. *I wish I had cut my damn hair.* The riders behind the commanding officer bore two flags—the 2nd Cavalry's and the American flag—its red, white, and blue colors smart and bright against the screen of dust raised by the plodding Army horses.

He counted twenty-four in the little troop. *Not much more than a heavy squad. And they must have been on the trail for a while. They look tired.*

As he neared the patrol, the commander, riding a muscular sorrel, held up his hand. "Hoooah."

"Troop halt!" his sergeant yelled in a thick Irish accent.

The two-by-two columns stopped and twenty-four pairs of curious eyes followed him as he reined in Bente.

Johannes and Bente faced the commander and his horse diagonally. The sergeant rode up and nodded to him, the black bill of his blue campaign cap bobbing in an authoritative manner. The epaulettes of the officer sported the double bars of a captain's insignia. He threw Johannes a lazy salute. *That would never do in my command.*

"I would be Master Sergeant O'Malley. This is Captain Henderson. We are C Squad, F Troop, United States Army 2nd Dragoons, excuse me, Cavalry." The master sergeant rubbed his nose with the back of his hand, then blew one nostril out over the side of his horse, pressing the other closed tight. "Can't get used to this name change between Dragoons and Cavalry—the Army is always changing its..."

"That will be enough, Sergeant," interjected the captain. His eyes shifted to Johannes, "And you are...?"

An image flashed into Johannes' mind, cutting through the pain in his heart. Another déjà vu. A cold, misty day on the border of the Alsace, the one hundred and sixty men in his company behind him in columns of fours. Two young and one older man stopped in the winding dirt road as they approached. The snap of the King of Denmark's flag, and the colors of his command gave texture to the silent mist that hung in the air. Sergeant Helgerjen, who had ridden up beside his captain, announced them. "We are First Company, Fourth Battalion, His Majesty, the King of Denmark, Heavy Dragoons."

Johannes remembered his own voice, authoritative, but not unfriendly, as it had mingled with the fog that day. *And you would be...?*

The captain's horse snorted and shifted his feet, and Johannes was again in the present. He hesitated, *What the hell.* "I am Captain Johannes Svenson, former commander of First Company, Heavy Dragoons, in the service of His Majesty, the King of Denmark." Johannes could feel a lifting in his spirits as he said the words, and sensed his chin jut slightly forward and his shoulders square. He snapped a stiff, brisk, perfectly executed salute, and Captain Henderson's eyes widened in surprise.

Captain Henderson straightened in his saddle, squared his shoulders, and returned the salute, this time as one professional to another. "You are a mighty long way from home, Captain Svenson."

Johannes looked the officer in the eye, "This is my home now. America. And an honor for it to be so."

"We're on patrol from Fort Laramie. I heard one of the wagon groups headed this way had some troubles with the Pawnee. When we didn't meet you headed west on the main track, we figured you cut south. Given the Platte Barge battle in '53 and the Grattan Massacre last August, we're particularly keen on finding out all we can about any hostile activity. Might be that we can't prevent it, but at least we can avenge it. The only thing those red devils understand is force."

Johannes kept his face impassive, recalling the Sioux who had ridden to their assistance. *A rather narrow view.* His eyes drifted down the line of troopers who had become attentive when they learned that Johannes was military. "Seems like a small patrol to be so far from Fort Laramie."

The captain laughed, "Yes, it is not often you see a captain leading a squad. We're short of men. Some have been pulled back to Fort Kearney to teach the Indians a lesson after the Grattan Massacre, and we have other patrols out west of the fort escorting some Mormon wagons down to the Great Basin."

Johannes smiled. "Would that Mormon group happen to have three families and twenty-two wagons?"

The captain laughed again. "Yep, indeed it does—sounds like you met up with them. They were escorted as far as Laramie by a light platoon from Kearney, and then we dispatched a heavy squad," he nodded behind him, "like this one, to bring 'em the rest of the way. The fort only has one company each of the Second Cavalry, the Fourth Artillery, Sixth Infantry, Fourth and Second Infantries." He chuckled. "But we found out that infantry escorting wagons on round trips of four hundred miles didn't work out all too well.

"I see you folks have cut south. Headed to Cherry Creek?"

"Yes, Cherry Creek."

"Well, you missed the traffic when you cut off on the South Platte trail. Not many trains go this way, but I think that is about to change. Up to now it's been Mormons on their Exodus, or whatever they call it, and a bunch of pilgrims..." He lowered his voice and leaned forward, "although I would only say this to another officer, they should have never left whatever city they came from back East. Fools are heading off to California absolutely convinced that they are going to strike the next twenty-ton vein of gold." He laughed. "From what I hear, few, if any, do."

"About how many do you expect to pass through the fort this year?" asked Johannes.

"More than a thousand folks will be headed down this east flank of the Rockies like your outfit. The main trail is another story. Between the Mormons and the folks hell-bent for California—if it's anything like last year—around thirty thousand men, maybe a thousand children, and about that many women. Maybe nine thousand wagons," he laughed, "and a whole bunch of mules."

Johannes chuckled, "Sounds like a lot, but given the size of this country, I'll bet you never know they went through here other than their wagon tracks and the scarcity of game."

"That's about right, Captain. They pass through, spend a few hours, maybe a day, and keep going. It's rare for us to ever see them again."

The sergeant gestured to the west. "Aye, this land just seems to swallow 'em up."

All heads turned at the sound of a horse approaching at a slow lope. Johannes quickly recognized Reuben, sitting comfortable in the saddle, riding with that easy half-Indian, half-cavalry grace.

Reining Lahn in thirty or forty feet away, Reuben came up at a walk to Johannes, the captain, and the sergeant. "Hello," he said, leaning across the saddle, shaking the captain's hand and then the sergeant's. "I'm Reuben Frank. I'm the assistant... I'm the wagon master. I see you met Mr. Svenson."

"We've met Captain Svenson and we were just sharing tales."

Reuben shot Johannes a quick glance when the sergeant called him captain, but the younger man played poker through it, turning back to O'Malley, "You are the first Army we have seen other than Fort Kearney. I dare say, it was nice see those blue coats coming in from the west. Fort Laramie?"

Captain Henderson was studying Reuben closely. His eyes dropped several times to the Prussian's Colt. What was on his mind was soon evident.

"Mr. Frank..."

"Call me Reuben, please."

"All right, Reuben. You're mighty young to be leading a wagon train. How'd that come to pass?" Reuben's eyes moved to Johannes and then back to Captain Henderson.

Johannes knew that Reuben was very carefully selecting his words so as not to upset him. As he opened his mouth to speak, Johannes cut him off. "Our wagon master, Mac, was wounded in a Pawnee attack. He died shortly after from a second Pawnee arrow. We buried him..." Johannes heard the catch in his own voice. He swallowed hard. "Along with the others."

The captain looked from Johannes to Reuben, his shock evident. "Mac? Mac's dead?" He recovered quickly, a slight suspicion in his eyes. "Anybody else die after the battle?"

"We lost one very sick man a week ago, Dr. Leonard, God rest his soul. But he was ill since the inception of this journey. We have three down with cholera right now, separated into one wagon. Tragically, one of the three is the deceased doctor's wife and another a fifteen-year-old orphan."

"Lucky it's only three. We've had trains come into the fort that we've had to quarantine. More than half of the poor devils sick and most of 'em dying. An entire field of wagons was burned to make sure that sickness didn't spread. Nasty thing, that fever. Who tends to the sick?"

Reuben's eyes flickered to Johannes. "Captain Svenson does." Both Captain Henderson and Sergeant O'Malley leaned back in their saddles imperceptibly, and Johannes was sure they would've backed up their horses if they hadn't thought it too obvious and rude. "Are you a doctor, Captain?"

"No," said Johannes, "But they need tending to, so there's no sense anybody more than one doing it. Mostly I bring them food, water, and supplies. They are all without family, as I am." He felt the last few words catch in his voice as he uttered them.

"Aren't you worried about getting sick?" asked the sergeant. Johannes shrugged and looked the Irishman in the eyes. "It will be what it will be. I've survived a lot. Bullets and sabers," he patted the saber on his side, "can't kill me, so I don't believe some little fever will."

The cavalry sergeant and captain exchanged glances.

Henderson's eyes again fixed on Reuben's Colt. He spoke slowly, "Come across an outlaw just about dead a few days back. Poor bugger had a hole from a Colt in his body. The pack of thieves he ran with just left him when his horse gave out. Before he died, he was raving about some young gun hand who kilt him and five others when they tried to attack some wagons," he paused. "Any idea who that would be, Reuben?"

Reuben's lips pursed. *Obviously surprised,* Johannes thought, *at the spread of news of their encounter with the Black Feather bunch.* Reuben held the captain's eye. "That would be me," he said softly.

The sergeant's eyes were wide. The captain measured his words carefully. "Well, Mr. Frank, the word is out." He nodded behind him. "My men are still talking 'bout that story. They thought the poor bugger was delirious. It will be all over the fort and the Oregon Trail and," his eyes flicked to the wagons, "Cherry Creek, too. You be careful."

Reuben looked unworried, "Thank you Captain. I will keep that in mind."

"May we ride in?"

Reuben smiled. "Of course. We have another hour before we get started moving again." He started to laugh, "We have a never-ending supply of buffalo chips, and our scout killed a buffalo cow a few days back, so we are stocked up on salted meat and jerky. Maybe the women can fix your troops some lunch. I'm sure they would be most pleased."

The captain glanced toward the wagons. "That third wagon set slightly offset from the circle is your sick wagon?"

Reuben nodded. The captain looked at him. "We would be obliged. My men could do with some food, and the coffee sounds good. Mind if we ride in on the opposite side from that Conestoga?"

Reuben nodded again, wheeled Lahn, and began to trot back toward the wagons.

Johannes was about to do the same when Captain Henderson called out, "Why don't you ride in with me. We can talk along the way." He smiled grimly, "as long as you don't mind me askin' you to be on the downwind side. I don't trust that fever."

Johannes laughed. "Downwind of you it will be."

The captain raised his hand, pointed at the wagons, and called out, "Forward Hoooah," and the troops began moving, the two captains from worlds apart riding side by side.

"What are your plans when you get to Cherry Creek, Captain?" Johannes realized the American officer was staring at him intently.

Johannes shrugged. "I promised Reuben to help him establish his ranch. I'll do that at the least. He will need the help. He's planning to hire some men in Cherry Creek and has our scout to help them, too.

"What's the scout's name?"

"Zeb."

The captain partially reined up, looking surprised. "Zebarriah Taylor?" The respect and recognition in his voice was undeniable. Johannes nodded. "Well, no wonder that young man can lead these wagons, and you folks survived that attack by such a large war party. That is one famous mountain man you're traveling with. Knows Indians, too. Spent time with the Sioux up toward the Big Horns it's my understanding. Never met him myself, but I hear he leads a mighty solitary existence down in the southwest part of the Territories. Hell of a trapper. Works the tributaries of the river they call the Uncompahgre. Supposedly he has a cabin in the Red Mountains down there, but no one knows exactly where."

Johannes felt himself start at the mention of the Red Mountains and the Uncompahgre. *That is why Zeb agreed to come with Reuben.* He kept his face expressionless. "He's a good man. Tough, steady, quiet, and he just gets it done."

Captain Henderson nodded, "Yep, that's what I've heard. Sure looking forward to meeting him finally after all these years."

"Probably won't happen, Captain. He is already a half-day's ride ahead, reconnoitering. We want to avoid a day like we had at Two Otters Creek with the Pawnee."

The squad was welcomed by the pioneers. Margaret, Rebecca, and Sarah, along with Elijah's wife and several of the women, whipped together a quick, but satisfying feast of beans, dried fruit, salted buffalo steaks, and coffee. The troopers lounged around, enjoying the respite from their saddles, talking amongst themselves and with the pioneers, and obviously relishing the movements of Rebecca and Sarah, as well as one or two other women on the train. *"Must be a lack of talent at Fort Laramie,"* Johannes thought.

"Damn." The captain downed his third cup of thick black coffee, stood up, and handed his cup to Sarah with a smile. "Thank you kindly, Miss Bonney." He turned to Reuben, "It's been a pleasure."

Reuben grinned. "Ours also, Captain." He looked up at the sun, "We best be moving, too. Are you headed our way?"

Captain Henderson shook his head and sighed. "No, we are only a week into a month patrol. We're headin' northeast, showing the flag, gathering information, and helping where we can. We will turn around somewhere this side of Kearney and come back roughly the same way. There has been little hostile action between here and Cherry Creek, but there are outlaws. Been several attacks on isolated farmsteads and one poor rancher, his wife, and all his hands were killed on their wagons in March down by a river they call the Cache la Poudre, just sixty miles southwest of the fort. Poor devils wintered with us. Fine people. We found their rigs, and what was left of them, but their daughter, she's fourteen, she was gone." He shook his head, "I shudder to think of her fate." His eyes rose quickly to Rebecca and Sarah, and he stiffened, "I'm so sorry ladies, I wasn't thinking."

"That is quite all right. We've seen enough thus far in our journey. The ways of the western part of your country are what they are," said Rebecca. Her eyes flickered to Reuben and she smiled. "But there is far more good than there is evil."

The captain nodded his head. "Yes, ma'am, thank you. Again, my apologies." He turned, lifted one hand to his mouth to amplify, and shouted, "C Squad. Mount up!" Sergeant O'Malley took it from there, "All right men, you've rested your sorry bones. It's time to get back to soldiering. In the saddles, the lot of you, and be smart about it."

The captain shook Reuben's hand and bowed to Rebecca, Sarah, and Margaret. "A pleasure meeting you all. I wish you Godspeed to Cherry Creek. Please say hello if you get to Fort Laramie."

He turned to Johannes, straightened to attention, and snapped a smart salute. Johannes did the same. "Perhaps we shall see you again, Captain Svenson. The Army needs good officers. There's trouble out here, and there's more trouble, bigger trouble afoot back East."

Johannes felt Reuben looking at him intently, and he could see the surprise in the faces of the three women gathered around. "I'll keep that in mind, Captain."

The captain nodded, walked over to his horse, which was being held by the sergeant, and mounted. "Keep your eyes out for savages." The bugler blew assembly. "Sergeant, form up the column."

The column formed in twos, flags flying. Captain Henderson turned in the saddle, looked at Johannes, and smiled. "We'll be seeing you, Captain." He turned and raised his hand, "Forward Hoooah."

May 17, 1855

*J*AGGED FRAME

REBECCA AND SARAH WERE TALKING, SHARING FAMILY STORIES FROM back in England. The wagon bumped and creaked. The day was cloudless, warm and bright. Rebecca, looking ahead of the horses, squinted and leaned forward.

"What is it, Rebecca?" Sarah asked, her voice anxious.

"I don't know...oh, it's Reuben."

Far out in front of the train, Reuben rode toward the wagons, waving his hat in the air like a mad man. Rebecca jerked the team to a halt, alarmed at his shouting. The other wagons followed suit. "Reach back and get my Sharps and the Enfield," she said to Sarah.

"Oh, please, not again," Sarah moaned, her complexion pale.

Reuben slowed at the first two wagons, pointing and shouting as he rode by, but he reined in completely at theirs. Lahn skidded to a stop. Reuben half rose out of the saddle, excitement spilling from his eyes, Lahn's bouncing, and partial turns and prancing, indicating he, too, had been infected by his master's exuberance.

"Look! The Rockies!" he exclaimed, pointing west, his hat in his hand. Sarah looked at Rebecca, her face a mixture of relief and startled excitement. They stood, shielding their eyes with their hands as they peered toward the horizon.

In the very far distance spread a line of uneven white. *Clouds?* As Rebecca focused, she could see the wavering bright, uneven tops of the great mountains, unsteady in reflected shimmers that radiated up from the rolling prairie, the snowcapped peaks forming a jagged saw-tooth picture frame between the paintings of the sky and prairie.

"I see them, I see them," Sarah almost shouted.

Reuben grinned, caught Rebecca's eye and stood in his stirrups, almost dragging her off the wagon as he kissed her, and then he was gone, at the gallop.

It was one of the few, carefree kisses they had shared since Inga's death, and Rebecca, her pulse racing, watched him ride down the line of wagons behind them, yelling. She suddenly realized how much she missed the full potent feel of his touch on her skin.

THEY CROSSED BEAVER CREEK AND CIRCLED UP EARLY, MORE THAN several hours before sunset. Reuben rode in, dismounted, and began to unharness the team. The men on night herd duty would drive the animals out to where they would be tethered or hobbled during the night. Sarah, not feeling well, was in the wagon.

"May I help?" Rebecca asked.

Reuben turned and looked at her, his eyes slowly dropping her full length.

"It will be difficult to be of assistance if I am undressed," she teased.

"Depends." He laughed. "Sure, some help would be great, thanks," Reuben replied.

She turned to head to the rear of the wagon to begin supper preparations, but he grabbed her hand, almost dragging her to the other side of the rig, away from the interior of the circled encampment.

"Reuben, for heaven's sake..."

He put his hand lightly over her mouth, insistent, and gently pushed her back into the wagon, his full length pressed tightly against her.

"Reuben, I..."

He put one finger to her lips and lowered his head until their faces were inches apart, the green of his eyes intense and smoldering. "There has been enough death and heartache, Rebecca, I want—I need—to remember life. I want you," and then he kissed her, his urgency sweetly smothering her. Her legs felt weak, and her own feverish desire erupted as she felt his need and realized she, too, was starved for something vital, something alive.

Wordless, they quickly saddled Lahn. Reuben pulled her up behind him, and they cantered off upstream, weaving along the edge of the cottonwoods to a sunlit clearing that opened to a broad expanse of prairie next to the creek.

He swung her down with one arm, leaped off Lahn, and tore the blanket from behind the saddle, throwing it not yet fully spread out onto the ground. She bent to straighten it but he caught her, drew her to him, and bent his lips to her neck.

The trees seemed to spin. She tore the buttons of his shirt, as his hand raised her skirt and chemise, slipped beneath her pantaloons, and his fingers found her. She heard herself gasp and she clung desperately to his neck, realizing that she *was* filled with the same consuming need to replace death with life, sorrow with joy. He whispered softly, urgently, over and over in her ear.

They struggled from their clothes, each helping the other. Reuben lay the Colt down by the upper corner of the blanket, and once naked, after devouring her with his eyes, he lowered her to the wool, her hand hungrily encircling him.

They clasped one another, her knees squeezing the sides of his upper chest, her heels digging into his lower back, her lips smothered by his. Their kisses grew in heated passion, and she felt his hips drive forward. Cocooned in his strength, she cried out, her body wracked with tremors, the universe seeming to collapse into them as she contracted with a groan and shuddered. He rolled her over, his arms strong around her back, supporting her, holding her to him, keeping himself in her, the primal wave washing her soul clean, the hot sun blazing down on her bare back, their position driving him even more deeply into her.

Her motions became more intense, rapid, not of her own volition, driven by a higher instinct, a more powerful urge. Grinding herself into him, spasms rocking her as she took his entire length, his hands on her hips, roughly clenching her to him until the prairie, the creek and the cottonwoods seemed to merge with their joining. She could no longer support herself on her arms and collapsed into his chest and they blended like the sky meeting the earth, the wind caressing them as she felt the searing heat of him fill her center in tandem with their mutual groans. They remained locked together, her clamped tight around him, rocking with sensual aftershocks, gently kissing, reluctant to let each other go.

THEY HAD FINISHED SUPPER, THE WHISPERS OF BEAVER CREEK JUST east of their wagon accented by the chirp of crickets, when Reuben, sitting by the fire, smiled, patted his belly and said, "You are turning into quite the cook, Rebecca. Would you grab some molasses? I am going to have another slice of that pan bread."

Rebecca's smile widened. "I should prefer to be called a chef," she laughed across the fire at him. "I'll get it from the wagon. We can't have a hungry man."

He looked up at her, his expression intense, his grin wolfish. "No we can't. If we get done early with the wagon maintenance tomorrow after we cross Badger Creek, perhaps we should saddle up and go for another ride."

The look in his eye, the radiant energy, cast her immediately back to just a few hours prior. She fumbled in the back of the wagon, momentarily forgetting what she had come to retrieve. She steadied herself with her hands on the tailgate, letting her heart rate subside and then returned with the molasses and sat beside him.

"I haven't seen that red sash on Johannes. Does he wear it just during battles?" she asked, handing Reuben his third cup of coffee, as he ate the pan bread.

He took one last gulp of coffee, and picked up a tablet of paper that rested on the ground next to him. Rebecca had watched him writing in it before dinner, holding it at an angle to catch the light, writing and thinking. He did the same thing now, his brow wrinkled in concentration. *Impressive,* she thought, *the way he makes lists and plans out things in advance.*

"I'm curious about Johannes' sash," she repeated.

He shot her a preoccupied look, began to speak, hesitated, then simply said, "He doesn't have it anymore."

He was going to say more. "Where did he lose it?" she pressed.

He sighed, looked up from the pad and held out his arm, "Come on over."

He was silent for a moment as she nestled into his side and leaned back against his saddle. Then he said, "You remember. Rebecca, when Johannes took Sarah and us to Inga's grave, that morning after the main service? When we were waiting for Preacher Walling and the rest to get there?"

Rebecca nodded. *He's trying not to upset me.*

"That is where the sash is. Johannes told me he had worn it in every fight since his first, at the age of fifteen." Reuben laughed softly, "He lied to get into the Danish Dragoons, of course. He said the sash carried a spirit which kept him safe. It was his father's."

He fell silent for a moment, looking into the flames. Rebecca heard his voice catch when he continued, shaking his head sadly. "He thought she should have that protection in her travel. And so that, if she had not heard his words at the end, she would know for sure now."

They sat for a long time without speaking, Rebecca nestled into him, the saddle supporting them both. When she finally rose, she said softly, "I think I'll add a piece of wood to the fire, and try that molasses and pan bread combination."

She tossed some kindling onto the fire and pried the last square of bread from the pan, dripped molasses over it, and took a bite, some of the heavy syrup catching the corners of her mouth. She reached up the back of her wrist and took two swipes across her lips, licking the sweet sticky topping from her wrist.

One of Reuben's eyebrows rose. She chuckled, "A procedure I have acquired from you men. Until this trip, I never knew the real purpose of the back of one's wrist."

"Let me see that wrist," Reuben said, reaching up from the saddle. As Rebecca extended her hand, he grabbed her and pulled her down, on top of him. He kissed her and she dropped the roll, the molasses forgotten.

CHAPTER

41

May 18, 1855

*B*ADGER CREEK

REBECCA WATCHED AS THE LAST WAGON ROLLED ACROSS BADGER
CREEK, the oxen fighting to keep their balance, sliding and unsure
in the fast, knee-deep current and slippery surface of the round cobbled streamed. Johnson's Conestoga was still proudly flying the
disheveled remains of the Betsy Ross Circular Flag as it bumped up
onto the bank and completed the defensive circle Reuben had
ordered. From more than a hundred yards across the circled encampment, Rebecca spotted the flash of Margaret's hand and she waved
in return.

The camp was animated, the spirits of the pioneers lifted from
the shock and despair of Two Otters Creek by the far distant sight
of the Rockies.

Outside the circled wagons, Johannes had a group of six horsemen
around him. He gestured to each in turn, pointed in a direction and
the rider sped off, rifle or musket at the ready. He had shaved and
cut his hair. *An air of command.* The saber dangled from his waist.

Rebecca took a deep breath, inhaling the day and the bustling
energy of the camp. She grinned as she recalled their first sight of
the mountains. And the casting off of death—the delicious primal
celebration of life that followed. She lifted her face to the late midday
sun. The radiant warmth on her face and pleasant soreness rekindled

the lingering, tactile memory of the hot spring sun on her back the previous afternoon, the vast emptiness, the backdrop to them taking each other again, the taper of his muscular torso when he rolled her over to the very edge of the blanket, placing her above him.

"Rebecca. Rebecca? *Rebecca!*"

She forced her eyes open. Sarah was standing in front of her, her head cocked, a concerned, but amused expression crinkling the freckles across her nose. "Are you okay?"

A vision of Inga answering this very same question just a month prior, back on the Missouri, flashed in Rebecca's mind. *I always thought she had been thinking about Johannes that morning, when she seemed so dreamy and removed.* Rebecca smiled, thinking of Inga. Sarah smiled back, unaware that Rebecca's mind was elsewhere. *Poor Inga.*

"I'm fine," said Rebecca, "in fact, make that grand."

The redhead's face cocked slightly again, and she laughed. "Judging by the expression on your face when I walked up, I'm not sure where you were, but I think I want to go there," she sighed, "particularly after Two Otters Creek."

———— ◆ ————

REBECCA, WITH SARAH AT HER SIDE, WATCHED AS ACROSS THE CIRCLE of wagons Reuben and several men got the forge fired up. His voice carried, then became indistinguishable in the hubbub of the encampment as he gave directions. "Spread a blanket under the wagons, and lay out the tools so we are not tripping over them. We're going to need..."

Rebecca felt Sarah's gaze from the side. "The looks that man throws in your direction," the redhead said softly, "particularly when you're not aware, are truly something to behold."

Rebecca took Sarah's elbow and gently nudged her arm. "You're one to talk. Zeb trips over his mustache every time he is around you."

Sarah giggled and blushed. "Zeb is such a nice man."

Nice man? That's all?

Sarah, still watching the men laying out the spare parts and tools, and firing up the forge over at the supply wagons, didn't pick up Rebecca's sharp, questioning glance.

Rebecca looked around her at the uneven landscape dotted with shallow buttes. One side dropped off abruptly, the exposed striations of different colored rocks each reflecting the sun in its own peculiar way, their abrupt bases softened by leafing cottonwoods and alders wherever there was a spring, creek or other water source. Badger Creek flowed north with a crystalline rush towards its rendezvous with the South Platte, which Reuben had said was miles north of them. Zeb said the Indians called the river, *Padouca*.

"Rebecca?"

"Yes, Sarah," she answered, feeling a twinge of annoyance at being pulled back from savoring the surroundings.

"Have you decided if you're going back to England?"

Rebecca stared at her. She was still looking across the circled wagons toward Reuben and the men who had begun their work, beginning with the supply wagons themselves. "That question came out of the blue. Why do you ask?"

Sarah's eyes moved to hers. "I was curious. I haven't decided what I'm doing either. I could stay in Cherry Creek. It's growing, and everyone, even the army captain, said the growth is bound to accelerate. I wonder if there's anybody doing seamstress work?" Sarah paused and looked up at the sky. "I could go on to Salt Lake. Those Mormons seem like very nice people."

The redhead's gaze returned to Rebecca. "So, have you decided?"

"Sarah, I have a question for you." Rebecca dropped her voice to a whisper. "Do you have a gold map?"

Sarah's jaw dropped open and her big blue eyes widened. She began to speak, thought better of it, then glanced over her shoulder and leaned closer, her voice a demanding whisper. "Who told you that?"

"Reuben and I were talking. Evidently, Inga had said something to Johannes who in turn mentioned it to Reuben."

Sarah glanced behind her again. "There is a map, Rebecca. I discovered it quite some time ago on the train, when Jacob was out playing poker and I was locked in the compartment dreading his return, and...and what would happen. I found a parchment gold map. Though I have tried to draw out of him where, and how, he obtained it, he has refused to tell me, even when he's drunk. I think he keeps it in his jacket—you know, the brown one he always has with him. And—I'm quite sure, in fact, I know—that he uses it for a pillow every night. Where Jacob goes, that jacket goes."

Sarah looked down at the ground, studying the toes of the elk moccasins Zeb had made for her, and sighed, "I hope you don't think less of me. It is the only reason, except one other, that I maintain any association with that scum Irishman."

Rebecca was startled by the venom in her eyes.

"I mean to have that map, Rebecca. I *will* have that map. Whether I shall ever find the place marked on the map, or sell it, or burn it, does not matter. I will have that map." Sarah was standing almost on her tip toes, her hands clenched fists at her side, and her jaw stuck out, and her freckles popped from the red flush over her nose and cheeks.

Rebecca made every effort not to react to Sarah's sudden, abrupt change in demeanor. "What was the second reason?" she asked.

"Revenge."

Rebecca looked sharply at her friend. "Sometimes, Sarah, it's better to let things go and move on. Life is too short," she swept her hand out toward the vast, rolling lands around them, "to become over invested in something so dark."

Sarah's eye lids were quivering, and her jaw clenched. "There are other times, Rebecca, I'm sure you know, when principle and justice demand that something started, *be finished.*"

Rebecca broke their gaze, an odd unpleasant feeling in her stomach. "May I ask where this map says the supposed gold is?"

Again Sarah glanced around, leaned into her, and responded in a whisper. "In the mountains southwest of Cherry Creek, quite far, I think. On the map, they're called Las Montanas Rojas. Jacob says the words mean *The Red Mountains.*"

Reuben was right! Rebecca was silent for a moment as she thought, then she put her arm around her friend, put her lips near hers, and whispered, "Yours is not the only map, Sarah. I have one too."

Sarah drew back, her eyes wide. "You do?"

Rebecca nodded. "It is a map to, and of, land my father was deeded by the King of Spain. His trading ships often visited Spanish ports. He bequeathed it to me..." She turned, looked around to make sure they were not overheard, and continued, "I shall tell you the story in detail another time." She fixed her eyes on Sarah's. "It describes potential gold deposits," she paused, "and like yours, the location is Las Montanas Rojas."

Sarah's eyes widened further, one hand flying to her mouth to cover a sharp intake of breath.

ACROSS THE CIRCLE OF RIGS, SITTING ON THE TONGUE IN THE SHADE of the wagon, Jacob watched the two women, looking down from time to time to time as the point of his boot knife scraped grime from under his fingernails. His chest felt constricted with a seething resentment and animosity as he watched them laugh and whisper. *Brunette queen and double-crossing redhead.*

He swung his gaze to Reuben and the men working on wheels at the far side of the circle, wiped the nail dirt from the knife on his pants, and spat. *One down, three to go.*

CHAPTER

42

May 18, 1855

REVENGE

REBECCA HAD LAID OUT ON THE TAILGATE EVERYTHING SHE NEEDED to freshen up. "Your vanity," Reuben liked to call the tailgate. Rebecca gathered her towel and a small canvas sack she had converted to a handbag for just such occasions. *Don't want to ruin my good purses.* As she sorted and the sun beat down on her cotton shirt, its heat permeated the cloth, warming her back.

She gathered the Sharps, made sure there were an extra five loads in the pocket Sarah had sewn into her riding dress, and decided to wear her light blue, wool jacket. The trees would be shady. She set off humming from the wagons. *Perhaps I should tell Reuben where I am going? No, Sarah knows.*

It was a short walk to the cottonwoods, the trees great crooked arms and their rough, textured trunks accentuated by the newly formed leaves. Rebecca wet her lips as she walked...*Dry. Very dry out here.* One hundred feet inside the cottonwood stand, completely hidden from the wagons, was a curve in the creek, its flow fifty feet across. Two large rocks broke the current, adding to the sound of the clear, rushing water.

Where the water drifted in a small eddy by the bank and stirred, rather than flowed, she could see her reflection, distorted in the movement of the water surface—a long, dark-haired woman wearing a tapered brown riding dress that heightened the curve of her delicate hips, blue cotton shirt underneath a light wool jacket of the same color, one hand holding a canvas bag, the other the Sharps.

She smiled down at the woman, laughing when she remembered how she had fallen in the water the first time she and Reuben made love, which seemed like ages ago. *Which Rebecca are you now? The Rebecca of trading ships and stately row houses, or the woman who has killed two men, looks forward to sunsets and sunrises in this wild land, carries a Sharps rifle...and is no longer a virgin.* She felt her lips widen and the brunette in the pool of water smiled back at her.

What does that scar look like? Her looking glass had long ago been broken, as had Sarah's. Reflections in the water kegs had sufficed for grooming since then. She leaned over and set the Sharps against a rock a few feet away, sank to her knees on the stream bank, and lowered her face, turning her head one way, and then other, to get a better look at the scar. She ran her tongue over the raised red line at her lip, and looked again.

She startled at a sudden image behind her and rushed to straighten up, but rough large hands grabbed her neck and arm and pushed her forward. She was no match for the man's strength as he shoved her head underwater. She struggled desperately but the grip around her neck and arm tightened, and the hand shoved her head deeper. Her forehead bumped twice on the rocks at the bottom of the creek. Her lungs emptied of breath. She felt herself weakening. *Oh my God, what is happening? Reuben!* A misty darkness began to fog her brain, red kaleidoscope swirls spinning in her eyes, the underwater rocks wavy in her vision, as the strong hand held her head under the water. A creeping blackness replaced the red swirls, and she felt herself drifting.

The first sound she heard was her own gasps, gulping, devouring air. The blackness receded, replaced by the savage face of Jacob O'Shanahan on top of her. Her dress had been lifted and her pantaloons ripped from her body. He had one hand over her mouth, the other between her legs. She was nearly anchored to the ground by his weight and the press of his shoulder on hers. One of his arms was behind her neck, the palm of his hand brutally covering her nose and mouth, the other palm pressing down her pelvis as his fingers touched her. One leg was pinned under his lower torso; the other waved feebly in the air.

He moved his lips from where they had been licking her neck, and let the full weight of his chest pin her completely, bruising her hips and lower back. Pain stabbed her. "Not so high and mighty now, are you Queenie? You brunette bitch. At least you will have a real man once before you die. And die you will."

Rebecca heard herself groan under the painful clamp of his fingers.

"Oh, like that, do you? I thought you would. It's always the hardest to get what has the sweetest taste."

She was having trouble breathing, his hoarse, rank breath in her ear. "Imagine how torn up that farmer's going to be—his woman dead and violated? He'll get stupid, and then I'll get him too. That'll be three down, one to go."

She was helpless under his bulk. His hand withdrew from her and she knew he was fumbling with his pants, both his legs now between hers, her thighs spread by the weight of his knees forcing them apart. *Reuben, oh my God, Reuben, where are you?* She flashed her eyes left and right, desperately looking for something, anything, to pick up and strike him with.

Jacob descended roughly down on her. "I've waited a long time for this." She felt him at the very edge of her and tried desperately to shift her hips. He cackled in a hoarse whisper, "I like it when they move." He raised his hips to thrust and then, suddenly, he shuddered, his body bearing down on her but his hips, instead of thrusting, relaxed.

She opened her eyes. Half-standing and half-kneeling above him, stood Sarah, her arm raised, the knife in her hand, a bloody red blur as she plunged it into his back, again and again, but Jacob's breath in Rebecca's ears had long ago ceased. With her free hand, Rebecca removed Jacob's hand from her mouth. "Sarah, oh my God, Sarah, he's dead! Stop! Stop!"

The redhead was crying, her face terribly distorted with a horrible look of hate, anger, and anguish. As if possessed, her arm kept rising and falling. Each time the blade entered his back, Rebecca could feel his body jerk. "Sarah, stop. Sarah, he's dead, he's dead!"

Sarah paused, bloody hand raised above her head, ready to yet again drive the knife downwards. Her eyes moved to Rebecca. She froze, then sank slowly to a sitting position, trembling violently, her arm resting on one knee, still holding the knife, the other hand covering her eyes. She began to sob.

Rebecca managed to slide herself, bit by bit, out from under Jacob's heavy, burly corpse. She lowered her skirt, covering where she had been exposed. His back was a red mass of torn, blood stained brown fabric and seeping blood, which mottled the torn pantaloons that lay partially beneath him.

Sarah had dropped the knife. Both her hands were pressed to her face, one of them bloody, smearing one half of her delicate features, accentuating her wild, animal look.

Rebecca tried to rise, but her legs were too weak. She felt bruised everywhere. She crawled on her hands and knees several feet to her sobbing friend, and put her arm around her.

"I...Killed...Him...I...Killed...Him," Sarah kept repeating, oblivious of Rebecca's attempts to calm her.

REBECCA WAS SHAKEN, AND STILL PARTIALLY STARVED FOR AIR. SARAH, still clinging to her, heaved great, deep anguished sobs. Gradually Rebecca's thoughts cleared. She glanced at Jacob's body.

"Sarah. *Sarah!*" The redhead's hysteria did not diminish. Rebecca drew her hand back and slapped her, then again. Sarah's eyes blinked through her tears, no longer crying—but taking great heaving breaths.

Rebecca inhaled, gathering her thoughts. "Sarah, didn't you tell me that he keeps the map in his jacket?" Sarah nodded faintly.

Rebecca pointed at the bloody corpse, "That jacket?"

Sarah blinked rapidly and nodded. In unison, they scrambled the few feet to his body on their hands and knees. Rebecca could feel her nose wrinkle as she reached out her hands and touched what had been the Irishman. There was blood everywhere. "Sarah, help me roll his shoulders up so I can check one pocket. If we don't find it, we'll do the same on the other side." Sarah strained, lifting Jacob's left shoulder six inches, then a foot.

Rebecca put her hand in his jacket, feeling the pockets, running her hands down the fabric. She looked up, and shook her head. "Let's try the other side."

They repeated the process, Sarah fighting with the weight of the body, and Rebecca rummaging through the dead man's jacket, feeling the cloth and lining. She was about to give up when she felt something, "Sarah get me the knife."

Without thinking, Sarah let go of Jacob. The corpse rolled over on Rebecca's forearms, and Jacob's lifeless open eyes stared at her, a sneer on his lips.

Sarah crawled back with the knife. "Pull this thing off me," Rebecca said, trying to free her arms. Using one hand, Sarah freed her, and then handed the bloody blade to Rebecca.

"Where did you get this?" Rebecca asked.

"Zeb gave it to me. He has my Deringer right now. It needed cleaning. Dirt got into the action somehow, and there is blood from the Indian..."

Rebecca yanked at the jacket and the lower corner came loose from Jacob's lifeless press. She ran the knife down a line that had been crudely re-sewn, felt inside with her hand, and drew out a folded piece of parchment. She grinned at Sarah. "I think, Miss Bonney, that you are now the proud owner of a gold map."

Sarah reached for the map but Rebecca held it back. "Wash your hands first."

Sarah blinked, stood unsteadily and staggered several feet to the creek.

A wave of nausea washed over Rebecca as she watched Sarah stare into the same patch of reflective water where, only moments ago, she herself had been kneeling. "Your face, too," she nearly shouted. "Get the blood *off* your face."

Sarah cried out, "Oh my, oh what a mess," and began frantically to splash water on her face, rubbing, then splashing, then looking anxiously back at her reflection. When she turned back to Rebecca, wet strands of red hair stuck to her cheek.

"Dry your hands, Sarah."

When Rebecca handed her the map, the redhead sat back on her heels, held the map to her breasts, and began to cry softly. "Rebecca, I wanted to kill him. I really did. I can't tell you how many times I thought about killing him." Sarah's eyes dropped to Jacob's body. "I'm sorry."

Rebecca eased around the body and over to Sarah. "Rest assured, if you had not, someone else would have. He was destined to die a violent death from the moment he was born. Think of all the people he has hurt. And the pain he caused Inga and Johannes. Think about what he did to you, and tried to do to me. He would have raped and killed me.

"I know what you are feeling. After killing those two Indians at Two Otters Creek, I know exactly how it feels to take another human life as do you. But he had it coming. And now, you have the map. Reuben says there are no coincidences, and..." Sarah looked at her attentively through her tears, "I don't know if you know this, but Reuben has maps, too."

Sarah's puffy eyes widened, "Reuben has a gold map too?"

"No, his maps were drawn by a scout. One concerns getting across the country, and the other maps out a perfectly suitable ranch," she laughed, "on the flanks of Las Montanas Rojas."

Sarah looked at her, speechless.

"Reuben told me that there was another map, too, a map that spoke of..."

Something clicked deep in Rebecca as she spoke. She could feel her eyes widen, and her heart race. She straightened up on her knees, reached over, and grabbed Sarah's arm. "When did Jacob first get this map?"

"He had it in New York, when we first got on the train."

Rebecca pointed at the map. "What is that darker stain? There, in the fold."

Sarah unfolded a portion of the map. "I noticed that right off, too. I had come to the conclusion, knowing Jacob, that its blood..." She looked up. "You mean...?"

Rebecca nodded. "Yes, I have a feeling. Reuben and I shared our maps the day after we..." She looked down, smoothed her hands down the front of her riding skirt. *Inga's habit!* She looked up at Sarah, "The day after we first made love. There's a name in the lower right-hand corner of the map. It's the signature of the scout his father and uncle hired."

Sarah's shoulders slumped, "Well then, its Reuben's map."

Rebecca shook her head. "I don't think so, Sarah. I think he might look at it differently. We'll take a look at it together and compare the names, but right now we have another problem," she nodded at the corpse.

Sarah clapped a hand over her mouth, "I didn't even think of that."

Rebecca looked at Sarah. "Obviously."

Rebecca settled back down to her heels. "He's much too heavy for the two of us to move. We would be here all day, and leave a blood trail that anybody could follow. Perhaps we should just tell Reuben what happened. You were defending me. Another few seconds and he would've..."

She felt his fingers inside her. A bitter taste rose in her mouth and she felt suddenly sick. She leaned over to the side and retched. Sarah scooted to her and put her arms around her shoulder, "It's okay, Rebecca. It's okay. The important thing is he didn't. You weren't raped. You are very much alive, and you aren't...thank God, you aren't pregnant with his child."

Rebecca straightened up and wiped her mouth with the back of her wrist.

"I don't think we should tell them, Rebecca," Sarah said. "The news will be all over the wagon train in a flash. Zeb calls it the 'sagebrush grapevine.' People will inquire. They will want the whole story." Her voice fell. "They will find out I was raped, and am now carrying the bastard child of that bastard. It will be all over Cherry

Creek. She reached over and grabbed Rebecca's hand, "I don't think we should. Really."

Rebecca looked at her friend, thinking. "We could roll the body into the creek. I wish it was a bigger river, but he might flow downstream far enough that nobody would notice."

"I have an idea," Sarah interrupted. "Let's..."

The women suddenly raised their heads. They froze at the distinct sound of muted splashing—a horse walking in the creek, headed downstream towards them.

CHAPTER

43

May 18, 1855

$\mathscr{S}$ACRED PACT

SARAH'S HEART BEAT WILDLY AND SHE KNEW HER LOOK MIRRORED that of Rebecca's, whose eyes were wide and fearful. The horse grew closer.

Wobbling, Rebecca stood and grabbed the Sharps. "Sarah, get my canvas bag. Make sure you pick up the knife. Let's get back in those trees." Still unsteady on her feet, she tripped, almost falling. Sarah clutched the canvas bag and, knife in one hand, put her arm around Rebecca's waist and the two moved into the protective cover of the cottonwood stand. They crouched behind a large tree, breathing heavily, hearts racing.

A squirrel in the tree above them chattered angrily as the sounds of the horse splashing through the water grew louder. "It's Zeb," Rebecca hissed. Sarah nodded, transfixed by the scene, her mind racing in a jumble of thoughts.

Buck stepped up on the bank just feet from the body. Zeb lifted his Sharps from his lap, and settled the rifle's buttplate on his thigh. Horse and rider stood silent and still, Zeb glancing keenly around the body, then out from it, his head and shoulder rotating slowly. He dismounted, his rifle at the ready, and knelt on one knee. He nodded and Buck backed up five or six steps.

Reaching out one hand, he felt around Jacob's corpse, not touching the body but seeming to feel the ground, letting his hand linger in certain places. He relaxed and stood, the Sharps now cradled in the crook of his arm. With his eyes glued to the ground, he took a few paces, cast a glance left, then right, then knelt down and felt the earth again. His head rose and his eyes followed their route into the trees. He stood. "Rebecca and Sarah, come on out."

The two women looked at each other. Rebecca's eyes were wide and bloodshot, her scar pronounced against the pallor of her skin. She started to rise, but Sarah pulled her down. "Let's wait. Maybe, maybe he's bluffing."

Rebecca shook her head. "He knows, Sarah, he knows. Maybe he will help us. He is likely the person who detested Jacob the second most on earth. And we both know that was prompted, in part, by you."

"Yes, but now? After I killed a man using his knife? And what happens when he finds out I'm pregnant?" Sarah fought the confusion and the surreal cold emptiness that gripped her. *There is no choice.* She sighed. "You're right, Rebecca."

They rose together and walked out to Zeb. He watched them, one hand busily stroking his mustache. They reached him and Sarah looked down, ashamed. "Zeb, I'm sorry, I didn't mean to..."

She was interrupted by the feel of his fingers under her chin slowly lifting her face, his long arm fully outstretched. "Sure you did. He had it comin'! If you hadn't, I probably would've and if I hadn't, somebody else certainly would've."

He swung his gaze to Rebecca, "Are you all right?" Rebecca's face was pale, but her eyes had that fiery look that Sarah had learned to respect since the very first night on the trail.

Zeb nodded behind him. "Looks like he jumped you from behind and pushed your head underwater 'til you passed out."

Rebecca's eyes widened, "Yes, Zeb. Exactly."

"Did he..." Zeb looked down at his moccasins, embarrassed, a latent seething just below the surface.

Rebecca reached out and laid her hand on his arm. "No, he didn't, but another few seconds and he would have, and afterwards he meant to kill me."

She reached over to Sarah, grabbed her hand and squeezed, "Sarah saved me, Zeb. She saved my life, and my honor. She was very brave." Rebecca turned and looked Sarah square in the eyes. "That's the second time you've come to my rescue in little more than a week."

Zeb turned his head sideways to examine the corpse for a long moment. His eyes moved back to Sarah, "My knife?" He smiled. "That pleases me. Sarah, sounds to me like you were here when you needed to be. Let's go tell Reuben."

"No!" Sarah took a step towards him and rested her palm on the leather at his chest. "No, Zeb, I don't want to. There'll be too many questions."

Zeb looked at her for a moment, then turned to Rebecca. "What do you think, Rebecca?"

"I think Sarah's right. The less people know, the better. It's not like there's anybody who will mourn or even miss him. Why should the heroine of the day," she gestured at Sarah, "be put in a situation of compromise and stress?"

Zeb's fingers worked his mustache as he looked from one to the other. "Anybody could happen on this body." He looked down at the ground, his eyes following where they had walked from the trees. "A child could read the sign." He looked down at Sarah's moccasins, then his own, and finally at Rebecca's boots.

"Got an idea." He whistled softly. Buck pricked up his ears and took the few steps necessary to stand next to them. Zeb handed Sarah his Sharps, "Hold this for me." He moved down Buck's flank, opened a saddlebag, and withdrew an arrow broken in two.

"Is that the arrow that..."

"Yep, sure enough is." He looked down at Jacob's corpse and spit. "I think that son of a bitch is who killed poor Mac. The sign was clear, but his boot prints didn't match the story in the dirt. Kept this for evidence, but don't need that anymore."

Sarah's head jerked up. "He has, I mean had, two pairs of boots."

Zeb nodded slowly, "I suspected he might. I talked to Reuben about doing a search of his wagon, hoping to turn the bastard into the Army at Cherry Creek. Anyways, for me to ponder about this plan, I gotta have a smoke." He reached inside his buckskin shirt, pulled out a small suede tobacco pouch, extracted a slip of rolling papers from his leggings pocket, and began to roll a smoke. Sarah and Rebecca glanced at each other. Zeb flicked his eyes up to them as he sprinkled tobacco on the paper. "Don't look so startled. He ain't going nowhere."

Sarah watched Rebecca dip her head, a smile playing on her face, then look up at Zeb. "I have a question for you. Might be out of place, but how on earth did you pack enough tobacco for this whole trip?"

Zeb grinned at her. "See them red willows over there," he gestured behind Sarah. "Up along the banks from the direction that me and Buck rode in from? Yep, see those spindly bushes over there? One is golden and those others are reddish barked. In case you ladies ever take up smoking, you don't need to buy tobacco. You just scrape the bark off them red willows and let it dry." He raised the paper to his lips, licked it, and held up the cigarette to them. "Best damn tobacco there is."

Sarah began to laugh and Rebecca joined in. Zeb chuckled, too.

"So here's my plan." He turned and stood over Jacob's body, holding the arrow with the stone broadhead secured to its tip by rawhide. *The work of Pawnee hands*, Sarah thought. He knelt down, raised his arm, and drove the arrow into Jacob's back.

Her stomach turned. She bent over and vomited. Rebecca was quickly at her side, holding her shoulders.

"Oh. Sorry. Wasn't thinking," said Zeb, looking concerned. "She'll feel better." He stood and surveyed his handiwork, glancing from time to time at the last half of the arrow. He turned it over in one hand, stroking his mustache with the other. He broke the half arrow more or less in thirds, and laid the pieces haphazardly by Jacob's side. He folded one of the dead man's arms over his back, bent at the elbow, and then rolled Jacob's body on top of the three pieces of arrow. The dead man's chest was strangely raised where the press of the broadhead through his spine and his arm arched his back from the ground.

Zeb stood back, the cigarette smoking in his mouth. Regarding the scene with a critical eye, he cocked his head from side to side. "Yep, poor Irishman came down here and got bushwhacked by Pawnees," he pointed across the stream, "probably from the other side of the creek. The bastard, clawing at his back, broke the arrow in the three pieces as he hit the ground."

"Sarah," he said, "please get me that knife."

Sarah still felt queasy. "It is back by the cottonwood where we were hiding."

"Okay, go fetch it. Don't step in the same track you made coming in and out of there. You can bend grass once, but you walk on it more and that track will be around for a long time."

Sarah felt as if she were in a dream. She walked, light-headed, back to the cottonwood, taking care to step only on untrammeled grass. She returned with the knife. Zeb put one moccasin foot on either side of the body, taking care not to get blood on the leather. He bent down, knife in one hand, Jacob's head lifted by its hair in his other.

He turned his head sideways at the two women, "You best look away." Sarah and Rebecca's eyes met and they quickly turned their backs. There was a wet, rasping sound, then again, and then a small splash in the creek.

"Okay—done."

When Sarah looked again, Zeb was wiping the knife on Jacob's pants. "Yep, and then after the ambush they came across the creek, leaving no track in the water, and scalped the poor Irishman. Then they snuck over to those trees," he pointed where Sarah and Rebecca had hidden, "to spy on the wagon train and came back the same way."

He looked at Rebecca's boots. "Take those off, Rebecca. Yours is the only sign we got to cover. I will put you up on Buck, get you back close to the wagons, and then you can put the boots back on and walk into camp from a different direction." He walked over to a small cottonwood and broke off one of the low-lying branches. He carefully backtracked their trail, taking care to brush out the track of

Rebecca's boots, but leaving the moccasin tracks belonging to him and Sarah.

He scooped Rebecca up and put her on Buck. "Just so happens, I took his shoes off two days ago. Two of 'em was bothering him. Truth is, I think he'd rather run unshod anyway." Buck flipped his muzzle up and down. "Leastways until we get to Cherry Creek."

"Zeb, I think that horse is the most important thing in the world to you, and you to him," said Rebecca, smiling slightly.

Zeb nodded, then turned his eyes to Sarah, softness in his deep-set stare. "I may be to him, but he's second most important to me now." The mountain man reddened and cleared his throat, and Sarah fought the impulse to bury her head in his leathers, and cry.

"Okay, let me walk around here a little bit with you on him and then we'll ease outta here up the creek and leave the site of this horrible ambush. If it is meant to be found, then Spirit will make it so."

Sarah watched as the mountain man created the scene he wanted. Then he led Buck over to her, lifted her up on the horse in front of Rebecca, and then splashed up the creek leading Buck. When he was satisfied with their location, he led Buck out of the creek. "Rebecca, let me help you off. Best you put on your boots here and walk."

They made their way through the cottonwoods until they could see the wagon tops through one narrow alley in the trees.

He helped Sarah down. "I suggest, Rebecca, you lend Sarah your jacket to cover the blood on her sleeves." He looked them up and down critically, then tried to joke. "Pretty clean for the mess you made, Sarah." She bit her lip, trying to hold back tears, but she could feel them trickling down her cheek. She stepped forward and laid her head into his chest. "Thank you, Zeb. Thank you."

"So what are we going to do or say if the body is found?" Rebecca blurted out.

Always practical, thought Sarah. Zeb looked at them. "What body?"

The two women exchanged looks. Sarah wondered if her expression appeared as puzzled as Rebecca's. "Jacob's body."

Zeb peered at them, his eyes slowly moving from one to the other, "Jacob's body? I don't know nothing about no Jacob's body. The redheaded lady, she's been down here with her dark haired friend gossiping or whatever it is women do at the river. The only folks know about any corpse is the Pawnee that killed him. Since we don't know about the Pawnee," he spit, "we can't know much else."

Zeb looked from one to the other and stretched out his arm, his hand extended, palm down. "Sarah, put your hand on mine, palm down."

Sarah reached out her hand and put it on top of Zeb's, stunned at how small her delicate fingers were compared to his.

"Rebecca put your hand, palm down, on top of Sarah's." Rebecca did as he asked. Zeb looked from one to the other. "This here's a sacred pact. We don't know nothing about nobody."

The two women looked at each other.

"Say it." There was an impatient edge to his voice. In unison, Sarah and Rebecca sang out, "We don't know nothing about nobody."

"And finally, we know nothing about no Pawnee ambush, so we don't know nothing about nothing." Both she and Rebecca didn't hesitate repeating the words this time.

He dropped his hand and flicked his finger in the direction of the wagons. "I suggest you just head on straight from here. I'm going to mosey up the river and come in the other side." He looked at Sarah, "What's for dinner?"

Sarah felt her smile growing, "Whatever you want Zebbariah Taylor. Whatever you want."

He nodded, swung easily into the saddle, and without looking back rode off into the cottonwoods towards the creek.

May 27, 1855

HERRY CREEK

REUBEN SMILED AT SARAH AND REBECCA AS HE SADDLED LAHN. The women stood shoulder to shoulder. Sarah was still in her sleeping gown, clutching a heavy shawl around her shoulders. Rebecca was already fully clothed in her brown riding dress and wearing one of Reuben's jackets, which she had grabbed when she scrambled out of the wagon. Her full skirt flared beneath the jacket, flowing around her boots as she walked.

After fastening the cinch, Reuben stood and looked around camp. "Quite the day," he said to the women, feeling a difference in the morning bustle, an anticipation that permeated the air and ran with a stiff breeze of excitement from one wagon to another. Pioneers talked with louder voices than normal, no one attempting to be quiet. There didn't seem to be a soul still left in any wagon. All were busy—sorting supplies, huddled over a few breakfast fires, or standing in groups, talking.

Over the eastern-most wagons in the circle, tendrils of clouds glowed with morning fire, tapering into a golden halo that rimmed the broken terrain, forming the horizon and signaling the coming sun. To the west above the rugged foothills and the sharp ridges of the high Rockies, retreating indigo danced around jagged snow-covered peaks, the last of the night clinging tenaciously to the spine of the continent. It's grudging retreat signaled a welcome to the wagon train.

Reuben watched the Kentucky boy, Abraham, limping, and his father harnessing up the team to Jacob and Sarah's wagon.

"Good thing, Sarah, that Abraham said he'd drive your wagon, when Jacob came up missing at Badger Creek. Wouldn't have even known it, except for his wagon standing there with the team milling around after the night guard dropped them off."

He turned and looked hard at the two women. Sarah became interested in plucking something from her shawl. Rebecca held his gaze but with unsteady eyes.

"I was just thinking," he said, pretending to adjust straps on Lahn's saddle, "what are the odds he would have wandered into some scalp hungry Pawnee down there on the creek?" He shook his head, "Those Indians certainly saved some people a lot of trouble."

He leaned on the saddle and stared at them.

"Well, we have all had experience with the Pawnee, but about Cherry Creek, I thought we were two days' out," asked Rebecca, her expression puzzled. "I thought we would be at Cherry Creek some-time tomorrow?"

Reuben shook his head. "No. We're this close, and, as Mac would've said, 'no sense dee-daddling. We're going to cut off a north loop of the South Platte. Zeb says he knows a little-used trail that'll get us in late today, maybe this evening.

"Sarah, you look a little green around the gills. Are you okay?"

The redhead nodded but kept her lips tightly closed. Rebecca glanced at her, then back at Reuben. "Are we going into town tonight?" she asked quickly.

Trying to divert attention again, she doesn't realize Zeb and I figured that out after Two Otters Creek. "No. Zeb tells me you couldn't really call Cherry Creek a town. There may be more Arapaho tipis than white man shacks and tents. Zeb is going in, though. He was good friends with Mac's brother Randy, who runs the Mercantile, such that it is. Zeb and Mac went way back, and he wants to break the news about Mac. Once any of this outfit gets into town, the news will be all over."

Rebecca's eyes dropped to the Colt. Reuben rested one arm over the saddle and held her gaze. "I suspect that will be news, too." He smiled at her and she smiled in return, but there was worry in her eyes. "Rebecca," he asked, "can we talk later?"

Her eyes softened. "Of course, Reuben."

"Excuse...Excuse me," Sarah raised one hand to her mouth and darted around the edge of the wagon. Rebecca peeked around the tailgate and then back at Reuben. "Poor Sarah, she's coming down with a cold..."

Reuben cut her off and looked her in the eye. "Uh-huh. Same as those dark spots around the hem of that riding dress of yours being boot polish." Rebecca looked down at the several blotches of dark irregular stains that had obviously been scrubbed on the lower third of her skirt. "One thing you have to know, Rebecca..."

"Yes?" her voice was apprehensive.

"You can trust me. With anything, about anything." He mounted Lahn and trotted out from the wagons, leaving her wide-eyed and open-mouthed.

There were hoof beats close behind him—Johannes on Bente, a serious look on his friend's face. As Bente fell into step next to the palomino, Reuben asked, "What is it, Johannes?"

"They're all dead. The fever got them all."

Reuben reined in, as did the Dane. Johannes shook his head, "I believe Thelma died yesterday. Perhaps last night. She was very weak and incoherent when I brought them their supplies yesterday morning. The lad with no kinfolk," Johannes dropped his head for a moment, "he was scarcely more than a scarecrow. And that widower fellow, Andrew, that was traveling on his own, I'm pretty sure died yesterday after my morning visit. Damn. Come all this way, and then they die just before getting to the destination."

Reuben looked at him. "My friend, Cherry Creek was the goal; it is not the destination."

Johannes' lips pursed, and he nodded, "True enough, Reuben, true enough." Then he added, "I told Daniel that he can drive his own wagon today, instead of the sick rig."

"You plan on burning it then?"

"I don't see any other choice, Reuben. We simply can't have other people moving those bodies and perhaps getting infected. If we bring the cholera into Cherry Creek, a couple hundred people could die." The tall blonde stopped and watched the glowing, fiery edge of the morning sun as it emerged on the uneven horizon.

"And we can't leave the wagon out here. It's got sickness all over it. Some other outfit comes by and climbs in, they're going to be sick."

Reuben couldn't keep the alarm out of his voice. "Did you go in the wagon or touch any of them?"

Johannes shook his head, "No, I was too much of a coward." Reuben looked at him sharply. *He's not kidding. He's serious.*

"Johannes, one thing I can definitely, without hesitation, tell you, one man to another and as your best friend, is that you are not a coward. Take three men and torch the wagon. Let's make sure anything burnable is cleared for quite a ways around. This is about the driest green grass I've ever seen. Then catch up with us. You can follow the wagon tracks. Zeb says this trail will save us a day."

Johannes looked at him, "I was hoping you would do that. Let's get there, already."

"We'll get supplies, get some men hired, and you and I'll go down south and see what we can do about buying some longhorns. If we can't find them closer, Mac told me there might be a place near the New Mexico Territory border that has some that come up from Texas."

Reuben paused and held Johannes' eye. "Then we have another big push—over those," he nodded at the Rockies looming above them to the west.

Johannes didn't say anything. Reuben studied him closely. "Are you coming down to the Uncompahgre with me?"

Johannes returned Reuben's stare. "Right now, I am going to burn that sick wagon and the poor souls in it. The rest we can talk about this evening or tomorrow." Johannes spurred Bente into a lope back toward the wagon train. Reuben watched his squared shoulders and retreating back, then fixed his eyes sadly on the solitary wagon two hundred feet from the circle. He breathed in and exhaled a large sigh. Lahn pricked his ears and flicked his eyes back at him. "Damn, Lahn, Damn."

REBECCA AND REUBEN RODE AT THE HEAD OF THE LINES OF WAGONS. They moved along briskly in the late afternoon, even the livestock seeming to sense the eagerness in the drivers. Zeb galloped up to them from ahead, leading Mac's mare, Red. "Rebecca," he nodded, and then turned to Reuben.

"Up this next rise a few miles, you'll be able to see it," he pointed. "This is the last of the high ground before the land starts dropping into the basin where the South Platte and Cherry Creek meet."

Reuben looked off in the direction of the basin and took a deep breath. "Hard to believe." Rebecca leaned over and smoothed her palm down his forearm, her eyes shining.

"Yep, we are more or less here," Zeb grinned. "You did a helluva job, son. It weren't the reason I originally said yes to you back in St. Louis, but I'll tell ya more on that later. I suspect you'll welcome the news," he grinned again.

His eyes drifted past them and Reuben was sure they were fixed on the third wagon in the line, driven by a certain petite redhead.

"Rebecca, Buck here is getting jealous of Red." Buck's muzzle moved up and down and Red moved her lips to the side, showing her teeth and whinnying. They all laughed. "Buck's gettin' new shoes too, and he ain't all too happy about that, neither." Buck rolled his eyes and shook his head. "Anyways, I know Mac was quite impressed with you. Said you was the prettiest marksman west of the Mississippi. I'm sure he'd like you to have Red, otherwise I'll take her down to Randy."

Rebecca looked startled. She blushed, throwing a sideways look at Reuben. "That is so nice of you, Zeb. I have always like that mare. I can appreciate her feistiness."

Reuben looked down to hide his grin and he noticed Zeb's cheeks twitch under his mustache, "But I don't know what my plans are," she continued, her eyes darted to Reuben and then back to Zeb, "and she deserves a long-term, stable home."

Reuben felt a deep chilly pang run through his gut, and he pretended to be absorbed in looking at the mountains, so she couldn't see his face.

Zeb stared at her for a long moment, then shifted his attention to Reuben. "Reuben, I'm gonna head down in. I think you might wanna camp tonight up on one of them shelves over that rim. Those that are going on can get a start from there tomorrow. You will only be an hour's ride in, and the ladies can stay away from...," he paused and stroked his mustache, "the rougher sides of the place. I got to make sure I talk to Mac's brother, Randy, before anyone else does." He sighed, "And I ain't looking forward to it—not one bit."

Reuben fumbled in his jacket, withdrew Mac's telescope, and offered it to Zeb. "Randy ought to have this." Zeb looked at the spyglass and shook his head. "Nope, I'm dead certain Mac would've wanted you to have it."

Reuben tucked the glass back into his jacket. "Could not have done it without you, Zeb."

Zeb smiled and began to wheel Buck around. Then the mountain man turned in his saddle, "Thanks," he said, grinning. "There weren't nothin' to it, and you and me son, we still got a fair ways to go." He nodded over Buck's ears at the mountains, then spun the tobiano. Let's go, Buck. You too, Red."

A short while later, Reuben and Rebecca crested the ridge Zeb had described, the settlement seven miles to the southwest spread below them. Reuben reached into his jacket, pulled out Mac's spyglass, and extended the brass. The image blurred. He lowered the glass slowly and wiped his eyes.

Rebecca edged the small sorrel she was riding, which had been part of the team pulling the sick wagon, closer to Lahn and put her hand on Reuben's thigh. "What's wrong?"

"I was just thinking about the folks we lost, dreams not finished, loves left dangling. It ought to be Mac looking through this telescope right now, from this spot."

He raised the spyglass again. West of the small, unorganized settlement, the Rockies rose rugged and inviting, their highest peaks swathed in clouds and intermittent sun, their flanks cascading down to steep but lesser and lesser foothills as the mountains spilled toward the prairie. East of the foothills were great hogbacks with reddish soil and rock, bearded with some type of brushy cover, which he couldn't distinguish from this distance. The town, dusty with haze, seemed to have several short dirt streets. Reuben could see movement and assumed that carriages, wagons, and horses were stirring up the dust. People, of course, too, but it was still too far to pick out details.

Spread out, apparently without thought, from the center of the settlement, were a number of small buildings and many tents. Wood smoke rose in lazy spirals from most of the structures. Between them and the fledgling town was a large cluster of tipis interspersed on the higher ground above the trees and meadows at the juncture of one larger and one smaller stream, which glistened a silver reflection from the west sun that hung suspended, its lower edge just kissing the tops of the snow-covered peaks.

He felt Rebecca's hand again on his thigh. She was looking at him with a dazzling smile. "Zeb is not the only one proud of you, Reuben."

He smiled and handed her the telescope. "Want to take a look?" She raised it to her eye. "You can steady it up some," he said, "if you hold it against the brim of your hat." *Damn I miss Mac.*

Rebecca followed his advice. "Oh, that is much better. It's not much of a town. In fact, it's far less than I expected."

He drank in her profile, allowed his eyes the luxury of traveling down the silhouetted curves of her body, and tried to ignore the gnawing uncertainty in his gut. She chuckled as she lowered the spy-glass. "It most certainly is not London."

Reuben had been about to pose a question he had been thinking about for some time. He stopped himself before the first word. She looked at him, her head cocked, "Were you going to say some-thing, Reuben?"

He shook his head. "Nope, was just going to suggest we get back to the wagons and call a meeting tonight. I expect a number of fam-ilies to be leaving in the morning. Might be some will just continue on today, although it's getting late. We can say our goodbyes and Godspeed, and folks can start getting organized."

She held his eye, her face impassive except for the curiosity in the rise of her eyebrows. Reuben wheeled Lahn, she turned the sorrel, and they loped back toward the wagons.

May 27, 1855

$\mathscr{S}$NAKE BITE

"PATRON."

Black Feather heard Pedro behind him, but neither turned nor stopped riding. The rotund Mexican sped up his horse until he was even with the black stallion, and abreast of Black Feather and Dot, who clung tenaciously, as always, to Black Feather's wool army jacket.

"Patron."

"What's on your mind, Pedro?"

The fat man's voice was intense, excited. "Patron, we must stop. González needs rest. He is bleeding again, badly. He is losing much blood."

"Well that's what he gets for getting in the way of a .36-caliber slug from a Navy Colt. We ain't stopping. Now that we are across the South Platte, I want to get into those foothills between the Big Thompson and the Poudre. We're easy targets out here for cavalry patrols in this open country."

"But Patron, González is my second cousin. This you know." Pedro's voice was plaintive, a vestige of surprise and anger in it. "That hombre with the pistolero, *este muchacho es un mal hombre.*"

Black Feather turned to look at Pedro for the first time in this short-lived conversation. "Don't know if he's a bad man, Pedro, but he's about the fastest I've ever seen with a Colt."

"But Patron..." Pedro's voice was louder and higher pitched, "just for an hour, so I can bandage him up again and stop the bleeding. We can find some cover."

Black Feather reined in the stallion abruptly, the horse flicking its muzzle up and down in disapproval, surprised at the sudden stop. Pedro had overridden a few feet further. He drew up and partially turned in the saddle to look back at Black Feather.

Without taking his eyes off the Mexican, Black Feather raised his voice, "González. González, get up here so we can take a look at you."

Pedro's face seemed to relax, and he nodded his head slightly.

That appreciation ain't warranted yet, compadre, thought Black Feather. González's horse approached from the rear of the scattered line of men. He swayed in the saddle, clinging to the saddle horn with both hands, and drew almost abreast of Black Feather, his mustang seeming to stop of its own volition. *You know, don't you horse?* Black Feather looked González up and down quickly. The tan was gone from the wiry Mexican's skin, replaced by pasty white. He seemed to lack the strength to even lift his head, staring down instead at his hands clasped around the saddle horn, a small pool of blood on the saddle dammed on either side by his thighs. Blood flowed with each heartbeat from where the young man's Colt had made a hole in the Mexican's belly. The entire front of his shirt was soaked in red, and the blood seeped halfway down his trousers. "How are you feeling, González?"

González shook his head very slowly from side to side. He partially lifted his chin, just enough so that by raising his eyes, he could look at Black Feather.

"Not so good, Patron. I am very thirsty." His eyes lowered and his head sank down again, the hole in his shirt pulsing blood.

"Well, González, we don't want you dying of thirst." Black Feather drew his Colt Army and, with one smooth motion, fired once, and then again, into González's body before it fell fully from the saddle.

"Patron!" wailed Pedro, shock, anger, and surprise serrating his cry, one pudgy hand moving slightly toward the pistol at his belt. He froze as Black Feather pointed the revolver at his head and pulled back the hammer.

"Pedro, we run this trail for a long time, you and me. You might be the only one I fully trust..." Black Feather paused, "mostly trust. So putting a hole in your head is not something I want to do, but I sure as hell will."

His lieutenant's hands relaxed reluctantly and crept back a few inches to their former position. Pedro said nothing, but his lower lip stuck out, his eyes were masked, and his heavy cheeks quivered with rage.

"Pedro, you know as well as I do, González was done for. Should've died two weeks ago. You couldn't even give him water with that gut shot. Did you want to see your cousin suffer? On top of that, he was slowin' us down. There could be three or four more of us like him. Maybe you. You ever think of that?"

Pedro shook his head, but Black Feather could tell his anger had not subsided.

"We seen two likely targets and they both had cavalry escorts." Black Feather spat on the ground. "Since when did the cavalry start accompanying wagons? It's only the smaller outfits, the ones we look for. That other train, hell, must've been eighty or ninety wagons. We couldn't take them on even if we weren't as shot up as we are. That was the last of the wounded. Perhaps we will be rid of the bad medicine of that youngster's Colt."

The men had gathered around him and Pedro. Their demeanor matched Pedro's eyes. *Dark clouds before a big rain.*

"I know we've been riding hard, men. Between them Indians, dragoons, the wagon trains, it was too damn busy back there for me. Only a fool disregards signs. We will be much safer up in the foothills. We will bide our time for stray wagons sure to come by, or maybe we will scout out a homestead or two, take them down, and set up camp there for a while until we get our medicine back."

Black Feather moved his eyes to Pedro and, with one deft motion, slid the Colt back in his belt. "Pretty fast, eh? Faster than that boy's Colt, don't you think? We owe him one. Next time..."

"We owe him six." It was Snake. He was staring at the red-stained corpse of González. There were already flies buzzing around the wounds.

"Good observation, Snake. If we want to be technical, maybe we owe him eight. That Colt gave the others time. That red-haired bastard wagon master had a chance to use that scattergun, and those marksmen they had to the side would have never had their shots neither."

Black Feather spent a moment closely studying the remaining twenty-three in his band. Some would not meet his eyes. All had looks of tired frustration and anger, and many exuded an air of restless enmity and mistrust.

"Snake, go fetch that mustang of González's for me. I think I will put Dot on the horse."

To his side, he heard Pedro mutter something in Spanish. He swiveled his head, "What do you want, Pedro? Let the horse wander around? You want a mustang riderless when I'm riding double? We don't have the luxury of doing things proper. We gotta get to them foothills, mend up, and plan our next move."

"We sure as hell hope this plan is better than the last one." Black Feather turned sharply to Snake. This time the man didn't look down.

Black Feather's eyes flitted momentarily to the others. They were all looking at him, tense, alert. *Dark clouds before the storm,* he thought again. He closed his mouth and forced a half-smile. "No matter, Snake." *If I ride over to the horse, chances are there will be ten lead holes through my body,* he glanced back behind him. Dot was looking up at him with those big green eyes, *and through the girl, or worse yet, what they'll do if she's not dead...* Black Feather nodded, showing no outward sign, but his hand was ready to make a grab for the pistol, and he was already calculating who would be first, second, then third.

Maintaining the partial smile took effort. Without taking his eyes off the men, he said in a level voice, "Dot, why don't you ease off the back of the stallion, go over there, and get that horse. You know how to ride, don't you?" He felt her nod "yes" against his back.

"Get on, then. We will wait for you." Dot carefully swung one thin leg over the rear of the stallion and then, supporting herself with her elbows, lowered her feet partially to the ground, dropping the last foot.

"Good, now get that mustang." Black Feather could tell Dot's progress by the eyes of his men, and he backed the stallion a bit so that Pedro was fully in his field of vision. He could see by the way the hungry eyes of some of them drifted slowly with the girl's movements that she was getting near the horse. "That's a good girl. Take those reins and pull yourself up in that saddle."

When the eyes were all focused on him again, he knew she had mounted.

"Pedro, you know the way to the Big Thompson. Let's stay low crossing the Pawnee. Take the lead. The girl and I will take the rear. It's only fair if we eat a little dust, too."

"Si, Patron." Pedro's words had a bite to them as he set off at a canter. The rest of the men exchanged looks and then, one by one, trotted by them. Tex was the last man. As he rode by he pulled his lips back from his teeth, pressed his tongue into the gap so that it protruded in an ugly pink boil, and cast a wild-eyed look at Black Feather.

Crazy as a drunk bed bug. Black Feather nodded another half-smile at the wild face as if he had not noticed either the warning energy the man radiated, or his lunatic behavior. He waited till Tex was a full fifty feet ahead of them then turned to Dot. "How's that saddle feel?" She looked up at him, and the first smile he had seen on her lips since that day on the Poudre, more than two months prior, wafted across her face.

"So, you like to ride? I bet you had a favorite horse? Maybe the one you learned to ride on. What was its name?"

The small, tender, tentative smile didn't leave her face, but she said nothing.

"That's fine. You can tell me another time."

IT WAS MIDAFTERNOON, AND UNSEASONABLY WARM. BLACK FEATHER peeled off the jacket he had stripped from the blue belly he killed in '54, his eyes roving the familiar hogbacks and buttes, and beyond them, the rugged foothills of the Rockies and the Rawah, just miles out.

He looked over at Dot. Her slight blond figure seemed especially small astride González's stocky mustang. He watched her for a moment. She rode with fluidity, a slight exaggeration in her hips. Black Feather watched her pelvis move to and fro in the bow of the saddle seat for a few seconds and then forced himself to raise his eyes. He had meant to lift them to her face, but they lingered where the west wind pressed the thin shirt against her small, petite, not fully developed breasts, slight accentuations in the fabric where her nipples pressed against the cloth.

Her face had a relaxed expression, though her posture was still guarded. She looked over at him, her lips creasing into that same partial half-smile she had revealed for the first time a few hours before. *Should have put her on horse long before this.*

"I'm going to ride up to talk to Pedro. We're gonna take a short rest and make sure the trail is clear. Get up a little closer to Tex—but not too close. I'll be right back."

Her light blond eyebrows frowned, shadowing the widening of her big green eyes. "I'll be right back. I promise." He kicked the stallion and the horse broke into a lope. As he passed his straggling band, he was acutely aware of the bitter stares that ricocheted off his back as he rode by. He reached Pedro quickly.

"Pedro, we'll turn into this canyon comin' up. Send Snake and Johnson up to the top of that ridge. Have 'em check out Big Thompson Valley before we cross. Then we'll head north into those rolling hills south of the Horse's Tooth Rock and camp up in there tonight. There are several good spots."

Pedro blinked and his eyes flickered with an unfriendly look. Black Feather wheeled the stallion and trotted back down his motley column. Behind him, he heard Pedro call out, "Snake and Johnson. When we pull up, climb up to the top there and see what you can see." Also audible were Snake's curses, not much more than a whisper, but meant to be heard.

As he neared Dot, her features, which been drawn and worried, eased and her face relaxed. Not a smile, but close. *We're making progress.* He smiled in return, loped the stallion around her rear, and rode next to, but slightly in front of her. Ahead of them, the men filed into a small rocky draw. Snake and Johnson were dismounting and pulling their long guns from their scabbards. Snake cast several furtive, less than friendly, looks in his direction.

He was shocked by the voice slightly to his left and behind him. A woman's voice, almost. A complete sentence, almost. He put his hand back on the rump of the black stallion and cranked his upper body around, "Did you say something, Dot?"

The soft skin of her eyelids fell twice in blinks, "Brush for the horse?" *I'll be damned. Horses. They really are the key.*

He shook his head slowly. "I'm sorry. I don't think there's a single saddle bag with a horse brush in it." He pointed, "But see that sage, part way up in that clearing between the rocks? Just grab a couple of handfuls and rub him down. Doesn't do quite so well as a brush, but horses seem to like it."

The girl nodded and Black Feather leaned down to hold her reins. She firmly pulled the leathers from his hands, wrapped them around the saddle horn with an air of practice, and dismounted, jumping from the stirrups to the ground.

Black Feather felt himself grin. "I guess you didn't need help, did you?" She looked up at him and shook her head, then began to pick her way toward the sage.

Black Feather slipped from the stallion's saddle, keeping the horse between him and his men. As he pulled the Musketoon from its scabbard, he did a quick hand-check of the Colt Army in his belt to make sure it wasn't hung up on anything, knowing his movements were shielded from prying eyes by the torso of the horse. During it all, his eyes were above the stallion's neck, surveying the men. *I better not sleep tonight,* he instructed himself.

There was a high-pitched scream from behind him. The men jumped up, some of them reaching for pistols, others grabbing their long guns. Black Feather drew the pistol and turned, his left hand gripping the rifle. Dot had collapsed next to the sage, rocking and crying, holding her left leg. *Snake bite!* He ran to her and rolled up the cuffs of the wool pants he had taken from Hank, one of the smallest men in the outfit before he was killed by that pearl-handled Colt that ill-fated day almost a month before.

He froze at the sound of the rattles and turned his head slowly. A four-foot diamondback was coiled just feet away; its pale pink, forked tongue flickering, searching, tasting; its opaque, reptilian eyes fixed on his. With the slowest of movements, he drew his knife. The snake struck, the blade flashed, and the twitching, writhing body of the rattler quietly coiled and uncoiled almost at his feet, headless. He wiped the sparse blood from the blade on his leggings and focused on the twin, welling punctures halfway up the side of her calf. Her face was white and her shoulders trembled. *What's it been, a minute? Maybe two?*

He untied the bandana from his head, wrapped it tight around her thigh, stuck a gnarled sage branch under the cloth, and twisted it. "You okay?" he asked. She nodded, her pupils beginning to dilate. "Hold this and tighten it when I tell you. Got it?" The blond head bobbed up and down.

He looked into her eyes. "This is gonna hurt. But if I don't, you'll die. You understand?"

The young woman bit her lower lip and nodded, tears rolling from her eyes. Black Feather steadied his hand and pressed the sharp point of the knife against her flesh, making two deep cuts in the form of a cross over the punctures. He lifted her leg and bent his head, fastening his lips to her skin and the ooze of blood. He could feel the leg muscle spasm under his mouth. *That poison is already working.* He sucked hard, turned his head and spat. Then again. And again.

Black Feather sucked and spat again. He glanced up. Her eyes were closed. There was a twitch in her check. Her skin was pale, very pale. The wound was beginning to swell and swollen tissue now extended several inches in all directions. A blue tint began to show around the punctures and the incision he had made with the knife.

The men had gathered below him, twenty feet away at the toe of the rise, watching.

"Pedro get a small fire going. No smoke. Tex, get some water and heat it up." He bent his head against the wound and sucked, grimacing at the bitter taste of combined blood and venom. He spat and wiped his mouth with the back of his sleeve. "Tighten that tourniquet, Dot." The girl did not respond. She began to ease her shoulders backward to lie down. He quickly scooped his arm around her back. "No! Don't lie down. The poison will spread faster. Stay sitting up." He could feel the bore and unsettling energy of twenty pairs of eyes on his back. He picked Dot up, turned her around, and faced the men, propping her up against a rock so that she could not lie down.

Pedro had not moved, neither had Tex. "Patron, you seem to care more about the skinny woman than you did about González. You rode with him for four years. She can't be that good in the bedroll." Pedro had pulled the worn serape back away from his pistol. Black Feather bent down, pretending to suck on the girl's leg again, and then straightened, suddenly, pulling his pistol from his belt as he did so. The shot caught Pedro between the eyes and he fell over backward without a sound. The men jumped, shocked.

Black Feather knelt over the girl, the pistol still extended. "Who's next?" he snarled.

Snake came running around from behind a rock, "What the hell was that...There's nothing doing, not even a rabbit..." He stopped and took in the scene, his mouth open.

Black Feather could feel the girl's arm beginning to shake under his left hand. Nausea would set in soon.

"Most of us have ridden together a long time. I have never forced anyone to stay or go. You make your own choices. But if you're with me, I demand loyalty, and you do what I say or you'll pay the price." He gave a sideways nod to Pedro's body. "I've been getting a bad feeling all day. Matter of fact, it ain't felt right for several weeks. I aim to save this girl's life. She ain't like us and she don't deserve to die like us. He shifted the gun from one side of the group to the other. "So here's a choice. You can ride with me or you can light out right now. No harm done, no grudge held."

The men, all silent, looked at one another. Black Feather stood. "I don't have a lot of time here. Every minute that goes by this poison goes more through her system. Who's in and who's out?"

Snake drew himself up, a vicious look on his thin swarthy face. "That girl is all you got on your brain. We ain't had nothing but bad luck since you took up with her. I'm going to head down to the Uncompahgre. Ain't supposed to be no troops down there, and not a lot of white men neither. Heard some rumors about gold. Maybe I'll find me some. Or, maybe I'll find someone who found some. That might be easier."

Several of the men laughed uneasily. Eight other bandits, including Tex, who wore his maniacal grin, stepped back from the circle. "We're going with Snake," one of them said. The others tensely nodded. Black Feather wagged his pistol. "Then git."

The men walked to their horses, muttering amongst themselves, shoved their rifles roughly into their scabbards, mounted up, and rode out of the canyon at a lope, not looking back.

Black Feather turned his attention to what remained of his band. "Bama and Chief, make that fire. Get some water on it." The two men nodded and scrambled to their tasks. "Tom, get yourself up to the top of that ridge and keep your eyes peeled. We're gonna be here at least a day to see how she does." He looked down at Dot. Her eyes were closed, her face pale and clammy. He leaned close to her ear. *Smells good, but maybe it's the sage.* "What I have to do is gonna hurt like hell. But, I got no choice. If I don't cut some of that poisoned flesh out of your leg, you'll die," he paused, "and that means no more horse riding. How are you feeling?"

"Burns, burns," she whispered, tears welling from beneath her closed eyelids. She turned her head and retched. Black Feather looked up at the men. "Anyone have any whiskey?" One of the men nodded. "Good, bring it over here, would you, Johnson?" The man ran off toward his horse. *The energy is already better. Good decision, can't ride with eyes in the back of my head every minute.*

Black Feather spoke softly to the girl. "You're going to start feeling dizzy. And, you're going be sick again. You're going to lose some skin up and down from that bite. It's just the way it is. I aim to pour a little whiskey on this leg, and then you need to take two big swallows. Can you do that?" Her eyes stayed closed, but she nodded a weak "yes".

Johnson handed him a small bottle of whiskey, which he unwrapped from a soiled, faded, red handkerchief. "Thanks, Johnson, I'll try and save some." The man smiled.

Black Feather held his knife over her wound, poured the whiskey on both sides of the blade, let it drip on her calf, and then smoothed it over the angry looking skin with the blade, covering the entire rapidly swelling area. He held the bottle to the girl's lips, "A good swallow now." She took a gulp and coughed. "Good, take another swig." She choked, coughed, and then turned her head to the side and vomited again.

"Johnson, hand me that bandana."

Johnson untied the bandana from his neck, and Black Feather wadded it up and pressed it against Dot's lips. "Open your mouth, bite on this." Her mouth opened, *straight white teeth*. She bit down on the dirty cloth.

"Johnson, hold her legs down."

He looked down at her leg. *Going bad quick.* He turned his head to check on her. One thin arm was extended, little fingers outstretched, reaching for him. He hesitated a moment, surprised, then closed one big hand over hers and squeezed.

He turned back to her calf, took a deep breath, and pressed the sharp, curved upper edge of the blade several inches to the side of the puncture wound, and three inches above it. *I've killed over forty men with this knife and sliced at least that many, and my hand ain't never shook before.* He took another deep breath and began to cut, Dot's moans of pain through the handkerchief hovering in the spring heat and echoing in his brain among older, more painful memories.

May 27, 1855

ℛAILS OF FREEDOM

HIDING INSIDE THE BARN'S WOODEN GRAIN BIN, WHICH WAS FILLED with oats, Israel felt like he was floating, suspended. *Reminds me of the lake. Hold my breath and just let myself sink.* Lucy squeezed his hand and he squeezed back. He listened to the faint indecipherable echo of voices, the words of the Nebraskan farmer muted by the wooden barn and the grain in which the farmer had hidden them.

"Charles, you know we get a complaint or report, we gotta check it out. We got laws and it's our job. Mildred ain't no liar."

"Marshall, I never said Mildred lied. She's a nice old lady with way too much time. Her imagination is bigger than the damn prairie. A breeze comes through her flower garden and she's screamin' down the road about a tornado. You know it, just like I do."

"We're sorry to bother you, Charles. We appreciate you letting us look in the house, root cellars and your loafing sheds. Last thing we gotta check is this here barn. You understand, Charles."

"That don't matter much, John, so have at it. My barn is your barn."

"Sam, Tommy—go and check the tool and tack rooms at the other end. One of you go check those stalls. I'll look around down here."

Israel squeezed Lucy's hand. She returned the pressure. He took another shallow breath from the canebreak stem that extended from his mouth upwards a foot, several inches above the level of grain in the storage bin.

"Nothin' in the stalls," one of the deputies called out.

A more distant voice shouted, "Ain't nothin' over here in the tack room, neither."

"John, get Charles' pitchfork and check them old hay piles by the door. Tommy, go on above and check them grain bins."

Lucy squeezed Israel's hand hard. He gave her two quick ones back. *If you can feel my thoughts, Lucy, you relax. Lord, I surely hope the stems ain't sticking up too high.* The grain dust tickled his nose.

Israel strained to hear. He could make out the occasional muted thud of boots as they hit certain loose, coarse planks on the barn floor, or when one of the lawmen jumped from one level to the next. *Sounds like one of 'em is comin' up this way.* Each step taken was more audible, closer, nearer. Lucy squeezed his hand again. The approaching sound of boots was dampened, but now he could hear almost every step. *Oh Lord. Definitely on their level.* Israel's mind raced. He could feel the sweat trickling down his sides. *He'll walk around the outside of the bins, then climb them outside ladders and peek inside.* Israel tried to remember which way the shadows fell from the lip of the eight-foot round, eight-foot high storage bins, but couldn't. Each stride of the approaching deputy was clearly audible now, eerily dull as the sound drifted and sifted through the grain. Then the steps ceased. Israel held his breath.

The steps resumed. *He's walkin' round the other bin.* The sound stopped again. Israel craned his ears. *We been in worse pickles than this over the last two months. Well, maybe not.* The steps circled their container, stopping twice. There was a rapping on the side. *Checkin' to see if it's full. He don't wanna climb that ladder.*

There was a muffled curse, then the creak of a ladder rung. Lucy squeezed his hand so hard one of his knuckles popped. *Lord, I'm talking to you. I may not have the right, and it surely ain't been earned. But me and Lucy, we come too damn far. God, don't let 'em hear my heart beat.*

Another creak and a second knuckle popped under Lucy's vice-like grip. *Easy woman, easy. Keep your head. Don't be getting' nervous and losin' that breathin' stem.*

Another creak.

Israel tried desperately to recall how many rungs there were on the ladder, *six or seven? He ought to be lookin' over the top right now.*

Another creak. *"Oh Lordy, what's he doin'? Has he seen somethin'? Lookin' closer?"* His hand ached where Lucy clamped down on it. He squeezed back twice. *Lord make my heart not beat so hard. He gonna see the grain rise and fall with every beat. Please, Lord.* He felt a slight shift in pressure in the oats above his head to the left of his left ear. *"Oh Lordy, he diggin' in the grain. He's digging in the grain! Lord make him stop."*

There was a sharp *crack* and a loud curse. Israel started despite himself. "Damn it, shit!"

Seemed like the voice was right over their heads.

"What is Tommy? What's going on up there?"

"The damn ladder broke. About broke my damned knee and ripped my damned pants. I just bought 'em last week at the mercantile."

Creak...creak...creak. *"He's goin' down. Goin' down! Lordy, thank you, Lord."*

"Anything up there?"

"Yep, three rats. Charles you know you got damn rats in your barn?"

"Ain't never seen a barn that didn't have a rat."

"Come on down, Tommy." The Marshall's voice dropped. "Sorry. Just doing our job. You understand, don't ya, Charles?"

"No, matter fact, John, I don't. But here's what I do know—it's getting' dark and I got six milk cows need milkin'. They don't much like lanterns, and I ain't partial to tuggin' on teats in the dark."

The Marshall laughed. "Well, there's several things I could say to that but bein' an officer of the law, I won't!" The other deputy laughed.

"I guess it's like you say, Charles. Mildred got overworked."

"Like I said, Marshall."

Israel strained his ears. It sounded, but he couldn't be sure, like they were walking toward the barn door.

"You playin' poker tomorrow, Charles?"

"I got too much spring work to do. But I'll see you in church on Sunday."

It sounded like they were outside the barn. Lucy's grip had loosened, but he could feel the agitation and tremble through her hand to his. She suddenly tore from his grasp. *She's frantic, tryin' to get to the surface.* He swam to the top, pushing grain away from his mouth. Just Lucy's mouth and nose were above the oats. She coughed. Israel wrenched his hand free and covered her mouth.

"What was that?" one of the deputies called out.

Charles sneezed, then hacked and coughed. "It's my damn spring cold. You can set your clock by it. End of May every damn year." He coughed once again.

There was a moment's silence, and Israel held his breath, Lucy's eyes above his hand wider than he'd ever seen them.

"See you on Sunday, Charles." There was a pause, then the distinct sound of three horses riding from the barn.

Israel scooped the grain from around his wife's face and neck, pushing it rapidly toward the walls of the bin. Her head and tops of her shoulders were finally clear, a cone of grain around her. He looked at her and started to laugh, covering the sound with the hand he had pressed against her lips.

"Israel, what's so damn funny? We been goin' for two months. Hid in rivers and with rats in root cellars. Been chased by Bushwhackers with torches and ropes. And dat hemp was way too thick for them to just tie our hands. And then I finds out, theys calls it, 'Bleeding Kansas'. Lord knows, I walked through a blizzard. Still got frostbite on my toes, and you think that's funny? One thing 'bout you, Israel. You ain't become a littler or bigger fool since the day I met you. You're just the same fool."

Lucy still had her eyes wide open, but her eyebrows furled down over them and an oat husk clung to one. Israel took his hand off his mouth and brushed it away, his laughter echoing in the bin.

"You better hope I stay stuck in here, Israel, cause if I get out..."

Israel looked at her, still chuckling. "It ain't that we're stuck or what we been through, although you gots to admit Lucy, that hidin' in that trash bin outside that restaurant in Holton in the Kansas Territory, when them Bushwhackers were huntin' us, you gots to admit, that was pretty smart.

"And smelly," she snapped back at him. He gently dug the grain from around her shoulders, and then helping her, they struggled, half swimming to the interior ladder.

"Be careful going down them outside steps. One of them rungs is broken."

They clambered down to the main level, Lucy wincing with pain on the steps, Israel holding her hand.

Charles was leaning on a pitchfork. He grinned as they walked up. "I'm not sure you'd pass for deputies, but on a dark night you'd most likely pass for white folks." He chuckled as he looked them over.

Lucy turned her face to Israel, her skin an off-white from the grain dust. He knew he looked the same.

She started to laugh. "After all these years, I find out now I done married a white man." The three of them laughed until their bellies ached.

Charles' face grew serious. "You're gonna have to move on in the next day or so, Israel. They'll be back. That damn Mildred does nothing but gab. She'll get folks riled up, and the Marshall will be back just to keep 'em happy. There's others behind you on these rails of freedom we gotta think of. We can't lose hideouts in the chain. Won't do no one no good to get pinched."

Israel turned to Lucy. Her eyes were wide and frightened. "We was hoping to rest up for a while. We've been on the go for two months. Poor Lucy here, she's havin' trouble walkin.' Her knees are getting worse. She got frostbite on one toe that ain't right yet."

Charles looked at him, then sank down to one knee, leaning on the pitchfork for support. "Lucy, if ya wouldn't mind, raise your skirt just enough so I can see your knees." Lucy flashed a startled glance at Israel, who nodded. She shyly lifted her threadbare heavy cotton dress until her knees were showing. They were swollen and wrinkled. Around the inside and outside of her joints, her dark skin had a purplish hue.

Charles pulled himself up by the pitchfork and leaned on it again, looking at Israel. "You told me you are handy with a leather awl, and know tack?"

"What's he up to? I don't fix up his tack and he turns us in?" Charles nodded over the top of his pitchfork toward the tack room. "Back there is ten saddles. Ain't one of them that don't need work, some more than others. Been meanin' to get to it," he chuckled, "about the only thing I told the Marshall that was the truth, is that there ain't enough time to get half of it done 'round here." He nodded his head to the side. "That there is a going on twenty-year-old mule. She's a worker, and there's a couple good years left in her."

Israel looked over at the mule who was watching impassively, one ear forward, one ear back, her muzzle more white than grey.

"I'll make ya a deal, Israel. I'll come down here this evening after dark. I got me a big tanned leather cowhide from a milk cow decided she didn't want to give milk no more. I'll bring down some awls, rawhide, stitching, and the metal pieces I bought about a year ago." He spit some chew on the rough barn floor. It hit the wood with a splat. "Them parts ain't left the bag I brought 'em home in." He looked at Israel, "You fix them up good and that mule's yours. Those knees of Lucy's don't look none too good to me. If you're headed all the way to the Rockies, she's gonna have to ride."

Israel stuck out his hand, "Thank you. You's got yourself a deal."

Charles shook his hand firmly and smiled. "Now before I leave, I'm gonna shutter every window in this place and when I leave, that barn door too. Don't poke your head out and don't touch them windows. Come hell or high water, you need to be on the road tomorrow night."

He reached in his pocket and held out a large pen knife. "You'll be needing this, Israel. When I come back tonight I'll bring you some supper along with those tools. You'll need leather shears, too. After that, I won't be back to the barn. Too many prying eyes. Just leave that knife on top of one them saddles when you're done." He pointed over to the corner, "And take that halter too."

He wheeled to go, then turned back to them. "That mule's name is Sally. She'll come to it, and she's pretty unflappable. The only thing that I know she ain't partial to is gunfire." He shook his head, "She don't like gunfire at all."

He nodded his head to Lucy, "I wish you well, Ma'am, the Good Lord look after you."

He held out his hand to Israel. The handshake was firm, warm and sincere. Charles looked him in the eye. "I know it's been tough. Every one of you brave people comes through here has their stories. Most of 'em ain't too good. But, remember," his eyes boring into Israel's, "if freedom was easy, everyone would have it."

Lucy and Israel stood silently as he shut and latched the shutters on the two open windows, walked to the barn door, and shut it behind him. Lucy turned to Israel. Tears, their downward slide slowed by the grain powder on her face, were working their way down through the white dust on her rounded cheeks, leaving jagged tracks. "He was like an answer to our prayers."

He hugged her tightly. "I love you, woman. And he," Israel painted at the roof, "loves us. And, it's more than that, woman. It's a job. It's my first job as a free man. Ain't gettin' no money, but we is gettin' a mule. With that mule we can go further. You know every place we stopped particularly, that last place in the Kansas Territory, Alton, they said further west you go the safer it'll be. Now we can go to that place with the river on the map that nice old lady shared with us in Topeka, you know, the night we slept in that carriage in the back of her livery. Looked like to me that map made that river to be on the other side of mountains, but still in 'em. I never read one of them types of maps before."

"Contour maps, Israel, that's what she called it. A contour map."

"Yep, but I'm telling you, Lucy, my eye went right to that river. Out of all them lines and drawings, something made me pick it out, right off. I'm not saying the good Lord spoke, but that map sure talked. Can't even pronounce the name of the damn river."

Lucy smiled. "For someone who knows readin' and writin', husband, you surely have a short memory. She said it was pronounced un-com-pag-grey. You 'member what she said it meant in Indian?"

Israel nodded his head "Yes, Lucy I surely do remember that. Uncompaghre. Where water turns rocks red."

May 27, 1855

SPIRIT WHISPERS

THREE KNIVES NUDGED HIS PONY WITH HIS HEELS, MOVING HIM beside Eagle Talon's mustang. "We must stop and find some water for Brave Pony."

Eagle Talon looked at his friend, nodded, and then gazed upward at the sun. "When we next see willows or the talking trees, we shall rest briefly. I will tend to Brave Pony. You can dig for water, and Pointed Lance can gather plantain for the poultice. It is early, but perhaps they can find some young shoots. Brave Pony is lucky the Pawnee bullet passed all the way through him."

Three Knives grunted. "If we can stop the bleeding with the poultice, I think he will live to count more coup."

He turned and smiled at Three Knives, "It was a good day for The People... and a good day to count coup. I saw you take four myself and will tell the Council."

Three Knives nodded, but his smile was shallow and his normally lively features subdued. "I saw you count five coups. Two were crippled when they rode off and three dead. I shall tell the Council. You almost doubled your feathers in one sun, Eagle Talon."

Eagle Talon glanced sideways at the other brave, "What bothers you?"

Three Knives gave him a quick but steady look, and then faced forward, his proud profile glistening bronze in the morning sun. "If the village has found tatanka, they will be stationary—skinning, cleaning, packing meat, and fleshing out the hides. If that is so, then we shall meet up with them before the sun sets today."

They rode in silence, Eagle Talon expecting Three Knives to continue, but he didn't. Mulling over the alternatives, he finally said, "You are worried with what the Council will say about our launching an attack on the Pawnee?"

"And what they will say about us leaving our positions. Flying Arrow's desire was clear," Three Knives snapped. "We were to shadow the Pawnee—to always know where they were." He paused and turned his gaze to Eagle Talon again, this time a hard look, his eyes narrowed. "He didn't say to help the hairy-faced ones. You do know, Eagle Talon, that today you might have saved the lives of white eyes that you may have to kill later, or die at their hands?"

Eagle Talon contemplated this thought. In the spur of the moment decision, excitement of the battle, and the inexplicable peace he found in the bond he made with the hairy-faced one with the white pistol, and his woman who reminded him of Walks with Moon, he had not considered this. He nodded slowly, "What you say may be true, Three Knives, but I believe we made the right decision. It is also entirely possible the white eyes in those wagons may someday help us."

He caught and held Three Knives' eyes. "Of this I am certain. The hairy-faced one who calls himself Roo-bin, and his woman, Ray-bec-ka, shall never be our enemies. I feel this in the Spirit. This," he pointed to his heart, "and this," he pointed to his head, "can be wrong. But Spirit," he pointed to the sky, "is never wrong."

Three Knives extended an arm, "Look—willows, and a lone cottonwood—shade for Brave Pony."

Eagle Talon signaled back to Turtle Shield and Pointed Lance, who rode on either side of their wounded comrade, to pursue the same slow pace. He and Three Knives cantered over to the lonely willow stand and dismounted quickly. Three Knives reached into the little patch, parting the supple golden branches, looking earnestly at the ground for water. He looked up, "None, but I can smell it. The ground is damp. I'll find a rock and dig."

Turtle Shield and Pointed Lance had reached them now, each of them with a hand on either arm of Brave Pony, who sagged weakly over the neck of his horse. Eagle Talon walked to them. "Lower him down to me." He gathered up Brave Pony in his arms and carried him over to the taller grass at the base of the cottonwood, laying him down gently, then examining the wound closely. The injured brave's eyes fluttered open. "Perhaps it is my time to meet Wakan Tanka."

Eagle Talon was concerned. There was puss forming around the uneven edges of both the entry and exit of the Pawnee bullet that had pierced his friend's side. He was sure the shell had not touched anything vital, but infection could kill just as easily.

He grabbed Brave Pony's shoulder and squeezed it hard. His friend's eyes opened again, "Are you trying to break my shoulder, too?"

Eagle Talon laughed with a humor he didn't feel. "You see, you feel pain. This is not your day to die. You will have to wait to see Spirit. You're stuck with the four of us for many winters."

Turtle Shield and Pointed Lance came running up, their hands full of young plantain leaves. They looked with concern at Brave Pony, then at Eagle Talon, with the question in their eyes.

A minute later they heard a low shout from Three Knives. "Water. Plenty of it!"

"He will live," he answered their voiceless query. "Three Knives, get the water over here. I will prepare the poultice." Using a rounded rock, he pounded and mashed the plantain to shredded fibers. Three Knives joined them from the willows, carrying two small buffalo bladders. The tough membrane was damp, but watertight. "Three Knives, give him some water."

Eagle Talon stripped off his shirt and made a shallow leather bowl within a circle of rocks he assembled. He looked up at his friends, "Walks with Moon will have my hide for this. She made the shirt for me just this winter."

The three warriors laughed, "I'm sure you will find a way to make her smile, Eagle Talon. It is well known in the village that if we can't find you, you are under the robes with Walks with Moon."

Eagle Talon chuckled and shook his head. "Winters are cold and long. One must stay warm somehow." They all laughed again, even Brave Pony, although his laughter was mixed with a hacking cough.

Eagle Talon carefully stirred the plantain, adding just a bit of water at a time. When it was a fine, mushy, fiber paste, he had Three Knives and Turtle Shield roll Brave Pony to his side.

"Three Knives, bring me some of the gunpowder for your musket." Three Knives looked at him, initially not understanding. Then his eyes lit up. "A good idea, Eagle Talon." He ran to his mustang and grabbed his powder horn.

"This will hurt my friend." Brave Pony nodded his head, gritting his teeth. He sprinkled gunpowder into both bloody red holes, then worked the tip of a finger in from each side, Three Knives adding powder as Eagle Talon packed the wounds. Brave Pony groaned through clenched lips.

"Bring a flint."

"Here." Pointed Lance reached into a small, beaded leather pouch that hung from his neck and handed the flint to Eagle Talon. Holding the flint close to the wounds, Eagle Talon struck the flint once, then again. A spark caught and an explosion of fire seemed to leap from both bloody apertures, diminishing to grey smoke and the acrid smell of exploded gun powder and burnt flesh. Brave Pony stiffened and bit into the meaty part below his thumb until it nearly bled.

"Now I will put the poultice on, and you'll feel much better." Eagle Talon applied the poultice lavishly, pushing into both sides of the wound. He sat back on his heels and sighed. Shaking his head, he cut a sleeve from the shoulder of his shirt, then cut it again, longitudinally. Turtle Shield and Three Knives held Brave Pony's shoulder up so Eagle Talon could bind the two strips tightly around his friend's midsection, over the poultice.

Brave Pony stifled a groan as they set him down. "I thought you said I would feel better." They all laughed, and Brave Pony smiled. "I do feel better. Spirit will have to wait."

UNABLE TO MAKE FAST TIME, THE SUN WAS LOW IN THE SKY WHEN they topped a golden ridge. The rolling country undulated in waves of spring grass, as does a pond in the wind.

"There they are!" exclaimed Three Knives.

Eagle Talon nodded and took in the scene, searching for Walks with Moon's graceful figure. Sixteen tatanka carcasses lay scattered across a wide valley, the nearest almost five or six arrow-flights from the furthest. Some were already just partial bones and remnants of flesh. Teams of women and older children worked on others, fleshing the great bloody hides, as others removed chunks and strips from the mountains of meat, cutting it carefully for storage, salting, and smoking. Others sloshed around in great piles of entrails, removed from the carcasses soon after death so that the meat would not spoil. The saving of hide, fat, and bone would come later. Camp dogs slunk around the edges, snatching whatever scraps they could.

Silhouetted on the higher hills all around the valley, braves stood guard over this ancient ritual—the difference between life and death for The People. Three Cougars pounded up the incline toward them, smiling. "We've done well. This was the second herd. We took fourteen in the first one and sixteen from this one. It was a great gathering of the brothers—probably thirty arrow-flights wide. He pointed out the mile-wide swath of trampled grass that receded up and down the hills, disappearing northwest into the twilight. His eyes fell to the Pawnee scalps and his face grew somber. "That is the good news. But there is other news."

Three Knives cast a nervous glance at Eagle Talon. "What?"

"I was instructed to tell you that the Council wants to meet with you as soon as you arrive. You're not to go to your lodges first." He looked down at the ground, hesitating, and then up at them again. He leaned forward and in a voice barely more than a whisper, "It was Flying Arrow himself who gave the instruction."

The five braves looked at one another. Eagle Talon swallowed. We shall get Brave Pony to his lodge. He is too weak to attend the Council meeting. Tell Flying Arrow we will be there immedi-ately after."

Three Cougars nodded, wheeled his horse, and with a shout, headed down the ridgelines toward—Eagle Talon supposed—where they had set up camp for the night—away from the valley of their dead brothers and the predators that would surely visit in the dark.

THEY TOOK BRAVE PONY TO THE LODGE OF HIS FAMILY. ANXIOUS not to keep the Council waiting, Eagle Talon promised they would tell him what happened the next sun. Eagle Talon emerged from the tipi, took a deep breath, and exhaled slowly, but his nerves would not settle. He looked up into a sky laden with stars, a bright half-moon perched on a distant rise, slightly higher than the one occupied by their encampment. One by one, his friends emerged from the tipi and joined him. The nervous tension ran like a strong wind between them. Eagle Talon breathed in deeply again, then exhaled, but his rapid heartbeat did not slow.

"Even deep breaths have no power to calm the nerves?" asked Pointed Lance.

"No," Eagle Talon sighed and the four braves exchanged glances. The soft lunar light accentuated the tension in their faces. Three Cougars appeared out of the darkness. "The Council grows impatient."

"Let's go, then," said Three Knives, his tone resigned.

He, too, would rather go anywhere else, thought Eagle Talon.

"Three Cougars, where has Flying Arrow set his lodge?"

Eagle Talon could see Three Cougars' head move negatively. "No, it is worse than that. They've set up the Council lodge for this meet-ing." The four braves exchanged looks. *This is not good. The lodge of the Council is rarely set up when the tribe is on the move, except for the most serious of circumstances.*

They followed Three Cougars slightly off the rim of the hill toward the middle of the encampment, a tipi bigger than all the oth-ers. The bright glow of the lodge fire shown through the smoke hole, its yellow-orange light rising above the main lodge pole only to be swallowed by the silver of the moon. *I wish I could talk with Walks with Moon. I know she would have good advice for how to handle this.*

They paused outside the flap to the Council lodge. There was not the usual murmur of voices. The four braves looked at each other, none of them wanting to be the first. Finally, Eagle Talon opened the flap and stepped in, followed by his friends. They stood respectfully, waiting for the invitation to sit in the circle that ringed the central fire. No such invitation was offered. Tracks on Rock caught Eagle Talon's eye. His almost imperceptible shake of his head radiated disapproval before he dropped his eyes to the fire. Flying Arrow stared at them. Not an elder spoke. A minute went by, then another. The fix of Flying Arrow's eyes was unwavering. Still, no words were uttered.

Eagle Talon had an overwhelming urge to shift his weight from one leg to the other. He could feel Three Knives to his left and Turtle Shield to his right, both struggling to remain still. Pointed Lance, the tallest of the four, peered over their shoulders, seemingly quite content to have the other three warriors in front of him. The silence extended for so long that when Flying Arrow did speak, it startled them. "Tell us what happened."

Eagle Talon stepped forward and told the story in great detail— when they encountered the Pawnee war party, the days they tracked the Pawnee, the soldiers they avoided—and, finally, their surprise attack on the Pawnee in the midst of their rival's battle with the white wagons.

Finishing the story, Eagle Talon paused, then stood as erect as he could. He held Flying Arrows eyes and said, "It is I who sent smoke to bring in the other scouts, and it is I who decided to attack the Pawnee. It is also I who talked Three Knives, Turtle Shield, Brave Pony, and Pointed Lance into joining me in such attack."

At the last of the speech, though he kept his eyes fixed on those of Flying Arrow, he saw the head of Tracks on Rock rise, and thought he detected a slight nod of approval.

There was another long silence. "It is, on one hand, a brave thing you have done. The amount of coup you counted in one day is very impressive. However, you were given specific instructions. He raised his arm and made a sweeping gesture. We're not a big village. We do not have many lodges. The safety of the village, our children," his eyes narrowed and bored into Eagle Talon's, "and our women, depends largely on knowing more than those who would do us harm, and gaining this knowledge sooner. Sometimes it is good to be the lone wolf, but even the wolf must know his place in the pack. When you made smoke and called in the other scouts, you left us without eyes in front of us."

Flying Arrow paused. "Tell us, Eagle Talon, more about this white man, Roo-bin and his woman Ray-bec-ka. Why do you think they might be friends of The People?"

Eagle Talon related what he had seen the evening they had snuck close to the wagons. He told the Council about the whispers he had heard from the Great Spirit, *Friend. Strength. Honor.* To his amazement, the heads of virtually all the elders nodded empathetically.

"We have all had similar experiences, Eagle Talon. Though never with hairy-faced ones. The future will tell you if you heard the whisper of Wakan Tanka, or merely the wind in the grass." Flying Arrow paused, then gestured toward the door of the lodge with a nod of his head.

Eagle Talon and the other young warriors walked sun-wise around the fire, and ducked through the door, out into the night. They could hear the current of the somber discussion inside. Several of the elders wanted to strip them of their coup. *Almost unheard of.* Two of the elders thought nothing should be done since no harm had come to pass. They believed merely being called in front of the Council would make the point of the recklessness of their decisions. Tracks on Rock and Flying Arrow said little, their voices lowered, their words imperceptible.

The lodge fell silent. The flap opened. One by one, the elders filed by them, speaking no words, not even casting a single glance at any of the braves, as they disappeared into the silver darkness.

Eagle Talon turned to his warrior friends. "We are being shamed. We will be ignored at Council meetings. If we speak to the elders, they will not listen. Our words will be like stagnant air." Thoughts pierced Eagle Talon, more painful than a knife. *What if I am no longer entrusted with guarding The People? Now I must hunt the tatanka alone.*

The braves dispersed. Eagle Talon began to turn toward his lodge, but a hand reached from the night and clasped his arm. It was Flying Arrow. "I wish to speak to you tomorrow of the white wagons and learn more of what you saw. Perhaps you can come up with further details of this Roo-bin with the white pistol." And then he turned away, leaving Eagle Talon standing alone in the gloom between tipis.

THOUGH NO DETAILS OF THE BRAVES' EXPLOITS WERE KNOWN, NEWS of their return had spread quickly. So had the ominous rumor of disapproval by the Council. Walks with Moon's joy at the return of her husband was diminished, almost extinguished by her trepidation over the Council meeting. She had gathered at the lodge of Talks with Shadows, wife of Turtle Shield, and with Deer Track, wife of Pointed Lance.

"What you think the Council will decide?" asked Walks with Moon anxiously.

"They could be shunned," said Deer Track, darkly joking.

Walks with Moon shook her head. "No, I can't imagine a serious enough offense for shunning."

Talks with Shadow was silent, staring intently into the fire. She looked up slowly, her eyes reflecting the flames, imparting a wild, almost unearthly look. Her eyes were enormous, and strangely fixed as if on some distant thing.

Walks with Moon and Deer Track glanced over their shoulders to see what Talks with Shadows stared at, but there were only the tipi walls and Turtle Shield's backrest to be seen.

"I know what will happen," the woman said, turning her eyes to the younger women.

Walks with Moon and Deer Track exchanged glances. Deer Track was biting her lip, trying not to giggle at yet another one of Talks with Shadow's premonitions. The other women teased Talks with Shadow unmercifully about her incorrect forecasts, but she usually shrugged off the jests, making excuses. *"I would have been right, if ...."* Walks with Moon had the uneasy feeling, though, that today was somehow different.

"How does the baby in your belly grow, Walks with Moon?" she asked abruptly. "Do you feel good? Does he feel strong?"

Walks with Moon was taken aback by the questions. *Completely out of place. What does this have to do with the Council?* The words seemed to come more from the wild look in the woman's eyes, than from her mouth.

"I feel wonderful, blessed by Spirit," Walks with Moon answered. "I think the baby is happy, as are we. But boy or girl? We do not yet know."

Talks with Shadows nodded. The fire flickered in her eyes again, her brown irises brightening, then fading. The whites of her eyes seemed to dance with an orange glow. When she spoke this time, it was almost in a monotone, like the voice of another.

"The men have brought shame upon themselves. It will be so for one moon."

Walks with Moon and Deer Track exchanged startled looks, their mouths open. Talks with Shadows seemed oblivious to their reaction, her face almost wooden in appearance. Walks with Moon listened as the woman continued with her prophetic announcement.

"Eagle Talon has bonded with a hairy-faced one whose woman reminds him of his love of you." Her shoulders were stiff and square as she spoke. Her voice, still strange, descended to a strong whisper, "The future of The People is not bright."

Walks with Moon returned Deer Track's wondering look. *Perhaps Talks with Shadows is tired or anxious about Turtle Shield,* thought Walks with Moon, trying to understand the woman's odd behavior. *What did she mean The future of The People is not bright?* Usually, her prophetic mutterings were lighthearted, her voice almost playful. Today, she spoke in the voice of a stranger.

The fire crackled, casting dark shapes on the hide walls that moved as the fire flared and ebbed.

"The hairy-faced one and his woman will play a role in the well-being of your son," she said, looking at the fire and then up at them again. Then Talks with Shadows seemed to relax, her face softening, as if she seemed not to remember the words she had just uttered, the flames no longer dancing in her eyes, and the normal cadence in her voice returning.

"We shall just have to wait and see what the Council decides, but I don't think it will be that serious," said Deer Tracks, doubt strong in her voice.

The flap of the tipi was shoved roughly open and Turtle Shield stepped in. One look at his expression, and Walks with Moon knew that the gathering of the Council had not gone well.

She could hear the anxiety in her voice when she asked, "What did they decide, Turtle Shield?"

"Your husband can tell you," he said, glancing at her, then at his wife. "The news should come from Eagle Talon."

He placed his shield, lance, and bow carefully against the wall of the tipi and sat heavily down against his backrest, legs crossed, his eyes fixed in a brooding stare on the lodge fire. Talks with Shadows sat down next to him, her hand on his knee.

"Thank you for opening your lodge to us," Walks with Moon said, already at the door flap, thinking that perhaps Talks with Shadow needed a few nights of good rest.

The woman looked up. "I'm not tired," she said.

How had she known what I was thinking? Walks with Moon and Deer Tracks exchanged glances again and then stepped into the growing darkness of the sinking moon, each running toward their lodges to hear the news. Along the way, Walks with Moon stopped to gather a few windblown twigs for the fire.

She arrived only moments before Eagle Talon, just enough time to grow the embers of the lodge fire to flames. The tipi flap opened and he stepped in. His face was dark and his eyes troubled. The smile faded from her lips.

"It did not go well?"

He did not answer, instead stowing his bow, shield, and lance, and then like Turtle Shield, sitting and staring morosely into the fire.

She knelt down behind him wrapping her arms around his neck and tenderly kissed his ear.

"Are you hungry?"

"No."

She nestled her breasts into his back and, moving her shoulders, pressed one, then the other into the muscles below his shoulder blades. "Are you sure you have no hunger, husband?"

Eagle Talon sighed, bent his head down, and kissed her forearm where it circled him to the side of his jaw. "I am sure, Walks with Moon. I ruined that shirt you spent so much time on this winter."

"Is that what is bothering you? I can make another. What happened to it?"

"No, that is not what distresses me...though I am very sorry," he added hastily. "And it did help save Brave Pony's life."

She took her arms from around his neck and began to knead the thick cords of muscles at the base of his neck. After a few minutes she could feel him relax. "Come to bed, Eagle Talon. I will hold you and rub you, and you can tell me the story."

He craned his head around to look at her, their eyes met and he nodded.

Under the buffalo hides, he lay on his side facing away from her. Walks with Moon wrapped one creamy, upper inner thigh over the tense muscles of his outer leg, snuggling her hips and growing belly into his buttocks. Her hands worked the stiff muscles in his shoulders.

He reached one hand behind him, over his shoulder, and closed it over hers.

"I am sorry, too. I was not here to take a tatanka for us. And now I must hunt alone. We have been shamed."

Walks with Moon froze and stopped her massage. Misunderstanding what had given her pause, Eagle Talon partially raised his head. "It's all right. The season is young. We shall have meat, wife."

"No, no, Eagle Talon. It is not the meat. Soaring Eagle killed three of our brothers..."

"Three!" Eagle Talon interrupted her and chuckled. "He is a great hunter."

"...And he gave us one. It is just he and Antelope Fawn you know. They seem to be unable to have children, and he was very appreciative of how long you have been gone."

"They are fine people. We shall have to give them a gift."

"Husband..."

"Yes, Walks with Moon."

"Tell me the story of where you went, what you saw...and," she hesitated, aware of the racing of her heart, "who you met."

He was silent for a moment. "We trailed the Pawnee, attacked them, I counted five coups. We evaded a small group of soldiers, but I shall tell you the details of all that and more later. The most memorable event was—please don't think me crazy, wife—I met our spirit brother and sister..."

His words distracted Walks with Moon, and the pressure from her fingertips lightened.

"Harder, wife."

She dug her fingers into him, working his muscle tissue. "Tell me about those people," she said, her heart pounding.

"They are...," he paused again, "hairy-faced ones."

Walks with Moon had a vision of the wild fire in Talks with Shadows' eyes.

"The woman's name is Ray-bec-ka. She reminds me much of you, and her man is called Roo-bin. They remind me of us—very much in love."

Talks with Shadow had, for once, been right, thought Walks with Moon. She spoke of this woman. But what of her other words? *The future of The People is not bright.*

Walks with Moon knew her husband could not see her wide eyes and open mouth, nor was he aware that she had dropped one hand, placing it protectively against the heat of her ever-rounding belly. But they both heard the call of a burrowing owl outside the tipi, soft and mellow. *Co-hoo. Co-hoo.* In the distance, the sharp yelps and howls of coyotes, feasting and fighting over the tatanka carcasses, echoed in the dark, melancholy energy of the night.

Walks with Moon remembered the owl outside the tipi at the winter camp on the Powder and the hawks as the village had trailed east. And the orange glow in Talks with Shadows eyes. What was the message? What did it all mean? *For The People*. For she and her husband? For....*your son*... Those had been Talks with Shadow's words.

She leaned forward, her lips lingering in a pensive, troubled kiss on the smooth skin of her husband's back, but Eagle Talon was asleep.

CHAPTER

48

May 27, 1855

*I*NDECISION

SARAH SNUGGLED INTO HER SHAWL AND WIGGLED HER SEAT INTO
the blanket she had laid over the rough ground of a small rise until
she was comfortable. Fifty feet east of her was the circle of wagons.
The customary small, cautious evening cook fires had been replaced
by several large fires, thigh-high flames licking the cool clear air,
excited pioneers clustered around each, trading stories, sharing
plans, reviewing goals, and saying goodbyes.

She hadn't wanted to be part of the jubilant crowd. She had had
little time to herself since leaving Liverpool, and she had much to
think about. Below her stretched the broad basin of the South Platte,
low-lying folds of lands that seemed to stretch and roll forever. The
fires and occasional oil lamps of the residents of Cherry Creek shone
far away, lonely flickers of light in a land of creeping shadows, their
luminescence, like the faintest stars, daring the approaching night.

To the west, the sun hung suspended behind dark, mountain silhouettes, the thin layers of softly glowing clouds laced with silver
and bold strokes of fiery orange-red. Underlying them, a deepening
purple sifted down from the highest peaks, curled around the
foothills, and spread like a fog of color across the rolling plains.
Transfixed by the sheer power of the scene, Sarah felt tiny and
insignificant, yet empowered at the same time. *So many choices.*

Her attention was diverted by three ground squirrels, a mother and two babies, thirty feet in front of her. Sarah cocked her head to the side and smiled. "Cute," she said out loud. The mother watched her two young kits, wiggling her nose with an apparent air of bored detachment.

As Sarah watched, she felt a sharp twinge in her belly. She held her hand to her stomach, trying to soothe the pain as the two young squirrels wrestled playfully. Suddenly, one turned and aggressively knocked the other one over, biting it. The injured sibling squealed and the mother chattered angrily. The three of them ran down the rise disappearing in the grass, the smaller of the two kits limping where the other had bitten it.

As she watched the animals disappear, Rebecca's voice came from behind her, "Sarah, may I join you?" she asked, smiling.

Sarah realized Rebecca had been standing, watching the antics of the squirrels. She patted the blanket beside her and Rebecca gathered up her riding dress and sat down heavily, slightly off balance, almost rolling backwards.

"That was graceful, Milady Marx."

Rebecca laughed, "Wasn't it."

The two friends sat silently side-by-side, watching the shadows lengthen as the high peaks seemed to devour the sun, one bright yellow bit at a time. "It truly is magnificent," Rebecca said, an unmistakable note of wonder in her voice. Sarah said nothing. The moment spoke for itself. She drew the shawl up over her shoulders, the temperature dropping as fast as the descending sun. The painful twinge in her stomach seemed to be gone.

"Sarah," Rebecca was looking at her with earnest, wide eyes, "can you remember England?"

"Sometimes it's difficult," she admitted. "I have flashes at times. The inside of our sewing shop, the jostle of shoulders when I walked to the market, but it wasn't long after we left St. Louis that I could not even remember the smell."

Rebecca nodded.

"And the sound. You know, Rebecca, that constant noise which you only notice when you don't hear it?"

"There was a night on the wagons," said Rebecca, with an unseeing stare at the last remnants of sun, "that I sat on the banks of the Missouri and realized I couldn't really recall what had happened only months ago, yet somehow it seemed like forever. London is like a book I read long, long ago. Not the place where I used to live."

"I know, Rebecca, I know. My anticipation of America was the hustle, bustle and throngs of New York, working in my Aunt Stella's shop, saving money to open my own. I really had no idea..."

"That this," Rebecca swept her arm expansively, "could exist."

Sarah turned to her friend, surprised at how effortlessly Rebecca had described her own feelings. She put her arm around the brunette's shoulders. Rebecca did the same and they leaned their heads together.

"It changes you somehow," whispered Rebecca.

Sarah nodded, feeling Rebecca's hair brush her cheek as she moved her head. "Perhaps more than change, it alters you—as if you've stepped into a bright sunny room with no walls and you can't go back." She paused for a moment. "Have you decided, Rebecca?"

Rebecca sighed. "There is so much to consider. For some reason I expected Cherry Creek to be more than it is..."

Sarah started to laugh, pointing at the sparse cluster of lights all but swallowed in the massive descending blackness, sweeping her arm with exaggerated grandeur, "Imagine a great city!"

Rebecca chortled. "Reuben let me look through Mac's telescope this afternoon when he and I rode. I couldn't hold it very still, but I got the impression that there are two dusty streets, less than a block long. I'm not even sure there is a solicitor there. I've no idea how I am going to conduct business or get this land sold...if that's my ultimate decision." She added after several seconds of silence, "It seems I have come a great distance, yet not arrived."

"I know. I shared your anticipation of Cherry Creek, but there seems to be but a few buildings. It's more an Indian village," Sarah sighed. "I had no idea. I'm not even sure there's a place to set up a sewing shop—or that there would be any customers. Maybe they are all like Zeb and they do their own sewing."

That thought made them both laugh. "I'm sure there are still plenty like me down there who wouldn't know," Rebecca said, "and who don't want to learn which end of the needle to use."

Sarah's head jerked with a thought. *The maps.* Jacob's map was now in the secret compartment at the bottom of her carry bag, along with her money. "Rebecca, did you get the opportunity to ask Reuben about the map?"

"No, he's been too preoccupied with the excitement of getting to Cherry Creek. And he has said some odd things. I think he knows good and well that we killed Jacob."

Sarah was startled. "Well, first, you did not kill Jacob. I did. But you certainly were a fine accomplice. Reuben's very much in love with you. You know that, Rebecca, don't you?"

Rebecca shook her head, "It does not matter. I know he cares for me. I'm not sure that it is love, though. In the end, Sarah, we all have our own paths."

Sarah fell silent, thinking about Rebecca's words. The chatter from the large campfires drifted in the breeze. Below the small hill where they sat, the dim form of a horse and rider moved across the land.

"It's Zeb," Sarah smiled. The mountain man dismounted where the ground squirrels had been, and walked up the shallow rise, Buck close behind him.

"Hello, Zeb," said Rebecca.

"Rebecca. Sarah. Purty night."

"I'm surprised to see you back, Zeb. For some reason I thought you'd stay in town, perhaps with Mac's brother, Randy." Sarah could see Zeb's head shake against the light of the first stars. His hands moved in the darkness, just thin flickers of skin when the fires behind the women occasionally brightened, their greedy flames feeding on yet unburned buffalo chips. Sarah realized he was rolling a cigarette.

"Oh, almost forgot," Zeb said, reaching into his fringed jacket, his hand fumbling underneath the leather. He drew out three envelopes. "Seems to be mail for you Rebecca, and Reuben. Got some for a few of the others, too. I'll go over and pass 'em out. There's one for Thelma and the Doc," he said in a low tone, "don't know whether to open it, or burn it."

He handed Rebecca two envelopes. "And this one," he flapped it back and forth, "is for Reuben. I can give it to him or you can, makes no never mind to me."

"How did these letters get here before us, Zeb?"

"Stages been running between Laramie and Independence since 1850. Occasionally, the Army drops down this way from Laramie, and when they do, they bring whatever's up there that belongs to fellas down in Cherry Creek."

He started to lift the cigarette to his mouth, then added, sensing Sarah's disappointment, "Sorry, Sarah that's all there was. I'm gonna go hand out these others. Would you walk with me?"

"How could any woman refuse such a gallant, well-mannered request?" Sarah answered in a teasing voice. "I would be delighted to Zeb."

He stretched out his hand. Sarah took it, and he pulled her to her feet. "I'll be excited to hear what's in your letters, Rebecca," she said as they turned to go. "I hope it's good news from home."

ZEB AND SARAH WALKED SIDE-BY-SIDE TOWARDS THE BONFIRES. Zeb stepped over the wagon tongue and held out his hand. *Such a nice man.* Sarah took it and he patiently helped her over.

The letters were quickly distributed, Zeb calling out "Mail!" and then the addressees' names, struggling with the occasional foreign pronunciation. The lucky pioneer generally ran to him, grabbed the envelope from his outstretched hand, turning immediately away, fumbling to open it with a muttered, "Thanks, Zeb."

Several of the people around one fire tried to engage him in conversation, but he would have none of it. "Got things I got to take care of. We'll talk in the morning before you pull out."

The chore dispatched, they walked toward the far side of the circled wagons. Sarah caught a glimpse of Rebecca, blanket tucked under her arm, about to climb in their wagon. Then she saw Johannes, striding rapidly toward them leading Bente. "Sarah! Zeb! I'm headed out, over the east ridge we crossed this afternoon. Got a night guard out in every direction, although we will rotate twice, instead of once tonight. Tomorrow's a big day and the men need time to get organized. He smiled. "All are excited, as well they should be. I don't want to keep anybody from their families too long tonight."

"What about you? Want me to spell ya later?" Zeb asked.

"No. I appreciate the offer, Zeb." Johannes looked up at the sky to the east. "I will enjoy the night out there. Would you tell Reuben where I am, and about the guard rotation for the night?"

"Sure thing," Zeb answered.

Johannes' eyes drifted down to Sarah. "I went through Inga's things," he said to her, pausing to take a deep breath. She noted a tremor in his voice as he spoke again. "Rebecca helped, but it was mostly me." He took another deep breath. "She doesn't think any of Inga's clothes will fit either of you."

Sarah could tell this was difficult for Johannes. He dropped his head, a catch in his breath. "But I know you and she were particularly close. There is one thing I found that I am sure she would like you to have." He raised his eyes to her, turned, walked around the horse, and fumbled with the saddlebag. He reached in and pulled out something. Leaning on his horse, she heard him clear his throat. A few moments passed before Johannes walked back to them.

In his outstretched hand, Inga's silver brush shone and reflected in the firelight. Sarah took it slowly, reaching out one hand and putting it on his arm. "Johannes...I...."

He didn't let her finish. "That was the only thing she had from the old country. She said it reminded her of her parents and the fjord where she grew up. I'm sure she'd want those happy memories to flow through to you."

Before Sarah could say anything, Johannes nodded to Zeb. "Tell Reuben, would you?" Then he abruptly turned, leading Bente away from the wagons and toward the east, Zeb and Sarah watching them both disappear from the firelight.

Sarah looked down at the brush and turned it in her hands, remembering. "Oh..." she said softly.

Zeb put his hand on her shoulder. "Let's go," he said quietly, leading her away. They stepped outside the curved line of rigs, the frontiersman's right hand holding the Sharps, his left arm hanging loosely in the darkness next to her. In a few paces, he stopped and turned. "We can walk around the wagons, or we can walk out to that little rise yonder," he pointed south to a raised portion of the shelf slightly more than one hundred yards from where they camped. "Your druthers, Sarah."

"Let's go up there, Zeb. I just have to make sure I don't trip and fall in the dark with this dress."

To her surprise, he took her hand. "I won't let you fall, Sarah," he said, shortening his steps. Her hand seemed lost in his warm, protective grip. She liked the rough and gentle feel of his touch. They reached the elevated area and stood silently, a vast blanket of stars over their heads twinkling with hope and promise. The mountain man did not take his hand from hers, and she realized she was glad.

"Always was partial to the sky," said Zeb quietly, looking up. "Tells you there's more."

She squeezed his hand, her fingers barely wrapping around the edges of his palm. "Me, too, Zeb. On both those thoughts."

Far in the distance she heard a long, lonely howl, shortly afterward answered by another from a different position, but close to the first. "Several people on the train said they don't like the sound of those coyotes, but I do."

She felt him look down at her from the darkness. "Ain't coyotes," he said. "Wolves. Not many this far south, though there's a fair amount when you get up north, or in the back country of those mountains."

"Wolves?" Sarah could hear the anxiety in her question. Apparently, so could Zeb.

He chuckled softly. "They won't bother us, Sarah. It's just the male and the female talking to one another," he paused, looked up at the sky and then down to her. "They mate for life, ya know."

She squeezed his hand again, and looked up at the dark rugged form outlined by stars. He turned toward her slowly, then seemed to hesitate. She took her hand from his, and wrapped her fingers into the folds of soft leather below the rawhide ties at his throat.

"Thank you, Zebarriah Taylor. You have been so very kind to me. Looking out for me. And, with Jacob..." She could feel his eyes on her face even through the darkness. He wrapped his arm around her back, below her shoulders, and bent down slowly, his kiss tentative as he drew her to him, his embrace firm yet not insistent.

Her surprise at the kiss quickly evolved—from questioning, to responsive as she felt the pressure of his lips on hers. She tightened her grip on his leather shirt. His mustache pleasantly tickling her, his lips warm, respectful, and gentle—particularly gentle.

He lifted his face from hers slowly and straightened up. Sarah dropped her arms, wrapped them around his waist and hugged him, and felt him wince, his ribs still sore. "Sorry," she whispered, the side of her face pressed against the bottom of his chest. Neither said a word. In the distance, the wolves sang their calls to one another under the faint glow of the silver moon.

Zeb cleared his throat. With her hands still pressed to his shirt, Sarah could feel the rumble in his chest. "I'd never let you fall, Sarah, in the darkness, or otherwise. The kid neither." Her eyes fluttered open, she jerked and began to pull away, but he held her to him, his grip tender but strong.

"Yep, I know. You bein' sick, and all. Knew for sure that day in the wagon, back there on Twin Otters Creek when...when I helped you with your clothes."

Sarah relaxed into him and began to quietly cry.

"No need to answer now, Sarah. We'll be here a week or two while Johannes and Reuben go fetch those longhorns. There's time to ponder, but know this, Sarah Bonney from over yonder, whatever your answer, I'm here for ya, and for the young-un too."

<hr />

REBECCA STOOD AT THE EDGE OF THE WAGON, TWO LETTERS clutched in one hand, the blanket tucked under one arm, her other hand lowering the ladder. She paused for a moment, watching the petite red-head in a traveling dress and the tall lanky mountain man, his fringed leather etched by the brightness of the fire as he stood passing out the letters. "That would be perfect," she murmured to herself.

She turned away, climbed the ladder swiftly, lit the second oil lamp, and found a comfortable perch on her bedroll. One envelope had the return address of their solicitors in London. It was addressed to her in formal, stilted letters:

To: Lady Rebecca Marx
Care of General Delivery, Cherry Creek Post Office
Kansas Territory
United States of America

Below that, *"Hold for recipient."*

Her eyes lingered for a moment on the words, *"United States of America."*

She put that letter in her lap and picked up the second, her hands trembling slightly. It was addressed in her mother's ornate scroll—formal, but warm—each letter with its own delicate curve. The address was the same as the solicitor's correspondence, except after the words *"Hold For Recipient,"* were the words (*"My Daughter"*).

She held the envelope up to the light, turning it to try and see the postmark date, well-worn after months en route. February 27, 1855. Her hand fell to her lap. *I was on the Edinburgh, just before New York.* Then Reuben's green eyes floated through her mind and she corrected herself. *We were on the Edinburgh...*

She held up the other letter. Its postmark was two weeks after her mother's. She held one in each hand, balancing them. "Which of you should I open first?" she asked them, and this time it was a vision of her mother's face and kind smile that floated through her mind. Her fingers shook as she carefully peeled back the envelope flap, which had been sealed with three small pressed wax seals with the family coat of arms. She could picture her mother's frail hand as she pressed down on the wax with the stamp months ago, *and five thousand miles away.* She pulled the two-page letter from the envelope. It was on the heavy, scalloped stationery her mother preferred, scribed with her Mum's favorite feather fountain pen.

My Dearest Daughter,

You've been gone only weeks, but I miss you, much as I miss my dear Henry. I've always been proud of you. You have great courage and your father's quick wit and strength. While I wish you were here, home with me, Adam, Sally and Eve—who miss you too—I realize our unfortunate predicament has left you no choice but to make this dangerous and difficult journey. It is, perhaps, the most brave I have ever seen you. Wherever this letter may find you, far from these shores, I hope that you are well.

Adam has tried to tell me, very gently, that you will not return. I pretend to ignore him, but in my heart, I know he may be right. Henry always said Adam saw the future clearly. I am old. Perhaps I should have departed this earth with or shortly after my dear husband, but God has seen fit to keep me breathing. I feel, Rebecca, I may not last through the year. Adam feels it too. I can tell by how he looks at me and the gentleness with which he and his family treat and care for me. I write you this letter not to worry you, nor to beseech you to return quickly. Quite the contrary, I may not be here when you get back, if you come back. As my life draws to a close, yours spreads out before you. Do what you must. Follow your heart.

The words blurred as tears came to her eyes. She folded the letter, saving the rest for later. Her elbow resting on her knee, her hand over her eyes, she hunched over and sobbed softly. Time passed. She got up and refilled one of the oil lamps that was flickering, wiped the tears from below her eyes and took a deep, breaking breath.

She picked up the letter from the solicitor. It was written on plain, white paper. Smooth linen without personality. Just like him, she thought as she began to read.

> *Dear Milady Marx,*
> *I write to advise you of the passing of your mother, Eliza-beth Marx, on March 18, 1855.*

The letter slipped from Rebecca's hand, her breath wrenched from her, her eyes lifted upward, she groaned. She swallowed hard, rubbed her eyes and bent over to pick up the letter again.

> *We shall handle your affairs as you instructed. You have been bequeathed the Estate in substantial entirety, some small items being left to your servants, Adam, Sally and Eve, no known last names.*
> *There are questions on the disposition or maintenance of your home, and, regrettably, on the remaining outstanding debts of Sir Henry Marx's trading business.*
> *We write further to inform you of an Offer to Purchase this office has received on your behalf for all lands to which you now travel, located in the southwestern part of the Kansas Ter-ritory, United States of America, consisting, more or less, of one thousand deeded hectares pursuant to Land Grant by King Ferdinand of Spain, 1847, location 107° 41' East and South of the Uncompahgre River, Kansas Territory, United States. The offer is for £100 per hectare or ££100,000 pounds, to be paid in cash upon the transfer of a deed. We understand this offer to be generous. We urge you to return to England with all due haste to handle these important affairs as soon as possible.*
> *This letter will...*

The letter went on for several paragraphs but her vision blurred. Suddenly exhausted, too tired to read another word, too overwhelmed, she put the solicitor's letter back in the envelope, and folded them in the blankets she used as a pillow. She untied her boots, pushed them off with her feet and lay down, drawing the other blanket over her head. *"Mother,"* she whispered. *"Reuben."*

May 27, 1855

*J*OHANNES' PROMISE

REUBEN RODE INTO THE DUSK IN SEARCH OF SOLITUDE. HE NEEDED time to think about the push over the mountains, and who might accompany him. The questions appeared more formidable than he had imagined. He talked them over with Lahn, leaning over to pat the palomino's neck. The horse moved surefooted in the moonlight, which cast a silver net across the land and back toward the wagon train's three large fires, half a mile out.

"Not much to say, Lahn, and damn few answers, but I appreciate you listening." The big horse's muzzle seemed to nod up and down, and he blew softly through his nose.

Reuben reviewed his mental list while he rode. He had to talk to Johannes and Zeb, and Rebecca. He sighed. And many goodbyes left to be said—the Johnsons were headed south toward an area they called Pike's Peak, the Kentuckians headed due west of Cherry Creek, and others in many directions.

He grimaced into the night. The longest, most difficult journey lay ahead of them. Could they find several hundred good head of cattle within a weeks' ride of where they were now camped? He clicked off the time that would be needed. Cattle. Hire three good men. Get supplies. Purchase additional wagon to haul building supplies. Perhaps a third wagon for provisions. Teams for the wagons. The list seemed endless.

His uncle and father's scout indicated on the map it would be a two or three-week journey. The scout had written the same words repeatedly in different areas on the map. *Rugged. Steep. Uninhabited. Ute Indians.* According to the scouts' letters, the first snows could blanket the Uncompahgre early September in some years. Would there be enough time to put up a decent shelter? If not, then what? The scout had written about winter temperatures well below zero, and snows over ten feet. He would have to acquire title or legal claim before building.

He patted his coat pocket and ran his fingers down the lower seam, pressing against the heavy wool fold until he could feel the six stones of Ludwig's diamonds, the family trust. *Almost there, father. Almost there.*

Completely distracted, Reuben rode back into the firelight of the wagons, and without realizing it, up to their prairie schooner—where Rebecca would most likely be found. Like a magnet, he chuckled to himself.

He tied Lahn onto the rear wheel with two quick loops. The oil lamps glowed inside the canvas. He knocked on the tailgate. "Rebecca? Sarah?" There was no answer. The flap was carelessly tied as if someone had been in a rush. He opened the tailgate, slid down the ladder and climbed in, intent on getting out his maps, studying them and then going over to the where others were still gathered by the fires. He needed to ask which wagons would be departing, and when, and where.

The blankets on Rebecca's bedroll stirred. So intent had he been on his plans, he had not noticed her slight figure, sunk in layers of bedroll. He sat beside her and peeled the blanket from over her head. Her appearance startled him, even in the dim light. She had been crying, and she was awake. "What's wrong? Is everybody okay?" A single tear slowly rolled from the corner of her eye, down the side of her nose.

He reached out and wiped her face gently with his thumb. "Would you like to take a walk? Or head over to the fires? We were going to talk anyway, and I'm not a bad listener." Again she shook her head slightly. "You are feeling okay, right?" She nodded.

He stood up. "Reuben," she said, "wait. There was mail for you in Cherry Creek at the Mercantile. Zeb brought it up." She stuck one hand out from under the blanket and pointed, "The envelope is on top of your map case in the forward corner of the wagon."

Reuben took an eager step forward, then stopped and turned to her. "Did you get mail?"

"Reuben, if you don't mind, I really don't feel like talking, but there's a problem in England."

That hollow feeling gnawed at him again. He looked at her, swallowed, turned, and made a long reach for the letter on the map case. He paused at the tailgate. "Rebecca, I'm here if you want to talk. Do you want me to stay?"

"No, Reuben. Thank you."

He stood for moment longer, jumped to the ground, closed the tailgate and tied the bottom of the canvas. He desperately wanted to read his letter. A quick glance told him Erik, his younger brother, had written it. The first word from Prussia in five months deserved attention, which would be difficult to give if he headed over to the fires.

A voice called out, "Reuben!"

Zeb and Sarah approached, one of Sarah's arms wound around his, her opposite hand fixed on his arm above the elbow, and her head leaning into his upper arm. Reuben grinned. *About damn time.* Sarah smiled up at him as they grew near, her face more relaxed than he had seen it since their first meeting on the *Edinburgh.* Zeb's expression was, as always, inscrutable, but Reuben thought there was a slightly different look in his deep set eyes.

Reuben was silent. "Johannes wanted me to tell ya he's out on the ridge east of here for the night. The night guards are getting switched out twice tonight, so the menfolk will have more time with their families."

"Thanks, Zeb."

"Sarah, there is something not right with Rebecca—the mail that came in today for her..."

"You received a letter, too, Reuben."

"I know—I am looking for some light to read by. But I think Rebecca received some bad news from England. She wouldn't talk to me about it."

He looked down the ground for a moment, fighting the constriction in his chest. "And she didn't want me to stay. But I think someone needs to be with her."

"I'll stay with her, Reuben," Sarah said, touching him lightly on the forearm. "Don't worry. Do what you need to do and if you need a private place to read your letter, use my wagon. There's an oil lamp."

She smiled up at Zeb, her face soft and radiant. "Thank you, Zeb. I'll think about that question."

"My pleasure, Sarah."

She lifted up the hem of her dress and walked quickly toward the wagon.

Zeb and Reuben exchanged a long look. "I think you ought to mosey on out and talk with Johannes. He seems a might down in the mouth to me."

"I'll do that Zeb, as soon as I read this letter."

"I'm gonna head down and camp maybe a third way toward those Arapahos down there. I probably know some of 'em. I'll head into their camp in the morning. Be back about midday and you can tell me what the plans are."

Reuben nodded and turned to go.

"One more thing, son."

Impatient to read letter from Erik, Reuben spun around. "Yes?"

Zeb held his eyes. "I ain't never lied to you, and I never will. But I didn't tell ya everything back there in St. Louis."

"Oh?"

"I'm a mite more than a little familiar with that country you're headed to. My trapping cabins are on the sides of them mountains, the Red Mountains."

Reuben stood, absorbing the information. Zeb continued. "Know the country like the back of my hand. I know exactly where those maps are at. Fact is, there's some mistakes in 'em. I aim to help you get set up. It'll still be a strange, wild land to you. But through me, you won't be a stranger."

Reuben began to say something but Zeb had already turned and was walking away toward the outside of the circle of wagons.

Reuben let his arm drop and shook his head. He hustled to Sarah's wagon. Not bothering with the ladder, he vaulted up on the tailgate, stumbling in the dark looking for the lamp, burning his fingers with the match. He got the lamp lit and looked around the interior. Two days before, Sarah had thrown all of Jacob's belongings, except his pistol and two marked decks of cards, into a heap and burned them. She had found his hidden, second pair of boots. After examining them, Zeb confirmed he was Mac's murderer. Sarah burned them, too, then moved her belongings back in to make more room in the prairie schooner, where she was spending the nights and days with Rebecca.

The wagon still held some of Jacob's malevolent energy. "We ought to burn you, too," he said out loud to the canvas. He thought about reading the letter elsewhere, but this first news, this first touch from his family back in Prussia, could not be delayed. Standing, he roughly tore open the envelope. The letter was only two paragraphs long.

March 10, 1855
Dear Reuben,
    I write to tell you that Father has died.

Still holding the letter with both hands, Reuben sat down on a crate, the letter on his knees, his legs shaking. He took a deep breath and blinked his eyes.

The rest of us are fine. Not yet knowing the town near the new farm, I hope this address is correct.

Reuben sighed. *Erik, you have no idea. There are no towns.* He continued reading.

The farm is prospering and Helmon and Isaac are the same. They will never change. There's talk of war with Denmark. The Jews, as usual, are being blamed for the unrest by those who need to do so. I'm thinking seriously about coming to America. Helmon and Isaac will never leave the farm. I have been reading everything I can on the United States, and missing you. I believe Father was right that night in the kitchen when he selected you to go. You are the right choice. I keep hearing his words, "America is the future. Where there is land, there is opportunity." I will write you soon again.

Love,

Your Brother, Erik

Reuben looked at the date. Erik must have posted it soon after he and Johannes had arrived in St. Louis, maybe while they were still on the train between New York and Missouri. He folded the letter carefully, shoved it deep in his pants pocket, blew out the lamp, jumped down from the wagon, secured the tailgate, and walked towards Lahn, a picture of his father's strong green eyes in his mind.

The muffled, sliding sound of Lahn's hooves moving through grass, and the occasional sharp metallic tick of his shoes hitting rock, cut through the chilled night air.

"Mississippi," came the voice out of the darkness.

"It's me, Reuben."

Johannes rode up to him, smoothly slipping his Sharps Carbine back into the scabbard.

"I see you're still using that password Mac gave us. Are you coming in tonight?"

"No, Reuben. As Zeb would say, this suits me just fine."

"I'll be direct, Johannes. Are you going to help with the push over the mountains and establishing the ranch down in the Uncompahgre?"

There was a long silence. "When Johannes Svenson makes a promise, Reuben, he keeps it. That's why I don't make many." He laughed in a self-deprecating sort of way. "That unfortunately includes some promises I should have made."

"And then?" asked Reuben quietly.

"And then, Reuben, my friend, I'm going to be what I am. A cavalry officer, but I'll make sure you're all tucked in before I bless the United States Army with my unparalleled presence." A small glimmer of true humor echoed in his laugh.

Bente and Lahn were standing side-by-side, their noses pointed at the Rockies, a looming forbidding mass of jagged, dark silhouettes rising without texture in the night, blotting out a third of the western sky.

"Have you asked her?"

Reuben's mind snapped back from where it had been somewhere on the other side of those mountains. "Asked who?" And, as he said the words, he realized what Johannes meant.

"That's what I like about you Prussians. A quick wit." The two men laughed.

"So? Are you?" Johannes' tone was serious. Reuben felt his friend's intent stare through the darkness.

"I thought about it. But every time I even inquire if she's going back to England, she avoids answering. I tried to bring it up twice in the last two days. Each time, something interfered and I have this feeling that she's glad she didn't have to respond."

"Remember back there, that morning at Two Otters Creek?"

Reuben nodded, silent. *All too well.*

"Are you in love with her?"

"Yes."

"Then, my friend, ask her to marry you. Moments don't come often, Reuben. It is the one thing I have learned since first looking in Inga's eyes, back there on the train to St. Louis." He sighed and looked up at the sky. "Don't let a moment slip by, Reuben. It might not come again."

Johannes reached a long arm over and slapped him on the back. "The worst she can say is 'No'."

Johannes turned his head in the darkness, looking at the Rockies. "It is an enormous, dangerous, wild, exciting, spectacular country, Reuben. Coming all this way we had the support and company of other wagons, more than a hundred brave, strong men and women.

From here on, it's just us. I have a feeling this next leg over that country up there is going to make what we've done thus far feel like a close column drill on a parade ground."

"I suspect so," said Reuben.

"You all right, Reuben? You seem quiet tonight."

"Got a letter from Prussia today. I just learned my father died in March. He chose me for this, you know. Even though he is...was, thousands of miles away, I had his support." Reuben felt his throat tightening again.

"We're all going to die, Reuben. It is the inexorable circle. That's why it is so important to live when you can."

Johannes' words struck a chord. Reuben's eyes widened. "Johannes, would you excuse me? I'm going to head back in and tell Rebecca about my father."

"I think, Reuben, that's exactly what you ought to do."

To BE CONTINUED...

Coming next, Book Three of the
Threads West, An American Saga Series,
Uncompahgre ©2012